THE CHRISTMAS WILL

THE CHRISTMAS WILL

PETE THOMAS

Contents

1	The Beginning of the End	1
2	Changing the Will	6
3	A Glimpse of the Past	10
4	Unraveling the Past	19
5	Finding Little John	23
6	Little John Learns the Truth	31
7	Train to Poplar Bluff	50
8	Little John arrives in Poplar Bluff	69
9	Christmas Morning	97
10	The Will	100
11	Christmas Lunch at the Mansion	119
12	First Day at JR's	132
13	The Bank	142
14	The Car and the Mansion	161
15	The Mansion and the Airplane	176
16	The Proposal	204
17	The Wedding	229
18	Delayed Honeymoon	241
19	Honeymoon The Days Before	254
20	The Honeymoon	267

This book is lovingly dedicated to my wonderful wife, whose encouragement was instrumental in its creation.

When the burden of life gets too heavy, you just have to get heavy with it.

My Father

1

The Beginning of the End

As John Roberts took his place at the head of the table, he straightened his tie and forced a smile. "Thank you all for joining me today. I know how busy we all are, especially with the holiday season fast approaching. Team," he began, his voice steady and positively charged, "we are on the brink of our biggest season ever. Every project we have nurtured and every task we have refined has led to this day. I am thrilled by what we are about to accomplish together!" Mr. Roberts greeted the team, his voice projecting confidence and authority. John's words did not just speak of hope; they were a rallying cry that promised victory and celebration in the years to come.

John's mind raced with thoughts of unfinished projects and looming tasks. He knew that this meeting held the potential to either stop his anxiety or worsen it further. As weak as he felt, he still had to show strength and stamina for everyone to see. John glanced around the room, taking in the familiar faces of his employees. Sarah started with John on the first day the store was opened. She was always very well dressed and unaffected by any challenge that came her way. And then there was Tom, the office joker, who found humor in even the most stressful situations. Their calm demeanor only heightened John's anxiety. "As you all know, this year's holiday season is crucial for our department store," Mr. Roberts continued. "We have set high sales goals, and it's up to every one of us to make it happen. Our success this holiday season will determine our bonuses and reputation." The weight of his words settled heavily on his shoulders. He knew the expectations were high, and failure was not an option. His mind wandered as he jumped into the specifics of the upcoming marketing campaigns and sales strategies.

He could not help but think about the countless hours he had spent poring over data, analyzing trends, and brainstorming new ideas. He was responsible for producing a winning strategy to gain customers and drive sales. The pressure was tremendous, and he felt the weight of the store's success on his back. He has been doing this for over 30 years and has always enjoyed and loved the holiday season. However, for some reason, he felt tired and run-down this year and could not shake off whatever bug he had. As the meeting progressed, John's agitation grew. He found himself fidgeting in his seat, unable to focus on the details he was presenting. Thoughts of missed opportunities and potential mishaps consumed his mind. He needed a breakthrough, a stroke of genius, to set his department store apart from the competition.

Finally, the meeting ended, and he felt relief and anticipation. He knew that he needed to channel his anxiety into action. With renewed determination, he told Sarah, his assistant store manager, that he needed a few minutes alone in his office. With that, he walked away to his office. As he passed by his secretary, he said, "Kathy, I need a few minutes alone," and continued to his office.

As the minutes turned into an hour, a sense of unease began to settle over Sarah. John had assured her he would only be there for a few minutes, so his prolonged absence was cause for concern. With a nervous hesitation, Sarah made her way to John's office, accompanied by Kathy, John's secretary, who had also started to worry. Upon entering the office, a scene of distress unfolded before them. John lay slumped over his desk, unmoving and unresponsive to their calls. Panic gripped Sarah's heart as she realized something was seriously wrong. Without wasting another second, she told Kathy to dial the emergency services and urgently request an ambulance.

As sirens wailed in the distance, time seemed to stand still. Sarah and Kathy watched with fear, hoping for a glimmer of improvement in John's condition. As the paramedics arrived, they worked swiftly and assessed John's vital signs. Concerned murmurs filled the air as they hurriedly loaded him onto a stretcher. Sarah and Kathy, their minds swirling with worry, trailed behind as they made their way to the waiting ambulance.

Sarah had been by John's side since they opened the store together over 20 years ago. They had built a deep bond over the years, and although they had both remained single, their friendship had grown into something more. They had fallen in love, and their love had stood the test of time.

The ambulance tires screeched against the pavement as they raced to the hospital. The blaring sirens pierced through the air, a stark reminder of the urgency. Inside the ambulance, Sarah clutched her hands tightly, praying silently for John's well-being while Kathy followed the ambulance in her car.

Upon arrival at the hospital, John was taken to the emergency room, his fate now in the hands of the dedicated medical team. Sarah and Kathy, their faces etched with anxiety, anxiously awaited any news, clinging to the hope that John would soon be on the road to recovery.

Time seemed to stretch endlessly as Sarah paced the sterile hospital corridors, her mind consumed with worry. Every passing second felt like an eternity, leaving her feeling both helpless and desperate. The minutes turned into hours, and the hours into an agonizing wait.

Finally, the doctor appeared from the emergency room, his face showing the seriousness of the situation. Sarah's heart skipped a beat, her breath catching in her throat. The doctor's words hung heavily in the air as he delivered the news. "John suffered a severe breathing problem with his lungs. This is what caused him to pass out. We are not sure what caused this problem, and he remains in critical condition. We have a lot of tests to run before we can find the problem. Sarah, it will take several days to get the answers."

Sarah's world seemed to crash as she listened to the doctor's words. The uncertainty of the future cast a dark shadow on her heart, but she was determined to stay strong for John. She would be by his side, offering unwavering support as he fought his illness. Kathy told Sarah, "I will return to the store and let everyone know the situation. Then, I will go through the office and make notes of where everything stands that Mr. Roberts was working on."

"That's a Good idea." Sarah explained, "When you have completed the information, please put it in a folder and bring it to the hospital so I can review everything." Kathy said, "On my way, Ms. Sarah, can I get anything for you while I am out?" "Not right now," Sarah said. "I may need something later; thank you, Kathy, and take care of things until I get back," she said, smiling and hugging Kathy.

Several days passed as the doctors diligently conducted test after test on John. It felt like an endless cycle of examinations and evaluations, leaving John and Sarah anxiously awaiting the results. Finally, the day arrived when the doctor entered the room to deliver the news. Sarah stood by John's side, her hand tightly clasped in his, supplying unwavering support. The doctor's face was grave, betraying the gravity of the situation.

"John, we have been friends for a very long time, which makes this more difficult to say," the doctor began, his voice gentle yet tinged with sorrow. "John, you have cancer." Silence hung heavy in the room as those words sank in, leaving an unbelievable mark on their lives. Sarah felt her heart clench as her mind raced to process the devastating reality they now faced. With a somber tone, the doctor continued, "We can start a very involved treatment plan, but I must be honest with you both. Despite our best efforts, this cancer is terminal. We estimate you have only three to six months."

Sarah's eyes welled up with tears, her grip on John's hand growing tighter. She fought to stay composed, to be a pillar of strength for her beloved partner. John's face mirrored her anguish, his eyes reflecting a mix of disbelief and acceptance. The doctor's words weighed heavily upon them, shattering their hopes and dreams for a future they had envisioned together. Time suddenly felt infinite and fleeting as they grappled with the harsh reality of impending loss. Amid their pain, they found solace in each other's presence. Sarah trembled as she whispered, "We'll face this together, John. We'll make every moment count." John nodded, barely above a whisper, "I love you, Sarah; let's make the most of the time we have left, cherishing every second."

As the doctor offered comfort and outlined the treatment plan, they held on to each other, finding strength in their love and determination. Their journey ahead would be hard, but their bond would remain unbreakable in the face of adversity.

2

Changing the Will

John Roberts, once a strong and vibrant man, now weak, found himself lying in a hospital bed, battling terminal cancer. His once vibrant spirit had become dim, but his determination to fulfill his final wishes burned fiercely within him. With shaky hands, he called his brother, sister, nieces, and nephews to see them all for the last time. He also called his dear friend and trusted attorney. As John's loved ones gathered around, he realized the inevitable truth that time was running out.

Though heartbroken and filled with grief, John's loved ones found comfort in the attorney's presence. He became a beacon of hope and stability during those trying times, guiding them through the legal processes and offering unwavering support. His calm demeanor and professionalism supplied a sense of assurance, even in the face of their impending loss.

John's siblings, Mary and James, exchanged worried glances as they watched their brother struggle to articulate his desires. They had always been a close-knit family, and the thought of John's departure was difficult to bear. But they knew they had to respect his wishes and support him in his final decisions. As the time to leave drew near, John's loved ones gathered around him.

They held his frail hand, offering love and gratitude for the time they shared. With every ounce of strength he had left, John expressed his love for each of them, assuring them that he would always be with them in spirit. As John watched his loved ones leave the hospital room, a sense of deep sadness and acceptance settled over him. He knew he had limited time left, and his only solace was knowing that he had taken the necessary steps to ensure his affairs were in order.

Sitting in silence, John's mind wandered back to the moments that had led him to this point. Memories of laughter, joy, and love flooded his thoughts, making him smile despite the gravity of the situation. He had always been a fighter, but now he had to face a fight whose outcome was already known. The reality that his time on Earth was coming to an end.

His trusted lawyer and friend sat by John's side, offering comfort and support. With a kind and gentle voice, he assured John that he would take care of everything, ensuring his wishes were fulfilled. It was a bittersweet reassurance, for John knew he would never see the outcome of his final decisions.

As the days turned into weeks, John's health began to decline rapidly. Each passing moment reminded him that life was slipping through his fingers like sand on a beach. Yet, amidst the physical pain and emotional turmoil, John found solace in knowing that he had done all he could to ease the burden on his loved ones.

Though his voice grew weaker, John spoke with his attorney regularly. He called his attorney and asked him to come to the hospital that day. John's attorney, Mr. James Thompson, sensed an urgency in John's voice. He knew there was something important that John wanted to share, and he was determined to ensure that John's wishes were fulfilled. When he arrived, he noticed that John's eyes were growing heavy from the medications; Mr. Thompson leaned in closer, eager to hear what John had to say.

"James," John whispered weakly, "there's something I need to tell you. It's about my will." Mr. Thompson wrinkled his eyebrow, his curiosity piqued. "Yes, John. Please tell me what you want to include in your will." John took a deep breath, gathering his strength. "I want to make sure that Sarah is included in my will and that she will always be a part of JR's Department Store. She has been integral to its success, and I want to honor her dedication."

Mr. Thompson nodded, understanding the importance of Sarah's role in the company. "Of course, John, I will ensure that she is included in your will and that her contributions are recognized."

John's gaze turned intense, a sense of urgency evident. "But there's more, James. I have a stipulation regarding the reading of my will. It cannot be read until Christmas Day, and it must be read in the large conference room of the department store. I want all of my heirs to be there."

Mr. Thompson's eyes widened in surprise at the unusual request. "Christmas Day? Why is that, John?" A weak smile crossed John's face. "Christmas was always my favorite time of the year. It is a time for family, for togetherness. I want my family to come together, not just for the reading of the will, but to remember the joy and love that our family and this store have brought us."

Mr. Thompson nodded, understanding John's sentiment. "I will make sure that your wishes are carried out, John. Your will reading must occur on Christmas Day in the large conference room of JR's Department Store, with all your heirs present." John's eyes closed, a sense of relief washing over him. "Thank you, James. I trust you to manage this with the utmost care." Mr. Thompson placed a comforting hand on John's shoulder. "You can count on me, John. I will ensure that your legacy and wishes are honored."

As the medicine took effect, John drifted into a deep sleep. Mr. Thompson gathered his thoughts, knowing he had an important task ahead of him. He would need to inform Sarah and the rest of John's family about the stipulations in the will and make the necessary arrangements for the reading on Christmas Day. It was an odd request, but he knew it would bring the family together and honor John's memory.

The attorney, overcome with sadness, steadfastly promised to honor John's wishes. "I'll be back soon, my old friend," he said to John, even though he was in a deep sleep.

3

A Glimpse of the Past

As the medicine gradually lulled John into a deep slumber, his mind journeyed back to 1914. The dream was so vivid that it was almost like it was happening again. It was as if he had first set foot in Johnson's clothing store, a small department store in Mountain Home, Arkansas, where he was employed as a men's clothing department clerk.

His passion for men's fashion was evident in every aspect of his life. From how he styled his outfits to his knowledge of the latest trends, he had found his calling in men's clothing. Every morning, as he dressed in his favorite suit and polished his shoes to perfection, he could not help but feel a surge of excitement. The thought of helping others achieve their desired style and confidence motivated him to excel in his career.

Walking into the store, he was greeted by the familiar scent of new fabric and the sound of bustling activity. The racks of neatly arranged clothing and the perfectly organized displays were a testament to his dedication to his craft. His eye for detail allowed him to match fabrics, colors, and patterns that suited each customer's personality and style. Whether it was a classic three-piece suit for a formal occasion or a casual suit for a night out, he could understand his clients' desires and translate them into impeccable outfits.

But it was not just about selling clothes to him. He genuinely cared about his customers and took the time to understand their preferences, body types, and personal styles. He believed clothing was a form of self-expression and wanted to help his clients make a statement with their attire.

His genuine passion for his work radiated in his interactions with customers. He patiently listened to their needs and provided honest advice, ensuring they left the store confident and satisfied with their purchases. This personalized attention to detail set him apart from other salespeople in the industry.

He loved the challenge of staying up-to-date with the ever-changing fashion trends and sought opportunities to expand his knowledge. He attended fashion shows, read industry magazines, and conversed with fellow fashion enthusiasts. His constant thirst for knowledge allowed him to offer his customers the latest and most stylish options.

His dedication and love for his work often led customers to return to the store specifically to seek his advice and expertise. He often received heartfelt thank-you notes and letters expressing gratitude for his exceptional service.

For him, it was not just a job but a career that brought him joy and fulfillment. He was living his dream of helping others look and feel their best. As he left the store at the end of each day, he could not help but look forward to the next, knowing that he would continue to make a difference in his customers' lives through the power of men's clothing.

His love for the job would only get better today, as fate intervened in the form of a beautiful young woman named Gail, who worked in the women's clothing department. Gail had a smile that could light up a room, and John could not help but be drawn to her joyful spirit. Their paths often crossed as they moved about the store, helping customers and ensuring the clothes were well organized.

One afternoon, during their lunch break, John mustered up the courage to talk to Gail. As they sat outside on a bench beneath the warm summer sun, he discovered they shared a passion for literature and poetry. Their conversation flowed effortlessly as if they had known each other for years.

John and Gail quickly discovered that they also shared a passion for success in the clothing business. Their conversations evolved into a daily routine of lunch dates, marked by flirtatious remarks and joking. As their bond deepened, love blossomed, going beyond their professional lives.

John eagerly awaited their encounters, cherishing every moment he spent in Gail's presence. She had a unique charm that attracted him, and he longed to get to know her better. Days turned into weeks, weeks into months, and months into years, and their friendship blossomed into something more. John fell deeply in love with Gail, and she returned his affection with equal intensity. They would spend their lunch breaks together, exploring the nearby park or enjoying each other's company in the quiet corner of the store.

Their love could not be denied, and John could not help but feel that Gail was the missing piece in his life. He had never felt this way before, which excited and terrified him at the same time. But he could not deny the happiness that Gail brought into his world.

As the months passed, John and Gail's relationship grew stronger. They talked about their dreams, fears, and experiences, creating an unbreakable bond. They supported each other through thick and thin, praising each other's triumphs and comforting each other during the difficult times.

John realized that his life had changed for the better since meeting Gail. She had awakened a passion within him that he did not know existed. Gail's support and belief in him inspired him to pursue his hobbies and interests with newfound enthusiasm.

But amidst all the joy, there were moments of doubt and uncertainty. John wondered if he genuinely deserved someone as incredible as Gail. He feared that his insecurities and flaws would eventually push her away. He could not bear the thought of losing her, and it weighed heavily on his heart.

One evening, as John and Gail sat on a bench overlooking the city lights, John took her hand and looked deeply into her eyes. His voice trembled as he confessed his fears and insecurities, sharing his soul with her. Gail listened attentively, her eyes filled with love and understanding.

"John," Gail said softly, "I understand your fears, but you need to know that I love you for who you are, flaws and all. We all have insecurities, but that doesn't mean we can't find happiness together. You deserve love just as much as anyone else."

Her words filled him with warmth and reassurance. At that moment, he knew that he had found his soulmate. They embraced, tears streaming down their faces, and John realized he had never been happier.

From that day forward, John and Gail faced life's challenges together, hand in hand. They supported each other's dreams, encouraged each other to grow, and cherished every moment they spent together. Their love was a beacon of light, guiding them through the darkest times.

As the years passed, their love only deepened and grew more assertive. They faced life's ups and downs with passion and resilience. And through it all, John knew he was the luckiest man in the world to have Gail by his side.

As the world plunged into the chaos of World War I, John and Gail found their love facing a new obstacle. They had built a solid and passionate relationship for three years, but now, duty called upon John to serve his country. The weight of responsibility rested heavily upon his shoulders, and he knew that enlisting was right.

John's heart was torn between his love for Gail and his sense of duty. He had always been a patriotic soul, deeply passionate about his country. The call to serve was not one he could ignore, despite the fear it brought to Gail's heart. He had seen the horrors of war through the newspapers and the stories of others, but he believed it was his duty to protect the values and freedoms they both held dear.

Gail understood the gravity of the situation and knew the war was more significant than their love or any individual. She respected John's desire to serve, and her heart swelled with pride in his selflessness. Yet, she could not help but worry about the dangers he would face on the front lines. Thoughts of losing him haunted her every waking moment.

One evening, as they sat together under a beautiful night sky, John took Gail's hand. The moonlight on his face revealed the determination etched in his eyes. "Gail, my love," he began, his voice trembling with excitement and trepidation, "I have something important to ask you."

Gail's heart skipped a beat as she looked into his eyes. She could sense the weight of his words before he even spoke. She held her breath, waiting for him to continue. "I know that the war has cast a shadow over our lives," John said, his voice filled with emotion, "but amidst the chaos and uncertainty, I am more certain than ever of how much I love you. Gail, will you marry me?"

Gail's eyes brimmed with tears, a mix of joy and fear. She knew their love was strong enough to endure the hardships ahead, but her worries for John's safety lingered. With a trembling voice, she replied, "John, I love you more than words can express, but I cannot deny the fear I feel for your safety. Promise me that you will return to me, no matter what."

John gently wiped away the tears streaming down Gail's cheeks. "I cannot make any promises about what lies ahead," he said, his voice filled with sincerity. "But I promise you this, my love: I will fight for our future, the world we dream of, and the chance to return to your arms."

Gail's heart swelled with love and admiration for John. She knew his sense of duty was unwavering, and she could not imagine a life without him. With a determined nod, she whispered, "Yes, John, I will marry you. Your love strengthens me, and we will face whatever comes our way together."

As their love deepened, the walls they had built around themselves slowly crumbled, allowing their true feelings to be revealed to one another. As the love in their hearts grew stronger, so did the intensity of their passion. Their kisses became more passionate, their embraces longer, and their bodies yearned for one another. They discovered a world of pleasure in each other's arms, losing themselves in their desires of love.

Yet, amidst the excitement of their intimacy, doubts and insecurities began to emerge. They questioned whether their connection was strong enough to withstand the challenges ahead. Fear of vulnerability and the possibility of heartbreak threatened to pull them apart.

Their journey towards intimacy was not always smooth sailing. There were moments of doubt, misunderstandings, and missteps. However, they remained committed to one another, determined to navigate their emotions and maintain their love for each other.

Ultimately, their intimacy was not a fleeting moment of passion but a profound bond that grew stronger with time. They discovered that true intimacy is a dance of vulnerability, trust, and open communication. It transformed their lives, bringing them closer together and making them feel alive in ways they had never imagined.

And so, as the world continued to be engulfed in war, John and Gail embarked on a journey to test their love's strength. They decided that as soon as he returned, they would get married. They held each other tightly, finding comfort in knowing their love would endure the trials ahead. Little did they know the challenges that awaited them, but they were ready to face them together.

When John left for the war, Gail's heart sank with mixed emotions. Their love had blossomed into something profound, a connection that seemed unbreakable. However, as John prepared to embark on this challenging journey, Gail was burdened with a secret she could not share. Their final moments together were filled with bittersweet longing, as Gail desperately wanted to seize the opportunity to tell John before he left. But fear and uncertainty held her back, clutching tightly onto the secret that had taken residence within her. She knew their lives would be forever changed if her suspicion proved true.

Gail had noticed subtle changes in her body over the past few weeks. Her usual routines had become a delicate dance of caution as she tried to conceal the telltale signs that her world was about to shift. The whispers of morning sickness, the faint glow on her cheeks, and the subtle tightening of her clothes all pointed towards one undeniable truth: she might be pregnant.

The realization left Gail in a state of both wonder and worry. How could she bring a child into a world ravaged by war? Could John handle the news, knowing the dangers ahead for him? These questions swirled in her mind, challenging her every thought and leaving her isolated.

As the days turned into weeks, Gail longed for John's return more intensely than ever. She yearned for his comforting presence, strong arms, and unwavering support. But she could not deny the fear that gnawed at her heart, the anxiety of how he would react to the news she had kept hidden for so long. Gail confided in her closest friend, Emily, who had been her pillar of strength throughout their entire relationship. Emily listened attentively, offering comforting words and a reassuring smile. She understood Gail's turmoil, conflicting emotions, and the weight of her secret. Emily encouraged Gail to trust in their love and to have faith that John would stand by her side no matter what.

Gail's heart ached as she counted the passing days, weeks, months, and years eagerly awaiting John's return. It had been three long years since he left for battle, and she had been filled with hope and longing. She occasionally sent and received letters, but it had been over a year since she had received a letter, and the last letter she had sent was returned as undeliverable. In his previous letter, he stated they were entering a major battle. Little did she know that John's journey home would be filled with trials and tribulations. The war had taken its toll on him, physically and emotionally. John had endured unimaginable hardships during his time away.

Gail had never known that John had been wounded in the heat of battle and taken prisoner. His body had borne the physical scars of war, and his spirit had been shaken to its core. As he fought for his life, he held on to the memories of Gail, finding comfort in the love they shared.

After the war ended, John was transported from a POW camp to a medical facility to receive the necessary treatment for his injuries. The journey to recovery was challenging, both physically and mentally. He endured countless surgeries and grueling rehabilitation sessions, determined to regain the strength he once had. However, it was not just his physical wounds that required attention. The trauma of war had left a lasting impact on John's mental well-being. He found himself plagued by nightmares, haunted by the memories of the battles he had fought. To aid in his recovery, he spent time in a mental hospital, seeking the help and support he needed to heal.

As the years passed, John slowly pieced himself back together, bit by bit. It had now been five years since he left Gail. He never forgot her, and the thought of her love gave him strength during his darkest moments. With every step forward, he dreamt of the day he could finally return to her, hoping she would still be waiting.

Finally, after what felt like an eternity, John was considered well enough to leave the confines of the medical facility. He longed to be reunited with Gail and hold her in his arms again. With a determined spirit, he returned to the town they had once called home.

Filled with anticipation, he set out to find her, unaware of the new path life had taken her on. Gail, determined to start anew, had moved to another city with her son, seeking a fresh start away from the memories that haunted her. John searched far and wide, but Gail was nowhere to be found.

Heartbroken and disheartened, John realized that the love he once shared with Gail had slipped through his fingers. The town that had once embraced him with open arms now held bittersweet memories of a love lost long ago. With a heavy heart, John made the difficult decision to move on, leaving behind the place that had given him so much love and hope in the past. Unknown to John, Gail moved back about one year after John quit searching and even went back to work at the same clothing store.

Though their paths had diverged, the love between Gail and John remained etched within their hearts. Each carried the weight of what could have been and the missed opportunity to rekindle their passion and share a future. But life had cruelly kept them apart with its unpredictable twists and turns.

As time passed, Gail and John found solace in their separate lives, yet both always wondered about the lost love. Each carried the scars of their battles, the invisible wounds that had shaped them into who they had become. And though they may never cross paths again, the memory of their love would forever linger, a bittersweet reminder of what could have been.

4

Unraveling the Past

John woke up in a daze, disoriented by the sudden intrusion of nurses administering shots and taking his vitals. He was momentarily confused, thinking he was still in 1914 with Gail. As he regained his composure, fragments of a life-like dream lingered in his mind. It was a dream about Gail, his long-lost love. With a sense of urgency, he asked his nurse to call Mr. Thompson, his trusted attorney and best friend.

"James," John said, his weak voice filled with excitement, "I need your help. Can you come see me?" Mr. Thompson said, "Yes, John, I will be there quickly." Mr. Thompson finished his current task, left his office, and headed to the hospital.

As Mr. Thompson entered John's hospital room, he could sense the urgency in his voice and the longing in his eyes. John's frail form lay in the hospital bed, his face etched with a mixture of hope and fear. Mr. Thompson approached him and gently touched his shoulder, offering a reassuring smile. Mr. Thompson tried to speak, but John was so excited that he started trying to tell Mr. Thompson something. However, his voice was so weak that Mr. Thompson could not understand him. He was trying to tell Mr. Thompson about his dream about Gail. The long-lost love of his life that he wanted to see before he died.

"John, my dear friend," Mr. Thompson said softly, "I'm here for you. Take your time, catch your breath, and then tell me about this dream you had about Gail." John nodded, taking a moment to compose himself. He took a deep breath and began recounting the details of his dream. As he spoke, his voice carried a sense of nostalgia and longing. It was clear that Gail held a special place in his heart, even after all these years.

"She appeared to me in the dream, James," John said, his voice filled with wonder and sadness. "Just like she was when we were young. Her smile, her laughter, everything was so vivid. I could feel the love we once shared, and it overwhelmed me. I realized I never stopped loving her, even after all these years."

Mr. Thompson listened intently, his heart going out to John as he understood the depth of his emotions. He knew reconnecting with Gail would mean the world to his friend, but he also understood their challenges.

"John, it's beautiful that you still hold such love in your heart for Gail," Mr. Thompson said, his voice filled with compassion. "I can see how much she means to you. It's not an easy task, but if it's what you truly desire, I'm here to help you reconnect with her."

John's eyes sparkled with gratitude as he looked at Mr. Thompson. "Thank you, James, you're a true friend," he whispered. "I know it won't be easy, but I want to try. Can you help me find her? I want to see her, to tell her how much she means to me before it's too late."

Mr. Thompson nodded, his commitment unwavering. "Of course, John," he replied, his voice filled with determination. "I will do everything in my power to help you find Gail. Together, we'll make this dream of yours a reality."

With that, Mr. Thompson embarked on a mission to find Gail, the long-lost love of John's life. He knew it would be difficult, but he would go to great lengths to grant his old friend's final wish.

Mr. Thompson enlisted the services of the most exceptional private investigator he had ever worked with. True to his word, Mr. Thompson soon arranged for the investigator to meet with John.

When the private investigator arrived, John wasted no time sharing his story. He recounted his past with Gail, their shared memories, and the life they had built together before he left for war. He explained that he needed to know what Gail was doing now and where she lived, but he clarified that the investigator should not approach her directly. John only looked to gather information about her current situation.

After weeks of tireless searching, the private investigator returned with a detailed report. Gail, it turned out, had remained in the same city where she and John had once lived. After John's departure, she worked at the same store for three more years. The investigator also revealed that Gail had given birth to a son a few months after John left. She had named him John, affectionately calling him Little John.

Heartened by this unexpected news, John discovered that Gail had never married and had dedicated herself to raising their son alone. After three years, she made the courageous decision to move to another city and start fresh, only to return to Mountain Home a few years later. The investigator informed John that Gail had passed away about a year ago, leaving Little John the house where she had raised him. After several months, Little John put the home up for sale and moved. None of the neighbors knew where he had moved to.

Overwhelmed by the revelation of a son he never knew he had, John felt a mix of joy, regret, and a deep desire to make amends. He thanked the private investigator for his diligent work and instructed him to send the bill to Mr. Thompson, then bid him farewell. With renewed purpose, John told his attorney, Mr. Thompson, that he intended to amend his will to include his long-lost son.

At that time, John also told Mr. Thompson, "James, I want you to go ahead and take control of my estate even though I have not passed away yet. This way, you can take care of some of the things you need to do and not have to wait until I'm gone. Can you do that for me, James?" "Yes, my dear friend, I can and will do that." Mr. Thompson said with tears in his eyes.

With a sense of sadness, he knew he would never see the day when his family would gather, not only to hear the reading of his will but to meet his long-lost son and hear about a love story that had been dormant for decades. Mr. Thompson called Sarah and asked if she could come to his office as soon as possible to discuss things John wanted done. Mr. Thompson said, "John has not passed away yet, but he has asked me, and I have agreed, to go ahead and take control as the executor of his estate." He conveyed the situation to Sarah with a voice that befitted the situation. The weight of his role as the executor of John's estate was not lost on him, nor was the gravity of the situation influenced by John's deteriorating health. He held Sarah's gaze as he spoke, his voice firm and steady, "Sarah, I am entrusting you with a huge responsibility."

His gaze gently scanned her reaction, the corners of her eyes twitching, her body language conveying a controlled astonishment. He continued, "I am appointing you as the department store manager." The words hung momentarily as if gaining weight by the second.

The announcement was followed by a pause, just a momentary lapse, before Mr. Thompson added, "This arrangement will stand until the will and estate are settled." His tone was final, an explicit confirmation that this was not merely a suggestion but a decision made by John.

5

Finding Little John

November 1946 arrived in a flurry of snowflakes, settling over the city like a white blanket, whispers of stories from previous seasons, and the promise of new beginnings for the future. Sarah's breath fogged up the glass as she stared out the window of JR's department store, her eyes seeing the untouched snow covering the vast parking lot. It was a stark reminder of the unforgiving grip of the year, which had taken more from her than it had given. It had been a little over a year now since John, her dear friend and the man she loved, was diagnosed with cancer and given a chilling three to six months to live. It has been a little over seven months since she had looked into his eyes for the last time. Each day since then, she had been shouldering the responsibility of the store, her only relief in a world without him.

In the bustling city stands a tower, a monument of enterprise, JR's Department Store. It would have been just another brick in the cityscape, except it was recently orphaned. Its heart and soul, John Roberts, had succumbed to cancer. Clutching the keys to this kingdom was not an heir but an attorney, aiding the owner in finding its rightful successor.

Meanwhile, Mr. Thompson, John's attorney, was on an urgent mission. They had so far failed to find Little John, the ghost of a son absent from his father's life. A young man, unknown to them all, whose

23

presence was essential for reading John's will. John never knew he had a son until a month before he died. The mystery of the son he had never met lingered as an echo of his past.

Sarah often found herself contemplating the existence of Little John. As the snowflakes gently landed on the windowsill, she could not help but feel a mix of curiosity and apprehension. What would it mean for JR's Department Store, the last piece of her connection to John, if Little John were found?

The snow continued to fall, crafting a beautiful yet cold world outside. As Sarah turned to face the store, her heart was heavy with uncertainty. She was a caretaker, caught at the crossroads of the past and the future, tasked with honoring a legacy and preserving the future.

In an office across town, Mr. Thompson found himself sifting through countless letters and documents, tracing the steps of a man who was seemingly everywhere and nowhere at the same time. Little John, the missing heir, is the last part of the puzzle needed to move forward. As night fell, he could not shake the feeling that he was running out of time. But he knew he had to keep trying, for John's sake and Sarah's. He owed it to them both. It was November, and if he found Little John soon, he could read the will on Christmas Day as required. It would be another year before he could read the will as needed at Christmas.

The snow continued to fall, veiling the city in a cloak of white, holding its breath in anticipation of what was to come. In the sanctity of his private office, Mr. Thompson sat behind a mahogany desk littered with case files, each bearing a tale of secrets and sorrows. But the early afternoon case under scrutiny held a particular place in his heart. It was about Little John, a name that echoed out of yesteryear. The name had been the mystery obsession of a man named John Roberts, who had left behind a legacy in the form of the famous department store, JR's.

Mr. Thompson knew his task was enormous. He was not just looking for a man, but a man who never knew he was being looked for.

He was to find a son who had never known his father, the one he was about to inherit. He was to reunite a legacy with its rightful heir, to mend a story torn apart by the world's wars and the heart's.

Mr. Thompson rehired the first private investigator he had used to search for Little John and reviewed what they already knew about him. Mr. Thompson told the investigator, "He should be about 28 years old and never knew his father. He was born in 1917, shortly after his father left for war, not knowing that his girlfriend and the love of his life was pregnant. After three years, Gail, thinking John was killed in the war, took her son and moved away from their home. John could never find her when he returned from the war."

Now, Mr. Thompson, John's attorney and close friend, is trying one last time to find him with the help of the first private investigator. John Roberts had been a charming man, a self-made entrepreneur riding the waves of the 20th century. His charm alone had lifted a humble general store to a sprawling department store known throughout the city. However, his life was marked by the cruel hand of fate. About seven months after cancer claimed him, the whispers of a forgotten past echoed in the corridors of his grand mansion.

Little John was not so little anymore. At the age of twenty-eight, he was a man in his prime yet unaware of the legacy his bloodline carried. John Roberts had never known he had a son, his love torn away from him by the horrors of the Great War. Gail, his beautiful Gail, had carried their young son away when the mayor of the little town was informed that many of the town's men had died in a major battle on the Western Front. Gail believed John was among this group and was heartbroken. Gail, unmarried to John and not a relative, could not get further information. Thinking this to be accurate, Gail took her son and moved away.

She was a woman of grit and grace. Believing John to be gone, she picked up the pieces of her shattered life, clutching the newborn Little John close to her chest, and moved away to start over. Her love for John was rekindled with every smile of Little John, a living testament to their undying love. A son John Roberts had never set eyes upon, a son he had never known to look for.

The cruel hands of time had claimed Gail no less than a year ago. Little John was all alone now, unaware of his late father's desperate search for him, which started in the last throes of his cancer-riddled life. The task was now in Mr. Thompson's hands: to find Little John and reveal the legacy that rightfully belonged to him. A task that was as personal as it was professional.

The clock ticked, oblivious to the tales unfolding under its watch. As the sun started setting, casting long shadows over Mr. Thompson's office, he sat back in his chair, a determined glint in his eyes. The search for Little John Roberts was about to begin again. The shadow of an old romance was rising from the ashes, revealing itself as a legacy that needed to be fulfilled.

Little John, oblivious to the chess game life was playing, was about to become the inheritor of an empire he never knew existed. A man born amidst the war was about to face another, a battle of self-identity, legacy, and hidden love.

So, in the quiet confines of his office, amidst the smell of old books and the rustling of legal documents, Mr. Thompson set the wheels in motion. At that moment, he was not just an attorney but a searcher for truth, a builder of bridges, and a writer of a story begging to be told.

Mr. Thompson had spent the last six months in his career's most spellbinding and complex case. The puzzle pieces were not aligning. He was on the verge of calling it quits with no hope of finding Little John.

He had been tirelessly scouring every possible lead, every hint that might lead him to Little John. After several futile attempts, he received a promising lead that appeared like a beacon amidst the uncertainty of his journey: A man named John had decided to sell his mother's house. The elusive Little John, the rightful heir to the department store empire, may finally be within his grasp. Mr. Thompson had received a long-distance telephone call from a lawyer, Mr. Daniels, in Mountain Home, Arkansas, who wanted to discuss a house for sale with him. Mr. Thompson explained, "I am swamped and do not have time to talk about a house for sale in Arkansas."

Mr. Daniels interrupted, saying, "I heard through the grapevine about the young man named Little John you were looking for." He told him, "I know it is a long way from Poplar Bluff, Missouri, but there is a young man here, about twenty-eight years old, with the first name of John. He is selling his late mother's house, who passed away about a year ago, and he no longer has any use for it. And the young man is from the same city as the Little John you seek. I am unsure if this is your man, but it seems like him. You might want to take a trip out here and talk to him."

Tonight, Mr. Thompson wrapped up his duties at his desk with anticipation beneath his hardened surface. A blend of eagerness and yearning stirred within him as the sun set for the day. The promise of a new acquaintance was on the horizon, a young man he was eager to meet.

The journey, however, could not be completed tonight. The winding curves of the mountain road, treacherous and unpredictable, commanded respect from the traveler. The twilight was no friend to those who dared traverse such paths without the sun's vigilant watch. The wisdom of the years cautioned Mr. Thompson that a night-time venture was not prudent. He glanced at the office, which had been his world for countless hours. The corridors echoed with muted conversations of days past, while the flickering lights in the hallway seemed to burn brighter in acknowledgment of tomorrow's trip. The eight-hour journey would be difficult, twisty, and long. But it was a small price to pay for what awaited at the end of the road. His house was silent as he walked in, a contrast to the clamor of his thoughts. It was an early night for him, punctuated only by the clock's ticking, reminding him of the time still left for him to wait. The dawn would usher in a fresh day, bursting with the promises of new beginnings.

The eight-hour trip had him driving into town late in the afternoon. The treacherous journey started in heavy snow and ended in light rain. Unfortunately, it was too late to meet the lawyer as planned. However, he quickly dialed up the lawyer, only to find out that his prospective young client, whom he secretly hoped was Little John, would only be available at 10 A.M. the following morning to discuss the house sale.

Mr. Daniels, in an assuring tone, informed him, "I will handle the preliminary stages of the business at hand, setting things in motion before calling you into the session." The lawyer also said, "By the way, the man's name is John Jenkins, and his mother's name is Gail Jenkins." Thus, he would finally have the opportunity to meet the elusive young man for whom he had traveled such a long distance. The anticipation stirred in him, brimming with expectancy of what the banner of a new day would unfurl. Thus, he checked into a hotel near the lawyer's office.

A light rain pattered against the hotel room window, a rhythmic complement to his thoughts. Mr. Thompson replayed every conversation with John, sifting through details, scrutinizing each word, and pausing. Like a gold miner, he hoped to strike upon a nugget of helpful information: a clue, a hint, anything that might link John to this Jenkins boy. Did he ever say Gail's last name? He could not remember John ever using Gail's last name. He knew he would not sleep tonight either. His mind was a cyclone, reeling with possibilities, each more unsettling than the last.

Gail Jenkins. He turned the name over in his head, and this was a mystery to unravel. Although her last name was never known, he had a feeling he couldn't shake that this was her. He could not help but wonder if John had intentionally left out the details. Could he have known that the time would come when Mr. Thompson needed to know? Had John merely been protecting him from the inevitable heartbreak that lay ahead?

The next day held the prospect of meeting Little John, a circumstance that ignited a strange mix of anticipation and dread within Mr. Thompson. The excited prospect of finally being united with Little John was equally countered by a potential disappointment.

The night grew darker as the rain grew heavier. In the dimly lit hotel room, Mr. Thompson reviewed the day's events, his plans for tomorrow, and a reminder of the gravity of the events that loomed ahead. He ordered a flask of whiskey from room service, hoping to quiet the raging thoughts that refused to let him sleep.

As dawn approached, Mr. Thompson anxiously awaited the morning and the meeting with the lawyer that would follow. He was on the brink of a surprise, about to enter the heart of a year-old mystery. His pursuit of Little John had led him thus far on a twisted path, and now the truth was within his grasp, only a few hours away. The future remained uncertain, yet he was a man emboldened by hope, teetering on the edge of closure. Hopefully, he would meet Little John tomorrow and clear up the mystery.

As dawn broke over the city, Mr. Thompson lifted the phone in his barely lit hotel room and asked the hotel operator to call his office in Poplar Bluff, Missouri. With heavy lids, he waited for the hotel operator to dial his long-distance number to his office, the stern rings echoing in his ears. When the other line was picked up, his rough, tired voice, thick with sleep, spoke almost instinctively, "I need you to make a call to check up on some information, please."

He raked a hand through his thinning hair, sitting heavily in the depths of his hotel chair. Though gruff from sleep, his voice was steady and demanding, leaving no room for discussion. "There's a little department store on 5th Street, here in Mountain Home, where John Roberts used to work in 1917. Please call and ask about a specific individual, Gail Jenkins. Confirm if she was working there at the same time as John Roberts. Also, find out if they know where she moved when she left. Call me back with the information at the hotel or the number I left on my desk for Mr. Daniels in Mountain Home, Arkansas."

Mr. Thompson's voice softened as he uttered the woman's name. His eyes stared blankly out the window, lost in a sea of thoughts as he waited for his instructions to be acknowledged.

6

Little John Learns the Truth

The sun rose over the horizon when Mr. Daniels sat at his beautiful wood desk in his corner office. He had just opened the door and let Mr. Thompson in for a cup of coffee to wait for John Jenkins to come in. Mr. Thompson's eyes were bloodshot from the long hours he had been putting in, but there was a strange excitement to his exhaustion. As the phone rang on Mr. Daniels' desk, the loud and shrill ringtone pulled him quickly from his trance. "Hello?" He heard Mr. Daniels say. He said, "Phone call for you," as he handed the phone to him. "Hello," Mr. Thompson said.

"Good morning, Mr. Thompson. I have the information for you," his secretary's voice filtered through the speaker. "Give me the information, please," he instructed, leaning back in his chair. The line clicked, and a gruff voice said, "Mr. Thompson, this is the private investigator. Got the info you've been chasing." A surge of adrenaline shook off some of the remnants of Thompson's fatigue. "What have you got?"

The private investigator's voice was gruff as he went straight to the point. "I made a phone call to Johnson's clothing store on 5th street in Mountain Home. I talked to a couple of people who had been there during that time, and they remembered both of them. Our girl! Gail Jenkins! She was employed at the same place during the same period as John Roberts. It's been a long time, but they think she moved away for a year or so after World War I, but moved back later and went back to work at Johnson's clothing store again. That's no coincidence, Mr. Thompson." The information sent a wave of relief coursing through Mr. Thompson. The puzzle pieces slowly fell into place, painting a picture more straightforward than he had hoped. But the private investigator was not done. "One more thing," he continued, a note of excitement creeping into his voice, "talking to some of the folks who worked with both of them, got a description of Gail. It might prove useful in comparing this description to John Jenkins's description of his mother."

Mr. Thompson grasped the edge of his desk, the wood cool beneath his fingers. The phone call had quickly turned into a breakthrough. "Go on," he urged, gripping his notepad and ready to write down every detail about Gail Jenkins. Whatever the private investigator had to share was sure to change everything. The morning was brisk as John Jenkins, a man in his twenties, strode purposefully into the bustling law office. Dressed in a dark navy suit, his dark hair a little rough around the edges, he was young but confident. His features were etched with a grim determination, hinting at the inner turmoil that lay behind his strong face. The chatter in the room hushed as he arrived, all eyes pivoting to take in his commanding presence. Everyone felt something was about to happen with this young man, but they didn't know what it was.

"Good morning, everyone," John said, his voice echoing through the quiet room. His eyes scanned each face, from the fresh-faced assistants to the seasoned veterans, making a point to acknowledge every individual in the room. In the corner office, Mr. Daniels awaited him, the heavy oak doors already open in an unspoken invitation. Mr. Daniels, a stern yet fair lawyer with sharp lines across his face, had spent years closing properties around the city and had a reputation for closing deals with an iron fist.

His gaze finally fell upon Mr. Daniels, a gentleman with silver-streaked hair and wise, steely eyes. Mr. Daniels was highly respected in legal circles and had been managing the sale of the house for John.

As he ushered John into the office, the stark contrast between them was evident. Mr. Daniels, with his graying hair and grizzled exterior, embodied the hardened face of the legal industry. On the other hand, John was the embodiment of a new generation: intelligent, sympathetic, and more focused on preserving his mother's legacy than the potential profit of the sale.

"John," Mr. Daniels greeted him, stepping forward and offering a firm handshake. "Good to see you." "Likewise," John replied, shaking his hand. "Can we get started?" "Of course," Mr. Daniels said, gesturing towards his office. This room reflected his years of experience with a meticulously organized filing system, walls lined with certificates, and a desk full of well-used tools of the trade. John followed him into the office with a sense of nervousness. He was here to complete the sale of his mother's house, the last remnant of his childhood memories. John's heart throbbed in his chest; he felt a lump in his throat, the bitter nostalgia of the impending sale hitting him hard. It was not just his mother's house he was selling, it was the bittersweet memories of homebound Christmas dinners, laughter echoing through the halls, warm bedtime stories, and whispered goodnights.

But it was a necessary step, a closure that he desperately needed. As he sat down opposite Mr. Daniels, he could not help but stare at the contract in front of him. It was more than just a transfer of property; at twenty-eight, John was about to sell a piece of his past and step into the uncharted territories of his future. Little did he know that this simple business transaction with Mr. Daniels would set the course for a story of unexpected twists and turns.

Once Mr. Daniels and John Jenkins completed their legal business of selling his mother's house, Mr. Daniels introduced Mr. Thompson. "John, this is Mr. Thompson, an attorney from Poplar Bluff, Missouri." Mr. Daniels told John, "He would like to talk to you about your father." John had never known his father. His mother only said to him that he was named after his father and that his father was killed in World War I. John's face showed an instant frown with a look of puzzlement. He was not expecting this and had no idea what it was about. "Hello, John," Mr. Thompson said. "If you are the person I think you are, I have information about your father. He was a very close friend of mine." At first glance at John, Mr. Thompson was slightly astounded at how much John looked like John Roberts. Was it real, or was it because, deep down, he wanted this to be his friend's long-lost son?

To John, Mr. Thompson appeared to be a contemporary of Mr. Daniels, standing at the side. He was a tall, lean man with salt-and-pepper hair, faithfully groomed, and the same tight-set jaw that spoke of a lifetime in courts and legal engagements. His glasses were perched on his nose, and his piercing blue eyes glistened with a guarded intelligence, mirroring a deep pool of knowledge and wisdom fostered through years of legal experience.

"Nice to meet you, Mr. Thompson," John said, extending his hand in greeting. John had never known his dad, and Mr. Thompson's words piqued his interest. Curiosity pierced through his initial shock, and he felt a whirlpool of emotions: anticipation, bewilderment, and a tinge of dread. "I'd like to hear what you have to say."

"Good," replied Mr. Thompson, his eyes resonating with a sincerity that was hard to find in most attorneys. "If this is your father, John, he was a remarkable man, as strong-willed as they come and with a heart as vast as the Mississippi."

Mr. Thompson's voice wavered slightly as he continued, invoking in John a sense of sadness he did not expect. "If this is your father," as he held up a folder thick with letters, pictures, military records, and other documents, "he was quite the entrepreneur; he was always looking at how things were and trying to figure out how to make them work better. He was the kind of person who would not rest until he had given his all."

Mr. Thompson explained to John that he needed to ask him some questions before they went any further. John said he understood and agreed with this and told him to go ahead and start asking his questions. Mr. Thompson asked him. "Did you have any other names used during your youth?" Mr. Thompson's questions tugged forth memories long buried in John's past, stirring within him forgotten emotions.

There was a hint of nervousness in his voice as he responded, "Actually, there was another name I used in my youth; people used to call me Little John." The excitement began to build in Mr. Thompson. He asked John, "What kind of work did your mother do when you were young?"

John said, "She worked in clothing sales," a wistful smile playing on his lips. "She used to work in a small department store here in town. She always loved working in a clothing store and raised me while putting in long hours at the store. " Then John said, "We also lived somewhere else for a while, not sure where that was." Mr. Thompson seemed absorbed in John's story, nodding as he continued questioning. "Did your mother ever tell you anything about your father's background? Any family ties or where he was from?"

John shook his head. "She never mentioned much about his family, except that his parents had already passed away before I was born, and she said he had a brother and sister that she had never met. As for where he was from, she only mentioned that he was from a small town in Missouri. Mr. Thompson then asked him what his mother loved most about his father. John replied, "She used to say he had the most infectious laughter that could lighten up a room instantly, and how brave he was to volunteer for the war."

Mr. Thompson thanked John for sharing his stories and asked if they could get together this afternoon at about three. John promised to get back to him once he had completed some other things he needed to finish before closing on the house sale. With curiosity and excitement in his stomach, John wondered what Mr. Thompson could find in his simple family history.

John gave a curt nod as he walked away; the image of his parents in the early years sprang to his mind. He turned to Mr. Thompson and said, "Back in my hotel room, I have a picture of my parents. Would you like me to bring the picture with me at three?" Mr. Thompson, with his eyes showing excitement, said, "Yes, please bring it with you." He was so excited now that he could hardly wait until three this afternoon. But he knew he needed to review all the information with the private investigator for their opinion. He also knew that John's picture would be the deciding factor, and there would be no going back once he approved it.

Mr. Thompson went back to his room to make some phone calls. He called the private investigator to inform him of everything he had discovered about John Jenkins. With all the information, the private investigator agreed with Mr. Thompson that this had to be the correct person. All this information could not have been a coincidence; it had to be accurate. Then Mr. Thompson told the private investigator that the young boy had a picture of his parents in his hotel room and would bring it to the three o'clock meeting. If the images looked like John Roberts, there would be no mistaking this, and the young boy would be the long-lost son of John Roberts.

In the hotel room, John picked up the picture. His mother, a woman with cascading brown hair, looked beautiful in her simple white dress, while his father, tall and handsome in his army uniform, wrapped his arm protectively around her. Behind their smiles were untold stories that he was not sure Mr. Thompson could shed any light on. John took a moment to rekindle the memories of his mother before laying down the weathered photograph. Held with a sense of respect, it depicted a happy couple, his parents.

At the three o'clock meeting, heart-pounding, John presented the photo to Mr. Thompson. The older man's hands trembled slightly as he reached for the photograph, his eyes entranced by the image of the couple. He traced their faces lightly and drew a shaky breath. They were incredibly young in the picture, but there was no mistaking the couple; he was seeing again the face of his old friend and, for the first time, the face of Gail, the love of his life. As Mr. Thompson's eyes welled up, John knew his journey was beginning. A trip that would unite him with his past, bringing closure to his present, and illuminating his future.

"John," Mr. Thompson began, his voice sincere and heavy with the weight of the words he was about to speak, "I won't mince my words, nor will I sugarcoat the truth. John, this picture and the contents of this folder prove that you are the person I am looking for. I will tell you now a love story that's remained untold for far too long."

"Your parents," he continued, "met more than three decades ago in a tiny clothing store tucked away in Mountain Home. It was a love story that bloomed at first sight. They decided they would marry as soon as your father returned from fighting in the war."

He took a deep breath, "But the narrative that you have known, that your father was killed in battle, is far from the truth. He was a war hero and was critically injured during a significant clash. He was captured and sent to a prisoner-of-war camp, where he endured hellish days. It took him years to recover from the physical wounds and mental scars. When he returned, hoping to find your mother, she was gone. She had believed the story of the city mayor that many of the men were killed in that battle, including your father. Since your mother and father were not married and there was no family she could contact, she was unable to obtain any additional information from the army. Believing this was all true, she packed you up and left to start a new life in a different city. Leaving no trace behind of where she was gone."

Mr. Thompson paused, looking up at John, "Your father relentlessly searched for her, but she was like a leaf lost in the wind. At that time, he had no idea that you even existed. He only discovered about nine months ago that he had a son."

"Here is what your father shared with me about nine months ago. I have written this down and will read it as your father told me." Mr.

Thompson stated, "Soon after he started to work at the small department store in 1914, a beautiful young woman named Gail began to work in the women's clothing department. Gail, as we know now, was your mother. She had a radiant smile that could light up a room, and he could not help himself; he was drawn to her cheerful spirit. Their paths often crossed as they moved about the store, helping customers and ensuring the merchandise was well organized."

"He and your mother quickly discovered that they also shared a passion for success in the clothing business. Their conversations evolved into a daily ritual of lunch dates and flirtatious teasing. As their bond deepened, love blossomed, transcending their professional lives."

"He eagerly awaited their encounters, cherishing every moment he spent in your mother's presence. She had a unique charm that attracted him, and he longed to get to know her better. Days turned into weeks, weeks into months, and months into years, and their friendship blossomed into something more. He fell deeply in love with Gail, and she returned his affection with equal intensity. They would spend their lunch breaks together, exploring the nearby park or enjoying each other's company in the quiet corner of the store".

"As the world plunged into the chaos of World War I, he and your mother found their love facing a huge obstacle. They had built a solid and passionate relationship for three years, but now, duty called upon him to serve his country. The weight of responsibility rested heavily on his shoulders, and he knew that enlisting was right."

"His heart was torn between his love for Gail and his sense of duty. He had always been a patriotic soul, deeply passionate about his country. The call to serve was not one he could ignore, despite the fear it brought to Gail's heart. He had seen the horrors of war through the newspapers and the stories of others, but he believed it was his duty to protect the values and freedoms they both held dear."

"Your mother, too, understood the gravity of the situation. She knew the war was more significant than their love or any individual.

She respected his desire to serve, and her heart swelled with pride in his selflessness. Yet, she could not help but worry about the dangers he would face on the front lines. Thoughts of losing him haunted her every waking moment."

Then Mr. Thompson said, "And that's how your father told me about nine months ago." He softly closed the folder, his eyes meeting John's, sharing the burden of a fractured past. "There is so much more I need to tell you if you are interested and want to continue." For a moment, silence fell in the room. "What happened then?" John asked, now fully invested in the story of his father.

Mr. Thompson sighed, his eyes distant. "That's where the story takes a turn, John. How about we discuss it more over dinner? You see, your father's story cannot be rushed. I want to make sure I do him justice." "OK," John said. "How about the local steak house at 7 P.M.?" "All right, John," Mr. Thompson said, shaking his hand. "I understand this may be a bit overwhelming. Your father was a good man. A complicated man, but a good one." John nodded, his throat dry. "What," he said, "what was his name?"

Mr. Thompson hesitated momentarily, his gaze dropping to the polished mahogany desk between them. "His name," he said as he looked back at John. "His name was John," he said. "John Roberts," he finally said as he continued to look into John's eyes. The name hung in the air, causing a ripple of emotion in the room.

John swallowed hard, his father's name echoing in his mind. He knew it was an experience he would never forget, the moment he finally learned about the man he had longed to know all his life.

It was 7 P.M., and John and Mr. Thompson were on time. They went into the restaurant and asked for a table for two. They were taken to a small room that could accommodate ten, and they both wondered why they were being given a private room. When Mr. Thompson asked why there was such a big room for the two of them, the owner said, "Mr. Daniels is a friend of mine, and he had called ahead and asked if I could give the two of you a private room. I was glad to help; your server is Spring, and she will take care of anything you need."

Spring served their drinks and said, "I'll check in with you every five minutes to see if you're ready to order." "Please, Mr. Thompson," John said, his voice choked with emotion. "Tell me everything and when or if I can ever meet my father." And with that, they began to talk.

John sat stiffly in his chair, his mind a whirlwind of apprehension and curiosity. He was unsure if he was ready to jump into the past or face the surprise about his father's life, but he knew this was a door he had to walk through. The secrets of his father were about to spill forth, and John was on the edge of a void filled with surprises. Little did he know that his life would take an unexpected turn. The day had started with selling his mother's house, and he would find out about the father he had never known. He had no idea that he was going to step into the role of the son of a multimillionaire. It was a monumental transformation; he could not conceive of the changes to come.

As John looked at Mr. Thompson, a thousand questions whirled in his head. His father had been a mystery, a shadowy figure from his past who now seemed to be infiltrating his life. He had lived in a void where his father's presence should have been. The suddenness of the moment was surreal.

John's heart pounded, and he felt a strange connection with his father that he had never known. Biting down the surge of emotions, he asked, "Mr. Thompson, there seems to be something else you want to tell me."

"First," Mr. Thompson said, "while he was in the hospital battling cancer and under heavy doses of medication, he would sleep a lot. He had a dream one night about your mother, Gail. He told me the dream was real, as if it had happened that day. So, he asked me to hire a private investigator to find her. So, it took us several months to find her, only to find out she had passed away about a year before. I had to ask all of these questions to ensure that you were the son of John Roberts."

Mr. Thompson opened his briefcase and removed a bundle of aged documents enclosed by a worn-out leather folder. His meticulous movements hinted at the value of the content nestled within the folder. Mr. Thompson slid the worn-out leather folder over to John. "These," Mr. Thompson said, "belonged to your father. From early years, when he was in the military, when he was starting his business, to just a few days before he was told he had cancer." Here is something your father wanted me to hand deliver to you," Mr. Thompson said. He opened his briefcase and took a color 8x10 photo of a three-story department store building with a vast parking lot. The parking lot was covered with snow, and the picture was beautiful.

John said, "That is a beautiful department store. Does my father work there? Is he the manager there? If so, maybe I can get a job there." Mr. Thompson said, "John, I am happy to tell you that your father owns that store, and he employs over one hundred people. Your father is one of the largest employers in the city, and on top of that, John," he said, "your father is a multimillionaire. And you are the heir to his estate.

"I must tell you another reason I am here. Yes, I am telling you about your father, but there is more to it than just telling you about John Roberts. As I said before, you are the only child of John Roberts and the heir to his estate." Mr. Thompson then said, "I am sorry to tell you all this information about your father, just to say to you also that your father passed away about nine months ago. And just about a month before he passed away, he found out he had a son, you. By the time we got started looking, he had passed away without ever giving me Gail's last name."

John sat dumbfounded at the dinner table in the local restaurant. The news hit him as if he had been knocked over by a speeding truck, leaving him breathless, struggling to gauge reality. His father, a man he had never known, was no ordinary man. He was a multimillionaire. "Your father was an extremely talented businessman and a friend. He has always been a man of high integrity, a charismatic man who cherished his loved ones," Mr. Thompson began, his voice laced with an unusual mixture of sadness and fond reminiscence. "Your father wasn't just my client; he was my closest friend. He confided in me about his deepest secrets, and it is time you knew one of them."

His thoughts immediately took him back to the countless nights he had spent wondering about his absent father. He tried to piece together an image of his father from the stories Mr. Thompson had shared. His mother had always told him his father died a hero in World War I, yet here he was trying to absorb this true information about his father. His father had lived through the war and was very wealthy.

His head was full of a thousand questions. How did his father amass such wealth? In the deafening silence of the private dining room at the restaurant, the only sound that echoed was the clicking of glasses and dinnerware in the main dining room. As the gravity of the situation began to sink in, a sense of unease washed over him. This inheritance, his father's legacy, was now his. He recognized the duty to preserve his father's legacy and understood that the employees depended on him for their livelihood.

Just like his father, he was now a millionaire. But unlike his father, he did not choose this life; it chose him. And now, he was left with no choice but to navigate this maze of newfound wealth and countless questions.

With a heavy heart, John rose from his seat and took one last look at the lawyer who had abruptly changed his life with a single piece of news. He said, "I need some fresh air. Give me a minute." He had much to think about, to process. As he stepped out of the restaurant for a breath of fresh air, he could not shake off the irony of his fate. Here he was, a man who had known nothing but the taste of struggles, suddenly thrust into a world of unimaginable affluence; his father never knew of him, so he could never include him. The revelation was both a miracle and a mystery; how would he ever manage this much money or, more importantly, the number of people that now depended on him?

After a few minutes, Mr. Thompson came to the door. "John, are you okay? " he said. "Yes, sir, I am okay. It is so overpowering that it is hard to understand what to do next." Mr. Thompson asked, "Do you want to continue or wait until tomorrow and try again?"

After a minute, John said, "I need to continue; I am now in a position where I can't just stop doing something because I am overwhelmed. I need to learn how to cope with adversity and stress. If it's okay with you, can we order dinner before we start talking again?" Mr. Thompson said, "Sure, John, I'm getting a little hungry myself." They walked back in, and Mr. Thompson asked Spring to take their order. When Spring entered the room, they ordered a regular steak, baked potato, asparagus, and salad.

As they returned to the conversation, John finally asked, "What do I do now? I'm unsure whether I should come to the store in Poplar Bluff, look for someone else to run it, or decide on a course of action. What do I do, Mr. Thompson?"

Mr. Thompson said, "That's why I'm here, John, to help you through it, just as I promised your father I would help make sure everything was taken care of with the department store." "Thank you, Mr. Thompson; I was so afraid I would be alone to figure this out," said John.

"John," Mr. Thompson said, "you have a woman named Sarah who will be the best person to help you get your feet on the ground and help you learn all there is to know about the department store." He also told him, "Under your father's directions, I, as the executor of his estate, made her the complete manager of the department store until further notice. I did this because I knew she was more qualified than anyone else who had worked or was working there. And, per your father's directions, she also owns 10% of the store. There are other holdings that you will inherit, but she only holds a 10% stake in the store.

Your father felt she was highly instrumental in the store's success and wanted her to share the ownership."

"From the moment your father turned the key in the lock of that first day, a dream leaping into reality, Sarah was there, his right hand, cornerstone, and unwavering support. She saw the seed of potential in what a handful of racks and one register could be, and a notion of what it could become, and she has been instrumental in nurturing it into the bustling department store it is today.

"Sarah and your father were the heartbeats of the store; their expertise showed in every department in the store. She has the knowledge and wisdom that only comes with years of dedication. "

"Working alongside your father, Sarah learned the ropes of retail from the ground up, mastering each task with a grace and enthusiasm that is nothing short of inspiring. She is versed in everything from merchandising to inventory, from customer service to crisis management, handling each challenge with a smile and confidence."

"And now, as you step into the legacy of the department store, Sarah will be there for you, just as she was for him. There is no question, problem, or customer request that is too complex for her to tackle. She is the ace up your sleeve and the guide you will need to steer the store into its next phase."

"John, your father's great foresight is nothing short of visionary. Picture this: a clause within the phrasing of the will that empowers you with an incredible choice. You stand at a crossroads, my friend, with the key to your destiny firmly grasped! The store has a passage just for you. With her 10% share, Sarah is a testament to your father's belief in unity and partnership. But here is the twist: the clause gives you the power to redefine the store's future. If you feel that your vision for the store is a solo act, you have the extraordinary opportunity to buy out Sarah's shares. And not just that, you would have to pay her a generous 25% of the store's value! That is not merely a buyout; it is a grand gesture of appreciation and respect for her involvement that your father felt she deserved.

"Your father's strategic move here is brilliant. It is about keeping the store within the family and giving you the latitude to make that pivotal decision. The numbers are in your favor, the terms are set, and the store is yours. So, what will it be? Will you embrace Sarah as a partner in your new venture, or will you take a bold step forward, ensuring that the store reflects your singular vision and ambition? Remember, with this clause, your father has not just left you a piece of the puzzle; he has handed you the power to complete the picture exactly as you see fit."

"John," Mr. Thompson said, "the opportunity is knocking with promise and excitement. Embrace it with open arms and let your decisions play out. This is more than a transaction; it's the next chapter in your life."

"John, what I am going to say now is very! Very! Important," said Mr. Thompson. "You have two years after you take control of the department store to make this decision." Mr. Thompson's face was very stern now. "After that time has lapsed, you can only buy her out if she agrees, and you still have to pay her 25%."

John's eyes sparkled with eager curiosity as he leaned forward, anticipating unraveling the mysteries of his father's will. "Mr. Thompson," he queried excitedly, "is there anyone else with a claim on the will?"

Mr. Thompson looked up from the stack of papers that held the secrets of a lifetime, a knowing smile playing at the corners of his mouth. "Yes, indeed!" he proclaimed with an explanation that seemed to add weight to every word. "Your father, a man of generosity and family love, has not forgotten his roots. He has left $25,000.00 to each sibling, a brother and a sister, tokens of his enduring affection and gratitude for the memories he has shared for many years."

"And that's not all," continued Mr. Thompson, his voice lifting with the kind of enthusiasm that was uplifting, "your father extended his generous heart to the younger generation as well, two nieces and two nephews, each one dear to him, each one remembered with a generous gift of $10,000.00!"

John's heart felt full, almost as if he could feel the pride and love his father had poured into every decision, every dollar allocated in his will. Mr. Thompson's eyes matched his tone, full of life, as he added, "This all comes from the treasure trove of your inheritance, a testament to the millions that your father amassed, not just in wealth, John, but in the rich friendships he valued above all."

The atmosphere felt electric with the spirit of generosity, clearly a mark of John's father's life. It was a moment of joy, a time to celebrate the man who had left behind not just a legacy of wealth but a legacy of love and kinship. For John, it was a newfound understanding that his inheritance was more than just money; it embodied his father's life, vitality, and a deep-seated commitment to family. "Mr. Thompson," John said, "what do you think I should do?" "Here's a good idea, my friend," Mr. Thompson said. "Dive headfirst into the partnership with Sarah; give it one or two years. Immerse yourselves in the process and give it 100% of your effort. Combining your talents is a brilliant opportunity; imagine the sheer potential. If you and Sarah click, if your partnership soars and sizzles, fantastic, ride that wave of success and embrace the incredible partnership you have forged." Mr. Thompson leaned in closer and said, "Hey, if it doesn't pan out, no worries, you'll have gained a wealth of insight from Sarah's expertise and knowledge. The things you learn will be priceless. And then, if needed, you can make a bold move and buy her out." Mr. Thompson gave a confident chuckle. "But think about this: the experience you'll gain during those one or two years, whether it's smooth sailing or a bit of a rollercoaster ride, will be enormous in shaping your future ventures." "Ok, Mr. Thompson," John said, "what do I do now to accept my inheritance?" Mr. Thompson said, "We will meet at Mr. Daniels' office at 8 A.M. and sign the paper attesting that you are John Jenkins, the rightful heir to John Roberts's estate. Once signed, you will own it all."

"Mr. Thompson," John exclaimed with anticipation, "I'll be there with bells on! It is like dawn brings a whole new part of my life!" Mr. Thompson could not help but smile at John's spirited response. "Bright and early, John! Ensure you bring that vibrant energy to Mr. Daniels' office. Once that paperwork is signed, you are not just John Jenkins; you are John Jenkins, the heir to the immense Roberts fortune!"

John's eyes sparkled with the promise of a future filled with possibilities. "Own it all, you say? That is more than a dream come true; it's like stepping into a world I have only ever imagined. I can barely contain my excitement! The thought of carrying on John Roberts's legacy is an honor and an adventure I am ready to embark on."

"And remember, John," Mr. Thompson added with seriousness, "great wealth comes with great responsibility. I am confident you will handle it with the same vitality and integrity you've shown."

John nodded, a determined and joyful look etched across his face. "You can count on me, Mr. Thompson. I will take this inheritance and build something meaningful, a testament to the legacy left behind. Tomorrow morning is just the start!" As they parted ways, the air was thick with the electricity of potential, all set to be unleashed at the stroke of eight the following day, when John would step into his new life, forever changed by the turn of fate's hand.

The hands of the clock in Mr. Daniels' office pointed at 8 A.M. sharp, the hour when fate would change young John's life, transforming it forever. Lined with law books and certificates, the walls stood as silent witnesses to the pivotal moment unfolding within.

John, a youthful and energetic 28-year-old with the vigor of a man stepping into the prime of his life, had a mix of nerves and excitement. With his heart pounding, he could not help but feel the world's weight shifting onto his shoulders. As a single man, the vast opportunity before him was both exhilarating and daunting.

Across from him, Mr. Thompson, the legal part of this transaction, confidently shuffled the documents that would seal John's destiny. His silver hair caught the light from the chandelier above, casting a glow of authority and assurance.

"John," said Mr. Thompson, "signing these documents is the first step in accepting your inheritance. You must understand that after signing these documents, the will must still be read out loud in JR's Department Store, in the conference room on December 25th in Poplar Bluff, Missouri, to the rest of the heirs before this officially takes effect. On that day, you become the official inheritor of your father's estate, and it will all legally be turned over to you after it is read."

The air was thick with the scent of leather and success, and as Mr. Daniels presented the pen, a polished instrument of change, John's fingers tingled as they wrapped around it. Each scratch of the pen on the paper was a fanfare, a heralding of a new era in John's life where he would become the inheritor of his father's vast department store empire and the custodian of a fortune that nudged into the millions. The presence of his father, with his passing over nine months ago and no longer present, seemed to fill the room with pride and expectation. John's hand was steady despite the tremors of anticipation that coursed through him.

Mr. Thompson's approving nods fueled John's increasing confidence as each document was signed. The last signatures found their place on the paper, and John capped the pen with a flourish of finality. It was done. The room seemed to pulse with the energy of accomplishment, and the men around him broke into broad, congratulatory smiles.

"Congratulations, John," Mr. Thompson said, his voice rich with genuine delight. "Your father would be incredibly proud of you today. His legacy is in capable hands." Mr. Daniels rose from his chair, the leather creaking like a round of applause, and offered a warm handshake. "To a bright and prosperous future," he beamed. John felt a surge of pride swell within him. He had stepped through a door that separated his past from his future, and as overwhelming as it might seem, he could sense the adventure of a lifetime beckoning him. This was his moment, a turning point etched in time, and he was ready to embrace it with open arms and a brave heart.

The inheritance was more than a transfer of wealth; it was the dawn of John's era, a testament to his father's faith in his son. Today, he had not just accepted an inheritance; John had stepped into his destiny. And oh, how things had changed in the last 24 hours!

7

Train to Poplar Bluff

John, you must remember," said Mr. Thompson, "the signing of this will is still confidential and cannot be discussed with anyone. The will must still be read on December 25th in the department store." "I understand, Mr. Thompson, not a word till I meet you in Poplar Bluff. When do I need to be there, and what do I need to do when I get there?" John asked in an excited yet still bewildered way. "John, I have set you up with a train ticket from Mountain Home, Arkansas, to Poplar Bluff, Missouri, leaving on December 21 and arriving on December 23," Mr. Thompson told John. "It is a three-day trip, so I have arranged for you to have a sleeper berth with a sitting room for your privacy. The ticket includes dining and lounge at no cost to you. Just show your ticket for anything you need. I have also set up a cover story for you. You are a clothing salesman going to Poplar Bluff to meet with Sarah about selling some clothes to JR's Department Store." It seems that Mr. Thompson has thought of everything, or at least it appears that way to John.

John asks, "When I get to Poplar Bluff, where do I go, or am I just on my own and need to find a place to stay? I know I cannot go to my father's house yet." "John, I have reserved a room for you at the Rivers Run Lodge, about three miles from town. The room is reserved for December 23 through December 31 with the option to extend it longer if needed," Mr. Thompson told John. He also told John, "I did it this way because I am not sure if any family member will push back or be upset and rude to you. They may go to the house after the will is read, and you may not feel the need to attend. It is my understanding, but I am not sure, that the servants are preparing a small Christmas celebration dinner for the family in honor of your father, John Roberts, to take place right after the will is read. Your father loved Christmas and always had a Christmas lunch at your father's house. It was lunch most of the time, but the will must be read at 1 P.M., so there will be no time for a regular lunch this year. It will be your house, so you can go if you want to, regardless of how they feel." Mr. Thompson watched John as he gave him all this information to see how he would react.

To his surprise, John said, "That's a good idea, Mr. Thompson. I don't want to start with so many bad feelings and have them turn against me." John said, "I want them to continue doing everything as they have always been. If they ask me to attend, I will probably go, but I will stay in the lodge for a while, or at least until everyone gets used to me and accepts me as my dad's son."

John asked Mr. Thompson, "Will I be able to meet Sarah before the December 25 reading of the will?" He looked like he wanted to meet her before he met the rest of the family. "I would like to talk to her about the store and reassure her that I am not looking to come in and start changing things. She must understand that I will look to her to continue things as she and my father have been for many years."

"That's a great way to start, John," Mr. Thompson said. "Bringing Sarah in to support you is a great way to get things moving in the right direction from day one." "Thank you, Mr. Thompson," John said. "Will Sarah be able to set me up with some transportation? I want to ride around the city a little to see where everything is located, and for Sarah to drive me around, showing the city to me, is asking for us to be seen and start questions."

"That would be a good idea to get you some transportation of your own," said Mr. Thompson. "When I get back to Poplar Bluff tomorrow,

I will tell Sarah that you will call her and set up a meeting to come out to the lodge so as not to be seen together any more than possible." Mr. Thompson also said, "I will ask Sarah to work with you to get you anything you need."

"John," Mr. Thompson said, "I do not mean to insult or upset you when I ask you the next question: How is your financial situation now? You will still need a little cash as you make the trip and for miscellaneous items until we turn everything over to you at the bank."

John said, "Thank you for asking; I have a few dollars left after selling my mother's house. My mom and I had a nice house with nice furniture and decor. However, Mom still owed a lot on the house, and I had to pay off several of Mother's bills that were still outstanding. What little was left from the sale has not yet been sent to me. I have money to get by for a while, but not for long," John said with an embarrassed face. "Funny," he said with a smile, "I am now a millionaire and don't have the money to ride a train."

Mr. Thompson laughed with him and said, "Well, John, I came prepared; here is $100 to help on your trip. You have a few $1 bills, $5 bills, $10 bills, and $20 bills. That should last about a month until we update the bank documents so you can access your inheritance.

"John," Mr. Thompson said. "Is there anything else you need to ask or anything I need to do before I start back to Poplar Bluff, Missouri? It's about an eight-hour drive, and I need to get started if I'm going to make it before dark. These roads get a little scary at night with all the curves and hills." "I think all has been said or asked that needs to be said or asked," said John. "If anything arises or needs answering before I arrive, I will send you a telegram."

"OK, John, I will arrange to have a taxi meet you at the train station on December 23 and take you to the Rivers Run Lodge. You will have to pay the taxi driver, so I am not giving away anything by paying for it ahead of time," said Mr. Thompson. With that, Mr. Thompson and John shook hands, and Mr. Thompson got in his car and drove off. As he did, he thought this had been a fantastic and stressful three days. He looked forward to returning home and sleeping for a day or two.

John returned to his hotel room and reviewed the past couple of days. It had been a nerve-racking couple of days, and he would take the three-day train journey to reflect on everything and start planning what to ask Sarah and what Sarah could recommend that he do during the reading of the will. There is a great deal to consider. Then he smiled and said to himself, "I'm a millionaire; there has been so much struggle over the years, and in two days, I have become a millionaire."

December 17 ended with the excitement of accomplishment; the house he had so painstakingly readied for the market had not only sold but was on the start of a seamless transition to its eager new owners. The deadline of December 21 to board the train seemed a long way off, yet it would be here in no time.

His hotel room, a temporary home, now echoed with the whispers of life on the verge of transformation. A few things still needed to be packed, a mere stone's throw away from being settled. Anything left behind was a minor detail against the backdrop of the awaited trip.

Looking around the room, he believed each item left would find its way to him in Poplar Bluff like loyal friends journeying across miles to reunite. There was no rush. Everything would find its place in time once he was nestled into his new surroundings; once the dust of change had settled, he could breathe in the scent of fresh beginnings.

Oh, and the train! Embarking on that locomotive sent a thrill through his veins. It would be a time to reflect and watch the world pass by in a series of picture-perfect scenes, each landscape a story whispered in the language of trees, rivers, and horizons.

He was almost there, just a few clock ticks from stepping aboard and steaming towards his future. Poplar Bluff, with all its promises and dreams, was just over the horizon, waiting for him with open arms. The countdown had never felt so exhilarating. December 21 was not just a date on the calendar; it was the start of his next adventure. And he? He was ready.

John's heart beat excitedly inside his chest, the bustling train station, and all the sounds that went with it. December 21st was meant to be the starting line towards his destiny, yet he stood rooted to the spot, his hand frantically patting down his pockets, his mind racing, panic setting in.

"Oh, what a fool I am!" John thought. "Did Mr. Thompson give me the ticket? Did I lose it, or did he forget? Either way, here I stand, ticketless!" Amidst his turmoil, he could almost feel the tick-tock of the clock hands, each second whispering urgent warnings. Poplar Bluff beckoned, a mere two days away, December 23, 1946, a date locked in his mind. The most important meeting of his life was within reach, a date with destiny, yet fate was determined to introduce hurdles.

But wait! The calamity had a savior clothed in blue, with buttons shining like beacons of hope. A conductor, expressing a kind mix of concern and authority, approached John amidst his distress.

"Saw the panic in your eyes, son," the conductor said with a grin. "Why don't you hurry over to the ticket office? If the purchaser is worth his salt, and you think he is, his noggin would've sent that ticket straight to the will-call area. It is a common mix-up; it happens all the time!"

John felt a surge of relief, his feet carrying him forward like a man on a mission. The conductor's words were like a lighthouse cutting through the fog of his worry. Ah, the will-call area! It was a beacon of hope that the ticket was just there waiting to be claimed.

The ticket office loomed ahead, a bustling hub of travelers and clerks. John waded through the crowd; his purpose renewed. He approached the counter, words pouring out in a rush, "John Jenkins, I believe there's a ticket waiting for me?"

A search, a smile, and then the sweet sound of success. "Here you go, Mr. Jenkins. One ticket to Poplar Bluff," the clerk announced, handing over the precious slip of paper.

It was too good to be true, and the relief washed over John like the warm embrace of an old friend. He gripped the ticket, feeling its texture and the weight of its importance. "Thank you, thank you ever so much!" exclaimed the man whose hope had been restored.

With the ticket now secure in his pocket, John strolled back towards the platform, a confident spring in his step. He could almost hear the train tracks calling his name, the steel rails shimmering with the promise of the future.

John's mind began to think of the future. Poplar Bluff, December 25, 1946; he could see it now. The most important meeting of his life was no longer a mere dream. John Jenkins was on his way to greatness, and nothing, not even the sneakiest of panic attacks or missing tickets, could stand in his way! The train whistle blew, and with a heart full of eager anticipation, he walked to the train with hope and determination.

As the hustle and bustle of the busy train station began to blend into departures and arrivals, John stepped onto the platform with an air of anticipation. Just at that moment, a porter sharply dressed and beaming with professional hospitality swooped in, graciously relieving John of his travel-weary bags.

"This way, sir," the porter chimed, ushering John towards his home away from home on the rails, his very own sleeping berth. The quarters boasted a plush bed that promised the sweetest of dreams and a separate sitting room that beckoned hours of productive solitude. A sanctuary on wheels made just for him!

With a flick of his skilled wrist, the porter opened a perfectly made bed with crisp linens. He unpacked John's luggage with grace, breathing life into this private nook, ensuring every item had its rightful place. John watched, impressed by the seamless service.

But wait, there was more! With the spark of a seasoned guide, the porter unveiled the crown jewels of the train: the lounge and dining room. "Open around the clock, every day of the week, for your absolute delight, sir," the porter said, his voice a lyrical promise of non-stop indulgence. Whether John craved a midnight snack or the company of fellow travelers, satisfaction was merely a step away.

And then, with a final gesture, the porter entrusted John with his name, a personal touch that transformed service into friendship, ensuring that every need was only a call away, no matter how small. John felt like royalty, and his journey was now set to begin on the most promising and exhilarating trip of his life. The adventure of a lifetime came to him, and he was more than ready to answer. As the night blended flawlessly with the sleeper berth, history was quietly being written. It was the year 1946, and the world was taking its first deep breaths after the war.

He had done it! With a dash of luck, our man had just entered the ranks of the millionaires. And yet, there was a twist in this newfound wealth; not a soul aboard the train knew of the change in his life. Was the difference paid to him merely the standard for those graced with a sleeper berth? Or was there a whisper of destiny in the air, treating him to a prelude to the richness that was to follow?

The train staff moved with efficiency, their uniforms crisp, their smiles genuine. They predicted every need and every desire of those lucky enough to slumber under the gentle sway of the Pullman car. The new million-dollar man watched as he was pampered with the same attention as those who might have been born with a silver spoon. It was as if the universe conspired to give him a taste of the life that awaited him.

Each clink of fine china, the sound of hushed conversation, and the sound of the steel wheels on the tracks seemed to celebrate the secret John held close to his heart. The experience was heightening for him, tinged with the thrill of his prosperity. It was a personal success, a world unaware of the monumental shift in his fortune, embracing him with the sheer elegance of the era.

The year 1946 would come to be known for many things. Still, to John, it would always be remembered as the year when stars aligned, and a sleeper berth on a train became a throne from which he could dream about his new life.

And so, with the whisper of the tracks beneath him, he journeyed on, surrounded by the unknowing miles of splendor, eager to embrace the new life that awaited him at the end of the line. What fabulous tales would unfold from this unexpected twist of fate? Only time will tell. But one thing was for sure: our millionaire in the making was already living his dream, cruising through the night with the stars as his witness, the world none the wiser, and his future as bright as the beautiful sunset about to fall over the horizon. What a marvelous ride it was going to be!

As John strolled down the narrow corridor of the train, the rhythmic dance of steel upon steel serenaded his every step. The evening was showing its starry sky, and with a light heart, he made his way to the lounge, a prelude to his anticipated gourmet experience in the dining car.

Upon entering the lounge, the atmosphere was abuzz with the soft murmur of friendly chatter and the clinking of glasses, a symphony of social harmony. The setting sun spilled through the panoramic windows, casting a warm glow over the plush interior.

Just as John contemplated the choice of fine spirits that beckoned from behind the bar, the door opened with a gentle swoosh, revealing a vision of youthful elegance. A beautiful young woman stepped in, eyes scanning the room for a solitary haven in the crowded space. Alas, not a single seat lay unclaimed.

Without a moment's hesitation, chivalry coursed through John's veins. Rising to the occasion, he caught her gaze with a friendly nod and gestured towards the seat opposite him, his voice a mix of warmth and welcome. "Hello, my name is John. Would you please join me?" he offered as if extending an invitation to a grand ball.

Her smile lit up the lounge as she gracefully accepted his proposal, gliding towards the table like a swan to its lake. As she settled in, John was captivated by her elegant composure and the subtle sparkle in her eyes. She said, "Thank you so much. I'm not quite ready to go to dinner and was looking for a place to relax; my name is Judy."

John said, "You are very welcome, Judy; I was doing the same thing, and having a nice conversation with a young lady will be much better than sitting here by myself just staring at the walls."

The conversation blossomed like a rare and delicate flower, their words weaving a tale of intrigue and enchantment. She excited him with her wit and wisdom, her laughter, a melody that played upon his heartstrings.

As the train continued its relentless march through the twilight, the two strangers found themselves lost in their journey, a trip into the realms of connection and friendship. A single chance meeting in the gentle roll of the railcar had ignited the spark of a compelling and mysterious bond that promised untold stories.

It seemed the night had stopped the hands of time from ticking on the clock, suspended in the soft glow of the lounge car as the world outside blurred into a starry night. The clinking and clacking of the train's steady movement whispered of destiny's hand, of a chance encounter into unforgettable memories. John could not help but enjoy his time with delightful passengers; the journey was made all the more thrilling by the companions we meet along the way.

After an exciting conversation, John was ready for dinner and said, "Well, Judy, I am ready. Would you like to join me?" Judy looked at John with a big smile and said, "I would love to have dinner with you, John, but I am not a fast eater. I like to take it slow and enjoy my meal." With a big smile, John said, "So do I, Judy, so do I." They stood up and started the short trip to the dining car. As the rhythmic clattering of the train blended with the distant chitchat of fellow passengers, John, with a beaming smile and a spark of excitement in his eyes, requested a cozy table for two. Soon enough, John and Judy were seated opposite each other in the warmly lit dining car that swayed gently with the train's motion, embarking on a journey as delightful as the one their train was charting through the countryside.

The atmosphere was electrifying, charged with the magic of new friendships, as the two kindred spirits prepared to dive into a feast of food, storytelling, and laughter. The table was set with gleaming cutlery and fine china, a prelude to the culinary symphony that awaited them.

With each dish served, from the appetizer to the main course and to the decadent dessert, John and Judy were immersed in exquisite tastes and aromas. Their conversation flowed as freely as the fine wine, sparkling with wit and bubbling with shared anecdotes. Each course was a tale, a fusion of flavors that mirrored the blend of their blossoming friendship.

The dining car, with its soft glow and the gentle hum of conversations around them, felt like a bubble of joy, disconnected from life's usual hustle. John and Judy savored every bite and every moment, their laughter mingling with the clinks of glasses and the murmur of the rails beneath them.

As the dessert fork finally rested on an empty plate, symbolizing the end of their splendid meal, they leaned back, utterly contented. Their faces were aglow with the joy of a shared meal, stories exchanged, and a friendship that, much like the rolling landscapes outside, stretched out before them, full of possibility and promise.

Indeed, it was a dinner to remember, not just for the flavors that danced upon their tongues but for the warmth and friendship that filled their hearts. Oh, what a splendid evening it was in the train's dining car, with the stars twinkling above and the world rushing by, where two new friends, John and Judy, sat down for an unforgettable meal.

As the evening began to wane and the scent of a delicious dinner lingered, John and Judy were enveloped in a comfortable conversation. The kind that springs up between two people whose chemistry is as undeniable as the stars in a clear night sky. One topic led to another as they effortlessly danced through dialogues about dreams, aspirations, and the winding roads of life that had brought them to this exciting point.

Then, as if guided by some playful twist of fate, they stumbled upon the subject of the immediate, thrilling future radiating with potential. With a spark in his eye, John said he was "going for a visit to Poplar Bluff," his voice with a touch of mystery and excitement. Imagine his surprise, his absolute astonishment, when Judy's face lit up brighter than a supernova, mirroring his destination.

"Oh, Poplar Bluff?" Judy's voice was a melody, a tune so ripe with enthusiasm it could make flowers bloom out of season. "That's precisely where I'm headed!" The air between them crackled with a cosmic coincidence, and John could hardly hold his curiosity. "What's pulling you to that neck of the woods?" he queried, the intrigue in his voice as noticeable as the pulsing energy of the universe. "Are you visiting someone?" Judy's reply shone with a determination that could only be matched by the morning sun creating a new horizon. "I'm on my way to JR's Department Store," she declared, her words an anthem of hope and resolve. "I'm going to ask for a job!" she said.

Judy was so excited that she could not stop talking. "Oh, John! You would not believe the coincidence of it all! The universe conspired to bring me to JR's Department Store. I had a roommate in college; her name is Kathy, and we were almost inseparable back then. She had an infectious laugh and a brilliant knack for predicting fashion trends. Well, she has been working at JR's, and guess what? Kathy caught wind of some exciting shake-ups within the store and unexpectedly sent me a letter. She wrote me this electrifying message, filled with her usual exuberance, telling me that JR's was on the cusp of something new. She insisted, no, she was adamant, that there was a place for me in this retail renaissance. Can you imagine? She even tempted me with the sweet nostalgia of our college days, suggesting we could reunite as roommates, diving back into those late-night giggles and early-morning coffee runs. I was already caught up in the thrill of the prospect of joining a team I was eagerly looking forward to! And the idea of rooming with an old friend again. That sealed the deal. It was as if all the puzzle pieces of opportunity fell into place, beckoning me towards

JR's, a future brimming with potential. So here I am, John, ready to embark on this adventurous journey to JR's with great expectations and a heart full of zeal! Isn't it fantastic?"

And there it was, the climax of our unfolding tale. Unknown to Judy, the man before her, John, was no mere traveler; he was the architect of her hopeful destination, the owner of JR's Department Store. The revelation hung invisibly in the air, a secret waiting to erupt like fireworks in July.

But for now, the secret remained just that, a delicate suspense poised with potential, as John's heart thundered in his chest like a drumbeat heralding a grand unveiling. Their shared journey to Poplar Bluff promises to be anything but ordinary when this truth becomes known. John's eyes gleamed with curiosity as he leaned in closer, his question hanging in the air like a note in a suspenseful melody. "Who are you going to see?"

Judy's voice was a cascade of excitement that could light up the dimmest of rooms. "Oh, John, it's about this incredible woman named Sarah; I'm pretty sure that's her name. I have jotted it down in my notes back in my cabin. You would not believe it; just a handful of days ago, I was on the phone with her, and guess what? She mentioned they might need an extra pair of hands soon. She was not entirely sure yet, but the thrill of it all!"

Her eyes danced with the spark of adventure, and she gave a slight, determined nod. "I thought, 'Why not? Why not just take that leap of faith and see for myself.' I will go out, knock on her door, and ask her. The worst she can do is say no, right? But imagine if she says yes! It could be the opportunity of a lifetime, an open door to something new, something exhilarating!"

John could not help but catch Judy's enthusiasm. She was all in, ready to embark on what could be an extraordinary journey. With optimism as her compass, Judy was set to sail toward the horizon of possibility, and who knew what unique treasures she would discover?

John smiled at Judy and said, "Judy, this is just a thought; the other side of the lounge car is a dance floor. Would you like to go and check it out and maybe dance a little before we call it a night?" The mere idea of whisking across the dance floor sent a thrill through Judy. With a sparkle in her eyes and a beautiful smile, she eagerly accepted the invitation. The two left their seats as if magnetically drawn to the promise of rhythm and movement, their hearts swaying to an unheard melody.

As they made their way to the lounge car, anticipation built. The customarily subdued clacking of the train seemed to change to a rhythmic clatter, almost a prelude to the music that awaited them. The doors opened to reveal a scene pulsing with life, a dance floor that invited freedom and joy, the air thick with the beats of jazz, swing, or perhaps a sultry Latin number.

The band, perched in the corner, seemed to sense new life in the room, the notes flowing through the air with an extra bounce as John and Judy approached. The first steps onto the dance floor were tentative as if dipping toes into a shimmering pool, but then, as if an invisible conductor had lifted his baton, they found their rhythm.

Laughter mingled with the strains of the music, and Judy's heart sang with every twist and turn. She was a natural, her body moving with graceful assurance as if each song were composed just for her. John matched her step for step, their movements a dialogue more intimate than words, a joyous celebration of the moment.

On this magical night, as the train wound through the sleeping countryside, John and Judy danced as though the world were theirs alone. Each step, spin, and dip was a story they wrote together, a memory etched in the night's tempo. As the last chord faded and the dance floor quieted, they knew this was a night neither of them would ever forget, a night where the simple suggestion to dance turned into an exuberant leap into happiness.

As the rhythmic clatter of the train on the tracks continued its steady serenade, John and Judy lingered in the narrow corridor, the afterglow of their dance still warming their cheeks. The evening had been nothing short of magical. It was a series of unexpected moments blooming into a connection neither of them had expected when they boarded the train at different stations, each absorbed in their solitary journeys.

Their dance had started as a playful challenge, a way to pass the time and break the monotony of the long journey. But as they moved together through the swaying car, the world outside the window melting into a blur of starlit landscapes, something shifted. The air between them crackled with electricity, each turn and step drawing them closer in a dance that was as much about the meeting of hearts as it was about the movement of their bodies.

And now, with the dance concluded but the melody of their encounter still playing in their minds, they stood hesitantly at the junction of their separate paths. John's hand brushed against Judy's, a silent question hanging in the space between them. Would the night's enchantment fade with the dawn, or had they stumbled upon the beginning of a timeless romance?

Judy's glowing and promising smile was the answer he had not realized he had been hoping for. She reached for his hand, her fingers entwining with his, and in that simple gesture, they silently acknowledged the profound impact of their shared evening. Words were unnecessary when their eyes spoke volumes, and John saw the reflection of his feelings in their depths.

With a reluctant yet hopeful sigh, they edged towards their respective berths. The promise of tomorrow's encounters hung in the air, as tangible as the warmth of Judy's hand still lingering in John's. The train continued its nocturnal journey as they retreated into their private sanctuaries, carrying them through the slumbering world outside.

But inside, in the quiet of their berths, sleep would be a coy mistress, for their minds were alive with the possibilities ahead. They were at the beginning of something new, something potentially life-changing, and the anticipation of what the next day would bring filled them with an exhilarating sense of wonder.

The dance on the train had ended, but the dance of their hearts was beginning. And as the train continued down the track to its destination, John and Judy were already dreaming of their next steps together in the stroll to romance. As John stretched out across his bed, the plush covers cradling him in comfort, a whirlwind of thoughts danced in his head, vibrant and persistent. Could it be true? He pondered; his heart fluttered with the notion. Did she harbor genuine feelings for him, or was it all just a twist of fate, a mere coincidence that their paths had crossed?

In the quiet of his room, with the moonlight casting silvery shadows across his face, John's mind replayed every moment, every glance she had bestowed upon him. Her eyes, bright and earnest, seemed to look right into his very soul, untouched by the pretense of wealth. He could not help but feel a surge of hope.

After all, he pondered with an inward smile, she had stepped into his life at the most unexpected time. He had been nothing more than a simple man, his days filled with simple joys, his pockets far from the depths of affluence. Yet, here he was, suddenly thrust into a world of wealth he had never imagined, all due to a father he had never known, a legacy unveiled mere days ago.

But she, oh, she was different. Unaware of the sudden turn of fortune that had befallen him, she had offered him smiles that sparkled with a sincerity that could not be bought, laughter that echoed with a warmth that no gold could warm. She had seen him, John, the man who existed before the dollar signs, who found richness in the sunset, not the jingle of coins.

The thought sent a thrill through him, a wave of excitement that banished any lingering doubts. She could not possibly know about the inheritance, the wealth that now lined his life like the pages of a fairy tale. Their connection was something more, something purer. It was as if the universe had conspired to bring them together at precisely the right moment, place, and time.

John's heart raced with anticipation for tomorrow, the opportunity to explore this budding romance unfettered by the shadows of his fortune. As he closed his eyes, surrendering to the comforting embrace of sleep, he could almost feel the promise of love's sweet adventure beckoning him toward the dawn.

As the train whistled closer to Poplar Bluff, Judy could barely hold the thrilling anticipation of what might come next with John. Oh, what a delightful thought it was! She envisioned the charming scenes that could lie ahead: stolen glances across a busy street, impromptu coffee dates, or strolls by the river, with their conversations continuing to bloom like the sweet magnolias of spring.

Wouldn't it be marvelous if John sought her once they reached their destination? Judy's heart fluttered at the thought. With a grin she could not suppress, Judy decided to make her move no matter what the future held. She would hand John her address and number, the key to unlocking more shared moments, leaving a trail of breadcrumbs for him to follow back to her.

Her optimism soared like an eagle in the Missouri sky, her hopes reaching high that John would use those little digits to whisk her away into a new part of their story, a few days, maybe less, it did not matter. Judy knew deep down that what they had was the beginning of something extraordinary, a connection that promised to be as grand and memorable as their unforgettable train journey.

So, as the train moved closer to the heart of Poplar Bluff, Judy's spirit danced in the air, giddy with excitement for what tomorrow would bring. Would John be her gallant beau, calling on her to embark on new adventures? Only time would tell, but one thing was sure: Judy was ready for whatever enchantment lay ahead, her heart open and eager for the possibilities that love had in store! But finally, sleep caught up with her, and she drifted off to dreams of the night's encounter.

As the sun's rays of dawn peeked over the horizon, Judy settled into the comforting rhythmic clatter of the train, her heart aflutter with anticipation. The dining car's plush seats and large windows revealing the countryside's waking beauty were the perfect stage for surprises. She was acting calm, but every tick of the clock made her more nervous about the possibility of a chance meeting with John. It has been 45 minutes of hopeful waiting, a small eternity for a heart smitten by the magic of chance encounters.

And there he was, as if drawn by an unspoken summons. He strode into the dining car, a beacon of warmth in the early morning chill. Their eyes met, and the world seemed still for a moment. The surprise on his face quickly transformed into the broadest of smiles, a silent acknowledgment of the delightful twist of fate that brought them together once more.

"Oh, Judy! What are the odds?" John exclaimed, his voice rich with genuine delight. They did not need to plan to meet; the universe seemed to conspire to weave their paths together.

With a menu in hand and an appetite not just for the morning's offerings but for each other's company, they nestled into their seats across from each other to see into each other's eyes, the doorway to their hearts and souls. The clinking of silverware, serving as a soundtrack to their conversation, made the moment all the more romantic.

The train sped on, mile after mile, the landscape outside a blur compared to the vivid scene inside. Their laughter mingled with the scent of fresh coffee and pastries. They shared stories and dreams, carving out memories from the remaining days.

John and Judy naturally synchronize their day without even realizing it. They're sitting at breakfast, laughing and chatting away, and their plans for the day magically align before they know it. It's like a dance they're doing without even seeing the steps.

So, there they are, deciding to take a leisurely stroll up to the high lounge area. It's the perfect spot to watch the scenery roll by as the train snakes through those beautiful curves and hills. They chat about everything and nothing, planning lunch, then dinner, and even some time in the lounge car for a bit of dancing and a drink or two. It's almost as if destiny had them penciled into each other's schedules.

Judy and John have quick, soft, and almost teasing kisses. Just enough to make their hearts flutter without diving headlong into the deep end. They're like little promises of maybe something more.

Judy turns to John with a warm smile as the day starts to fade. "John," she asks, "how about meeting for breakfast tomorrow?" John grins back and says, "I would love to have breakfast in the morning, would seven be too early?"

With a sparkle in her eye, Judy assures him, "No, that would be perfect," and gives him one of those light, breezy kisses. "See you in the morning," she adds, leaving him with a smile.

As seven A.M. arrived, they both walked into the dining car at the same time. They sat at a secluded table for two and enjoyed the breakfast and each other's company. They smiled all morning, talking, laughing, and talking about Judy's plan at JR's Department Store. John listened with a big smile and said he thought her plan was a good idea.

Poplar Bluff was drawing nearer with each passing moment, and they both felt the tug of the inevitable goodbye. But for now, for these precious few hours, they were here together, making the most of the joy that life had thrown their way.

Time would rush on, but Judy and John were determined to ride this newfound friendship wave and bask in each other's presence until the last call to the station. With the end of their trip near, this breakfast would shine as a joyful moment, a testament to the extraordinary power of fate and the unwavering hope of a future meeting.

And then, the moment everyone on the train had been waiting to hear! The anticipation was electric as the train's speaker system crackled to life, sending waves of excitement through every cabin: "Poplar Bluff fifteen minutes, Poplar Bluff fifteen minutes!" The announcement hung in the air like a promise of adventure, a signal that heralded the end to their journey.

"Your porter will take your luggage to the baggage claim area," the voice boomed, authoritative yet comforting, like a captain steering his ship into port. Passengers glanced at one another, nodding, their eyes alight with the shared acquaintances of those who have traveled the rails together.

The train began to slow in its final approach to Poplar Bluff, as if paying homage to the quaint town awaiting its arrival. Judy's heart skipped a beat, her mind racing through the memories she would carry from this trip. To her left, the porter would carefully handle her bags, treating each piece like treasure.

And John, dear, brave John, his luggage would be to the right, a slight quirk in the otherwise seamless perfection of their travels. A testament to the notion of life, the delightful unpredictability that makes each story unique!

Regaining their composure, Judy and John prepared to disembark. They could already feel the cool embrace of Poplar Bluff, a town that seemed to call out to them with open arms, eager to be part of their new life. This was not just an end but a bright new beginning, an invitation to continue exploring the endless possibilities beyond the train's doors.

So, with hearts pounding and spirits soaring, their eyes sparkling with the unspoken promise of what was to come. With its charm, character, and welcoming spirit, Poplar Bluff was ready for Judy and John. And Judy and John were prepared for it!

8

Little John arrives in Poplar Bluff

The snow crunched under their feet as they stepped down the platform from the train, the frosty breath of winter nipping at their cheeks, a sharp reminder of winter's embrace. Their gazes locked, two souls connected by a journey, their hearts skipping in tandem. The moment, so ripe, so raw, was about to bloom into an embrace when an exuberant cry pierced the air, "Judy!, Judy!, Judy! over here!"

Like the trumpet of old friends reuniting, Kathy's voice was a beacon of warmth in the chill. Judy whirled around, her eyes lit with the sparkle of a thousand Christmas lights. There stood Kathy, her silhouette framed by the swirling snow, a monument to years of laughter and secrets shared in whispers.

The happiness on their faces was nothing short of contagious, a visual symphony celebrating the timeless dance of friendship. Once the glee settled into gentle smiles, Judy turned and introduced John to Kathy. "John," Judy said, "this is Kathy, my best friend and the only roommate I ever had in college." She turned to Kathy and said, "Kathy, this is John, we met on the train, and he has become a perfect and dear friend on the three-day trip." They shook hands while Kathy looked at Judy with a puzzled look on her face.

Kathy studied John with a curiosity that touched the corners of familiarity. "Sorry to stare, have we met somewhere before?" Her question hung in the frosty air, mingling with the mystery that John carried like an aura about him. "I don't think so," John said. Kathy recovered quickly and said, "I am sorry, but you just look like someone I have met before, but just cannot remember. Probably not, sorry," and turned to Judy and said, "Let's go; there are more friends of ours waiting for us at the apartment. You will never guess who else lives here in Poplar Bluff."

With a start, the trio started their walk, but not before Judy, in a whirlwind of emotion, called out, "John! Wait a minute!" Her feet carried her back to John as though they were going in that direction anyway, and then, something electric. She gazed into John's eyes, a fleeting moment that held the weight of eternity, and then she threw her arms around him, kissing him with a prolonged kiss that would indeed leave an imprint on his soul. And then, like a magician revealing her trick, she slipped a piece of paper into his hand. "If you want to use this," she whispered, a compelling offer wrapped in mystery.

With a final wave, she dashed back to Kathy, leaving John with the promise of possibility clutched in his fingers. Kathy looked at her with a big smile, but was also puzzled at the same time. Then Kathy said, "I think we have a lot to talk about tonight." With that, they hugged again and started walking faster to escape the cold snow. The train behind them may have reached its destination, but their stories and journeys were beginning to unfold.

John's heart fluttered like a captive bird eager for release as he watched Judy's retreating form. The soft sway of her dress was like the gentle dance of leaves in a summer breeze, even though it was snowing. As her silhouette merged with the afternoon sun, he slowly uncurled his fingers, revealing the delicate treasure she had entrusted to him, a scrap of paper that held the promise of new beginnings.

The crisp edges of the note brushed against his palm, a tiny whisper of potential. John's eyes admired the elegant curves of her handwriting, each loop and line a testament to the grace with which she carried herself. It was more than ink on paper; it was a verse of hope.

A broad and unrestrained smile broke across his face, lighting up his eyes with a spark he was trying to hide. Her name is Judy Martin, and she is at 369 Oak Street, Poplar Bluff. Her phone number is Poplar Bluff 6838. They were the keys to unlocking a future he had only dared to dream of. The digits of her phone number danced in his head, a melody that he longed to play out.

But patience held him back. The reading of the will loomed over him, a solemn affair that needed his undivided attention. John knew he must have been excited, for the revelation of his ownership of JR's Department Store was a closely guarded secret.

John looked for the taxi Mr. Thompson said would be waiting for him, and there it was. John could not help but feel a surge of excitement as he approached the taxi. The sign with "Jenkins" painted across it was a beacon, a promise of the new beginnings that awaited him at Rivers Run Lodge. The taxi driver greeted him with a nod and a warm smile as if understanding the importance of the journey John was about to embark on. John asked, "Could you please take me to the Rivers Run Lodge?"

"Yes, sir," said the driver, "step inside the taxi out of this snow, and I will put your luggage in the trunk." In a moment, they drove off, starting the new adventure. As the taxi drove through the streets, John's mind raced with thoughts of the lodge, the retreat Mr. Thompson had raved about. The anticipation rose within him, a simmering pot of hope and curiosity. The drive was picturesque, of natural beauty that whispered promises of peace and a hint of romance in the air.

Upon arrival, the lodge was even more breathtaking than John had imagined. The location had a rustic appearance, situated peacefully within the natural surroundings. The clerk at the reception desk welcomed him with a bright smile, and John was touched by the seamless efficiency with which everything had been prepared for him. It seemed Mr. Thompson had thought of everything, confirming John's belief that this was the right place to rest, relax, and find inspiration for the reading of the will.

Then, there it was, a message from Sarah. The mere mention of her name sent an unexpected panic through him. He had not seen her yet, and she was already woven into his new adventure. Her message, a simple request to call, felt like a nudge from fate. It was as if the stars aligned, setting the stage for something extraordinary.

John entered his room and stood on the balcony, taking in the scent of the fresh pine in the air. The small river that ran beside the lodge was beautiful. It was a new beginning in his life, and the message from Sarah was the first step.

He picked up the phone, and the hotel operator asked, "How may I help you, Mr. Jenkins?" John asked, "Would you please connect me with Sarah at JR's Department Store?" The operator said, "Of course, Mr. Jenkins, one moment, please," as the line connected, his heart skipped a beat in optimistic anticipation. Whatever lay ahead, John was ready to embrace it with an open mind, and it all started with a simple, "Hello, Ms. Sarah, it's John. I've just arrived."

Sarah said, "Hold on just a minute, John; I need to close the door." His heart was racing as she said those words. He was unsure of what to say or whether he should say anything at all. Maybe just let Sarah do all the talking. "Hello, John. Did you have a good and relaxing trip?" said Sarah. "Yes, ma'am, it was a great trip, and I met many nice people on the train," John told her. Sarah said, "You didn't say anything to anyone on the train about the store." "No, ma'am, definitely did not say anything," said John.

"Today is Monday, and the lodge restaurant has a great catfish special tonight. If you'd like, I can come to the lodge, and we can have dinner there tonight, visit each other for a little while, and start making preliminary plans. We must review several things, including getting you some temporary transportation." "That would be great, Ms. Sarah. Would seven tonight be ok with you?" said John. "Yes," said

Sarah, "that would be perfect. I'll meet you at the restaurant. See you at seven tonight."

As Sarah hung up the phone, she wondered how she could get transportation for John. Then she smiled; the last time John Roberts had his car serviced, Jimmy, owner of the local Ford dealership, would let him use a Ford sedan until they finished servicing his vehicle. She would call Jimmy and explain to him, not everything, that an important person was coming to Poplar Bluff today and needed some exceptional help.

"Hey, Jimmy! This is Sarah over at JR's Department Store. How is everything at your end? Marvelous, I hope!" Sarah chirped with a sunny cadence that could brighten even the cloudiest days. Her voice rang enthusiastically, making you want to smile just by hearing it.

She listened with a patient ear as Jimmy expressed his condolences on the passing of Mr. Roberts, the owner of JR's, her head tilting slightly, her eyes twinkling with understanding and positivity. "Oh, Jimmy, you're always such a gem. Seriously, your kindness is truly remarkable! However, I'm calling with a favor to ask. Jimmy, there's a lot I can't tell you right now, but I'll tell you everything in a few days. If you can help me, I would greatly appreciate it. And could you please keep this confidential? A significant person is coming to Poplar Bluff today." Sarah's laughter rang through the line, a light-hearted melody that warmed up the conversation. "So, we are in a bit of a bind, and I remember the last time Mr. Roberts's car was in your care, you were a knight in shining armor with that sleek Ford sedan you loaned him. It was just fantastic!"

She paused for effect, her enthusiasm building like a wave before crashing over the shore. "Do you think we could borrow a car for a few days? I know it's a big ask, but if anyone can save the day, it's you, Jimmy. Who else has an entire fleet of shining chariots at their disposal, ready to swoop in and make things right?"

Sarah's voice danced with excitement, her optimism infectious. "You'd be helping us out so much! John would be over the moon, and

I would be forever in your debt. We could even display the car right in front of the store! Think about the exposure! Customers come in for their shopping and leave, dreaming of a new Ford. It is a win-win, don't you think?"

The warmth and energy in Sarah's voice embodied a smile that no doubt mirrored on Jimmy's face. Her enthusiasm was not just a mood but a persuasive force, a bright beacon in the fog, impossible to ignore or decline. She waited eagerly for Jimmy's response, ready to add another sprinkle of cheer to seal the deal.

"Sarah, you don't need to explain anything; I am glad to help." A big smile appeared on her face. "I probably owe John Roberts more than anyone will ever know. Where do you want me to drop it off?" Jimmy asked.

"Oh, thank you, Jimmy, thank you so much. Can someone drop it off at Rivers Run Lodge and leave the key under the driver's seat? I will take care of it from there," Sarah said, almost with tears in her eyes. "I will be glad to, Sarah, and again, I am so sorry about John's passing. Just let me know when you need me to pick it up."

John's heart raced as the finality of the call with Sarah settled in his chest like a stone, sinking slowly with the weight of the future. His palms were slick against the phone, a testament to the nerves dancing like live wires beneath his skin. The department store, JR's, was more than just a building filled with goods; it was a vessel for his father's legacy.

As the sun dipped below the horizon, the sky was filled with a beautiful sunset; the gravity of the impending 7:00 P.M. meeting with Sarah pulled at him. His mind, a storm of thoughts and questions, looked desperately for an anchor. What should he ask? The breadth of his responsibility loomed large, and the fear of inadequacy whispered in his ear.

John could almost hear the echo of his father's voice, the man who had once stood where he stood now, full of hope and ambition. He needed to know the heartbeat of the business, the pulse of its daily operations. "How does the store currently engage with the community?" he would ask Sarah, looking to understand the soul of JR's, the essence that had kept it standing through the many years it had been in business.

He would tenderly inquire about the staff, the lifeblood of the store: "What are the strengths and challenges that our team faces?" To him, this was not just a transfer of ownership; it was the passing of a torch, the beginning of a new era in a great history.

And with the night slowly replacing the sunset, the soft glow of the parking lot lights casting long shadows on the pavement, John would ask about the future, his voice steady but laced with the vulnerability of one standing on the precipice of change. "What is the vision for JR's, and how can we innovate while honoring our past?" Because this was not just a business transaction; it was a promise to carry forward a legacy, a commitment to nurture and grow a community pillar.

The clock ticked closer to 7 P.M. with each passing second; John felt the weight of his new role settle more firmly on his shoulders. He would step into that meeting with Sarah not just as a businessperson but as a custodian of dreams, as a man ready to leave his mark on the rich history of JR's department store. And in his heart, where nervousness had once reigned, now showed tender moments of courage, ready to face the future head-on.

John was a bundle of nerves, his hand quivering ever so slightly as he fidgeted with the condensation on his chilled drink. His eyes flicked to the entrance every other second, betraying his attempt to be nonchalant. Tonight was the night he would meet Sarah, the powerhouse who had been steering the department like a legendary captain at the helm. And John felt more like a greenhorn than a seasoned sailor in her formidable presence.

The restaurant buzzed with patrons' lively chatter, but the sounds seemed to quiet down to John as the host led Sarah through the maze of tables. There she was, confident, experienced, and the linchpin of the business he was about to dive head-first into. With every step she took, John's heart seemed to match the tempo, pounding louder and faster.

As Sarah approached, John found his feet, an adrenaline rush propelling him upward. His chair scraped back gracefully, and he straightened his posture, smoothing out the front of his shirt as if to wipe away the jitters clinging to his frame like lint. Cooled from the glass but warmed by anticipation, his hand extended forward.

"Hello, Ms. Sarah. I am John," he declared, his voice bright and welcoming. His nerves melted into a sincere enthusiasm for bridging the gap between inexperience and mentorship. Sarah's presence was magnetic, but John's readiness to learn and his fervent resolve to succeed shone through his eyes and the eager handshake that followed.

The future was uncertain, the challenges ahead formidable, but in that handshake, John conveyed his respect for Sarah's impressive tenure and eagerness to embark on this new adventure with her guidance. A new partnership was beginning tonight, among the clinking of glasses and the soft hum of conversation, and John's excitement for what was to come was nothing short of contagious.

Sarah's eyes sparkled with surprise and enthusiasm as she extended her hand, her voice a cocktail of warmth and excitement. "It's so nice to meet you, John," she beamed, unable to peel her gaze away from his familiar features. Time seemed to slow momentarily as she took in every detail, her stare fixed, her mind whirling with thoughts.

Quite perplexed by the intensity of her observation, John could not help but check himself with a touch of humor. "I'm sorry, Ms. Sarah," he chuckled with a light-hearted grin, "did I spill something on my shirt?"

There was a pause, a delicate beat in their new acquaintance, during which Sarah seemed to awaken from a trance of memories. "Oh no, I'm so sorry for staring at you," she said, her cheeks colored with a hint of embarrassment. Her voice softened, taking on a note of wistfulness as she continued, "It's just, well, that you look just like John Roberts, your father." The room hummed with the energy of recognition and remembrance as if Sarah's words had cast a spell, bridging the gap between generations. Her heart was beating in rhythm with the echoes of the past, seeing in John the living legacy of a man she had loved, admired, and held in high regard.

John's smile widened, a light of curiosity and intrigue igniting in his eyes. Here stood someone who knew his father, who could perhaps share stories and moments he had never heard. This was more than a meeting; it was a connection to the parts of his father's life that had remained, until now, whispers and shadows.

So began their conversation, a lively dance of past and present, each word spinning a vibrant thread in the colorful history of John Roberts' life. Sarah was full of stories and laughter, and John was eager to drink in every tale to discover the father he never knew. The enthusiasm in the air was unmistakable as two generations collided in the joy of remembrance and the thrill of discovery.

Sarah's eyes sparkled with the vividness of cherished memories as she turned to John, her voice ripe with excitement and nostalgia. "John," she began, her voice infusing the room with a warmth reminiscent of a summer's embrace. "I worked with your father from the first day we opened the store doors. Oh, and what a glorious day that was! It feels like a lifetime has danced by since then."

She leaned in, her gaze fixated on John with an intensity that only actual reminiscence could raise. "I want to tell you this straight from the heart," she confessed, her enthusiasm undimmed by time. "The reason I couldn't help but stare at you is that you are the spitting image of your father; the very essence of him seems to live on in you!"

Her hands moved expressively as she continued, a smile unfurling like a banner of joy across her face. "And there's something magical I must share with you: your father and I were in love for many years. It was a love that blossomed and grew from day one in the department store, among the aisles and the shelves of our little store."

Sarah's voice reached its highest point with intensity, "We weren't keeping our love a secret. No, far from it! The entire world, or at least our small part, knew we were deeply in love. They knew we were a pair, a team, a couple utterly devoted to one another." With a twirl of her hand and a heartfelt chuckle, she added, "We just never got married. Can you believe it? We basked in the now, in every shared smile and whispered dream. We always thought time was a friend that would linger indefinitely."

Her eyes gleamed with unshed tears of joy and lost time, "But let me tell you, John, every moment was a treasure. And seeing you now, seeing him in you, I am swept right back to those precious days. Your father lives on, not just in my heart, but in the wonderful legacy he's left in you." "John, your father never knew he had a son. He found out about a month before he passed away. We talked several times about what to do if or when you were found. I told him I would do everything in my power to ensure that everything went smoothly with the reading of the will and your taking over the company. That is a promise I plan to keep. John and I were never married, so you aren't my stepson, but if it's OK with you, that's how I would like to treat you. I think your dad would like that." "I would like that very much, Ms. Sarah," John told her. "Now," said Sarah, "let me tell you about your transportation."

John's eyes sparkled with unbridled anticipation as Sarah relayed the details about their mode of transportation. "Let me give you the scoop on your wheels!" Sarah began, her voice ripe with excitement, as if she were unveiling a grand prize. "You're not going to believe this, but Jimmy, a stellar friend of your dad's and the bigwig over at the Ford Motor Company, has tossed us the keys to a beautiful new Ford sedan!"

She leaned in as though about to disclose a state secret. "We've got our hands on a 1946 Ford sedan, John. It is a beauty!" Her hands gestured as if she could sculpt the car's curves from the air between them. "Imagine this gleaming tan paint that catches the sunlight, making it look streaked with gold. And get this: the way we're getting it... It is like something out of a spy novel. The key is stashed under the driver's seat, waiting for you to take possession. It is a beauty, John."

"We will look at it after we talk and have dinner. It is yours to use for a few days or until you make other arrangements," Sarah told him. "Let's order, and then we can get back to talking and planning," Sarah said with a delighted face. After they ordered, they began discussing the Will. "John," said Sarah, "the reading of the will is going to take place on December 25, 1946, Wednesday at 1 P.M. I suggest you get there about thirty minutes before anyone else so I can unlock and let you into my office, sorry, your father's office or maybe your office." John felt that Sarah had thought everything out particularly well. "Everyone else will go straight to the conference room down the hall once everyone is seated and ready for the reading of the Will. I will come to the office, get you, and you will wait outside the door where you can hear. Mr. Thompson will address everyone and explain the process for reading the will. After reading the will, he will explain how long it will take for it to go through probate. Mr. Thompson will begin reading the will with the standard introductory verbiage that typically precedes most wills, then outline the specific bequests to each person. The first ones to be read aloud will be the two nieces and nephews. He will ask them if there are any questions. If none, he will move on to the next two: your father's brother and sister. He will explain what they will get and how long it will take them. After that, he will call for me, and I will be just outside the door with you. I will walk back in then, and you will remain outside. He will read the stuff about my inheritance at that point. After that, he will tell a quick story about your father and his long-lost son. He will explain how he only found out about a month before he died, and ordered Mr. Thompson to search for you. At that time, I will walk to the back and stay in the room, but I will say, Little John, yes, that is what I will call you, Little John. Could you come in, please? At that point, I will introduce you to everyone as little John, the son of John Roberts. We will give everyone a minute to calm down at that point. He will continue reading the will. He will read aloud the parts that you will get. After he finishes, he will ask if you have any questions. You will not; whatever you think, you have no questions. If you have a few questions, we will get with Mr. Thompson after everyone leaves, and he will answer them. We do not want your private and financial information to be publicly available. After that, he will ask everyone to come up one at a time and sign some documents. Although you have already signed the documents, you must re-sign them on that day to become official. I'm not sure exactly how it will go then. But the reading of the will must be completed at that time." John said he understood completely.

As the aroma of golden-fried catfish drifted through the cool air, their minds wandered with the delightful anticipation of their meeting. The hushpuppies, those little orbs of crispy perfection, sat beside the fish waiting to be discovered. With each bite into their crunchy exteriors, a soft, savory center emerged, melting on the tongue, a testament to the culinary magic of Southern comfort food.

The coleslaw, a crunchy cabbage and carrot mixture, was dressed in a creamy dressing that was a balance between tangy and sweet. It was the perfect counterpoint to the rich flavors that adorned their plates.

Baked beans simmered to a thick, hearty consistency offered a smoky sweetness infused with molasses and a whisper of bourbon. Each spoonful was a warm embrace, a reminder of lazy summer picnics under the shade of old oak trees.

And then there was the tartar sauce; you could say that it was just tartar sauce, but it was so much more than that! At The Rivers Run Lodge, nestled in the bend of the Rivers Run, something miraculous was happening, as the beautiful flowing water revealed a remarkable sight. The tartar sauce, a seemingly simple condiment, had become the talk of the town, the jewel in the crown of this bustling river establishment.

Imagine this: a creamy and tangy concoction that had the power to transform any ordinary dish into a masterpiece. It was not good; it was divine. It was the kind of tartar sauce that made you want to stand up and applaud after the first taste. The type of tartar sauce that had people lining up around the parking lot, come rain or shine, just for a dollop of that golden goodness.

CEOs and entrepreneurs studied the phenomenon in boardrooms across the city, eager to bottle the magic for themselves. But the secret to the sauce was more than its ingredients: the passion, care, and love that went into creating it daily. The product captured the essence of the restaurant's commitment to excellence, a beacon of its dedication to delighting every customer.

With another cold beer to wash it all down, the frothy liquid was a refreshing cascade, the perfect companion to their feast. Each sip was an incredible delight, a bubbly punctuation to the rich flavors that dominated their meal.

As they sat there, basking in the beauty of the night lights on the winding river, they knew they were experiencing some of the best catfish the town had to offer. It was not just a meal but a celebration of flavor and a moment of joy they would savor in their memories for years to come.

"Ms. Sarah," John said, "I am so full of catfish. I'm not sure if I can stand up. I spent three days on the train and arrived just this afternoon. I am about ready to stop for the day. Dinner with you and discussing the plans on Christmas Day have taken their toll on me. Let me pay for our dinner, look at the car, and get the keys so I can go tomorrow, and then call it a day."

John's energy was starting to run low, his words dashing out slower than before. "Imagine, after three days chugging along on the train, the endless tracks unfolding like the stories of a mysterious novel; I've finally arrived at this marvelous afternoon! And lo and behold, our delightful dinner meeting was spectacular. The will reading is like something out of an Agatha Christie book!"

His hand reached into his pocket and pulled out some of the cash that Mr. Thompson had given him. With that, he said, "I will pay the server, and then we can go into the cold, snowy evening air to see my temporary wheels." They stood up and walked towards the lodge's front door. Just outside the front door was a beautiful tan Ford sedan waiting for someone to get in and take it for a spin. But that would have to wait till tomorrow; he was too tired to ride tonight. John said, "Where did you say the keys are, Ms. Sarah?" Sarah said, "Look under the driver's seat". And there they were, the keys to this beautiful tan Ford sedan, just waiting for him to climb in and start looking over the city.

John said to Sarah, "Thank you so much for taking time out of your schedule today to come out and talk to me. This will make Wednesday's meeting much better and calm my nerves."

Sarah said, "You are very welcome, John; when you have time tomorrow, call me, and we will talk more and let you know how everything is going. I will also let you know if there are any changes to the will reading on the 25th. Besides that, take the car, ride around the city, and take a look at things. If you need anything or require help, please don't hesitate to call me. You have my number at the office." With that, they shook hands, and Sarah got in her car and drove off.

As Sarah drove off, she could not help but think that she could tell this was John's long-lost son, as he had many of the same traits that John had. She looked forward to working with him at JR's and hoped everything would work out. She would also check on him late tomorrow afternoon to ensure he had settled in and everything was going okay. After all, that is the least she could do for John's son, the man she had loved for so many years, and he had loved her in return. Discovering about Little John shocked her, and she was sure it would shock everyone. On the 25th, during the will reading, she would ensure everything went as John wanted, and nobody would harbor any animosity towards Little John.

John decided to look around the car and get a feel for everything before using it the next day. He opened the door and sat in the driver's seat, and a big smile appeared on his face. He and his mother had never owned a car, which was a new experience. John could not help but let a wide, grateful smile stretch across his face as he watched Sarah's car shrink in the rear-view mirror, her generosity and thoughtfulness fueling his admiration for her even more. Her taking the initiative to resolve his transportation logistics warmed him with indescribable comfort.

He gazed around at the spacious interior, running his fingers over the plush seats, the new-car scent enveloping him like a promise of new beginnings. Sarah was right when she said Jimmy, the owner of the local Ford Dealership, did us a big favor by selecting this Ford Sedan. It was sleek, powerful, and had an air of casual sophistication that resonated with his style. The thought of driving this beauty on the open road was exhilarating, each mile to be savored like a gripping novel.

"Oh, Ms. Sarah, you really took care of me with this car!" he thought, his heart fluttering with a sense of adventure. The dashboard beckoned to him, the polished steering wheel ready to guide him through twists and turns yet to be discovered. This was not just a mode of transportation but a way for memories to be etched into his life.

The sparkle of the car's exterior seemed to mirror the twinkle in his eye, both sparked by anticipation and shining reflectors of the joy his late father brought into his life. It was more than he could have ever dreamed, a tangible reminder of his care and connection with the department store, a nod to the future he was building, one mile and one moment at a time.

John felt a surge of eagerness to start the car. With a quick check of the mirrors and a slight adjustment of his seat, he started the car. As he turned the key, igniting the whisper-quiet engine, a sense of boundless gratitude and excitement danced in his chest. The road was calling, and he was ready to answer, but it could wait till morning. John headed back to his room to sit on the balcony and relax for a while. As he settled on the balcony, the crisp mountain air nipped at his skin, starkly contrasting with the warm, amber liquid that swirled in his bottle, a craft beer obtained from the charming lodge lounge. He tipped the bottle to his lips, feeling the soothing bubbles dance against his palate. With each sip, he gazed at the winding river, his eyes tracing the silhouettes of towering pines against the twilight sky. The stars began their nightly show, sparkling like distant lanterns, celebrating with him. The snow started to come down lightly again and would cover the parking lot by morning.

Just a week ago, the world's weight seemed unbearable, the relentless pressure of financial woes suffocating his every thought. But as fate would have it, the winds of fortune had shifted dramatically. John, once struggling financially, is now a multimillionaire. The revelation was as staggering as the jaggy mountain peaks that surrounded him. And the source of this seismic shift? A father from a past he had never known, a man whose absence had been a silent constant, now echoed by a legacy of untold wealth.

With each sip, John could not help but marvel at the turn his life had taken. The balancing act of overdue bills, the chorus of 'insufficient funds', the vise of living paycheck to paycheck, all of it was now relegated to the annals of his history, a distant memory to be recounted with disbelief and, perhaps, a tinge of nostalgia.

The future unfurled before him like the vast night sky, limitless, mysterious, and laden with twinkling possibilities. Investments, charities, travel, worlds of opportunity reachable with the flick of a pen on a check. Now, he could make amends, forge new paths, or even investigate the mystery of the man who had unwittingly altered the course of his destiny.

John raised his bottle in a quiet toast to the father he never knew and the adventures ahead. The night hummed with promise, and John, with a heart swollen with newfound enthusiasm, was ready to meet it head-on. Cheers to the unexpected, cheers to new beginnings, and cheers to the rich life that never ceases to surprise and delight.

As the first light of dawn pierces through the crisp December skies, John awakens with a vigor that only the anticipation of a pivotal day can bestow. Today, he thought, might tilt the axis of his world. But first, a most crucial endeavor awaited: breakfast.

With a spring in his step, he makes his way to the lodge's restaurant, a sanctuary of delightful aromas and the promise of a morning feast. The atmosphere buzzes with holiday cheer, a prelude to the feast. The restaurant, adorned with festive garlands and twinkling lights, seems to welcome John personally, whispering tales of culinary delights.

The menu, a testament to fine dining, boasts an array of dishes crafted to ignite the senses. And does John relish the thought of indulging in such an exquisite breakfast? He chooses with care, knowing that today's adventures require the sustenance of champions. Each bite is a symphony, each sip of rich, aromatic coffee a sonnet. This is no mere meal; it is a celebration on a plate, the perfect fuel for a day marked by destiny's hand.

John's mind dances with schemes as forks and knives clatter softly against the china. The reading of the will, that impending ceremony laden with revelations, hovers just on the horizon. But for now, he basks in the moment, in the simple yet profound joy of a delectable breakfast at the lodge. He savored it, knowing that every good day begins with a great meal, and today, he was off to a spectacular start.

As he slid behind the wheel of a beautiful 1946 tan Ford sedan, John could not contain his excitement. Its chrome accent sparkled like diamonds under Poplar Bluff's winter sun, and the engine hummed as he turned the key. Today was no ordinary day; it was the day before everything would change. The vibrant streets of his new hometown beckoned, and he was eager to answer the call.

As he rolled down Maple Avenue, the world seemed to slow down so that he could admire the beauty of his new hometown. He took particular pride in knowing that tomorrow, Christmas Day 1946, his life would take a fantastic turn; he would inherit JR's Department Store, a landmark in this close-knit community. Its grand windows, now dressed in festive garlands and twinkling lights, reflected the dreams and aspirations that his inheritance symbolized.

His first destination was preordained: He cruised by JR's without stopping, yet was ready to unravel the surprise that lingered in the air like the scent of pine and cinnamon. The citizens of Poplar Bluff went about their last-minute holiday shopping, unaware that the man behind the wheel would soon be the owner of their beloved store. JR's Department Store is the cornerstone of his inheritance and a treasure trove of the community, gleaming amidst the humdrum of Main Street. Its windows were like the eyes of the town, reflecting the bustling life of hopes, dreams, and the everyday pursuit of happiness. John felt a deep sense of pride, knowing that his efforts and vision would soon be a part of it.

Yet, he remained quiet, a silent sentinel to the legacy that bubbled beneath his composed exterior. The patrons and employees were unaware of the change on the horizon, the shifting tides that would bring a new captain to the helm. But for now, John was content to be an observer, letting the store bask in its innocence for just one last day.

With JR's shrinking in his rearview mirror, John felt the urge to explore further, to allow the road to guide him wherever it may lead. Should he point his Sedan toward the mighty Mark Twain National Forest, one of nature's finest works? Or perhaps he should go down to the bustling rail yards, where trains exhaled plumes of white into the wintery air? The possibilities were as limitless as his rising joy.

With a future full of possibilities, John pondered where to venture next on this ride. He considered the outskirts, where the landscape turned to rolling hills and frosted trees, the perfect backdrop for a newcomer in town. Or perhaps he would drive through the heart of Downtown, where the laughter and cheer spilled out of diners and boutiques, already inviting him to be part of their community.

The decision was at the tip of his thoughts when whimsy took the wheel, urging him to explore, to become one with Poplar Bluff's yuletide spirit. So, he took a left, then a right, following the winding roads with no destination in mind, just the pure joy of anticipation mingling with the freedom of the open road.

Tomorrow, his journey as an heir will begin. But today, it was just John, his Ford, and the endless promise of adventure, turning an ordinary December drive into a prelude to his new life. On that crisp December morning, with the sun shining on the frosted earth, John, brimming with new beginnings, eagerly drove his Ford sedan. Today was no ordinary day in Poplar Bluff; it was the eve of Christmas and the dawn of John's legacy. With an eager heart, he embarked on his first voyage around the town that would soon become his hometown.

Yes, today was more than a simple drive; it was an overture to John's future, a prelude to the grand adventure that awaited. As the Sedan hummed and the town rolled by, John could not help but feel that this Christmas would indeed be the merriest and the brightest it had ever been.

John's eyes sparkled with anticipation as he took the final turn toward Rivers Run Lodge. The clock hands were inching towards the 3 o'clock mark, a silent reminder that his day of adventure was transitioning into an evening of cozy refuge. Now swirling down with tremendous enthusiasm, the snowflakes painted the landscape in a cloak of winter wonder, a sight that offered both a breathtaking view and an ounce of concern for tomorrow's plans.

He pulled up in the lot, parked, and turned off the car. It was more than just a car; it was his lifeline for the next few days in a world blanketed in white. The heavy snowfall framed it in a picturesque scene, worthy of a snapshot straight from a holiday card. John could not help but pause, admiring the view, feeling a surge of appreciation for the car that had carried him reliably throughout the day.

With a lightness in his step, John made his way into the warm embrace of the lodge, shaking off the chill as he strode through the welcoming doors. The lobby had a rustic charm with a large fireplace at the front facing the clerk's desk, and the clerk behind the desk was the picture of mountain hospitality. Several chairs and tables were between the clerk's desk and the fireplace. It was as if the fireplace was beckoning anyone to sit down and enjoy the warmth. John sat in front of the fireplace to enjoy the sound of the wood popping and the heat from the fire on this cold, snowy day. It was almost mesmerizing, and then, "Mr. Jenkins!" the clerk called out with a chipper tone, leaning over the counter with a smile. "I have a message here for you. It is from Sarah. She wants you to call her when you get a chance."

Sarah! Just hearing her name sent a wave of eagerness racing through him. He thanked the clerk, his mind already racing with possibilities. What could Sarah have to say? The message had an air of mystery, a secret note passed in class that promised an unexpected turn in his day.

He bounded upstairs, two steps at a time, his spirits undampened by the winter weather. The room welcomed him with open arms, a sanctuary of calm after the day's escapades. He sank into the desk chair, giving himself a moment to revel in the serenity, the silence punctuated only by the muffled sounds of the snow against the windows.

The anticipation was too great; he could not wait another minute. He reached for the phone, and the desk clerk said, "May I help you, Mr. Jenkins?" With that, John asked, "Would you kindly connect me to Sarah at her office at JR's Department Store?" His voice showed curiosity and excitement. The dots were connecting, leading to a new adventure waiting to unfold with the simple act of a phone call.

"Hello!" Sarah's voice sounded warm as she answered the phone. The familiar jingle of the store's daily routines echoed in the background, a testament to another bustling day of business. "Hey, Ms. Sarah, this is John Jenkins." "John! Oh, I am glad you called back," Sarah exclaimed, her tone lifting with genuine delight. "I trust your day has been filled with wonderful things?" "Yes, ma'am, I had a perfect day, Ms. Sarah," John responded, his words infused with a downright infectious positivity. "I certainly hope your day was just as fantastic, and the store has been buzzing with happy customers!" "Oh, you've hit the nail on the head, John!" Sarah was enthused, her voice dancing with excitement. "Today has been splendid, and the store, well, it's been a beehive of activity, a perfect day! Maybe the best day before Christmas in years, and John, please feel free to drop the formalities, and John, Sarah will do just fine."

"Yes, ma'am," John said, though his voice held a hint of a chuckle, acknowledging the old-fashioned habit. "It's just a bit hard not to show my respect to my elders."

"Well, John, I called for a rather specific reason," Sarah continued, now brimming with anticipation. "Would you like to meet me after hours to look at the store? We are closing shop at 5 P.M. today because it's Christmas Eve. Once the last customer has left and the staff has headed home, I'd be thrilled to meet you at the door around 6:30 P.M. to tour the store with no one else around! What do you say? You can pull up to the door at 6:30, and I will just be inside to open and let you in."

Sarah's invitation was energetic, clearly reflecting her passion for the store and the community it served. It was an offer wrapped in the joy of sharing something special, a behind-the-scenes glimpse into a place that undoubtedly held countless stories and treasures.

"Thrilling!" Sarah exclaimed, her eyes sparkling with the excitement of a thousand twinkling stars. "I can show you JR's Department Store, a treasure trove of wonders from the moment you step through the front door to the very instant you find yourself at the back door."

She beamed with pride, her voice promising and anticipating. "But wait, there's more! Imagine the sanctum of strategy, where decisions come to life, your dad's office, a realm of resilience and resolve, which I now guide with honor and dedication. It's a space that's seen dreams crafted and challenges conquered, a true testament to the legacy of JR's."

With a gentle, inviting gesture, she continued, "And it will be your very own office after the will is read. A place where your hands, heart, and ingenuity will shape the future of JR's Department Store."

Sarah's enthusiasm was infectious; her words painted a vivid picture of a business empire's past, present, and future, which stood as a cornerstone of the community. Her offer was not just a tour; it was an odyssey through time, a celebration of heritage, and an initiation into a legacy that was as much a part of Sarah as it was of him.

She urged, with a twinkle in her eye and a smile that could light up the darkest of rooms, "Let me show you the heart of JR's Department Store, where every corner holds a story, and every story is waiting for you to write its next page. This will allow you to see it all before tomorrow, which may alleviate some of the jitters. After that, I will take you to dinner to repay you for dinner last night." Sarah finally breathed and said, "Oh, how I wish you would, John; after reading the will tomorrow, it will be a real fast-paced few weeks." "Ok, Ms. Sarah, I mean Sarah. I will be outside the door at exactly 6:30 P.M."

The steady beat of his heart seemed to synchronize with the rhythmic fall of snowflakes against the ground, each flake like a whisper of the past, ushering in the present, a present where John stood on the precipice of a new life, the life his father had built but never shared with him.

JR's Department Store had always been a city landmark, a beacon of commerce wrapped in the festive glow of Christmas lights. The windows portrayed holiday cheer, but the joy seemed distant to John, overshadowed by the sheer weight of the legacy he was about to accept.

Sarah. Her name echoed in his mind like a promise. She was the glue that held the store together, the one who would bridge the gap between the giant figure of his father and the empire he had built, and John. He had learned that she was more than just a manager; she was the heart of JR's, beloved by staff and customers. He imagined her to be a woman of poise and grace, moving through the aisles with quiet confidence. He was about to find out if his imagination aligned with reality. A gust of wind swept down the street, stirring the snow into ghostly swirls as the clock continued to count down to the half-hour.

It was 6:15 on December 24, 1946, and John was waiting for precisely 6:30 to meet Sarah at the front door of JR's Department Store. At 6:29, he drove to the front door and saw a shadow in the window beside the door. He knew the only person there was Sarah, so he exited the car in the snow and walked to the door. He stuffed his cold hands into his overcoat pockets, the fabric slightly damp from the relentless snowfall. Through the muffled silence, the sound of the door unlatching from within jolted him from his thoughts. A sliver of warm light cut through the darkness, growing steadily as the door swung open. Sarah opened the door and said, "Glad to see you again; come in." The illuminated clock face of the department store's grand entrance towered above him, its hands showing 6:30 P.M., a minute that marked the beginning of his unforeseen inheritance.

"John," she said, her voice steady and welcoming, "I'm glad you made it through the storm. There's a lot to see inside. Let's get you out of the cold." With a nod, John stepped over the threshold of JR's, leaving behind the chill of uncertainty. The warmth of the store enveloped him, the scent of polished wood and the lingering fragrance of holiday spices drifting through the air. Sarah closed the door to the winter's night, and with it, an old part of his life sealed itself away.

She led him through the grand foyer, past the ornate decorations and the towering Christmas tree that was the centerpiece of every holiday season. The store was silent, starkly contrasting with the bustling corridors on a typical business day.

As Sarah guided him through each department and section, the giant store began to shrink into something more manageable, more human. Through her eyes, John saw the lifeblood of JR's: the fine-tuned symphony of commerce and care that his father had conducted daily by her side.

Tonight, the store was more than a building; it was a legacy that John was about to step into, with Sarah as his teacher, his ally, in the profound stillness of Christmas Eve. And then, with a mix of trepidation and curiosity, they entered the conference room, a chamber of secrets where the reading of the will would take place, altering the course of their lives the next day at 1 p.m. "Your father remodeled this conference room about a year before he passed away." "It is a beautiful conference room, and it tells a lot about the person who decorated it, my father," said John.

"Now, John, I saved the best for last," said Sarah. "Would you like to go ahead and see your father's office? I have used it since your father died to run the store." "Sarah! I would be honored to see where my father spent so many of his days shaping the business that has become a pillar of our community. His dedication and passion for his work have inspired me, and stepping into his space, where he made countless decisions and strides for the company, feels like the next part of a legacy I am excited to continue. It is both a privilege and a great responsibility to follow in his footsteps, and I embrace it wholeheartedly. Seeing the office as a reminder of his absence and a beacon of what can be achieved with hard work and vision will fuel my desire to continue his remarkable work. Lead the way, Sarah. I am more than ready to connect with my father's spirit and wisdom that lingers in the heart of his office. Let's continue the journey that he began with so much hope and ambition, and let it be a place of innovation, success, and warm memories as we move forward." Sarah's voice rippled with an undercurrent of excitement, a pitch of intrigue that lured us toward the looming doorway. "Let's go into your father's office," she said, smiling as if she knew the treasures awaited us. Flourishing, she pushed open the giant door to reveal a realm of wooden splendor. The office was finished in tongue-and-groove oak, its grain adding warmth to the walls. The air was heavy with the scent of aged timber and whispered secrets.

The large mahogany desk seemed to anchor the room with its stately presence. Beautiful chairs, their curves and lines speaking of expert craftsmanship, circled the desk.

Antique items dotted the office's landscape everywhere he looked, each placed with a curator's eye for detail and design. They were not mere decorations but silent narrators of history, each with a story to tell.

In one corner stood its restroom, a nod to the blend of comfort and privacy that only true power and wealth could afford. And then, as if this office were not impressive enough, there was the dining area, a small, intimate space where deals were undoubtedly brokered over fine china and crystal glasses that chimed like bells toasting to success.

The entirety of the office was not just a room; it was a testament to the man he had been. It was a fortress of solitude where decisions were made that could change the fates of many. Sarah's invitation was not just to a room but to a legacy, and as they walked inside, the legacy enveloped them, eager to share its tales of triumph and toil.

Every corner seemed to pulse with life despite the absence of its creator. John's spirit resonated through the office, and the past whispered to the present, promising that the story was far from over.

Sarah's voice held a boundless warmth, like sunshine spilling over a meadow at dawn, as she spoke to John. Her eyes sparkled with the memories that danced behind her lids, painting the picture of a life so full of love it could fill up the oceans.

"John, isn't it just breathtaking?" she exclaimed, her arms gesturing grandly to the space around them as if embracing the beauty of it all. "This place has such an incredible energy, doesn't it?" John's gaze wandered, soaking in the splendor, feeling the echo of times past and moments shared. He turned back to Sarah, his voice rich with a mixture of awe and a touch of longing. "It is magnificent," he agreed, his words thick with emotion. I can almost picture him here, you know? In this very room. The conversations we could have had..."

Sarah stepped closer, her presence a pillar of support as sturdy as the oak trees that lined the path to this very place, her eyes soft yet filled with an indelible strength. "John," she said, her voice as tender as a lullaby, "when you need to talk, remember, laugh, or even cry, I'll be right here. There is no distance too far, no hour too late. You see, your father was the greatest love of my life. We shared everything, from the most mundane tasks to the grandest adventures. We were inseparable, two halves of a whole."

She took his hand in hers, a lifeline, steady and sure. "So, believe me when I say I probably knew him better than anyone else. Every dream he whispered in the dark, every fear he confided, I hold them all right here," she said, placing a hand over her heart.

"And I am here for you, John. To share stories, offer insights, and remember the love of your father lives on in us, in the legacy of love he left behind. And together, we will keep his memory shining bright as a beacon of the love that never fades and that defies time and space. You and I will be okay because we have each other. And with every step we take, your father's spirit walks with us, guiding us forward on this magnificent life journey."

And then John said, with a hint of tears in his eyes, "Sarah, where and when can I go see my father's grave?" Sarah smiled with tears beginning to run down her cheeks," John, I would love to take you to your father's grave site. We can meet here about an hour and a half before the will reading and go to the cemetery. That will give us time to be back about half an hour before the will reading. Does that sound ok with you?" "That would be perfect, Sarah." As a small tear ran down John's face,

Her enthusiasm was contagious; her words were not merely spoken, but felt, a testament to a shared history and a future yet to be written. There was a power there in her unwavering support, an unspoken promise of continuity and steadfast friendship, offering a kind of solace that only proper understanding and shared memories could provide. "John," Sarah spoke to get him out of a trance in the office, "it is 8 P.M. Are you ready to go to dinner? I promised you dinner tonight, and it is time for me to pay up."

John said, "Is there anything open now? I would think everything would be closed at this hour." "There is," said Sarah. "The lodge restaurant where you are staying is still open. Many people are traveling and staying at the lodge, so they still must have a place to eat." They left in their cars and headed to the lodge for dinner.

As they drove to the lodge, the sky was clear, and the stars were bright, as if looking at a picture. John and Sarah found themselves heading towards the welcoming glow of the lodge, nestled in the heart of tranquility. Eager anticipation fluttered in their stomachs, not just for the delectable meal awaiting them but also for the discussions that would take place during their meal.

Upon arrival, the aroma of sizzling steak and the earthy scent of baked potatoes enveloped them in a warm embrace, setting the stage for an evening shaped by comfort and camaraderie. The crisp and fresh salad was a symphony of colors, a perfect sidekick to the hearty main course. And oh, the cold beer! Its chilled embrace was the ideal foil to the rich meal, offering a tantalizing tickle to their taste buds.

Their conversation meandered from the mundane to the magnificent as they enjoyed their meal. They spoke of the store, that bustling hive of activity where life's small necessities and joys could be found. They reminisced about the office, a place pulsing with the heartbeat of ambition and the whip-smart snap of productivity.

Finishing their meal with satisfied sighs, they could not help but think of the speech John would craft later that night. Not just speech but thoughts and responses woven with the threads of consideration and foresight. This was not merely about delivering words but about encapsulating a moment, a sentiment, a connection with those who would listen.

In this tranquil setting, John and Sarah ended their day with the peace of a good meal and the electric buzz of anticipation for what the next day would bring. Their hearts and minds aligned with the promise of possibility; they stepped toward the future, ready to embrace it with open arms and resolute spirits. As Sarah left to go home and John retreated to the comfort of his room, the day's exhaustion whispered to him, promising the sweet surrender of sleep. But John, with a mind racing with thoughts of tomorrow, could not sleep.

He went outside on the balcony to enjoy the quiet of the night, trying to compose his thoughts under the sky full of stars. He was putting together a speech for tomorrow, or some words after the lawyer reads the will. A light snow had started, so John returned inside, changed clothes, and went to bed. As he fell asleep, he hoped the snow would stop before morning so he would have no problems getting to the department store to read the will.

9

Christmas Morning

John bolted upright, his heart racing with the thrill of Christmas morning; it was as if the universe had conspired to wake him with a glimmering spectacle of light snow. The sun, a beautiful sunrise, and John could not help but feel invigorated by the sheer beauty of the day. It was a beautiful 8 A.M., the kind of start that promised magic and a touch of destiny.

He sat up on his bed, a big smile on his face, his mind already racing with the events ahead. Today was no ordinary day; it was a day steeped in mystery, where the past would meet the present at the reading of a will that could change everything.

But first things first, breakfast! John's stomach growled in agreement, and he chuckled, thinking that even the most enchanting mornings must bow to the siren call of a hearty meal. He walked downstairs with his thoughts already savoring the eggs, the sizzling bacon, and the steaming coffee that would soon grace his table. And then, he would make his way to the department store, a tower of bygone eras, where at 1 P.M. sharp, the future would unfold in the palms of eager heirs. John's heart pounded with exhilaration, his stomach was full, and his spirit soared high.

After satisfying his hunger with a feast fit for royalty, John's plan was crystal clear: He would retreat to his room and pour his essence into crafting the most stirring speech. The words would flow from his heart, cascading like the winter's first snowfall, gathering weight and purpose until they formed a message of depth and passion.

As the clock's hands marched steadily forward, the moment would soon arrive for him to leave. He would need to leave around 11:00 to ensure he arrived at the store by 11:30, so he and Sarah could visit the cemetery before the reading of the will. He would meet with Sarah; from there, they would go to the cemetery, then return to JR's, where she would take him to the office and stay until she came to get him.

John worked on his speech all morning and completed it to the best of his ability. He hopes to have no problems with anyone or that the group will not cause any issues. John has never had an immediate family and hopes to have one now. He puts the paper in a folder and looks at the clock, and to his surprise, it is 11:00, time to go. John puts on his shoes and heads to his borrowed car.

John's heart thundered with a potent cocktail of nerves and excitement as he revved the engine of his trusty car, the wheels crunching determinedly over the freshly fallen snow. The world was wrapped in a pristine blanket of white, and the road ahead was a challenge he was more than ready to meet. Six miles, a mere stone's throw for such a steadfast traveler, stretched between him and the legendary JR's Department Store, the keeper of secrets and declarations that will alter the course of his life.

He felt a surge of adrenaline as he navigated the slippery road, his mind full of curiosity about the will's contents. As the familiar structure of the department store loomed out of the snowy scene, a smile quirked his lips. One lone car in the parking lot, Sarah's. A sense of relief washed over him, warming him despite the frosty air that nipped playfully at his cheeks. It was such a short ride that the heater had no time to warm up. The presence of others had been a nagging worry; their early arrival through the snow was a possibility he could not dismiss. But not today, it seemed.

With a confident stride, John approached the building, his boots leaving a trail of hearty footprints in his wake. Sarah instantly spotted him, as if she had been waiting for this moment; her face was a beacon of welcome. Together, they drove to the cemetery and visited John's grave. Sarah talked about John's father, laughed, and cried as the stories were told. Time seemed to fly as Sarah said, "John, we have to go, it's 12:15 and we need to get you into the office before anyone gets to the store. We can come back anytime you want or need to." John smiled, hugged Sarah, and said, "Thank you, Sarah, this means more to me than I could ever say." They walked to the car and left. A short time later, they arrived at JR's.

Sarah ushered him into his father's office, a room steeped in memories and silent anticipation. This would be the office of his destiny, where he would sit, his patience a silent sentinel until the time came for revelations and truths to be unveiled. John settled into a genuine leather chair, where the very fibers of the room were a reminder of the past, and the clock slowly ticking towards the moment that could change everything. Enthusiasm, bright and bold, coursed through him, for John stood on the precipice of the unknown, and he was ready to meet it head-on with open arms.

10

The Will

In the mahogany-laden conference room, the air buzzed with the excitement of secrets held tight within the Will of John Roberts. Mr. Thompson, the distinguished attorney and executor of the late John Roberts' estate, cast his practiced gaze over the family members who anticipated unveiling their loved one's last wishes. The room held different relations: two siblings whose faces were etched with the roadmap of shared history and silent rivalries, two bright-eyed nieces and two robust nephews, all wearing the cloak of youthful optimism and barely concealed greed. Then there was Sarah, the love of John's life, whom everyone knew, and she had been with John since he opened the store. Beside her was a vacant chair for someone unknown to anyone except Mr. Thompson and Sarah.

Peeking from behind his notes was Mr. Thompson's legal clerk, a keen mind wrapped in an earnest desire to see the drama that would unfold. And there, offset from the central drama, sat Kathy, Sarah's secretary, her eyes the quiet custodians of untold stories and confidences that might now see the light of day. Next to Kathy was Judy, who would provide a little extra help if needed. Kathy was to help with anything Mr. Thompson might need, such as typing, shorthand, different papers, or anything that needed doing.

With a throat-clearing, meaning that we will start, Mr. Thompson prepared to draw back the curtain on the reading of the will, that ritual where words on paper had the power to unite or divide, to bring joy or despair. As the last whispers of anticipation hushed into a respectful silence, the attorney unfurled the document that would lay bare John Roberts's previous intentions to his gathered kin.

"Thank you, everyone, for being here today," Mr. Thompson began with the warm enthusiasm usually reserved for heralding great news. "I stand before you today not only as the attorney and executor of John's estate but as a dear friend to a man whose generosity and zest for life knew no bounds. Today is a sad and joyful occasion, a gathering brimming with the vibrant spirit of a truly remarkable soul."

"With immense privilege and a heart full of reverence, I officially bring into effect the last will of John Roberts. This document is a testament to his unwavering kindness and commitment to enriching the lives of those around him." Mr. Thompson hesitated to clear his throat and regain his composure. As he had said before, John Roberts was not just any client but also a dear friend. He continued, "A little over nine months ago, John Roberts passed away from a battle with cancer, and today, I shall voice the wishes of John, each word a beacon of his intent and each sentence a melody of his legacy. I will read the will, and with each name called, know that it sings of John's affection and gratitude for your presence in his journey through life. If you wonder why we waited so long to read the will, here is the reason. One stipulation in John's will is that it can only be read on Christmas Day and must be read in this grand conference room. Most of you know Christmas was a significant part of John's life; he loved this day more than any other, and the season was always his favorite. As we traverse the path of John's final wishes, may you feel enveloped by his warmth and gratified by the recognition of your unique bond with him. John Robert's impact on life continues through you, his beloved friends, and his family. And as his will is read, let us celebrate the joy of being a part of this incredible man's life, which continues to flourish even as we honor his memory. Now, without further ado, let us begin by telling you some of my final expressions of our dear friend John Roberts and then officially notifying all beneficiaries of their legal inheritance."

"John Roberts was not just a man of considerable means, but considerable thought and love for his family. It is a great honor and privilege to reveal the contents of his will, as each of you holds a place in his heart and now, in his legacy."

The room leaned in, the air thick with breaths held tight, and Mr. Thompson felt a thrill at being the bearer of words that would dance the fine line between joy and despair. Within this room, John Roberts's voice would echo from beyond the grave through a will that promised to be anything but ordinary.

With a nod to Sarah, whose eyes glistened, and her cue to get Little John and bring him outside the door to wait and listen, Mr. Thompson embarked on the reading that was sure to etch this day into the annals of Roberts' family lore.

"Let me take you on an extraordinary journey through time, resilience, and the unwavering spirit of a visionary! The story of John Roberts is not just about a department store; it is a tale woven into our history, a narrative marked by courage, perseverance, and a dream that refused to dim even in the darkest of times."

"In the bustling year of 1914, a young and vibrant John Roberts set foot in the clothing business, and oh, how he thrived! With each thread and each sale, his passion for fashion and customer service fluttered through the aisles, igniting a dream that would one day illuminate the world of retail. His dream was not merely to open a store but to create a sanctuary of style, a haven for quality, and a symphony of delightful shopping experiences. But little did he know the path ahead would be a journey of trials and triumphs!"

"As the world plunged into World War I, our very own John Roberts volunteered for service as many other men did then. He was not only a businessperson but also a decorated war hero who showed courage beyond measure. Many of you may not have known this, but amidst the clamor and chaos of the battlefield, our John fought with a heart of steel, exemplifying heroism that would etch his name in the annals of bravery. Yet, fate had its trial by fire in store for John. He was grievously wounded by a test of the flesh and the spirit and, after being captured, endured the harrowing ordeal of a POW camp. But even as his body was trapped, his dream remained."

"Each scar he bore was a testament to his unwavering determination to survive, fight another day, and return home. His brothers-in-arms speak of him with a reverence reserved for the most hallowed warriors, recounting tales of his bravery that could turn the coldest hearts to fire! But do not let his steely resolve fool you, for beneath that brutal exterior beat the heart of a guardian angel whose heroic deeds were fueled not by the desire for glory but by an undying love for peace for the country. For the precious lives he safeguarded through his actions."

"It would take years for John to knit his body and mind back together to heal from the scars of war and captivity. Yet, he appeared not embittered but emboldened. With each step back toward civility, John's determination blazed a trail straight to the heart of his dreams. And here we stand today, 34 years after that fateful beginning in the clothing business, amidst the splendor of a dream realized, a dream that grew into this magnificent department store we are all a part of. This store is not just bricks and mortar; it is a testament to John's will, impeccable taste, and unwavering commitment to excellence."

The nieces and nephews sitting in front of Mr. Thompson started talking to one another and said that they never knew their uncle John was a war hero from World War I, and they sure never knew that he was in a POW camp and was severely wounded.

Mr. Thompson said, "OK, let's get started with the reading of the will. I, James Thompson, attorney and executor of the will, officially break the seal on this will and place it into effect. I will read each beneficiary's name and ask a couple of questions. You will then answer each question. All questions, answers, statements, and comments will be placed in the record as of this time."

Mr. Thompson started, "Today is December 25, 1946. We are reading the will of the estate of John Roberts, who passed away on March 10, 1946. The will itself:"

Last Will of

John Roberts

I, John Roberts, a resident in the City of Poplar Bluff, County of Butler, State of Missouri, being of sound mind, not acting under duress or undue influence, and fully understanding the nature and extent of all my property and of this disposition thereof, at this moment make, publish, and declare this document to be my last will ("Will"), and at this moment revoke any other wills and amendments previously made by me.

PERSONAL REPRESENTATIVE

I appoint James Thompson, Attorney, a resident in the City of Poplar Bluff, County of Butler, State of Missouri, as Personal Representative and executor of my estate.

DISPOSITION OF PROPERTY

I appoint and bequeath my property, both real and personal, and wherever situated, as follows:

1st Beneficiary

James Raymond Roberts, brother,

"Are you James Raymond Roberts?"

"Yes, I am," said James.

"James Raymond Roberts, you are the beneficiary of $25,000 from the estate of John Roberts. Do you have any questions?"

"No, sir," said James.

"2nd Beneficiary, Jamie Roberts Henderson, sister.

Are you Jamie Roberts Henderson?"

"Yes, I am," said Jamie.

"Jamie Roberts Henderson, you are the beneficiary of $25,000 from the estate of John Roberts. Do you have any questions?"

"No, sir," said Jamie.

"3rd Beneficiary, Allison Jill Roberts, niece.

Are you Allison Jill Roberts?"

"Yes, I am," said Allison.

"Allison Jill Roberts, you are the beneficiary of $10,000 from the estate of John Roberts. Do you have any questions?"

"No, sir," said Allison.

"4th Beneficiary, James Raymond Roberts Jr, nephew.

Are you James Raymond Roberts Jr?"

"Yes, I am."

"James Raymond Roberts Jr, you are the beneficiary of $10,000 from the estate of John Roberts. Do you have any questions?"

"No, sir," said James.

"5th Beneficiary, Janice Gail Henderson, niece.

Are you Janice Gail Henderson?"

"Yes, I am," said Janice.

"Janice Gail Henderson, you are the beneficiary of $10,000 from the estate of John Roberts. Do you have any questions?"

"No, sir," said Janice.

"6th Beneficiary, Jimmy Max Henderson, nephew.

Are you Jimmy Max Henderson?"

"Yes, I am," said Jimmy.

"Jimmy Max Henderson, you are the beneficiary of $10,000 from the estate of John Roberts. Do you have any questions?"

"Yes, sir," said Jimmy.

"What are your questions?"

"Can I buy a car with this money?" everyone laughed, and Mr. Thompson, smiling, said, "You will need to talk to your parents about that."

"Everyone knows the next beneficiary here. From day one, when JR's Department store doors swung open to the promise of endless possibilities, Sarah stood shoulder to shoulder with Mr. Roberts. The store was brimming with potential: just a few racks of carefully purchased clothes, a cash register, and an unwavering commitment to excellence. The air was electric with anticipation, and Sarah's smile was a beacon of the warm customer service that would soon become the store's trademark."

"Sarah was not just an employee but a dynamo, a force of nature. With every sale, with every satisfied customer, she wove her magic. The register's merry chime sang a chorus of success, thanks to her skillful touch with sales and her natural ability to connect with people from all walks of life. Her smile, expertise, and passion for fashion all became the department store's signature."

"And as John ran the gamut of responsibilities, from sourcing the latest styles to meticulously arranging each display, Sarah's relentless spirit kept the engine running. She was the maestro of the sales floor, orchestrating transactions with the ease of a seasoned conductor. The store did not just grow; it blossomed, flourished, and surged forward on the tides of Sarah's dedication. With a twinkle in his eye and the utmost certainty, John himself would tell you that his empire, this beloved local landmark, would not be what it is today without Sarah. With heartfelt gratitude, he often says that success has a name, which is etched in every corner of the store: Sarah Johnson. Sarah has been the cornerstone, irreplaceable confidant, and trusted partner for twenty years, transforming a modest space into a thriving hub of commerce and community."

"This is not just a story of a department store; it is the saga of a partnership that defies the odds, built on unwavering trust and mutual respect. The twenty years or more that they worked together slowly brought them closer and closer to each other's heart, till one day they realized that they were in love. They both laughed and said there was no better way to fall in love than to become friends and then fall in love. Over the years, they said they were going to get married. They were both so dedicated to the store that the day to get married, just never came."

"7th Beneficiary, Sarah Julie Johnson, is the assistant store manager and the love of his life. Are you Sarah Julie Johnson?"

"Yes, I am," said Sarah.

"Sarah Julie Johnson, you are the beneficiary of 10% of JR's Department Store from the estate of John Roberts; you must read section 5 for more information on your inheritance. Do you have any questions?"

"No, sir," said Sarah.

Mr. Thompson continued, "Now, I want to tell you a short story about John Roberts as he told it to me. He has loved two women in his life. You already know about Sarah, and now I will tell you about the first one, which was many years ago. Sarah just found out about this story just before John passed away. The first was in 1914 when he started working in the clothing business. He fell deeply in love with a beautiful girl named Gail Jenkins and dated for three or four years. It is essential to understand the emotional landscape of John Roberts' life, a man profoundly changed by ill-fated love and the chaos of war. His narrative begins with a tender romance with Gail Jenkins, a relationship that rooted itself deeply in his heart during the early years of his venture into the clothing business. Their plans for a shared future were a testament to a love that was both earnest and hopeful. The first woman he loved, Gail, was a significant figure in his life, an emotional cornerstone and a symbol of what could have been a life of time-honored bliss disrupted by the outbreak of World War I."

"The war's intervention was both cruel and transformative. Like many of his friends, John was swept up in a tide of patriotic duty that saw him enlist and leave for the front lines, tearing him away from the possibility of marriage and fatherhood, a future that would remain unrealized. Gail discovered she was pregnant about four weeks after John had been shipped out to the army. Gail Jenkins' resulting pregnancy and the decision to withhold the news in her letters were motivated by a desire to protect John from added strain amidst the horrors of war. Her silence on the matter would have lasting repercussions, adding a layer of tragedy to their story."

"Upon receiving the mistaken news of John's death, Gail was left to navigate a reality marred by loss and societal stigma, a reality that led her to move with their child, severing ties with their past. John's return started his desperate search for Gail, and upon discovering his profound misfortune and the agonizing consequences of her misinformation, he made the heart-wrenching decision to cease his search and return to Poplar Bluff. That marked the end of his quest, albeit with a heart still laden with unanswered questions and a longing for the life he almost had."

"John Roberts's love for Gail Jenkins was not simply a tale of romantic affection but also a narrative full of the complexities of wartime communication and the enduring impact of personal loss. His experience symbolizes countless stories from that era, where lovers' fates were often left to the mercy of circumstances far beyond their control. This account offers a window into the human cost of war and the enduring nature of love amidst the most trying of circumstances."

"About a month before John passed away, he found out that Gail had passed away a year earlier and left behind a son, John Roberts' son, that he never knew he had. He tasked a private investigator to find him, and they did, but not before he passed away." Mr. Thompson looked at Sarah and said, "Sarah."

She nodded as if she knew what he needed. Sarah stood up, left the room for about one minute, and returned. When she walked back in, she went to the front of the room with a young man beside her, turned to the group, and said, "Ladies and gentlemen, it gives me great pleasure to introduce to you, John Roberts Jenkins, the long-lost son of John Roberts."

Sarah's voice pierced the tense atmosphere with unwavering conviction, her words a beacon of acceptance in the storm of shock that had swept through the room. "Calm down, everyone," she urged, her gaze sweeping over the faces of John's family, each a mix of confusion and curiosity. "We found out about John's long-lost son about a month before he passed away, and let me be clear, it hasn't shaken the foundations of our love, not one bit. John said he knew we never got married, and he can't change it now. He also said he wanted me to treat his son as ours, and I intend to do just that."

Her declaration hung in the air, as potent as the fragrance of blooming roses. "My heart hasn't wavered, and neither has John's. This young man," she continued, her voice imbued with warmth and certainty, "is part of our family now. He's one of us, and I won't have it any other way."

The room remained silent, and the family was caught in the gravity of her words. "I know it's a lot to take in," she acknowledged, her tone softening, "but we will get through this. We must. John wanted it this way, and I promised him that I would do everything possible to make sure that his son was treated fairly, welcomed into this family, and embraced openly. It's time for us to unite and show the world the strength of our love and unity." Her speech was a testament to her unyielding spirit, a promise of unwavering support, and an invitation to her family to rise to the occasion. There was no room for doubt or hesitation in Sarah's heart, only the boundless ability to love and the determination to honor John's legacy. After Sarah finished, Mr. Thompson continued with the last part of the will reading.

"The 8th Beneficiary is John Roberts Jenkins, long-lost son of John Roberts and Gail Jenkins; I leave the rest of my estate; ninety percent of JR's Department Store and all things associated with it; a twin-engine airplane with ten passenger seats; my main house here in Poplar Bluff and all the properties, land and buildings surrounding it; a vacation house in the Florida keys; stocks, bonds, and cash worth about $15,000,000."

Mr. Thompson said, "Little John, I mean John. Sorry, Little John is the name I started using for you after we first met to keep you apart from your father. "That's quite all right," said Little John. "I hope so," said Mr. Thompson. "You look so much like your father; many people will call you Little John."

"It will be an honor to use that name," said John. "Little John, I am now going to play a recording made by your father for you. Remember, he was extremely sick and weak, so the voice is going to sound weak." Mr. Thompson placed a record on the turntable and started playing.

"My dear son, I will call you son because I did not know your name when I asked the private investigators to find you. I am so sorry that I cannot use your name. My heart beats with mixed emotions as I say what will likely be some of my final words on this earth. Joy, regret, hope, love, a mixture of feelings, whirl inside me, centered on the most critical revelations: that you, my dear son, exist."

"I am told that you are 28 years old. Not a single day of the days I have left will pass without me wondering about the precious moments lost, the milestones missed, the laughter, and the life lessons we never got to share. But within this whirlwind of discovery and parting, I want to leave you with more than words."

"You are about to inherit a legacy, an inheritance in an amount that will serve as a sturdy foundation upon which you can build a towering life. But even as I arrange these financial affairs, I am acutely aware that these numbers bear no weight against the true wealth I would like to impart to you, a treasury of ideals and love, albeit from afar."

"Embrace this world with the courage I know courses through your veins. Stand with integrity, as I believe you will, and let your kindness be the currency that enriches your days. My dear son, it is a grand adventure for life, and this fortune is merely a vessel to carry you through the rough seas and into ports vibrant with your dreams and aspirations".

"Know with every fiber of your being that, although absent, I am proud of you. With this inheritance, I pass on not only my worldly assets but a piece of my spirit, a flame of enthusiasm, and a boundless belief in all you can accomplish."

"Live boldly, love fiercely, and leave trails of joy in your wake. And should you ever doubt your place in this world, look to the stars and know that our stories intertwine somewhere in the grand design."

"And last, my son, you are not alone as you work your way into this inheritance. Mr. Thompson, my attorney, is not just my attorney but also my dearest friend. Last is Sarah; besides your mother, Sarah is the only other woman I have ever loved. She will be a guiding light for you. JR's Department Store would not be where it is today without Sarah. I trust her with anything she says, but that trust for you must be your choice over time, not just because I trusted her."

"You have other family members here in Poplar Bluff: an uncle, an aunt, four cousins, and many friends. It will be up to you to decide who your friends are and who wants to be friends because of the money. Be careful, my son; many people want money and will claim to be a friend to get cash. Real friends will do things for you and help you, and they will never ask for money; that is the true definition of a friend. When in doubt, talk to Sarah. Goodbye, my son; remember, I will always be with you in spirit. I love you."

Mr. Thompson stood up with tears in his eyes. "Little John, do you have anything you want to say?" And with that, he made a gesture with his hand, offering him the floor to speak. "Thank you, Mr. Thompson," Little John said, his voice a mix of awe and dignity, his eyes reflecting a world turned upside down. "Life had never been easy for me and my mother; money was a stranger that seldom graced our doorstep. But we had each other, which had always been enough to push through the tough times."

He glanced down at his suit, the fabric a bit worn at the seams, a silent testament to his simple life. "I've never owned a car, only have this one suit," he said with a humble smile that reached his eyes but could not hide the years of hardship behind them.

"This inheritance is a life-changer, an unexpected twist that I would not have imagined in any amount of time. It is not just about the money, however. It is about the legacy, the weight of carrying on my father's and the family's dreams, a man who was more of a mystery than a memory."

"I pledge, with every ounce of my strength," he continued, his voice steady despite the storm of emotions brewing within, "to work with everyone to ensure that JR's, my dad's legacy, this department store continues to thrive as it always has."

At that moment, Little John was not just accepting an inheritance, but also taking on a new identity, journey, and purpose. The legacy of the department store was not just a business; it was a symbol of hope, a vessel carrying his father's dreams and, now, his visions. And he was ready to give it his all to ensure that the department store, much like his resilient spirit, would endure and flourish against all odds. "Thank you all; I look forward to meeting and talking to everyone, even today, if we have time," Little John said.

Mr. Thompson said, "That completes the reading of the will. Please let me know if anyone needs to speak with me, and we can meet in the office. Thank you all, and Merry Christmas." Then he turned to Sarah, "Sarah, if no one has any questions, could you get someone to let me out the door? I will excuse myself and let your family have this time to let everything sink in."

Sarah turned to Kathy and said, "Kathy, would you please let Mr. Thompson out? Thank you."

As Little John's eyes looked around the room, his heart skipped a beat; there she was, Kathy, the mystery from the train station, whose gaze had lingered just a touch too long, as if she knew him. But the puzzle pieces clicked; she was a familiar face from JR's, a store infused with the essence of his father's presence, a man whose shadow he had learned to embrace. "Aha!" he thought. "The mystery of her recognition is solved!" But life was not done with its unexpected games, not by a long shot.

Just a whisper away, barely an arm's length from Kathy, stood Judy. Judy, with the laughter that echoed over the train's rumbling, Judy, who made the hours dissolve into a haze of joy and connection. The memory of their journey danced vividly in his mind, a treasured story he had carefully tucked away, hoping it was not a once-in-a-lifetime coincidence. The look on Judy's face was one of shock. She looked as if she would run away, not understanding what was happening. But she stood still, right next to Kathy, as they talked in a low voice.

Now, they were both in a twist of fate that could only be orchestrated by the universe's most playful puppeteer. His lips curved, almost of their own accord, into a small smile. It was a moment too perfect, too deliciously unexpected, that his spirit soared on the wings of anticipation. What were the chances? Indeed, life had a knack for the dramatic, and he was all in for the ride. He looked a little longer at Judy, gave her a big smile, and in a way that he knew she would understand. His smile was the unspoken invitation to stories yet to unfold. And Judy, finally, returned a big smile to John,

As Little John began talking to Sarah, his Aunt and Uncle, Jamie and James, started walking towards them. Sarah realized they wanted to speak to John and said, "John, here comes your Aunt Jamie and Uncle James. I have a few things to take care of before we leave." John asked Sarah, "Is there anything that I need to be doing?" "Oh no," said Sarah, "I'll take care of everything."

"OK," John replied. "When do we open back up, and when do you want us to get together?" Sarah told John to come to the store at 8 tomorrow morning to get the ball rolling, and she would meet him at the door. With that, he turned to his aunt and uncle to talk to them, unsure how it would go. He had never met them before and had just inherited a substantial amount of money, so he was confident that they thought they should have received it.

John's heart was a sea of emotions as he stood there, the weight of his newfound wealth pressing down on him like a heavy cloak. As his Aunt Jamie and Uncle James approached, the air around him thickened with unspoken words and expectations. He could feel their eyes on him, appraising, calculating, perhaps even coveting the fortune fate had whimsically tossed into his lap.

John was calm as they approached, but Sarah sensed the tension that clung to the air like a persistent fog. Her voice was soothing as she turned to introduce his relatives, John felt a flicker of warmth in the otherwise incredible moment. "John, this is your Aunt Jamie and Uncle James," Sarah said, her voice a gentle thread weaving through the awkwardness that threatened to unravel the fragile beginnings of their family reunion.

John's mind was a whirlwind of questions and doubts as he turned to Sarah before she excused herself to address the tasks that awaited her. "Is there anything I need to be doing?" he asked again, his voice barely above a whisper, betraying his need for guidance.

Sarah's response was a gentle reassurance, a lighthouse guiding him through the fog of uncertainty. "Oh no," she said, her smile a soft caress against the sharp edges of his anxiety. "I'll take care of everything." John's gratitude was a silent wave crashing within him as he nodded, his voice echoing his inner turmoil. "OK," he replied, his mind already racing ahead.

Sarah's promise to meet him at the store's front door the following day was a lifeline thrown across the unknown. It was a promise of a new beginning, a chance to start the ball rolling on a path as uncertain as it was inevitable. With a heart full of hope and nervousness, John turned to face his aunt and uncle. This was their first meeting, and he was aware of the inheritance that could be a problem between them.

As he engaged in conversation with Aunt Jamie and Uncle James, John could not help but feel the delicate balance of their interaction. Each word was measured, and each smile was cautiously offered. He was navigating a minefield of unfamiliar expectations, acutely aware that his inherited wealth was a double-edged sword that could unite or divide them.

In the back of his mind, Sarah's presence lingered like a promise, a reminder that she was a place where he could reach out and hold on to amidst the chaos of fortune and family. And as the conversation with his relatives unfolded, John held onto the hope that, with Sarah by his side, he could weather any storm that life might throw their way.

James reached out, his hand steady and welcoming. "John, it's a pleasure to meet you," he said, his voice warm despite the surprise rippling through the room upon John's unexpected arrival. "I think we were all a bit taken aback, that's all. None of us knew about you, and it's quite a revelation."

John accepted the handshake, his grip firm yet slightly hesitant. "I understand," he replied, his eyes reflecting the whirlwind of emotions he had grappled with. "I was in the dark myself until just over a week ago. To think that my father was out there, living his life until nine months ago... it's a lot to process. I have thought many times in the past week that I wish I could have at least met my father before he passed away. As I learned more about him, I realized he was a remarkable man. I hope that I can live up to his expectations."

Aunt Jamie stepped forward with her characteristic blend of assertiveness and warmth, taking John's hand. "We'll have plenty of time to unravel this mystery later in the week," she assured him, her voice tinged with the season's spirit. "Right now, it's Christmas, and if Sarah has shared anything about our traditions, you'll know we always gather for a Christmas lunch at John's house on the 25th. I insist you join us. And Sarah," she added, her gaze softening, "you're expected as always." Her eyes then drifted to the two young women helping Sarah, their holiday plans undoubtedly disrupted. "And those two sweet souls over there," Aunt Jamie continued, "they've likely missed their celebrations. Why not extend the invitation? Ask them to join us for lunch."

John's heart swelled with a mix of gratitude and nervous anticipation. "I'd be honored to attend," he said, his voice barely above a whisper, "but I'll need the address." Aunt Jamie turned to Sarah without missing a beat, her eyes imploring. "Sarah, dear, could you ensure that John and the two young ladies make it to the house for lunch?" Sarah nodded; her smile was genuine and reassuring. "Of course, Jamie. It would be my pleasure."

At that moment, the room seemed to glow with the warmth of newfound connections and the promise of a Christmas lunch where the table would be graced with unexpected guests, each with their own story, each a part of their shared history.

As the will's final words resonated through the grand old room, a sense of unbelief washed over John. It was as if fate had dealt him its most generous hand, offering a life he had never dared to dream of, a life bursting with promise, wealth, and a surprise reunion that set his heart racing. Like a vision from the past, Judy, the spirited young girl who had shared three magical days with him aboard a train, where every mile they traveled together felt like a step towards destiny.

Glancing over at Judy, whose presence on this Christmas day felt almost unbelievable, John's pulse quickened. She was chatting idly with Kathy, his father's secretary; their heads tilted towards each other in quiet conversation. The air was thick with the aroma of Christmas, the room awash with the warmth of family tradition, and yet, for them, it might have been just another workday. But not if John had something to say about it!

With a heart full of newfound generosity and a spirit encouraged by the surprising inheritance, John approached Sarah with a twinkle in his eye. "Sarah," he said, cheerful with excitement, "do you think you could extend an invitation to Kathy and Judy for Christmas lunch? The more, the merrier, right? And I suspect they've missed their family celebrations because of work."

The idea was perfect. The mansion, which seemed like the birthright he was only discovering, would now be the backdrop for a lunch that promised to imprint upon the memories of all who attended. Their acceptance would breathe life into the house's dormant halls, filling the rooms with laughter and festivity. He recalled the train trip to Poplar Bluff, recalling how he and Judy had sparked something undeniable, an electric connection that energized every word they shared. John hoped they could pick up where they had left off and turn the page to a new beginning in this grand adventure.

As for his sudden elevation to the heir of the vast fortune, the JR's Department Store, and the breathtaking mansion, John sensed that things were only beginning. With the Rivers Run Lodge as his temporary home, he would slowly ease into his new role. He wanted to ensure the transition went smoothly so the people around him could see beyond the wealth and the title and understand the man he was meant to become.

John's heart was set alight by a boundless optimism, and with this unexpected Christmas twist, the house that held so much history was on the cusp of hosting new memories, one grand lunch at a time. With Judy alongside and the community coming to know the man behind the fortune, this Christmas was shaping up to be one that no one would soon forget.

Kathy and Judy's faces lit up like a Christmas tree as Sarah extended the sparkling invitation from John and Aunt Jamie. "Imagine that!" Kathy exclaimed, her eyes twinkling with the same vibrancy as the festive decorations around them. "A late Christmas lunch at the mansion? That would be simply magical!"

Judy nodded in agreement, her smile warming the chilly winter air. "Oh, how delightful! She had already heard about their holiday gatherings at the mansion, which were always woven with such splendor and joy. It is like stepping into a Yuletide fairy tale!"

The only cloud looming over their excited chatter was the prospect of transportation due to problems with Kathy's car, but Sarah quickly swept that worry away with her reassuring words. "Transportation hiccup? No way! That will not dull our festive spirits," Sarah said with a beaming smile. "John has transportation, and I will ensure he knows how to get there. Kathy, you can take your car back to your apartment, and I will pick you and Judy up and go to the mansion."

Kathy said, "OK, but give us a few minutes to freshen up and change clothes." Judy clapped her hands excitedly. "A lunch with friends, singing Christmas songs? Count us in! The more, the merrier, I always say!"

Sarah's smile was infectious, and it was clear that her master plan included a luxurious lunch and a heartwarming drive together. "Fantastic! It is settled then," she declared with a smile. "A festive ride to the mansion, good cheer included, and to cap it off, John will ensure that you both get home safe and sound, nestled in the comfort of his car."

Kathy and Judy exchanged a look of pure joy, already visualizing the day ahead, the laughter, the stories, the togetherness. It was more than just an invitation; it was the promise of memories that would twinkle in their hearts for many Christmases. With eager anticipation, they all looked forward to what was sure to be a splendid way to extend the season's festivities. Kathy smiled at Judy and said, "Maybe your three-day train trip will be rekindled, and the spark will spark into a heart-loving fire."

Sarah said, "John, after I pick up the girls, we will meet everyone at the mansion." John smiled and said OK as Sarah locked the door to the department store, and they all left. Aunt Jamie said, "Be sure everyone is careful in the snow; see y'all in about one hour." John smiled as he left for the lodge to shower and put on some relaxing clothes with a hint of Christmas. He was excited that the drive to the mansion would only take about twenty minutes.

11

Christmas Lunch at the Mansion

The snowflakes danced gracefully outside, dressing the sprawling gardens of the mansion in a delicate white coat. John, with a mixture of enthusiasm and anxiety, approached the massive oak doors. Today, the mansion and the department store had unexpectedly become his.

As the mansion door opened, John looked over the grand threshold, revealing a foyer that twinkled with the warm glow of Christmas; the butler's professional nod was a silent welcome to a world he had only ever imagined. Garlands laced with holly berries cascaded down the grand staircase, and a towering fir tree adorned with sparkling ornaments and golden lights stood as a monument to the season's joy. John stepped inside, a flutter of excitement in his chest, the air rich with the scent of pine and the distant sounds of Christmas music. The air was thick with the smell of polished wood and a story that whispered secrets from the ornate walls. With each step toward the library, John's heart throbbed with nervous anticipation and excitement. The will reading had been nothing short of a fairy tale; suddenly, he was not just John, but John, the heir of a mansion, JR's Department Store, and many other things that were part of his inheritance.

The butler guided John through the maze of corridors. The soft murmur of conversation grew louder as they approached the library, where the family had met, a mixture of faces that were both new and familiar, all connected by the reading of the will that had taken place just hours before. As he entered, the room hushed momentarily, all eyes turning to appraise the newcomer. Uncle James, with his hawkish gaze and a sharp suit that looked like it could cut glass; Aunt Jamie, her eyes twinkling with mischief and warmth; the four cousins, a spectrum of curiosity and skepticism in their young eyes. Others believed his father's life was something he did not yet understand.

Sarah stood by the mahogany bookshelves, her elegance as timeless as the books surrounding her. Her love for his father had been a legend, their unwedded union a testament to a bond that transcended titles and conventions. Her smile was a silent promise of stories to come, of secrets she would share when the time was right.

Kathy, the ever-efficient secretary, offered John a professional and warm smile, accompanied by a firm handshake. Her eyes held the spark of someone who knew the inner workings of a world that was still a maze to John. Her presence provided reassurance, acting as a stabilizing force amid the complexities of inheritance. Her loyalty to his father had been unwavering, and now, it seemed, it would extend to him. John met Judy, a vivacious friend, on the train to Poplar Bluff, and her laughter and smile filled the three days with joy and excitement. She stood slightly apart from Kathy and John, the new owner, to give them the privacy that an employee and the new boss deserved, but her eyes were bright with curiosity. Her eyes met his with a spark of shared adventure, a connection that was as unexpected as welcome. She was the wild card, the friend of a friend who might just become something more. Their conversations during the journey had been the highlight of his travels, her wit and charm sparking an interest he was anxious to explore.

As the butler discreetly closed the door behind him, the room seemed to hold its breath. John cleared his throat and stepped into the heart of the gathering. "Thank you all for inviting me," he began, his voice steadier than he felt. "I know this is as strange for you as it is for me, but I hope we can come together, not just as a family bound by blood, but as people who share a remarkable legacy."

Uncle James nodded, the first to break the silence. "Well said, lad. Your father would be proud of you." With his silver hair and commanding presence, his hearty voice enveloped John in a welcome as warm as the crackling fire. "A toast to our newest family member!" he declared, raising his glass with a smile that crinkled the corners of his eyes.

Aunt Jamie approached with a composed demeanor, offering a gentle embrace. Her eyes showed signs of emotion, but she maintained a welcoming smile. One by one, the cousins shuffled, sizing him up, their youthful minds already turning with questions and possibilities; each, with their vibrant personalities, introduced themselves, their youthful energy infectious, their laughter a melody that danced through the air.

Sarah approached with the grace of a bygone era, her hand extended. "Welcome home, John. We have much to discuss." Kathy then stepped forward and handed him a folder containing information about JR's Department Store, the house, and many more things his inheritance had given him. "There is a lot in here to digest, Mr. Jenkins. I'm here to assist you with this process if you need anything." She indicated her ability to help with navigating the upcoming responsibilities.

And Judy, dear Judy, stepped forward last, her hand finding his in a gesture that was both familiar and thrilling. "Looks like we're in for quite the adventure, aren't we?" Her eyes danced with the promise of shared secrets and the thrill of the unknown. "Looks like we didn't need the note I gave you at the train station after all, did we."

John looked into her eyes and smiled. "No, looks like fate is trying to put us together." He pulled the note from his pocket and showed it to her, saying, "I was planning to call you tonight after reading the will. I did not know you would be at the department store today."

At that, Judy replied, "And I had no idea who you were at the train station or on the train." They looked into each other's eyes, and both smiled big. Then Judy said, "You can still call me tonight, can't you?" John smiled and replied, "I can, or you rode here with Sarah and Kathy, didn't you?" She smiled and nodded. "Maybe I could just drive you to Kathy's apartment." She smiled and said, "I think we can do that; I'll tell Kathy when we or they get ready to leave."

John felt the weight of his new responsibilities, the mansion, the department store, and all the trappings of his inheritance, but at this moment, surrounded by what was now his family, the weight felt lighter. There was potential here, not just for business, but for love, connection, and a future as bright as the star atop the Christmas tree.

In the heart of the library, surrounded by the scent of old books and new possibilities, John realized that this inheritance was more than wealth and property; it was a chance to weave his own story into the rich history of his father's legacy. With Sarah's wisdom, Kathy's guidance, and Judy's vibrant spirit by his side, he was ready to turn the page on a new beginning, one filled with romance, mystery, and the promise of tomorrow.

As they were ushered into the grand dining room, where the table was set, the china gleamed, and the aroma of a feast filled the air. Uncle James motioned for John to take his place at the head of the table, and with this jester by Uncle James, he felt his life unfold in new directions. This Christmas lunch was not just a meal but the first part of a tale of unexpected paths and new beginnings. The air was thick with the promise of new beginnings as they took their places, where the table groaned under the weight of a festive feast. The clink of silverware and the clatter of dishes supplied a lively symphony as stories were shared and memories were made.

The family, his new family, whom he had never met until that day, filled the room with joyful music that would lift the spirits of anyone who came in. With his spirited laugh and glowing cheeks, Uncle James raised his glass in welcome. Aunt Jamie, elegant and with a smile that reached her eyes, followed suit. His cousins, a fantastic mix of personalities ranging from the bookish to the bold, eyed him with curiosity and mischievous glee.

Then there was Sarah, a vision of warmth, her eyes holding years of dedication to the department store. Then Kathy, who went to work straight out of college at JR's Department Store, had dedicated over five years of work to John's father at JR's and was prepared to do the same for John's son, also named John. But Judy, the unexpected friend who met on the train trip from Mountain Home, Arkansas, to Poplar Bluff, Missouri, had him smiling. Judy and Kathy were roommates through four years of college, and their friendship was the link to him and his new world. That friendship with Sarah, Kathy, and Judy will be the anchor that keeps him steady in the rolling sea of new faces.

As glasses clinked and the room resonated with stories and laughter, he realized that these people, this house, and the very spirit of the season were weaving into his life. The department store, a titan of commerce that he now helmed, felt less daunting with Sarah and Kathy as his guides, both of whom shone brighter than any holiday decoration.

The lunch unfolded like a dance, an intricate ballet of passing dishes and shared memories. Each mouthful was a revelation; each smile was a promise of unity. And there, amidst the clatter of silverware and the glow of the grand chandelier, something beyond gratitude blossomed in John's chest.

A magnificent roast turkey sat at the heart of the table, glistening under the chandelier's warm glow. Its golden-brown skin cracked with the promise of succulence. Around this centerpiece, an array of delectable dishes vied for attention. The turkey had an aromatic smell, rich with sage, pecans, cranberries, and a sweet, smoky crust from the honey-glazed ham. A harmony of spices drifted from the glistening cuts of meat, igniting the appetite.

Traditional side dishes were reimagined as culinary marvels, each a testament to the chef's ingenuity. Creamy mashed potatoes were whipped to perfection, swirls of butter pooling in little wells on top, while the roasted Brussels sprouts had been transformed by a drizzle of balsamic Glaze and a sprinkle of toasted pecans. A medley of roasted root vegetables, including carrots, parsnips, and sweet potatoes, was caramelized to perfection; their edges were tinged with a delicate char that enhanced their natural sweetness.

But let's not overlook the cranberry sauce, oh, no! This was no condiment but a jewel-toned masterpiece, its tartness perfectly balanced with a hint of orange zest and a whisper of cinnamon. It was the ideal complement to the savory richness of the meats. And for the showpiece, steaming boats of gravy, with a depth of flavor so profound, it seemed to hold the very essence of the festive season itself. Of course, there were bread rolls, fluffy as a fresh snowfall, and an assortment of cheeses, each bite a journey through textures and tastes, ranging from the creamiest milk to the sharpest aged cheddars.

With the clinking of crystal and the joyful hum of conversation, guests indulged in this abundance of Christmas delights. Each dish was a feast for the palate and the eyes, artfully presented with sprigs of holly and berries, which added a natural touch of color to the display.

As the meal drew to a sweet conclusion, the dessert spread was revealed, and it was breathtaking. A tower of delicate pastries, fruit tarts with glistening glazes, and a majestic plum pudding set ablaze with brandy, its blue flames dancing like sugarplum fairies. Alongside the silken eggnog custard and an assortment of spiced cookies and gingerbread men, their playful shapes delighted both young and old.

The Christmas lunch at the mansion was a true masterpiece. A symphony of flavors harmonized to create a culinary experience that would be etched in memory long after the last crumb had been savored. The joy of the holiday mingled with laughter and satisfied sighs, echoing through the halls of the mansion like the most musical of carols.

John looked out over a transformed world as the sun stretched its rays over the vast snow-covered estate. It seemed like he was juggling bills and mundane worries just yesterday, and today, his existence was nothing short of a fairy tale!

The majestic mansion that now belonged to him was nestled in the heart of an awe-inspiring garden, winding pathways leading to secret gardens and hidden terraces covered with snow. It was a home that whispered tales of magnificence and echoed with the laughter of generations. The department store he had inherited was a local treasure, a bustling hub where every shelf and aisle sparkled with promise, where every customer left with a satisfied smile and a plan to return.

Amidst this whirlwind of good fortune, John hoped the bond between Judy and him would grow stronger. Judy's laughter was the melody in the symphony of his new life. Her presence was like a lighthouse, guiding him through the sea of his newfound affluence. Their friendship was the anchor keeping him grounded, a treasure far more valuable than the riches that now filled his world.

John was falling in love with Judy, and he could see the department store, with its glistening window displays and elegant counters, becoming part of their daily lives together. Each visit with Judy was like a celebration, a shared wonder at the curiosities they would find. He smiled when he thought about the future and the memories they could share, and their laughter would become an integral part of the store's very essence.

Every day, John will discover a new way to appreciate his new fortune and how it will give his life new meaning. From the crisp morning jogs around his estate, where the fresh air is so refreshing, to the parties that dance well into the night, his life will be a continuous parade of joy.

The inheritance was not just a windfall but a heart full of gratitude and eyes wide with excitement. John embarked on this new adventure, graced by the glow of happiness and the richness of true friendship. If Judy were by his side, the world would not just be his oyster but a world of endless possibilities. And oh, how he planned to savor every single one of them! With Judy and life itself, the chaotic beauty of family, and the sense of purpose that now coursed through his veins. John realized that the inheritance was more than assets and square footage; it was a legacy of connected lives, a heartbeat that sustained more than just the walls of the mansion and the aisles of the department store.

As the flames in the fireplace flickered and cast a warm glow upon the meal's conclusion, John felt compelled to speak, his voice carrying a newfound conviction. "Today, I've discovered not only the dignity of this place but also the legacy that we share," he began, his gaze sweeping from one attentive face to another. "I have also found a family I never knew I had and a home waiting to welcome me. I may have arrived as a stranger, but I stand before you now as one of your own, ready to uphold the traditions that make this season, this mansion, and our family so special."

He raised his glass, his heart full, his eyes bright with the reflection of the season's joy. "To new beginnings, to Christmas, and to the unwritten stories we're about to create together!" As the family echoed his toast, the mansion seemed to settle around him like a cloak, warm and protective. Christmas lunch at the mansion was more than a meal; it was the starting point of John's most incredible journey, one that promised as much love and connection as the romances he had only read about before.

The mantel clock chimed, weaving its melody into the day, and John knew that the Christmas magic had only just begun. As the laughter swelled and the afternoon waned into evening, John knew this Christmas would be one for the ages. It was the start of a new life filled with the warmth of family, the spark of potential romance, and the season's magic. His father's legacy would live on, not just in the tangible assets he had left behind, but in the bonds forged in the heart of this grand old mansion.

The entranceway of the mansion loomed over John as he prepared to leave, the echoes of Christmas cheer still warm in his heart. The festive garlands seemed to glow brighter as he bid farewell to the family he had just discovered. Each goodbye was a delicate thread weaving him into each of their lives, a life that, until a week ago, he had not known he belonged to.

He turned to Uncle James, whose laughter still rumbled like the comforting bass of a familiar song, and Aunt Jamie, whose eyes twinkled with the same merriment that sparkled from the chandeliers above. Their embraces were hearty and sincere, a promise of the many family gatherings.

Sarah stood slightly apart; her smile was tinged with the sweet sorrow of memories. John could see her love for his late father, a passion that had been a steadfast flame, never fully able to ignite into the blaze of matrimony. He took her hand with a gentleness that spoke volumes, acknowledging the years she had devoted to a man he had never known, who was part of who he was.

Kathy, efficient and ever-present, held the secrets of his father's life in the neat stacks of paper that lined the study. Her handshake was firm, a testament to the strength she had upheld JR's Department Store and the estate's affairs. Even in their brief interactions, John could sense her respect and admiration for his father, a respect he hoped to earn for himself.

And then there was Judy. With her laughter, Judy seemed to dance through the air like the snowflakes outside. Their chance meeting on the train had felt like a twist of fate, an unexpected encounter that John was reluctant to end. As he prepared to leave, he approached her with a heart beating rapidly like drums.

"Judy," he began, his voice a mix of hope and desire, "I can't think of a better end to this day than for you to ride back to town with me." Her eyes, a clear and vibrant blue, met his with an intensity that matched his own. In them, he saw the reflection of their newfound connection's potential. Judy told Kathy and Sarah she was riding back to town with John and would return home later. Kathy and Sarah just smiled and said, "Okay."

The world seemed to hold its breath as they walked out into the crisp winter air. The silent night was punctuated only by the crunch of their footsteps on the snow. The majestic and quiet mansion watched over them like a guardian of the past and a beacon for the future.

In the privacy of the car, with the world reduced to the soft purr of the engine and the intimate wrap of warmth against the cold, John dared to reach for her hand. Their fingers entwined in a simple touch that held the promise of countless tomorrows. Judy said, "I told Kathy I would be home later if we wanted to get a cup of coffee or soda. If there are any places open." John said, "The restaurant at the lodge where I am staying is open, and they have dinner items, snacks, and coffee, if you'd like to?"

Judy smiled and said, "I would love to, John." And with that, they drove to the lodge, only about twenty minutes from the mansion. The drive was a journey not just through the snow-dusted streets but through the possibilities that lay ahead. The snowflakes danced like a flurry of winter as John and Judy approached the Rivers Run Lodge, a picturesque haven nestled amidst a winter wonderland. With its rustic charm and smoke rising from the chimneys, the lodge promised warmth and magic on this crisp Christmas Day of 1946.

A cozy heat greeted them as they stepped inside, chasing away the chill that clung to their skin. The lodge was alive with holiday spirit; garlands draped over the hearth, and the gentle glow of the Christmas tree lights bathed the room with soft, colorful lights. The air was scented with pine, and there was a subtle hint of cinnamon from the kitchen, where something sweet was undoubtedly baking.

John, whose life was transforming with an unexpected inheritance, was more intrigued by the woman beside him than the fortune he had just inherited. Judy's easy smile and eyes that sparkled with curiosity were excellent companions on this yuletide evening.

They found a secluded table by the window where they could watch the snow continue to blanket the world in white. The server, a cheerful woman with rosy cheeks, took their order for coffee and left them with a plate of freshly baked cookies, a little festive treat on the house.

As they sipped their steaming cups, the conversation flowed as effortlessly as the river that gave the lodge its name. They spoke of dreams and memories, favorite Christmas traditions, and the little things that brought them joy. Judy laughed at John's tales of boyhood shenanigans, and he found himself utterly captivated by the warmth of her laughter.

Time seemed to stand still for the pair; the outside world faded away as they delved deeper into each other's pasts, hopes, and fears. They shared stories of family and the unexpected twists of fate that had led them to this moment. John found himself sharing things he had never told anyone, and Judy listened with an understanding that made him want to tell more.

The lodge's patrons came and went, but John and Judy remained in their little bubble, their connection growing stronger with each passing moment. They were two kindred spirits, thrown together by chance on a snowy Christmas Day, finding comfort and perhaps the beginnings of something more in each other's company.

As the hours waned and the lodge began to quiet, John realized that his inheritance could not compare to the treasure he had found in Judy. And Judy, who had walked into the lodge with a stranger, now looked at John and saw the possibility of a future she'd never dared to imagine.

The snow outside had stopped, and a peaceful silence enveloped the world. They stood up, reluctant in their movements, not wanting to end the enchanting evening. But as they walked toward the door, their hands found each other, fingers entwined with the promise of tomorrow. With hearts full of newfound joy and the sparkle of Christmas magic lingering in the air, John and Judy stepped out into the night, the world around them transformed. Like the fresh snow blanketed the ground, their love was untouched, pure, and full of endless possibilities.

John drove Judy to Kathy's house, her best friend and old college roommate, where she stayed during her visit to look for a job at JR's. As they neared Kathy's home, John felt the sad tug of parting, yet he knew this was merely the beginning of something extraordinary. "Judy," he whispered, the emotion evident in his voice, "would you like to have lunch with me tomorrow?"

Her smile was the only answer he needed. It was the spark in the dark, the warmth against the cold, the first note in a symphony yet to be written. Judy said, "I would love to, John, but tomorrow will be your first day at the department store. Will you have time for me tomorrow?" "It will be a hectic day," said John, "but I will make time for us to have lunch if you think you can be flexible."

At that moment, Judy remembered that Kathy had asked her if she wanted to go to JR's Department Store with her tomorrow and help with some things she was behind on. "Kathy has asked me to go to work with her tomorrow to help her a little; I said I would, so I will be in Kathy's office all day. I will tell Kathy about our lunch date, and we can leave when you have time." John liked that idea and leaned over in the car, kissed her, then smiled and said, "I can't wait till tomorrow." And as they bid each other goodnight, the world around them seemed to sing with the promise of a love story waiting to be told.

John drove the fifteen-minute drive from Kathy's house to the lodge. The fireplace still crackled with a beautiful fire as the last twilight drops cascaded over the little town. He found himself pacing the polished wooden floors of Rivers Run Lodge, each step echoing the rapid drumming of his heart. His mind, a whirlwind of anticipation and nerves, replayed the day's events like a cherished movie reel. Seeing the mansion he had inherited for the first time was an experience that words could not describe, as he met his newfound family in the library before lunch. The extraordinary lunch in the elegant dining room and the coffee date with Judy had been nothing short of magical; her laughter was a melody that now played an endless loop in his thoughts. Tomorrow promised another glimpse of her, another chance to delve deeper into the connection that seemed to spark effortlessly between them.

But it was not just the promise of Judy's company that had his pulse racing; tomorrow marked the beginning of a new life, one penned by fate's hand. The keys to JR's Department Store, a legacy left by a father he had never known, now rested heavily in his pocket. It was a new world to conquer, a challenge he was determined to meet head-on.

The lodge's grandfather clock struck midnight; its chimes reminded John that the future was at his doorstep. John finally surrendered to the night, allowing dreams of what lay ahead to cradle him into a restless sleep.

12

First Day at JR's

The morning dawned bright and clear, waiting for John's story to unfold. He donned his only suit, the fabric hugging his frame, and the years of use showing. John went downstairs to the restaurant for coffee and breakfast before leaving for the department store: eggs, bacon, grits, and toast. The restaurant consistently delivers a great meal experience. With his appetite satisfied, he left for the department store and drove the fifteen minutes it takes from the lodge. Arriving at the store with a snow-covered parking lot, John put on a heavy coat and started for the entrance. With each step toward JR's Department Store, his confidence swelled. This was his legacy, his chance to build something extraordinary. John's hand found the store's front door as the clock neared eight. Pushing it open, he was greeted by the scent of polished wood and fresh ink. The department store, a kingdom of commerce and dreams, stretched before him. It was in this very place that he would carve out his destiny. And there she was, Sarah, the store's manager. Her presence was commanding, her eyes reflecting the years of dedication she had poured into the store's success. She extended her hand, her grip firm and welcoming.

"Good morning, John. It's a pleasure to help you get started as an owner. I have heard so much about you from Mr. Thompson," Sarah said, her voice blending strength and warmth. "The pleasure is all mine, Sarah. I am eager to learn everything there is to know," John replied, his voice steady though his heart raced with the thrill of the unknown.

"First things first," said Sarah, "we will open at 10 A.M. today, and we must go to the men's clothing section. We can review everything in that section first, and while we're there, you can try on some new suits. Although you have a nice suit, it is not what you must wear as the owner. I do not mean to insult you, but you need to start off looking the part."

"Thank you so very much, Sarah," said John. "That's what I need, for you to be straight up front with me and not hold any punches." John tried on several suits until Sarah said, "That's perfect, John, you look like a million dollars. And that is what you want to look like, a model of success."

Together, they walked through the aisles, Sarah imparting knowledge that only years of experience could bestow. John listened intently, absorbing every detail. He was not just an owner in the title; he was a student, ready to embrace the wisdom of those who had woven the very fabric of this establishment.

As the morning passed into the afternoon, John felt more at ease, the store's rhythm becoming familiar. He was ready for this, prepared to honor the past while steering the ship toward new horizons.

And then, as the clock signaled the approach of 1 P.M., Judy's face flashed in his mind, a reminder of the other adventure that awaited him. A lunch date with her was just the reprieve he needed, a moment to step away from the weight of responsibility and bask in the simple joy of budding romance.

John told Sarah, "If you don't mind, I'm going to take Judy to lunch and give my brain a chance to relax for a little while. Where is a good place for lunch that is quick, good, and close by?" John asked; his brain needed a little downtime to unwind.

As they walked to Kathy's office, Sarah said, "JJ's steak and seafood. About a mile from here." When they entered Kathy's office, John asked Judy if she was ready for lunch and suggested JJ's steak and seafood. John's suggestion of lunch sparked a visible excitement in Judy's eyes, which made the corners crinkle with genuine delight. "That sounds wonderful," she replied, her voice tinged with anticipation. "I've heard their seafood is the talk of the town, and I've been meaning to try it." Her smile was infectious, and John found his own growing wider in response.

As they prepared to leave, Sarah chimed in with an approving nod. "You two will love JJ's. It is the perfect spot to unwind, and their lunch specials are out of this world!" she exclaimed, her hands gesturing animatedly as if to underline her point. "Make sure you try their grilled salmon salad; it's my favorite. And the atmosphere is just so cozy and inviting, perfect for a midday break!" John prepared to return to the world outside JR's Department Store with a newfound sense of purpose and a heart brimming with possibility. He was at the crossroads of love and legacy, ready to embrace both with open arms.

With Sarah's enthusiastic endorsement ringing in their ears, John and Judy made their way out of the office, the promise of a delightful meal ahead fueling their steps. The idea of a light yet savory lunch in a place where friends gather daily was precisely what they needed to recharge. As they walked, the air between them was charged with a clear sense of connection, the simple act of sharing a meal laying the groundwork for something potentially more profound. The prospect of what the afternoon might bring hung tantalizingly as they stepped out into the sunshine, heading towards John's car and JJ's Steak and Seafood. As Judy settled into the passenger seat, the soft fabric of the car's interior brushing against her skin, she couldn't help but feel a flutter of excitement in her chest. The simple gesture of John opening the car door had sparked a warm glow in her heart, a gesture so chivalrous it seemed ripped from the pages of a timeless romance. Her radiant and wide smile was the kind that could light up the darkest of nights, and it was all for the man who stood before her, a gentle knight in modern attire. With a big smile, she acknowledged, "Thank you, kind sir."

John's response, a playful dance of words, "You are so very welcome, dear lady," was accompanied by a twinkle in his eye, one that hinted at a growing affection, a shared secret between them that the world had not yet been privy to. As he closed the door behind her and made his way to the driver's side, Judy felt the air buzz with visible excitement, the kind that whispered the potential of what could be.

Behind the wheel, John's hands found their place with practiced ease, yet his heart raced with an unfamiliar rhythm. He glanced at Judy, her profile outlined by the sun's soft glow through the window, and felt a surge of something daring, something bold. This was no ordinary drive; it was the beginning of a journey that promised laughter, whispered dreams, and perhaps, if the fates were kind, a love story for the ages. As the engine hummed to life, so did the melody of their adventure, a tune they were both eager to explore, note by beautiful note.

The drive was smooth, the silence comfortable, punctuated only by the soft hum of the road beneath them. Judy found herself stealing glances at John, each sending a surge of anticipation through her veins. How he navigated the busy streets with care and purpose told her this journey was more than just a drive; it was the beginning of an adventure. And as the city blurred past them, Judy knew, without a shadow of a doubt, that wherever this road might lead, she wanted to explore every twist and turn with John by her side.

As the afternoon sun was shining bright over the bustling city, John and Judy stepped into the warm embrace of JJ's Steak and Seafood Restaurant, a mere stone's throw from the grand department store that now bore John's responsibility. The establishment, with its polished silverware and crisp white tablecloths, displayed an air of timeless elegance that seemed to slow the pace of the world outside its doors.

As the afternoon sun filtered through the delicate lace curtains of JJ's, John and Judy found themselves comfortably nestled in a cozy corner booth, the kind that whispered of privacy and intimacy. The restaurant, a beacon of elegance in the heart of Poplar Bluff, hummed with the gentle clatter of china and the soft murmur of satisfied diners. With their impeccable manners and crisp uniforms, the staff moved like a well-rehearsed ballet, adding to the ambiance of understated luxury. With smiles as inviting as the aroma drifting from the kitchen, the waiter presented them with a pot of steaming tea and a basket of freshly baked rolls, their crusts singing of the hearth's embrace. As they sipped the fragrant brew, the clink of china and the soft murmur of conversation around them supplied a soothing backdrop to their dialogue. John's inheritance had thrust him into a world of responsibility and expectation; he could not help but feel a sense of ease as he sat across from Judy, a vibrant spirit with eyes that sparkled like champagne.

As they sipped their tea, the conversation flowed as smoothly as the tea in their cups. With a hint of vulnerability that contradicted his usual confidence, John confided in Judy about the whirlwind of emotions that came with his new role as the owner of the city's most beloved department store.

Judy listened, her gaze unwavering, her interest genuine. She shared her journey, the years since college that had been a mosaic of adventures and misadventures. She spoke of her jobs since she and Kathy graduated from college in 1941, the places she had seen, and the dreams she harbored in her heart. Her voice, tinged with both wisdom and wonder, captivated John. It was as if she carried with her the freshness of spring, the promise of new beginnings.

Their conversation meandered through topics as varied as the books they loved and the places they longed to visit. They spoke of art, music, and simple pleasures that made life worthwhile. And as they did, the world around them seemed to fade away, leaving only the two in their little sphere of connection. Time, that ever-persistent thief, ticked away unnoticed. With a discreet cough, the waiter reminded them that the world outside their bubble still turned, and menus were offered once more. With a shared smile, they turned their attention to the culinary delights that awaited them, each suggesting dishes the other must try. As they finally placed their order, the promise of a shared meal before them, it was clear that this was the beginning of something special. In a world still reeling from the echoes of war, John and Judy found a rare peace in each other's company that spoke not just of friendship but of the possibility of love. The afternoon waned, the shadows grew long, and the restaurant's lights cast a warm glow over the two figures still deep in conversation. And though the future was uncertain, one thing was clear: in the city's heart, a new chapter was being written in a restaurant that knew a thousand stories. Time, however, was a relentless chaperone, and as the clock hands swept toward 3 P.M., the reality of their responsibilities beckoned. John, with a reluctant yet determined smile, signaled for the check. They had enjoyed their leisure time, but the department store awaited its aisles and ledgers, a siren's call to the custodian of its future.

With a promise to return, they stepped out of the restaurant's embrace and into the crisp afternoon air. The store, a monument to commerce and community, loomed ahead, its doors wide open to the possibilities that lay within. John, with Judy by his side, felt a surge of determination. Learning the ropes would be a Herculean task, but he was ready to give it his all, to pour his heart into the very foundations of the establishment.

As they crossed the threshold, Sarah, ever the beacon of support, greeted them with a knowing smile. Together, they would navigate the intricate dance of retail, each step a note in the symphony of success. The journey would be long, the hours demanding, but John was persistent. With Judy's friendship and Sarah's guidance, the department store would thrive and soar, a testament to the power of dedication and the magic of new beginnings.

And so, amidst the hum of commerce, their lives intertwining within the walls of JR's, John embarked on his quest. With each passing day, the store would become more than a mere brick-and-mortar structure; it would become a home, a legacy, and a love story penned with the ink of hard work and the boundless optimism of a dreamer.

John and Judy strolled back inside as they opened the department store doors, their hearts still skipping from the intimate lunch at JJ's. They were on their way to the office, their minds swirling with the delicate dance of new romance, when Sarah, John's business partner, intercepted them with a bright smile and news that buzzed with urgency.

"John!" Sarah exclaimed, her eyes sparkling with business savvy and excitement. "Kathy caught me just before you two walked in. She mentioned that Mr. Thompson, the attorney, had called and arranged a special after-hours meeting for us at the bank at 5:00 p.m. today. It's all about privacy and getting our paperwork in order, including signatures on banknotes, loans, and checking accounts, you know the drill. I know my part is minor, but I've heard you have quite the portfolio to manage."

Still basking in the afterglow of his lunch date, John nodded with a confident grin. "Yes, we had a wonderful time," he said, his voice tinged with the warmth of shared laughter and quiet confessions over an exquisitely prepared meal. He turned to Judy, his eyes locking with hers, a silent promise of countless more moments like the one they'd just savored.

He escorted Judy back to Kathy's office; each step they took together was one more step in their love story. As they reached the threshold of the office, hidden from the prying eyes of the bustling store, John leaned in, his lips meeting Judy's in a tender, fleeting kiss, a promise sealed with a whisper. "I'll try to call you tonight," he murmured, anticipating hearing her voice again, sending a thrill through him. "It all depends on how long we're tied up at the bank."

Judy's reply came as a soft chuckle, her eyes alight with understanding and affection. "No matter how late, John, you can still call if you want to." The words hung between them, a delicate invitation, an assurance that time held no power over their shared connection.

With a final shared smile, they parted ways; John navigated the complexities of finance, and Judy went to the quiet hum of the office, each carrying the warmth of their newfound bond. The afternoon sun cast long shadows through the store's large windows, hinting at the evening to come as John strode confidently toward the tasks at hand, his heart buoyed by the knowledge that a simple phone call would bridge the distance until he could see Judy again.

As the snowflakes fell outside the grand windows of JR's Department Store, John stepped into a world utterly alien to him. The scent of polished wood passed through the air as he made his way to Sarah's office, the heart where the financial lifeblood of the store pulsed. The store, an empire of commerce and dreams, now rested on his unacquainted shoulders. The weight of it was immense, yet the thrill of the unknown quickened his pulse.

Sarah's office was a sanctuary of order amidst the chaos of post-holiday sales. She was the store's chief financial officer, a woman whose reputation for sharp wit and sharper quickness preceded her. As John entered, her eyes lifted from the ledger, igniting a spark of curiosity. "John," she greeted, her voice a melody of warmth and professionalism. "Welcome to the nerve center of JR's. Are you ready to learn the financial ropes of your new kingdom?"

John nodded, his gaze sweeping over the room, taking in the stacks of papers, the antique calculator, and the charts that covered the walls. "I am, Sarah. I'm more at home with the open skies than the ebb and flow of commerce, but I'm here to learn and am a quick study."

Sarah's smile was encouraging as she gestured to the chair across from her desk. "Then you've come to the right place. Let us start with the basics: pricing and sales. The art of retail is a delicate balance between enticing the customer and maintaining a healthy profit margin."

She explained the intricacies of markup, the percentage added to the cost of goods to cover overhead and profit. John listened intently, absorbing her words like a sponge. She spoke of the dance between wholesale and retail prices, the ebb and flow of the market, and the keen eye needed to set a price that whispered temptation into shoppers' ears.

"And what of sales?" John asked, his mind alight with newfound knowledge. "Ah, sales are the things that enhance the success of retail," Sarah said, her eyes gleaming with the thrill of the game. "They are a strategic tool used to entice customers to move inventory and keep the store's offerings fresh and exciting. Timing is everything. Post-holiday sales, for instance, capitalize on the desire for bargain hunting after the Christmas rush."

She walked him through the calendar, pointing out the critical periods when sales were most effective: the end of seasons and back-to-school. Each sale was a carefully orchestrated event designed to maximize foot traffic and convert browsing into buying. As the hours slipped by, John lost himself in numbers and strategies. Sarah was a masterful teacher, and her passion for the store's success was infectious. He could see the patterns forming, the logic behind the seemingly random chaos of discounts and deals.

John felt confident when the shadows grew long and the time approached 5:00 p.m. The store was more than a building; it was a living entity, and he was beginning to understand its language. "Thank you, Sarah," he said as they stood to take a break. "We need to leave for the bank. How long will it take for us to get to the bank for our meeting?" Sarah reassured John, "We will be there by 5:00 P.M. It is just one block from the store. We can walk it in five minutes." They left the building and began talking as they walked.

"Today has been invaluable. I feel as though I am beginning to see the store through my father's eyes." Sarah was reassuring. "You have the makings of a fine proprietor, John. Your father would be proud. Remember, the heart of JR's is its people, customers, and staff. Treat them well, and they will steer the store to prosperity."

13

❧

The Bank

John and Sarah walked down the snowy sidewalks of Poplar Bluff, feeling the December chill. The Christmas decorations displayed in the shop windows continued to twinkle cheerfully. With her coat buttoned up to her chin and her hair pulled back in a practical bun, Sarah carried the weight of memories in her eyes. "I know," she said with a conviction that seemed to borrow from decades of love and loyalty. "Your father had an eye for potential, and John, you've got that spark. I can see it." They turned the corner, and the bank's stone façade loomed ahead. John felt the nervous flutter in his stomach. His life had changed overnight, and he was about to step into shoes much more significant than any he had ever worn. Sarah's heels clicked on the pavement, a steady rhythm against his tentative steps. "I just wish I could've met him, you know? Before he..." John's voice trailed off. It was a sentiment he had repeated often since the lawyer, Mr. Thompson, had arrived in Mountain Home with news that had turned his world upside down.

With her sharp wit and a heart full of memories, Sarah clutched her coat tighter, the fur lining brushing against her cheeks. "John," she began, her breath forming a misty veil before her, "I think you're going to do a great job with everything." There was a tremble in her voice, a mix of chill and emotion, as she continued, "The store, the mansion, the money; your father would be so proud of you."

John, his face still wearing the soft edges of youth yet marked by the lines of life, offered a shy, appreciative smile that was not entirely straightforward. He hesitated. "Thank you, Sarah, that means a lot coming from you. You worked with my father for almost as long as I have been alive. You are part of the reason the store is so successful."

"Thank you, John. Your father and I worked together for so many years that we fell in love over time, but never got married. He was the love of my life, and I promised him I would do everything I could to help you. So, remember, I am here for you anytime you need me."

The heavy snow slowed their walk, each step sending a crunch through the silence that settled between them. "Strangers," Sarah said, her eyes focused on the path ahead. "Maybe once, but not anymore. A part of him lives on right here these past few days." She reached out tentatively and touched her hand over John's heart. He felt a jolt, an electric spark from her touch that seemed to illuminate the shadow of loss within him.

Sarah used her hand to smooth her hair, a nervous gesture. They were about to walk into a new part of their lives intertwined by the web of another making. "I suppose we'd better get this started," she said, her voice steady though her heart was a drumbeat against her chest.

John nodded, feeling the same unstoppable momentum. "Together?" he asked, partly because he was not ready to let go of the warmth between them and partly because he was unsure whether he could do this alone.

John, who had just landed in this new life like a bewildered parachutist, was still grappling with the enormity of his inheritance. His father, a man he had never known, had left him a legacy that felt as heavy as it was grand.

"I think you knew my father better than anyone." John's voice was a mixture of hope and uncertainty as he glanced sideways at Sarah.

She had been the heart and soul of JR's Department Store for as long as anyone could remember. If anyone knew about his father's pride, it would be her.

Sarah reached out, her gloved hand briefly touching his arm. "Even though he didn't know about you until a month before he died, in his way, he was reaching out, trying to make amends."

The bank doors opened, and the warmth from inside rushed out to greet them. Mr. Thompson and Mr. Smith were already there, their faces a blend of professional sympathy and ready to get on with the business at hand. The marble facade stands majestic and imposing, a keeper of fortunes and secrets. Their lawyer, Mr. Thompson, alongside the bank president, Mr. Smith, greeted them with curt nods, their faces etched with the day's fatigue. The chill of the winter air was still clinging to their coats as John and Sarah stepped into the bank lobby, starkly contrasting with the warmth that greeted them inside. "Together," she said softly to John, her eyes smiling in a way that made John's heart gather courage. The time on the grand clock in the lobby marked the end of one era and the beginning of another. The marble columns rose to meet the ornate ceiling, and their footsteps echoed with the hushed whispers of their anticipation. It was the day after Christmas, yet the festive spirit seemed to have been left at the threshold; what lay ahead was strictly business.

Mr. Thompson, their attorney, a man with a hawkish nose and eyes that missed nothing, held a briefcase that seemed as old as the law itself. Beside him, Mr. Smith, the bank president, stood with a friendly smile that revealed the steel of a man accustomed to the weight of financial empires on his shoulders.

"Good afternoon, John and Sarah," Mr. Smith greeted, ushering them into a private room reserved for the most confidential meetings. "I trust you had a pleasant Christmas?" "It was... reflective," John replied, the weight of his inheritance casting a long shadow over the holiday festivities. Sarah nodded in agreement, her mind a whirl of numbers and responsibilities about to become a significant part of their lives.

As they sat in the heavy leather chairs of the bank's private meeting room, Sarah leaned in, whispering, "Remember, we're in this together. I'll help you navigate through all of it." As they sat down to sign the papers, the moment's gravity was not lost on either of them. Each signature was a promise to uphold their responsibilities and to the memory of a man they both loved in their unique ways.

The room was set with a large mahogany table, atop which lay stacks of documents, each a testament to the wealth and complexity of the empire that John's father had left behind. As they sat, Mr. Smith asked Mr. Thompson, "Do you have all the documents signed and verified that everyone here is the rightful heir to the John Roberts estate?" "Yes," said Mr. Thompson. "Great," said Mr. Smith, "may I have them please?" Mr. Smith verified all the names and their signatures for accuracy. He then explained each paper methodically, his voice a steady drone against the ticking of the grandfather clock in the corner.

For Sarah, the process was relatively swift. Her signatures were needed on several documents, tying her to the new financial reality they would both navigate. John's co-signature is required on all checks written on JR's department store account if the withdrawal is over $1,000.

John's task was more Herculean, with each document linking him to his father's legacy. The checking account for JR's, his father's checking account, the personal savings account, and the investment accounts for stocks and bonds. Every signature affirmed his new role and every initial step into his father's shoes.

Mr. Smith watched John with a practiced eye, sliding one document towards him with a knowing look. "I took the liberty of approving a check design for you that had your full name, John Roberts Jenkins," he said, his voice showing the importance of the gesture. "That will tie you to your father and make things easier for you to get established here."

John felt the weight of his name, the legacy it carried, and the expectations that came with it. His signature on that document was more than ink on paper; it was an acceptance of his heritage, a commitment to the future, and an embrace of the past.

A couple of hours had passed, the room growing darker as the sun dipped below the horizon, the only light from the banker's lamp casting a glow over their work. When the last document was signed and the final page turned, John said, "Mr. Smith, I would like to use one of these nice checks you just gave me and cash a check for $200, if it is not too much trouble. I need to pay Mr. Thompson the $100 he loaned me while we were in Mountain Home."

"No trouble at all, John; I kept some money out just to do that, thinking you might need a little cash in your pocket. Here is your money, and I will take your first check." John turned and gave Mr. Thompson the $100. Mr. Thompson said, "Thank you, John, you are just like your father. He also made sure any debt he owed would be paid." Then, John and Sarah stood up, ready to leave, their hands cramped but their resolve firm.

"Thank you, Mr. Thompson, Mr. Smith," John said, his voice steady despite the fatigue. "For everything," Sarah echoed his thanks, her eyes meeting John's with pride and determination. They were a team, united by a will and now by a shared purpose. As they left the bank, the door closing with a finality that echoed in their hearts, the night had fully taken hold, and the stars above twinkled with the promise of challenges and triumphs to come. John and Sarah walked together, their breaths visible in the cold air, their path lit by the glow of street-lamps, and the unspoken understanding that together, they could face anything.

The sun was beginning to set, the day's end promising a night of reflection. "I think I will talk to Judy when we return to the store and ask her for dinner?" John said, the first hint of a smile tugging at his lips. "I'll take her to JJ's Steak and Seafood Restaurant. We had lunch there today, and she said she would love to return at night when it would be so romantic. My treat, of course; I think I can afford it now."

Sarah laughed, a sound that seemed to dispel the nervousness that both had on the way to the bank. "I think that would be a great idea, John; it's obvious that the two of you have feelings for each other," she said. "And maybe, over dinner, you can start planning your future. Remember, John, JR's has always been more than a store; it's a part of this town's soul, and now, so are you."

Together, they walked back towards the heart of Poplar Bluff and JR's Department Store, their footsteps coordinated, a testament to the new partnership that was beginning. It was the day after Christmas, but it felt like the first day of a new year, filled with the promise of enduring spirit and friendship for John and Sarah. The lights from JR's Department Store spilled out into the streets like a beacon calling them back to where their journey had indeed started. The day's weight was lifted by shared jokes and tentative dreams for the future, and it was clear that something special was unfolding. The kind of story that, were it not for the undeniable reality of their breaths in the cold air and the ink drying on legal documents, would feel like the stuff of fairy tales. And maybe, just maybe, it was. John had barely crossed the threshold of JR's when the air seemed to shimmer with anticipation. The store, alive with the quiet hum of evening shoppers, felt like a stage set for the night's unfolding drama. With each step, the mundane became magical, the lights above casting a glow that might as well have been moonlight for all the electricity in the air.

"Kathy," John's voice was a steady beat in the quiet office, "may I have a word with Judy, please?" His request, simple yet charged with an unspoken promise, hung in the air. Kathy's reply, "Sure, Mr. Jenkins, I'll go get her." It was formal and respectful, starkly contrasting their usual easy jokes. It was a nod to the shift in their world, John's new status as owner reframing their interactions. And yet, the undercurrent of warmth remained unchanged, a testament to the bonds they had all formed within these walls.

When Judy entered, she walked over to John. "Mr. Jenkins, Kathy said you needed to see me." John looked surprised that she hadn't used his first name. However, she did have a smile on her face.

John looked at her with a frown and asked, "I was wondering if you would like to go to JJ's tonight? You mentioned you would like to do so during lunch today." Her use of "Mr. Jenkins" was a pebble in the pond of John's expectations, ripples of surprise and confusion spreading through him. But the moment he extended the dinner invitation, the formality washed away, replaced by the unmistakable thrill of new possibilities.

Judy told John, "I would love to go to dinner tonight. When would you like to leave?" "When you can get off, just let me know. I will be in Sarah's office," John said as he walked towards Sarah's office; the future seemed to unfurl before them, bright and beckoning. Judy looked at Kathy and asked her, "Should I do this? He is the owner now and very wealthy. Just not sure how he feels now."

Kathy had watched the exchange, a knowing smile playing on her lips. "He'll be the man you fell for when you met on the train. You didn't know him, and he didn't know you, and the two of you were getting along great," she assured Judy, who was caught in a storm of doubt and hope. In Kathy's eyes, the love story was quietly writing itself, within the walls of JR's department store. Tonight, JJ's would become more than just a dining spot, where two lives, intertwined by day-to-day familiarity, would start to explore the depths of something much more profound.

As John walked to Kathy's office, his mind was still puzzled by Kathy and Judy using his last name. He was playing the day over in his mind. Did he say or do something that would make both stop being his friend, or was it the money or owning the store now that changed them, or him? He hoped not; he did not want to stop seeing Judy. He lightly knocked on her door when he got to Sarah's office. She looked up and said, "Come on in, John; well, is Judy going to dinner with you?"

"Yes," he said, "but I am confused; we have been getting along very well until now. She called me Mr. Jenkins, and that confuses me." John leaned casually on the edge of Sarah's cluttered desk; her office was an oasis amid the post-Christmas retail chaos, papers and decorations jumbled together in a strange order that only she seemed to understand.

Sarah laughed with a big smile. "I am not laughing at you, John. I remember when I started working with your dad over twenty years ago. We started by referring to each other by our last names. I called him Mr. Roberts for several months until one day we talked, and your dad said, "Sarah, would you like to go out to dinner tonight after we close?" I was so surprised that it shocked me. I stuttered and then said I would very much like to. And that is where it all began for us. You see, John, she is just trying to feel her way through this, and I am sure she does not want to cause you any problems. Do you want me to hire her to work for us? Kathy said she was looking for a job, but has not said anything. Maybe you can talk to her about it tonight." "Ok, I'll try to bring it up. So, what time are we thinking of starting tomorrow?" he asked, eyes scanning the room, intrigued by Sarah's organized disarray. Sarah looked up as she replied, tapping a manicured nail on the desk. "The department store doesn't open until 10 A.M. tomorrow, so an 8 A.M. start would give us a good lead. Plus, it's usually quiet, right after the Christmas frenzy."

John nodded his thoughts already on the tasks for the next day when the soft knock on the open door drew both their attention. It was Judy, her cheeks flushed with the cold or perhaps from the flurry of activity in the store. She was still in her work attire, a sensible blouse paired with professional and elegant slacks.

"Hey, Mr. Jenkins, I've finished up with Kathy. If you are ready, we can leave now?" she offered, with that hopeful upswing in her voice. A smile spread across John's face; it was not just the date but the sight of Judy standing there, ready for an evening with him, that lifted his spirits. "I'm ready if you are," he replied, standing up straight, eyes lingering on her just a moment longer than necessary. "Ok, Sarah. I'll see you at 8:00 A.M." John and Judy walked out of Sarah's office, went down to the first-floor area, and headed for the front door.

Together, they walked through the echoing halls of the store, where customers were rushing around with a small number of things that were needed right after Christmas and taking advantage of the after-Christmas holiday sales. As they pushed through the glass doors into the crisp evening air, the snow fell softly, like a cascade of tiny whispers, covering the city in a blanket of white. John and Judy walked to his car, which was parked a short distance away. Snowflakes were catching in her hair, glinting like tiny stars.

As they approached his car, he quickened his pace to reach the passenger side door before her, pulling it open with a flourish. Judy's smile, as he did so, was worth all the chivalry in the world. This simple action, a tradition his mother had taught him, gave her a big smile. John felt a warmth that had nothing to do with the biting winter air.

"Such a gentleman," Judy teased, her breath forming clouds as she gracefully slid into the seat. He closed the door behind her and jogged to the driver's side, feeling a little buzz of excitement at the prospect of the evening ahead. The car was cozy, a sanctuary against the cold night, and as he started the engine, the heater hummed to life.

They drove through the softly lit streets to JJ's Restaurant, an intimate little place they would both come to favor. Its warm glow was inviting, a beacon in the snowy landscape, promising a refuge from the cold and a chance for the evening to unfurl in ways neither of them had planned.

Nestled in the heart of a bustling town, JJ's was a beacon of culinary excellence, its reputation for sizzling steaks and fresh seafood echoing every food lover's dreams. Tonight, the cozy glow of the restaurant welcomed two patrons, John and Judy, whose palates were set for a symphony of flavors only JJ's could provide. They were seated at an intimate table for two, where soft-spoken words could be shared and a hint of privacy was possible. Judy hesitated, a shadow of uncertainty crossing her face before she leaned in and whispered, "Would it be all right if I had a glass of wine?"

John met her question with a pleasant grin. He was ever the picture of ease, his loosened tie and casual demeanor conveying a sense of ease. "Of course," he replied, signaling the waiter with a nonchalant wave. I think I'll join you with a beer." Their orders were dispatched into the restaurant's busy stacks of paper; their evening began with the quiet simplicity of things unfolding between them.

When the waiter returned, bearing beverages and a basket brimming with the restaurant's famed rolls, glistening with butter, and still sizzling from the oven's heat, the comforting smells seemed to underscore the charm of this small-town haven. Judy cradled her wine, allowing it to breathe and blossom as she watched John through the dance of reflections in her glass. The setting was filled with a blend of potential and the slight tremor of nerves. Their conversation began with witty banter and unknown facts about each other. Their work personas gently unraveled, revealing the genuine spirits beneath the surface. Stories and barbs were exchanged, each laugh peeling away layers, bringing them closer to something real.

John tipped the balance, his inquiry direct yet tinged with a vulnerable curiosity. "Why did it become Mr. Jenkins today and not John?" He was earnest, seeking the truth behind her formality without a hint of challenge.

Judy let her finger trace the lip of her glass; her response hung in the air like an autumn leaf, caught for a moment in suspense before it descended. "Because you're the boss now," she murmured, her tone walking the tightrope between respect and familiarity. "It is about perception. Until everyone knows about us, I must maintain some professional distance if there is to become an us."

Their dialogue, wrapped up in this delicate balance, was a clever dance where each step was measured, and the intention was cloaked in consideration. Her eyes held his, communicating her hope that he would appreciate her need for prudence and see the quiet affection beginning to unfurl behind the decorum.

The server's arrival to explain the virtues of marbled steaks and the night's "chef's specials" momentarily halted the progression of their revelation. Her enthusiastic pause gave them both a chance to digest the significance of their conversation.

Their order was magnificent, a meal for their first full date that they would never forget. It is almost indescribable. The shrimp cocktails! Not just any appetizer, but a JJ's masterpiece. Each succulent shrimp, a jewel of the sea, was lovingly cradled in a cocktail glass brimming with a zesty, tangy sauce that promised to tease the taste buds and ignite the appetite. With a synchronized nod, John and Judy gave their orders, their voices tinged with the thrill of the first act of their dining experience.

But what is a starter without the main event? The best to come is JJ's great T-bone steak, which is next on their culinary itinerary. The mere thought of the steak, seared to perfection, caramelized char on the outside, yet promising a tender, juicy heart within, was enough to make their mouths water with unbridled desire. To accompany this magnificent cut of beef, sautéed mushrooms were the chosen accompaniment. Each mushroom had soaked up the essence of garlic and butter, enhancing the robust flavors of the steak.

And what is a steak without the baked potato? But not just any baked potato; this was the loaded kind, brimming with a molten core of cheddar, a cloud of sour cream, a crumble of crispy bacon, and a final flourish of fresh chives, a true comfort in every bite. A side salad, fresh and crisp, provided a refreshing interlude. Greens lightly kissed with dressing, a colorful array of vegetables offered a crunch that whispered secrets of the fertile soil from which they sprang.

The choice of another round of drinks to wash down this feast. Judy's wine, a luscious red, swirled in its glass, the aroma of dark fruits and a whisper of oak promising to complement the hearty flavors of the meal. And for John, another beer, the frothy head releasing the scent of hops and barley, a faithful companion to quench the thirst and cleanse the palate.

This was to be their meal, a testament to the culinary arts, an ode to the joy of dining. They raised their glasses in a silent toast to JJ's, the chef, and each other; tonight, the world outside faded away, and all that remained was the adventure on their plates.

As they awaited the arrival of their order, John and Judy leaned back, their eyes closing briefly in satisfaction. With the server's departure, John met Judy's eyes, his look radiant with understanding. In his soft nod, there was an unspoken covenant; he would not rush her, and the name John would wait for its proper unveiling until the mutual unfolding of their private and professional lives considered it appropriate.

Their conversation circled back, inevitably, to the path that had led them here. "What was your major in college again, and have you finished?" John asked with genuine interest.

"Oh, I finished five years back, same time as Kathy did," she replied, the memory softening her tone. "I have a double major, accounting and math. This would open many fields for me with a math and accounting degree," she told John. "That's a great Strategy, Judy," John expressed. "What have you been doing the last five years?" "Well, I have spent a lot of time with my father. He was a pilot in the war and had been away for a long time. I also worked part-time at an accounting firm while attending college part-time to earn my master's degree in accounting. I finished my master's degree about 6 months ago, and not long after that, I received a letter from Kathy about a possible job at JR's Department Store." John said, "So, are you still looking for that job?" Judy looked a little confused. His tone softened into something between a joke and an offer. "I remember on the train you said that you were going to JR's Department Store to see an old friend and that she had said that there may be a job available soon. Are you still looking for that job at JR's?" Judy said, "Well, you know I did not know who you were while we were on the train, and I was just being honest and conversing just to be around you more. I liked you at that point." John now smiled big and said, "If you want a job there, I suspect I might have some influence. I could put a good word in for you." Judy smiled a smile that could brighten up a dark day and said, "I have finally reached the point in life where I know someone with influence."

John continued, "Well, I was thinking, just thinking now, that Kathy will be my secretary as she was for my father, and Sarah has her plate loaded pretty good now, trying to be a manager and take care of a lot of the accounting duties. There is an office just outside Sarah's office, which could be for her assistant." He smiled big. "Give it some thought; maybe we will need to go to dinner tomorrow night to discuss it in more detail." At that point, Judy gave him a big smile and stated, "Yes." She smiled even more significantly. "For dinner tomorrow night. But as for the job, we still need to talk about that."

Judy laughed, a sound that held both warmth and the caution of the complexities their situation promised. "Let me sleep on it," she said, her smile hiding the whirlwind of thoughts. "It would be wonderful to work there and see you daily, but I would not want it to create any issues. Nor do I want to stop seeing you." She spoke the last with an earnestness that John felt in his chest, a hopeful note for them both to hold onto as the night ended.

The meal began to come to the table, and they were both astonished at how much food there was and how it looked. As the first dish made its way to their table, they knew they were about to have a meal that only JJ's could prepare, which would linger on their palates and in their hearts forever. Each bite was amazing, a perfect sear, a flavor that was fantastic. John and Judy made each moment at JJ's a memory that would forever be etched in their minds.

Indeed, JJ's had lived up to its reputation and then some. It was an experience that combined the simplicity of good food with the complexity of fine cooking, an ode to the love of steak and seafood. For John and Judy, it was more than a meal; it was a celebration of the senses, one that they would return to time and time again. The evening at JJ's was not just food on a plate; it was a story served on a silver platter that they were all too happy to read over and over. The evening lay before them, a picture of possibilities, each moment painting another brushstroke of what would come. Sitting across from each other in the dim light of the restaurant, the two seemed suspended in a space between the past and the potential of their shared future. As dinner gave way to dessert and dessert plates whisked away, John's hand found Judy's across the table. It was a silent pledge, a testament to his deepening sentiment. Judy's heart answered with a squeeze, her eyes lighting up with the promise of something profound and the budding hope of a shared future.

As the beautiful evening turned into a romantic night, John asked his server for the bill and paid for their meal, smiling at Judy across from him. She could not help but smile back. The air was filled with the tantalizing aroma of perfectly grilled steaks and seafood, and the lingering notes of soft music. The night's ambiance was electric, as if the stars were conspiring to add a touch of magic to their date.

With a smile that could light up the darkest nights, John said, "I enjoyed our dinner tonight," his voice warmed with genuine pleasure. Judy's eyes sparkled in response, a mirror to the twinkle of the city lights. "So did I," she replied, her voice an unforgettable harmony to the soft hum of the city around them.

Their conversation flowed effortlessly as they strolled toward the car, their words weaving dreams of tomorrow and their growing romance. As they approached the door, John, with the grace of a gentleman from a bygone era, opened the door for Judy. Her smile bloomed like a rose kissed by the dawn, and she said, "It means a lot to me when you open the door." Her appreciation was genuine, feeding the silent promise growing between them.

Slipping into the car, the world outside seemed to hush in anticipation. John turned to Judy, his gaze an ocean of deep and infinite emotion. "I did enjoy this more than I know how to express," he confessed, his voice a whisper against the sounds of the night.

The space between them was charged with an electric current, a pull neither could resist. Slowly, as if drawn by an unseen force, John slid across the seat toward Judy. Their eyes locked, two souls speaking without words, in that singular, electrifying moment, their gaze intertwined, and oh, how the sparks flew! It was as if the entire universe conspired to silence the mundane of everyday life, to mute the world around them.

Each heartbeat is a drumroll: each breath, a symphony. And then, in a moment suspended in time, their lips met. The kiss eclipsed all the others, a crescendo of passion and tender vulnerability. It was the kind of kiss that spoke of uncharted territories and whispered promises, a kiss that held the power of a thousand words and the gentleness of a blooming flower. This kiss was more than a mere expression of affection; it marked the beginning of a story yet to be written, a tale of two hearts embarking on a journey where each moment was a treasure waiting to be discovered. A kiss that marked the beginning of something extraordinary, a romance that would unfold with the beauty and mystery of the rising dawn.

As they pulled away, breathless and exhilarated, the world came rushing back. But for John and Judy, nothing would ever be the same. They had tasted the sweet nectar of a love that promised to grow stronger each day, a passion that would dance on the edges of tomorrow.

The beautiful white snowflakes danced around the Ford as it hummed back to life, its engine breaking the serene silence of the winter night. John's heart was still racing from the kiss, a sweet, lingering promise of something more profound. He turned to Judy, his eyes reflecting the soft glow of the dashboard lights, and the sincerity in his voice wrapped around her like a warm blanket. "You are so beautiful; it almost takes my breath away."

Judy's cheeks flushed a rosy hue, a perfect contrast to the ivory snow outside. She could not help but slide closer to him, the leather seat creaking softly under her. Her lips brushed his cheek in a tender kiss, and she nestled into his side, her head finding its perfect spot on his shoulder. The world outside the car seemed to fade away, leaving only the two in their little wrap of warmth and affection.

She tilted her head to look up at him, her eyes shimmering with unspoken words and dreams yet to unfold. "Can we ride around for a while before you take me home?" she whispered, barely above the falling snow.

John's heart swelled. He could deny her nothing, especially not on this enchanted evening that felt like the beginning of their forever. "Yes, darling, we can ride till the sun comes up if that's what you want," he replied, his voice steady and sure. When he said, "Yes, darling," her heart swelled with so much joy that she had tears in her eyes and snuggled closer to him.

And with that, they were off, the car's tires crunching over the fresh snow, leaving behind the world and its expectations. The streets were empty, and the Christmas lights in the windows of the houses they passed twinkled like distant stars. They spoke of everything and nothing, their conversation meandering as the roads they took, with laughter spilling into the night.

As they drove, the boundaries between them, built up over time and circumstance, seemed to melt away. They shared stories of their childhoods, hopes for the future, and the fears that sometimes kept them awake at night. Judy spoke of her love for painting and dreamed of capturing the world in vibrant colors and bold strokes. John truly listened; his admiration for her grew with every word.

The hours slipped by unnoticed, the moon tracing its path across the sky as they lost themselves in each other. They only found solace in the comfortable silence when two souls were in perfect harmony. Occasionally, Judy would point out a constellation, her finger tracing the shapes against the car window, her breath fogging up the glass.

John parked the car in a place where they could see the valley below with the lights of Christmas shining like stars. They sat cuddled up to each other, watching the lights twinkle and talking until they both fell asleep. Finally, they woke up as dawn approached; the first hints of light began to paint the horizon in pink and gold. They were both startled at first, trying to grasp their surroundings. They smiled at one another when they realized they were still parked where they had gone to sleep the night before or this morning. At that point, Judy reached up to John, kissed him, and said, "Good morning. I don't see how life could get any better than this."

With a big smile, John said, "This is a morning we will remember forever, and it is one of many more to come." They were on the outskirts of town, overlooking a valley, slowly waking up to the new day. John opened his door, and they both stepped out of the car, the cold air biting their cheeks.

They stood side by side, watching the sunrise, the sky ablaze with color. Judy leaned into John, her hand finding his, their fingers intertwining naturally. They did not need words; the look they shared said it all. In that moment, they made an unspoken promise to each other, a vow to take on the world together, no matter what it might throw their way.

As the sun climbed higher, they returned to the car, the heater's warmth a welcome relief from the chill. John finally turned the car back towards town, towards Judy's home, but they both knew this was just the beginning. They had all the time in the world and intended to spend it together, no matter what the future held.

It was still incredibly early as John drove Judy home through the quiet streets, the world around them muffled by the thick blanket of snow. The Christmas lights from the houses they passed by cast a warm, festive glow, but the light inside the car felt warmer still, filled with the soft laughter and the lingering joy of the evening they had spent together.

Nestled comfortably next to John, Judy watched the snowflakes settle on the windshield before the wipers swept them away. As John drove Judy home, he said, "Why don't you tell Kathy that you can't help her tomorrow, I mean today, and sleep till about lunch? When you get up, call the store and ask Kathy to message me so I can call you. I will call you and schedule a time to pick you up for lunch. How does that sound?"

She turned to John, her eyes reflecting the myriad of lights they passed. "That sounds perfect," she said, her voice a soft melody over the hum of the car engine. "I can't remember the last time I allowed myself such a luxury. Sleeping in, a leisurely lunch with a charming man... It's like something out of a dream."

John smiled at her, his eyes never leaving the road, but his heart was very much attuned to her presence. "Well, dear, I believe everyone deserves a bit of a dream now and then, and I can't think of anyone I'd rather share such a dream with." The car stopped in front of Judy's house, the engine idling as neither seemed eager to end the night. Judy reached for the door handle but paused, her hand hovering as she turned back to John. "Thank you, John. For tonight, for the laughter, for making me feel... alive again. It's been so long since I've felt this way."

John reached across the space between them, his hand covering hers. "Judy, you've brought so much light into my life since we met. I was walking around in a fog, but you have made things clear again. I want to be there for you, make you happy, and see your beautiful smile every chance."

Their eyes locked, and for a moment, the world outside ceased to exist. The two of them were surrounded by the soft glow of the dashboard lights and the quiet intimacy of shared emotions. Judy's heart fluttered like a butterfly's wings caught in the first rays of dawn.

Finally, Judy nodded, her voice barely above a whisper. "I'll call Kathy first thing. And then I'll be waiting for your call." She quickly kissed John and opened the door, stepping out into the snowy night, but not before squeezing his hand in a promise for later today.

As she walked up the path to her front door, she turned back to see John in his car, watching her. She raised her hand in a wave, and he waved back. With a contented sigh, Judy entered her house, expecting the sound of his voice on the phone and the promise of a new beginning that today would hold.

Inside, the house was quiet, the Christmas tree still twinkling in the corner of the living room. Judy hung her coat and kicked off her shoes, her mind replaying every moment of the evening. Before she went to bed, she left a note for Kathy where she knew she would find it. She climbed the stairs to her bedroom, her steps light, her heart more golden. As she slipped under the covers, she could not help but think this was the best day she had ever had. As she drifted off to sleep, Judy's dreams were filled with laughter, the touch of a hand, and the soft promise of a lunch date that felt like the start of something truly magical.

14

The Car and the Mansion

John did not have much time to waste this morning; when he left Judy, he just had time to return to his room, shower, change clothes, and head to the store. Not even time for breakfast today, but the time he spent with Judy last night was worth little sleep. He was rushing to the store to meet Sarah at 8:00 A.M. to continue training. When he arrived at the store, the door was locked, and he had to tap several times to get someone to come to the door. A night security guard went to the door and said, "Sorry, sir, we don't open till 10:00 today."

John said, "Okay, please tell Sarah that John is at the door." "Yes, sir, I'll tell her; I was just going to her office." "Thanks," John said. Sarah rushed to the door and explained to the guard, "This is Mr. Jenkins, the new owner." The night guard kept apologizing, but John told him, "Hey, stop apologizing. You were doing your job, and I thank you for that."

Sarah and John walked to her office and started reviewing today's plans. She told John she planned to leave after lunch today and that Kathy would lock up tonight at closing. "Unless you would rather I stay till closing and lock up myself." "No, that's fine," John told her. "I am planning to leave at about 12 or 1 myself. I need to visit the Ford dealership and talk to Mr. Jimmy about the car. And then I would like to go to the mansion and look around for a little while, maybe make plans to move in, if you think that would be ok?"

"John," said Sarah, "the mansion is yours, and everyone there works for you. You can move in at any time you wish. I will call Mr. Wainwright shortly and tell him you will come by today. He is the head of the staff at the mansion, and he will look after any of your needs. After that, I will call Jimmy at the Ford Dealership and tell him you are coming by." With a smile, she said, "Are you going to take Judy to see the mansion? You should take her with you to have someone you know and trust to discuss things."

"Thanks, Sarah. I am so thankful you are here; we work incredibly well together. I talked to Judy last night about the job you and I were discussing, and she said, just like you told me, she was worried about how things may look if we were dating, and she did not want us or the store to have any problems." "That's great," Sarah commented. "That shows she can see the overall picture and wants everything to work out between you and the store. She also does not want anyone to think she got the job because she is the boss's girlfriend. I know she and Kathy went to college together, but I would prefer not to have them working in the same office if we hire her. I am sure it would be fine, but sometimes old friends working together can create a problem we do not need. What type of degree did she graduate with?" John replied, "She has a double major, one in accounting and one in math. And listen to this: She also spent part of the past five years working part-time for an accounting company while she went back to college and got her master's degree in accounting."

Sarah smiled and said, "First, experience with an accounting firm will go great here. I do not want you to think I am trying to get out of work, but I am currently overwhelmed and could use some assistance from an accounting professional. The office outside my office would be perfect for an assistant." John started laughing with a big smile. Sarah said, "I'm sorry. Did I say something wrong?"

"No," John said, "I just like how we both think; when I talked to Judy last night, I told her that you had a lot on your plate, and I felt like you could use some help. If Judy is your assistant, she would use the office outside your office." "Wow," said Sarah, "it is like I am talking to your father; we always had ideas that were, most of the time, close to the same thing. We would always look at each other and start laughing."

John said, "I will tell Judy to come talk to you about this position, and if you say you're okay with it, then I am ok with it. "The next thing I want to talk to you about is my father's office. I want to move into his office and keep Kathy as my secretary or assistant; I'm not sure what you all call her. I would prefer her to be my assistant because I am sure I will depend on her a lot, just like I depend on you."

"That sounds good; I will let Kathy know you will move into that office. You can talk to her about anything you might need help with. Kathy is up to date on just about everything we do."

"Thanks, Sarah," John said as he saw Kathy waving at him and went to see what she needed. She told him to call Judy as soon as he could. While in Sarah's office, he used her phone and said, "Judy, this is John." John could hardly contain the warmth that spread through his chest at the sound of Judy's voice on the other end of the line, the corners of his mouth pulling into a smile that he could not suppress, even as he caught Kathy's knowing look from across the room.

Her laughter, light and musical, filled his ear. "Good morning, Mr. Early Bird. I did not expect to hear from you until later. Did the dawn catch you well?" "Better than well, thanks to the company I had last night," he replied, the image of their evening together, a soft glow of candlelight and the sweet scent of her perfume still vivid in his mind. "Listen, I will be free around one. How about I pick you up for lunch?"

There was a brief pause, a rustling sound as if she were covering the receiver to share a secret with the universe. "I would love to, John. It will give me time to look presentable." He chuckled, the sound echoing softly in the confines of Sarah's office. "You always look presentable, Judy. But it is a date. And afterward, I have a couple of er-rands to run. Would you like to join me?" "Errands with John Jenkins? How could I resist such an offer?" Her voice was playful, teasing, but he could hear the undercurrent of eagerness.

"One of those errands involves the mansion where we had Christ-mas lunch. Sarah told me today that the mansion was mine, and I needed to go ahead and move in. Everyone who worked there was also an employee of mine. So, I need to review it and see if I want or need to make any changes or fixes. I want your opinion on the place."

The line went quiet for a heartbeat longer than expected, and he wondered if he had overstepped. After all, they had only begun to ex-plore the depths of their relationship.

"John, are you serious? You want me to see it with you?" Her voice was a mixture of surprise and delight. "Yes, Judy, I am serious. There is no one else whose opinion I trust more. And besides," he said, his voice dropping to a softer, more intimate tone, "I want you to be a part of my new life in whatever way you're willing to be." He could almost hear her smile. "Then it is a date, Mr. Jenkins. I will be ready at one."

They exchanged a few more pleasantries before hanging up, and John returned to the main floor of the store, a spring in his step that had not been there before. Sarah caught his eye, a knowing twinkle in hers, and he just nodded, unable to keep the grin off his face.

The morning passed in a flurry of activity, with John absorbing the intricacies of the business, his mind occasionally drifting to the lunch that awaited him. When the clock neared twelve-thirty, he excused himself, anticipation quickening his heartbeat.

He picked Judy up promptly at one, and they enjoyed a cozy lunch at JJ's. Today, they had hamburger steaks covered with Swiss cheese, mushrooms, onions, gravy, and fries. They talked and laughed for an hour until they had to leave for their first appointment at the Ford dealership.

After lunch, they drove to the dealership, where Jimmy greeted John with a firm handshake and a slap on the back. "John, you look a lot like your father," Jimmy said as he looked at him. "He was a very dear friend of mine. Many years ago, my dealership was having some problems, and your father is the only one who believed in me and stepped in to help. He has never asked for anything in return, so every two or three years, I would call him to come pick out a new car. That was my way of saying thank you for believing in me. Now, I have several dealerships around the state, and I owe it all to him. I want to extend the same offer I gave to your father, reflecting my appreciation for what he did for me. And, I have had your father's car here since he got sick. It's yours now, and the car's all tuned up for you, John. The car runs like a dream."

Judy admired the sleek lines of the vehicle, and her expression conveyed genuine admiration for its beauty. It was another shared moment, marking their growing relationship. With that, John gave Jimmy the keys to the car that Sarah had borrowed for him. "Thank you, Mr. Jimmy," John said as he and Judy walked to the car. He opened the car door for Judy, and she slid in, leaned over, and unlocked the other door for John. She smiled at John and said, "Your father had great taste. This car is lovely, and I'm so happy for you." Then she snuggled up next to him, kissed him on the cheek, and they left for the mansion.

The snowflakes continued to fall, a beautiful scene against the gray sky, as John and Judy made their way from the Ford dealership to the mansion that loomed ahead. Inside the warmth of John's car was a kind of electric anticipation that only a new beginning could bring. With her eyes reflecting the snow-covered landscape, Judy turned to John, her heart filled with a mix of excitement and nervousness. Sensing her inner turmoil, John reached for her hand, a reassuring anchor, as she struggled with her doubts.

"Judy," John began, his voice as steady and comforting as the hum of the car's engine, "I know you've been wrestling with the idea of working at JR's. But believe me, your talents would shine there, regardless of our relationship." Judy's gaze met his, searching for the confidence she felt she lacked. "John, it's not about my capabilities. I don't want to be the subject of office gossip or, worse, be discredited for my accomplishments." John's smile was gentle yet filled with unwavering conviction. "Sweetie, you underestimate the respect Sarah has for true talent. She has seen your work; she knows your worth. And as for the rest of the staff, they'll come to see what I see in you every day: brilliance, dedication, and integrity."

The car turned onto the long driveway. The mansion was now in full view, its windows aglow with the promise of warmth and comfort. John continued his words, vividly painting the future he envisioned for them.

"Imagine this," he said, his enthusiasm infectious, "you'll have your own space right outside Sarah's office. She is eager to mentor you to bring out the best in your abilities as an accounting assistant. And I'll be just down the hall, taking the helm in my father's office."

Judy's heart swelled. She could almost see it: the bustling corridors of JR's Department Store, the friendly nods of acknowledgment from the staff, the sense of purpose that came with being part of something greater. And there, in the heart of it all, was Sarah, a woman of poise and professionalism, ready to take Judy under her wing.

"And Kathy," John added, a playful twinkle in his eye, "she's been with the company for five years, and she'll make sure everything runs smoothly for me, just as she did for my father."

The car stopped gently before the mansion, the engine falling silent. For a moment, they sat there, the future hanging before them like the delicate snowflakes outside, full of potential and ready to settle into place.

Judy turned to John, her decision made, her fears melting away like snow under the morning sun. "All right, John. Let's do this. Let's start this new part of our life together." A beaming smile spread across John's face, mirroring Judy's own. Hand in hand, they stepped out of the car and into the crisp winter air, their hearts as one, their journey just beginning. As they walked towards the mansion, each step was a promise of love, growth, and a shared future built not on expectations but on the solid foundation of their unwavering bond.

The estate was breathtaking, and the gardens were meticulously kept, even in the chill of winter. Mr. Wainwright, a dignified older gentleman, met them at the door, his demeanor lukewarm but respectful. John took Judy's hand as they toured the expansive rooms, and her insights and enthusiasm made the experience even more meaningful. They stood together in what would be his, or perhaps their, living room, the late afternoon sun casting a glow over the space.

"This could be a wonderful home, John," Judy whispered, her eyes shining with unspoken possibilities. He turned to her, his heart full, knowing that any place could be home with her by his side. "Yes," he agreed, his voice steady despite the emotions that swirled within him, "a wonderful home indeed."

They continued to tour the mansion while Mr. Wainwright started downstairs to meet the rest of the staff waiting in the kitchen. Just as he walked down the hall, he stopped at the door of one room, looked at Mr. Jenkins, and said, "This room was your father's room, sir; he had it decorated very beautifully." With that, he continued downstairs. John and Judy went into his father's room to look around. Mr. Wainwright was right; it was terrific. As they looked around the room, they sat down on the bed simultaneously. They smiled at each other, touched their foreheads together, and then shared a slight kiss that led to a kiss like the night before. The passion was so great that it was almost breathtaking. They slowly laid back on the bed, feet on the floor, and looked into each other's eyes for a few minutes. John said, "Darling, are we moving too fast?"

Judy looked deep into his eyes and said with a big smile, "We may be, I am not sure; anytime you leave, I cannot wait to see you again. John, I am falling in love with you, and I cannot stop myself." John looked into her eyes, then kissed her with more passion than ever before, and then said, "I love you, Judy. I don't know how to stop loving you and don't want to." They sat up on the edge of the bed, smiled, and talked about everything they both had been feeling.

Judy put her head on John's shoulder, looking at her hands, and said, "I love you, John; I think I have since the first time we met, but I'm scared!" In a slow, soft voice, John looked at her and said, "What are you scared about, sweetie?"

With a weak, shaky, and nervous voice, she said, "I am afraid you may think I said that because of the money. I am afraid that people will think I am a gold digger, and I am also concerned that those at the store might believe I coerced you into taking the job by doing things to get it. I am afraid that."

"Hold on! Wait just a minute; that is enough of being afraid," John said. "We both know that none of this is true. You and I had feelings for one another while on the train. You didn't know me then, and I didn't know you. I know we fell in love with each other faster than we could have believed possible, but here we are, in love. I know we make each other happier than ever, and I do not want to stop."

Judy smiled at John, gave him a big kiss, and, with playful flirting, said, "Well, let's go downstairs and see more of the house, Mr. Jenkins." John said, "Ok, Ms. Jenkins, maybe one day." She looked so happy as they stood up and began to walk downstairs to the kitchen. The magnificent staircase spiraled like a seashell, descending into the mansion's heart, where history whispered through every corner of the manor. John's hand was a gentle pressure at the small of Judy's back, his touch both steadying and possessive as they descended.

The Christmas decorations in the mansion's grand entrance looked like they had just been set up, their vibrant colors and sparkling lights a testament to the joy and warmth still lingering in the air. The festivities may have reached their crescendo just days ago, but the season's magic had not yet waned. The entrance was a sight to behold; it was aglow with the warmth of a crackling fire. A magnificent Christmas tree, awe-inspiring in silver and gold, reached up to kiss the high ceiling, its twinkling lights reflecting off the polished marble floor. The ornaments, each a tiny masterpiece of craftsmanship, told stories of Christmases past and whispered promises of the joy yet to come. This was not just another holiday season; it was the beginning of their forever, a story that would be recounted with fondness and hunger for generations to come. For in the grand entrance of the mansion, beneath the boughs of the Christmas tree, a new love had taken root, destined to blossom through the ages.

The kitchen was bright white and clean, like a hospital or doctor's office, and the staff, a small group of individuals, were aligned with the kind of precision that spoke of old-world discipline and respect.

Mr. Wainwright, the head of the staff, was a dignified figure with silver at his temples and the bearing of a man who had served the household for more years than he cared to count. He stepped forward, his voice rich and welcoming. "Mr. John, Ms. Judy, welcome to your new home," he announced, his gaze flickering with the barest hint of curiosity as it landed on Judy. "Allow me to introduce you to the staff aiding you in your new home."

"First," he said, turning to the first person, "this is Molly Jefferson, the head cook and housekeeper, whose hands have shaped the dough of countless loaves and whose eyes hold the wisdom of someone who knew the mansion's rhythms better than her heartbeat. You will find no better shepherd's pie this side of the Thames," Mr. Wainwright declared, his pride in his team evident. "Beside her is Maria Goldstein, the assistant cook and maid, whose youth is offset by a keen intelligence, promising new recipes, and the courage to blend tradition with innovation."

"The outdoors is cared for with equal passion. This is David Jefferson, Molly's husband and the head groundskeeper. His hands are the architects of the estate's rich green beauty." At that point, he explained more about the Jeffersons: "The Jeffersons live here at the mansion in the servant quarters. They have been here about ten years and call this home. "And Michael Johnson, the assistant groundskeeper," Mr. Wainwright continued, nodding to Michael, whose youthful vigor was matched only by his eagerness to learn from his seasoned counterpart.

The staff each offered a slight nod, their faces etched with the anticipation of serving the new lord of the manor and his lady. Judy felt the weight of their gazes, the unspoken assumption of her role as John's wife wrapping around her like an unexpected shawl.

John cleared his throat, and in that moment, Judy felt the tenor of their relationship shift, a silent understanding passing between them. They were partners in this grand adventure, and if the staff believed them to be married, so be it. The masquerade had a certain romance; in the play-acting of life, they were still dancing around the edges.

"We are grateful for your welcome," John said, his voice steady and sure. "Judy and I look forward to getting to know each of you and becoming part of this home's rich history."

The words hung in the air, a vow of sorts, binding them to the staff and the walls surrounding them. Judy's heart raced with the thrill of it all, the sense of beginning, and the undercurrent of something more profound, a love that was only beginning.

As they turned to take in the rest of the mansion, Judy's hand found John's, their fingers entwined with the ease of two people standing on the edge of forever. With its secrets and legacy, the manor was a blank page on which they could write their story, a tale of love, adventure, and the home they would build together, one day at a time.

But before they walked off, Molly said, "Ms. Judy, is there anything special you want us to prepare for tonight?" "Molly," Judy said, "I hate to ask, but do we have any ham left from the Christmas lunch?" "Yes, ma'am, we sure do. How would you like it prepared?" Judy said, "I would like just an old-fashioned ham sandwich if that is okay with you."

"That would be fine, Ms. Judy; what time would you like it served?" With a big smile, Judy said, "Will 6:30 be enough time to fix it? And can we get mayo and mustard, please?" "Yes, ma'am. It will be ready at 6:30 in the small dining room."

With that, she turned to John with a big smile and said, "Are you ready to look at the rest of the house, Mr. Jenkins?" With a big smile, John said, "Yes, I am, Ms. Jenkins." He reached out his hand to her, and they walked off.

Upon stumbling into the billiard room, a hidden jewel within the heart of the manor, their spirits soared. The room echoed timeless elegance, housing a pool table that beckoned with the allure of leisure. The soft lighting cast a warm glow over the emerald expanse of the table, while plush chairs promised comfort, and the TV and stereo system hinted at a modern touch amidst the classic charm. Laughter bubbled between them, a carefree melody as they playfully took their shots, the clinks and clatters of balls a harmonious backdrop to their escalated cheering. Each strike, every maneuver around the felt-covered table, drew them closer, Judy's smile a bright beacon to John's admiring gaze.

And then, they met at the end of the table and embraced each other. The following embrace was as inevitable as the sunset beyond the manor's walls, a perfect union of arms and hearts. When their lips met, it was more than a kiss; it was a seal over the vows they had yet to speak, the silent promise of forever that flowed through them with each heartbeat. In that single, lingering moment, the world outside ceased to exist; only John and Judy were entwined by the bonds of growing love that grew stronger with each sunrise.

A glance at her watch prompted Judy to break their tender moment of passion. "Honey, it's 6:25," she murmured against his lips, her voice laced with the slightest hint of reluctance. Even momentarily, the idea of leaving their secluded paradise seemed a hard task. Yet, the prospect of their first meal together in the mansion, a christening of sorts, was equally enticing.

Her laughter, a musical chime, filled the room as she playfully chided, "Let's not be late for our first dinner in our new home." She emphasized the 'our,' a simple word that encapsulated the enormity of their shared future.

Ever the gentleman, John entwined his fingers with hers and echoed her joy. "Of course, Ms. Jenkins, to the dining room we shall proceed," he replied with a dramatic flourish, a sparkle of humor in his eyes. They were no longer just Judy and John but partners in life's marvelous dance, lord and lady of the manor.

As they walked towards the dining room, each step was a promise, each shared glance an affirmation of their love. The dining room itself was anything but small, its table set for two, crystal gleaming under the soft glow of the chandelier. Yet, in their eyes, it was the perfect size for two souls to share meals and dreams in their love story. Tonight, they would dine on the beautiful dinner that awaited them. With the manor as their witness, Judy and John's journey began a trip of passion, laughter, and an enduring love that would last through time.

As John and Judy finished their ham sandwich dinner, they realized it was time to return to town. Both of them had very little sleep in the last two days. They had stayed out all night, and John barely had time to shower and go to work this morning. They enjoyed the meal so much that they wanted to thank the cook. They stood up and walked to the kitchen, where Molly and Maria were cleaning up after making the meal.

Judy, as the lady of the house, took the lead. "Molly, Maria, thank you so much for fixing our dinner. The ham sandwiches were delicious, and spending time with you was a pleasure. We are leaving now and going back to town."

"What?" said Molly. "We were preparing your room for you. I assumed the main bedroom would be ok." Molly looked and said, "Mr. John, tell Ms. Judy that you all will stay here tonight. It is snowing heavily now, and driving back to town might be too dangerous. We have already prepared the main bedroom with towels, bathrobes, soap, shampoo, and any other essentials you may need in your bathroom, which is connected to your bedroom. I will not take no for an answer. Sorry, I must help Maria finish in the kitchen."

When Molly walked off, she looked at John and said, "This backfired on us. I hadn't thought it would go this far. What are we going to do, Mr. Jenkins?" John looked at her and said, "Well, Ms. Jenkins," smiling and looking into her eyes, "Do you trust me?" She looked into his eyes for a full minute and said, "John, I trust you, but are you sure what you are thinking? We are not going to do anything; do you understand that? No exceptions, right?"

"Judy, I love you, and if you truly love me, you know I will not try anything." Judy said, "Ok, we will do this, but I probably will not sleep. I will tell Molly we will be staying here tonight. What time do you need to go to work tomorrow?" "Well, Ms. Jenkins, are you taking on the responsibility of getting me to work on time?" "No," she said, "we are in one car, and I have to go in when you do." John said, "Oh, I did not think of it that way. Tomorrow is Saturday, and I need to meet Sarah at about 8:00 A.M." Judy kissed him and said, "I'll go tell Molly we are staying; love you, sweetie." She looked back at him, smiled, and said, "Wow, that came out so easily and felt natural and good. I will meet you in the room. Is that, ok?" "Yes, sweetie, I will see you in our room shortly. I love you, too."

John headed upstairs while Judy went to the kitchen. "Molly," Judy said, "we have decided to take your advice and stay here tonight." "That's great," Molly said, "what time would you like breakfast served in the morning?" "We need to be at work at 8 in the morning, so would seven be ok?" "We will have breakfast ready at seven," said Molly. "Since you didn't bring any extra clothes with you, please leave all your clothes in the laundry bag in your room in the hall by the door, and we will clean them and have them hanging outside your door when you wake in the morning." Judy said that was unnecessary, but Molly said, "Ms. Judy, we are not going to let you leave here with wrinkled clothes. Just leave them in the hall, and we will take good care of them. If you need anything, there is a buzzer next to the bed.

Push, hold the button, and ask for it; we will deliver it. Good night, Ms. Judy." Judy said good night and went to their room.

When Judy returned to the room, the door was closed, so Judy knocked on it. John came to the door already in his bathrobe. She went in, closed the door, and kissed John with a passion that they had become accustomed to. She went to the bathroom, changed her clothes, and put on her bathrobe. She did everything she usually does before bed since everything they needed was there. Molly had taken care of everything just like she said she would. When she left the bathroom, she had all her clothes in a laundry bag. John said, "What is that bag?" Judy explained, "Molly said to put all our clothes in the laundry bag, and she would have everything cleaned and hanging outside our door before we get up. She will have our breakfast ready at seven, so set the alarm for six." John smiled at Judy's efficiency, so he put all his clothes in the bag and placed them outside the door. He turned out the lights, and they got into bed; a dim light was showing through the windows, giving just enough light to act as a night light. They kissed a gentle kiss that gradually became passionate, lasting two or three minutes. They held each other tightly for several minutes, then rolled over, said good night, and went to sleep.

It was 5:45, and they had both woken up before the alarm went off. They were both surprised and happy to be cuddled up to each other. They said good morning to each other, lay there, and talked for a few minutes before Judy said she needed to get up, shower, and get dressed.

Judy looked at John and said, "Okay, turn your head; I'll stand up and put on my bathrobe." John rolled over and looked the other way while she slipped on the bathrobe. John went to the door, and their clothes hung where Molly said they would be. John brought the clothes in and hung them by the bathroom door.

It was 6:50, and John and Judy were ready and went downstairs for breakfast. Molly had scrambled eggs, bacon, grits, and toast on the table for them to sit down. They laughed and talked until 7:45, and it was time to leave. They said goodbye to Molly and the others and left for the store. John opened the car door, and Judy said, "I have never been so happy; I love you."

John said, "Sweetie, I love you so much, I can't find the words to express it." John walked to the driver's side as Judy slid across the seat to unlock the door. When John sat down, Judy sat beside him and continued cuddling. John told Judy, "When we get to the store, I think you should check in with Kathy for anything she needs help with today, and I will go to Sarah's office and tell her you will take the job as her assistant. She will get in touch with you as soon as she gets a chance. Meanwhile, I am going to my father's office to redecorate, make it my own, and start using it. I will use Kathy a lot to set everything up, or use her as she has time to spare. You may be able to help her until Sarah has time to talk to you and get you started."

Judy said, "Can I tell Kathy about last night? She is going to know I did not come home last night." "You may as well," said John. "She will not let the day go by without asking." After driving most of the way to the store, Judy kissed John on the cheek and slid back over to the right side of the seat.

15

The Mansion and the
Airplane

In the calm pre-dawn quiet of December 28, 1946, the humming engine of John's Ford sedan moved slowly through the snow as it made its way to JR's Department Store. A fresh layer of snow blanketed the world in a solemn white, covering John and Judy's tracks as if to preserve the sanctity of their night spent at the grand old mansion. As Judy stepped out of John's car, her cheeks touched by the morning's crisp embrace, her breath dancing before her in fleeting clouds. Judy, with her blond hair pinned neatly under her hat, and John, tall and straight-backed in his pressed suit, walked together with the kind of closeness born of shared secrets and unspoken promises. They parted at the entrance; he would prepare for the day's business, and she would seek the counsel of her friend, Kathy.

As Judy walked into Kathy's office, she said, "Good morning, Kathy." "Well, if it is not the lady of mystery herself," Kathy teased from her desk, her typewriter sitting idle, the click-click-click of its keys stilled for the moment. Her smile was as if she knew something, crinkled at the edges by the hint of sleep in her eyes. She gestured to the chair across from her. Kathy continued, "Judy, I noticed that your bed was not slept in last night, yet your clothes look like they have

176

been dry cleaned. This is almost impossible since there were no cleaners open yesterday or today. I will gladly listen if you need to explain how this happened."

Judy took the seat, a blush warming her cheek from more than the coal furnace. "Oh, Kathy, you wouldn't believe the evening we had," she began, her voice a blend of excitement and restraint. She spoke of the mansion, of the silence in its halls that spoke volumes more than the day's busy chatter ever could. And, almost shyly, of sharing the main bedroom with John. "We were together, just together, nothing else, and yet... it was as if the walls themselves held their breath, watching over us as we slept."

Kathy twirled a pencil between her fingers, her eyes reflecting the fragments of a daydream. "Sounds hauntingly romantic," she murmured. Judy nodded, her eyes looking away from Kathy's to peer out the office window, where the day had begun to reveal itself in shades of gray. She confided in Kathy about her decision to work at JR's as Sarah's assistant; the position would be in the small office, just outside Sarah's office.

"And John," Judy's voice grew warm with pride, "he is stepping into his father's shoes, and he wants you there with him, Kathy. He sees the brilliance in you, as we all do."

Kathy's penciled eyebrows arched in playful skepticism. "Are you sure he's not just sweet on my filing system?" But her eyes danced with the excitement of sharing in their new beginning.

The women laughed, rippling through the quiet office and echoing off the walls like hope. John stepped in then; his presence was commanding but tender, like the soft thud of heartbeats within a chest.

"Ladies," John greeted them, with a respectful nod to Kathy and a glance towards Judy that held all the promise of a rosy future, "I have spoken to Sarah. We are turning the page on a new phase here at JR's, and I could not be more certain that the two most brilliant minds I know will guide us through it. Judy, Sarah said that you should come to her office as soon as you can get away from the work you and Kathy have lined up for today." Amidst the clatter of typewriter keys and the rustle of papers, a silent observer might have noticed the glances between Judy and John. A spark unnoticed by most but as noticeable as the chill of the winter air, a silent promise of a love that would grow alongside the business, nurtured by shared ambitions and mutual respect. With evident enthusiasm and her blond hair tied back in a ponytail, Judy had made her way down the hall to Sarah's bright office. Sarah, with the exact meticulous nature but with more of a motherly touch, welcomed Judy into the fold. Their conversations weaved through the personal and professional, and with each shared story and advice exchanged, Judy found her place within the store's family.

The office that awaited Judy was an empty room, a space yearning for life and laughter. Its walls, stripped of memories, were soon to bear witness to the tireless work of two formidable women. The task was to breathe life into this dormant corner of JR's, which Judy enthusiastically embraced.

Together, Judy and Sarah rolled up their sleeves, their movements harmonious and purposeful. They lugged in desks, not just as pieces of furniture but as foundations of their future success. They arranged filing cabinets with the precision of seasoned artists, each drawer a testament to the order and efficiency they sought to uphold.

Laughter echoed off the walls as they debated the merits of a notebook versus a ledger, their friendship growing with each passing moment. Every detail, from the placement of a telephone to the choice of a desk lamp and the chair's cushion, was meticulously crafted to reflect the seriousness of their Mission and the warmth of their friendship.

Judy's office, once but an idea, now stood ready, a proud symbol of progress. It was more than a physical space; it was a realm where dreams could be charted and goals manifested, where Judy could shine under Sarah's guidance, and where, perhaps, the seeds of love could find fertile ground.

Judy looked around her new realm as the sun dipped below the horizon, casting a beautiful sunset over the city. She felt a surge of pride for the office they had built, for the future they had crafted with each turn of the screwdriver.

In the heart of JR's department store, amidst the soft hum of activity and the promise of tomorrow, Judy's journey had just begun. With a mentor like Sarah and a partner like John, she was poised to become not just an employee but a force to be reckoned with in a world where love and ledger books were not mutually exclusive but intertwined in the most enchanting of ways.

By that afternoon, John's office was in a flurry of activity. Kathy's wit and John's steady hand proved a powerful combination, making the transition seamless, as if the very walls of the building had been awaiting their touch. Together, they were more than just stewards of JR's legacy; they were the beating heart of a vibrant future, tightly woven into the fabric of the department store that had become so much more than just a place of business. It had become a testament to love, ambition, and the quiet magic that lies in new beginnings.

John stepped into the late afternoon light streaming through the dusty windows, which cast long shadows across the space soon to be his new domain. His father's office was a capsule of an era gone by, with heavy mahogany furniture that seemed to groan with old memories and walls lined with overbearing bookcases filled with leather-bound volumes that no one had dared to move for decades.

Kathy, her red hair looking like fire in the sunlight, followed behind with a worn cardboard box cradled in her arms. "I can't believe he's gone," she said softly with a tear in her eyes. "It was more to me than just a room. We spent several hours here, planning, replanning, and executing our plan." John heard the soft words and was glad his father had such a great friend and employee until the end. He felt himself getting a little emotional in his heart.

"I can't believe he is gone either; I would have liked to have met him." John's voice was a subdued echo, his gaze lingering on his father's empty chair, a throne awaiting its new king. He glanced at Kathy and managed a small smile, an unspoken sign of mutual understanding and grief. "Let's give this place a bit of our spirit, shall we?" said Kathy.

For hours, they worked in tandem, the generational changes unfolding as the old gave way to the new. They shifted the heavy desk toward the window to catch the light, arranged the books by relevance, and cleared out the clutter of years past. Kathy had an eye for efficiency, ensuring every item had its place and purpose, while John admired her thoroughness, the gentle way her fingers turned each page of his father's extensive ledgers before deciding where it belonged.

As dusk approached and the sunset spilled into the room, Sarah made her way to John's office, her heels clicking with authority on the polished floor. She found John and Kathy in a space that had been transformed, modern, and alive with potential.

"How did your day go, Sarah?" John queried as he stood to greet her, wiping his hands on his trousers. "It was productive. Judy is going to be a splendid addition," Sarah said, her eyes taking in the changes with a mixture of surprise and approval. "And this," she gestured around, "is remarkable. You've done well."

John looked at Kathy, and their eyes met, silently celebrating their teamwork. "We had a good day," John concurred. Sarah took a seat, smoothing the fabric of her skirt as she did. "I just wanted to remind you that tomorrow is Sunday, and the store will be closed."

"Your office is looking great, but there's something else," Sarah said, her tone shifting as she clasped her hands together. "Your father left you more than just this office and company. At the airport, there's an airplane under your name now." "My father's plane?" The sudden revelation stirred an unexpected thrill within him.

"Bill is the airport manager, and he was a perfect friend of your father's. He can answer any questions about the plane; his number is Bluff Field 369. I have known Bill for years; he is as reliable as they come," Sarah informed him, retrieving a small book from her purse and passing it across the desk. "Your father was quite the pilot; here is his logbook, and he saw to it that I could fly too."

John's brows rose in surprise. "You're a pilot?" Sarah chuckled, a sound tinged with a hint of nostalgia. "Your father believed in being prepared. He made sure I was licensed." Her eyes held a memory as she added, "He loved the Florida house. You should see it; it's beautiful, peaceful; you'll find pieces of him there." Kathy, who had been respectfully quiet during the exchange, now spoke up. "Sarah, I know you and Mr. Roberts used to fly together quite often. Have you been flying much lately?"

"Occasionally," Sarah said, with a modest tilt of her head. "The skies offer a unique kind of freedom." John touched Sarah on the shoulder and said, "Sarah, as long as I own the plane, you can fly any time you want to." "Thank you, John, that does mean a lot to me. Your father and I spent many hours flying together. He and I enjoyed flying; it was always so peaceful."

John rubbed his chin thoughtfully, visions of distant shores and open skies growing within him, a legacy that awaited beyond the horizon. "Maybe we should fly down sometime, see the place," he suggested, a spark igniting in his voice, the idea of new adventures stirring unknown desires within him.

Sarah smiled and stood, her presence encapsulating the warmth of the legacy John's father had left. "Just let me know when, and we'll take to the skies." As she turned to leave, John caught her wrist gently. "Thank you, Sarah, for everything." "You're welcome, John," she said, placing her other hand over his. "Remember, you are not just inheriting his assets. You are stepping into his dreams. Make them your own." And with that, Sarah left John and Kathy in the office, the remnants of the day settling around them like the dust they had swept away. Tomorrow held the promise of rest, and the day after that, the promise of flight. "Kathy," John said, "how do I call on this phone?"

Kathy said, "I will get Bill on the phone for you, Mr. Jenkins; when I get him, I will tell you the line number. Press that number, pick up the phone, and he will be there." "How do you know that's who I want to call?" "Just a guess," Kathy said. "Was I right?" "Yes, thank you." John could hear her through the door. "Mr. Bill, this is Kathy at JR's Department Store. How are you today?" Kathy said. "That is great, Mr. Bill. Yes, I'm doing fine. Thank you for asking. I have Mr. John Jenkins here, Mr. John Roberts's son; he would like to talk to you if you have a minute." "Mr. Jenkins, Bill is on line three." "Good afternoon, Mr. Bill; this is John Jenkins. Hope I haven't called at a bad time." "No, the timing is perfect," said Bill.

"I heard you were here; I took the liberty of pulling your plane out of the hangar and getting it washed, serviced, and ready for you to look at it. After completing your inheritance matters, I figured you would come to the airport." "Thank you so much, Mr. Bill. Would you have time to show me the plane tomorrow?" Bill said, "Sure, would 10:00 A.M. be, ok? I will have completed my morning tasks and have the rest of the day open on Sunday."

John said, "Thanks, Mr. Bill; I will see you at 10:00 A.M. tomorrow." Bill said, "Again, John, I am deeply sorry about your father; he was a very good friend. Several years ago, he helped me several times when things were slow. He has never asked for anything in return. He was a great friend; I will always owe him, and now you. That is how much I think of your dad. See you tomorrow." John hung up the phone, walked to the door, and said, "Thanks, Kathy; this is the first time that anyone ever dialed a phone call for me. That was great. I am going to walk over and see Sarah for a minute." "She left about 5 minutes ago, Mr. Jenkins." "Okay," said John, "I'll just drop by and see how they've redone the office space." Kathy smiled widely and said, "Yes, sir." John walked down the hallway and turned in at Judy and Sarah's office. "Hello, Ms. Martin, how are you today?" John said, "The office looks great. Is Sarah still here?" Judy said, "No, sir, Mr. Jenkins, she left about five or ten minutes ago." "Good," John said, "I needed to talk to you."

"I know," said Judy. "What are we going to do tonight?" Judy continued. "Well, I was going to ask you the same thing," John said; then he added, "Would you like to go to the lodge for dinner tonight?" Judy smiled and said, "Yes, Mr. Jenkins, I really would, and I am starving; what about you?" John said he was also, and they were ready to leave. As they walked by his office, he stopped for a moment and asked Kathy if she was locking up tonight. "Yes, sir, I am locking up, Sarah asked if I would. Have a good evening and a great weekend, sir." "You too, Kathy," he replied and walked out.

Judy stuck her head in and hugged her goodbye as usual, and Kathy whispered in her ear with a smile, "Are you staying out tonight?" Judy replied, "Not sure yet." With that, Kathy said, "OK, I am so happy for you. I am, but be careful." Kathy smiled as she said that. Judy hugged her and then said, "I will, I promise. I may call you later if you are going home." Kathy told her, "I should be home after I lock up; it's too late to go out then. Bobby said he might come over tonight; I'll talk to you later.

As Judy and John walked to the car, the click of Judy's heels on the pavement was a familiar sound. The crisp December air was filled with the remnants of yesterday's snowfall over JR's department store parking lot. Yet, among the silent cars and the whisper of winter, Judy approached the car with a grace that could melt any frost. Despite the turmoil of his newfound responsibility, the gallant gentleman hastened to open the door, his heart skipping at her warm smile. "Thank you, kind sir," she chimed, her voice soothing his anxious spirit.

"You are so very welcome, my little angel," he replied, the endearment slipping from his lips like a prayer of gratitude to the heavens for putting her in his life. Circling the vehicle with a sense of purpose, John felt the electricity in the air as Judy leaned across to unlock his door and then slid back to her side of the car. It was a simple act, yet it spoke volumes of their intimacy, a shared secret in a world where their love was yet to be declared. Settling into the driver's seat, he could not resist teasing her, and desire danced in his eyes. "What! No snuggling up next to me?"

Judy's shy grin was his undoing, her modesty a testament to their unspoken agreement: to keep their romance from the prying eyes of the department store. "Now, honey, you know that until we let it out that we are dating, we must keep everything above board," she said, her voice laced with the sweet agony of their restraint.

As they drove off, the playful banter continued, their laughter mingling with the engine's hum. "What's in the bag, sweetie?" John inquired, his curiosity piqued by the mysterious parcel at her side.

A blush crept over Judy's cheeks, the color of roses in bloom, as she clutched the bag a little tighter. "I had a few extra minutes at lunch today," she began, her voice a whisper of excitement, "so I went out in the department store and bought a few things that I might need... and some extra clothes, just in case." John's puzzled expression reflected his confusion. "I'm sorry, honey, just in case what?" The car was filled with a silence thick enough to slice through, Judy's embarrassment a noticeable entity between them. John's heart clenched; the last thing he wanted was to cause her distress. "I'm sorry, honey, I'm not sure what I said wrong. Please let me know so I can fix it. It breaks my heart to know that I have hurt you somehow," he pleaded, his voice thick with concern.

"It's nothing you said, darling," Judy reassured him, her eyes meeting his with a vulnerability that made him love her even more. "I wasn't sure if we were going to the mansion tonight, so I bought some things... just in case." John's heart soared as understanding dawned on him. "Oh, Oh! I understand now; I am sorry; I had not even thought of tonight," he admitted, his excitement for their evening together reigniting.

Judy's eyes sparkled with anticipation. "Well, it's time we started thinking about it. Do you still want to go to the lodge for dinner?" she asked, her voice brimming with eagerness. "If you're okay with eating at the lodge, then so am I," John replied, his decision clear.

Judy's voice was more determined, "Well, if you want to stay at the mansion tonight, we can eat at the lodge, pick up some of your clothes and things from your room, and then go to the mansion." Her smile was a radiant sunburst, her following words a promise of a future filled with love and shared secrets. "Or, I guess I could say we can get some of your things from your room at the lodge and go to our! Mansion home. If we do, I will need to call Kathy later tonight after she closes the store and goes to the apartment that we share. So that I can let her know I will not be coming home tonight."

Home. The word hung in the air, ripe with possibility, a sanctuary they could build together amidst the shadows of the past and the light of the future. Tonight, as they drove under the stars towards a destiny of their own making, John and Judy's hearts beat in unison, a melody of intense passion and unbridled hope.

As the lodge came into view, its windows aglow with welcoming light, Judy's heart fluttered like the delicate wings of a butterfly in spring. With a twinkle in his eye that rivaled the stars above, John shared his exhilarating news about the airplane waiting at Bluff Field Airport. "I hope this is okay. You know I now own an airplane at the Bluff Field Airport, and I set us an appointment to see it at 10:00 A.M. tomorrow."

Judy was so excited she could hardly contain herself. "Yes," she said, "I can't wait to go to the airport; I love planes." The air between them crackled with excitement, charged with the electricity of adventure and the unspoken depth of their growing affection.

Dinner at the lodge was an unforgettable experience. The table for two, set with fine linen and glowing candles, seemed to float in a space of its own, apart from the other diners. Their steaks, cooked to perfection, were accompanied by the rich, velvety notes of vintage wine, enhancing the night's flavors.

As they dined, their conversation danced from dreams to desires, of shared moments and quiet confidences. Judy, her eyes shimmering with the soft glow of candlelight, broached where the night would lead.

"Well, are you going to take me to my apartment, and you stay here at the lodge tonight, or are we going to the mansion for the night?" Her voice, though shy, carried the weight of her hope and the tenderness of her trust.

Feeling affection for the woman before him, John responded with a smile that spread across his face like the dawn. "I know what I want to do, honey, but I need to know what you want to do," he said, his voice a gentle caress.

Judy's response was a whisper, yet it echoed through John's heart with the clarity of a bell. "Well, I want to stay with you, John. I want that so much." Though laced with the promise of closeness, her words also held a boundary she was not ready to cross. "But I also need you to understand there is nothing extra going to happen. I am not ready for anything else yet. Just like last night."

John's respect for her wishes shone in his eyes as brightly as the love he felt. "That's what I wanted also," he said, his heart swelling with joy. "After dinner, we can go to my room, get some of my things, and head to the mansion."

Their plans were set, and they finished their meal, savoring each bite and each moment of togetherness. They went to John's room for him to pick up a few things to take to the mansion. John opened his room door, and they went into a very well-organized room with everything in its place, just like he had done at his office at the store. She smiled; he was a very well-organized person, even in a hotel. Judy said, "You sure keep everything extremely organized and clean."

He said, "Yes, I do; that was the one thing my mother always made sure of, always being clean and organized." Judy hugged John and said, "I'm so sorry about your mother, John; I wish I had known her." John said, "You would have liked her, and I know she would have liked you."

As they exited the lodge, wrapped in their coats against the cold, Judy mentioned a brief stop at her apartment to gather a few things for their airport adventure. "Kathy will be home by then, and she can talk to you while I get my stuff." With a sense of anticipation, hand in hand, their hearts beating to the same rhythm. The promise of the airplane, the adventure awaiting them, was just a prelude to the journey they were embarking upon together, a trip not just to the airport but through the uncharted territories of love, where every moment was a treasure and every glance a story to be told.

As they drove off, the lodge faded into the background, but the warmth of the evening lingered, a testament to the beginning of a love that would soar as high and as far as the airplane they were set to explore. The mansion awaited a silent witness to the tale of two hearts in the dance of romance, poised under the watchful gaze of the winter stars.

But first, they had a quick stop at Judy and Kathy's apartment to pick up a few things she may need at the mansion. As they walked up to the door, Judy quickly knocked on it so Kathy would know she was coming in, just like they used to do in college. Judy told Kathy she was picking up a few things and then told John, "Honey, have a seat on the sofa, and I'll be back in a few minutes." "Ok." Said John. With that, Judy and Kathy walked to Judy's room as they talked.

As Judy and Kathy walked up the stairs, the chatter of their conversation became a distant hum. John let the soft cushions of the sofa embrace him, his mind awash with the warmth of the evening. The scent of Judy's apartment, a blend of vanilla candles and her signature floral perfume, lingered in the air, wrapping around him like a comforting shawl.

Judy's voice danced excitedly in the other room as she recounted the night's events to Kathy, telling Kathy all the details: "The steaks were excellent, and our conversations flowed like a smooth and refreshing vintage wine." John's heart swelled as he heard Judy tell of their night; it was as if their bond had deepened with every shared experience, the threads of their love woven more tightly.

Kathy's eyes shone with genuine interest as Judy spared no detail, her hands animatedly moving as if to paint the scene in the air between them. They went on to gather Judy's belongings, a symphony of soft rustles and whispered giggles emanating from her room as they packed.

Upon their return, Judy's presence was a beacon to John; her smile was the light that guided him home. "Ready to go, sweetie?" she chimed, singing a melody that plucked at his heartstrings.

Kathy, ever the observant roommate, leaped into the conversation with the enthusiasm of someone sharing a well-kept secret. "I understand y'all are going to the airport tomorrow to see your airplane," she said, her eyes sparkling with shared excitement.

John answered with a nod, and Kathy, who could no longer contain the news. "Did she tell you she loved airplanes?" Kathy posed in a playful, teasing tone, hinting at the coming surprise. "She said she likes planes and would enjoy going to the airport tomorrow," said John.

And then, with the force of a secret that could change the very orbit of his world, Kathy announced, "She doesn't just like planes; she is a pilot. Has been a pilot for several years, and I have always loved flying with her." The room seemed frozen around them as John's gaze found Judy. Seeing her in a new light, a woman of the skies, a conqueror of the clouds. Amazement etched itself into his features, his voice carrying the weight of newfound awe. "Just when I thought I couldn't love you more," said John.

Judy's cheeks flushed a rosy bashfulness and pride as Kathy's statement hung in the air. "Oh, hush, Kathy," she playfully chastised, her eyes dancing with secrets now shared. "I'm ready to go."

As they made their way to the door, the anticipation of the following day's adventure bubbled within them. The prospect of touching the wings of their shared dreams, of soaring together above the world they knew, promised an intimacy that words could scarcely capture.

And as the night continued, John knew that with Judy by his side, there was no horizon they could not chase, no sky they could not claim as their own. Love seemed not just a feeling but a journey they were only beginning to navigate, with hearts as their compass and the stars as their guide.

John's excitement was evident, contagious, and sparkling, bubbling up like champagne in a wine glass. He could hardly contain the grin that seemed to permanently reside on his face as they strolled out of Judy's apartment, the evening air kissed with the promise of adventure. With every step towards the waiting car, his heart did a little skip, not just at the thought of spending the night at the mansion but also at the prospect of learning more about the woman who had captivated his every waking thought.

"So, I heard from Kathy you've been a pilot for years?" John inquired, his voice wrapped in genuine interest. The streetlights cast a soft glow on Judy's face, illuminating the sparkle in her eyes as she turned to him.

Judy nodded, her smile a mirror of his enthusiasm. "Yeah, my dad's been flying for one of the airlines forever, and he would take me along whenever he could." She chuckled; the sound was like music to John's ears. "I was practically raised in the skies, so he started teaching me when I was about thirteen. It's been about fourteen years now."

John's admiration for Judy soared to new heights, much like the planes she piloted. "What kind of planes do you fly? Anything with wings?" he teased, his eyes glinting with delight.

Judy's laughter rang out, clear and bright. "Not just anything. I can handle single and twin-engine planes with ease." She shot him a playful glance. "What about your plane? What type of plane is waiting at the airport for you?"

John's smile bloomed into a full-blown grin, his cheeks aching with the force of it. "Well, OUR plane, according to Mr. Thompson, is a ten-seater plus pilot and copilot. I am not sure about the engines." Judy said, "Our plane, our plane?" "Yes, honey, our plane," said John, and then Judy said, "I'm guessing that with that many seats, it's got to be a twin." At that moment, he was filled with a warm glow of mutual respect and love. John reached out, his hand finding Judy's, their fingers intertwining naturally.

"Honey, I love you more than you could ever imagine," John said, his voice earnest and thick with emotion. "I'm so proud of you." The sincerity in his words was the key to the floodgates, and Judy felt the tears well up, the overwhelming sense of being seen and cherished too much for her heart to hold. She moved closer, her head finding the crook of his shoulder as she snuggled into his embrace on the sidewalk. Tears flooded from her eyes, but Judy did not care who might see them, who might witness this moment of vulnerability. Because with John, she felt safe and loved.

And John, with the protective circle of his arms around her, felt as if he could take on the world. He did not care about prying eyes or the gossip of the town. All that mattered was the woman in his arms, who had stolen his heart with her courage, passion, and love for the skies.

They stood there, two souls anchored in a single moment, under the evening sky. The stars above them twinkled in approval, acknowledging their rare and beautiful connection. As they eventually pulled away, their eyes met, and a silent promise passed between them, a promise of forever, of adventures yet to come, and a love that would soar higher than any plane Judy had ever flown. With one last squeeze of their hands and hearts full of anticipation, they continued to the car, ready to face whatever the night at the mansion would bring. But no matter what, they knew they would face it together.

When they got to the car, John opened the door like he always does, and Judy, with tears in her eyes, very softly said, "Thank you, my love," and sat down in the car and slid over to unlock John's door. John came around, got in the car, and started it up.

Judy still had tears of love for John in her eyes. She snuggled up as close to John as possible and let a few more tears flow from her blue eyes. As they drove down the street, John put his arm around her and said, "It's ok, honey; I've got you and will never let you go."

The tears came again when she said, "I'm so sorry, my love; I don't know why I can't quit crying; I'm just so happy, I can't even describe it." He gave her another big hug with his right arm and just let her relax against his shoulder. Judy's response was as natural as the sunrise, a confession of pure happiness that could only be expressed through her tears. They were not just drops of saline; they were liquid diamonds, each a treasure born from the depth of her soul. And John understood the language of her tears as if he were born fluent in it. His hug was not just an embrace but an anchor, a haven where all her worries could be moored and forgotten.

The mansion loomed into view, a testament to their love. John, ever the gentleman, swept around to Judy's side and offered his hand as an invitation to step into the life they would build together. With grace, she emerged from the car, and they embraced, two hearts beating as one, ready to cross the threshold of their future.

When they walked to the door, John had to ring the bell, realizing he didn't have a key. Molly opened the door almost by the time he had pushed the doorbell. Molly, the ever-attentive caretaker of the mansion, was a beacon of warmth. As she opened the door, the light spilled out onto the couple, wrapping them in the comfort of being truly home. Molly had seen the lights and was already headed to the door. John told Molly, "Please leave the door unlocked. I have some bags in the car and will return shortly to get them." Molly said she would take care of the bags and leave them by their bedroom door.

And so, with their hearts full and the promise of forever etched in their embrace, they stepped into the mansion, not as two individuals but as one unstoppable force of love. In this haven of romance, John and Judy would write their story, a tale of love that promised to be as timeless as the walls around them.

As John and Judy ascended the grand staircase of the mansion, their arms interwoven with an intimacy that spoke volumes of their deep connection, the air around them was thick with the scent of blooming love. The evening had left Judy's heart brimming with emotions so potent that tears shimmered in her eyes, threatening to spill over in a silent testament to the joy John had fostered within her.

Upon reaching the sanctuary of the main bedroom, they found solace on the plush sofa amidst the room's vastness. With a tenderness that seemed to resonate from the depth of his being, John gathered Judy into his embrace. The world outside their embrace ceased to exist as they held each other, basking in the warmth of their closeness. John's voice, a soothing melody in the quiet room, broke the silence, "I think Molly just put our bags by the door, sweetie. Do you want me to get them so we can go to bed?"

Judy, clinging to the moment, to the sense of completeness that John's presence granted her, whispered, "Please don't, honey, don't leave me right now." With reassurance as steady as the beat of his heart, John replied, "I will be right here beside you, my love, right here beside you." Time seemed to stand still within the confines of the main bedroom, and the stroke of midnight finally stirred Judy from the comfort of their embrace. As her eyes fluttered open to the sight of John, vigilant and ever-present, a gentle concern laced her voice, "Honey, have you been awake all this time?"

John replied with unwavering devotion, "Yes, my dear little angel, I have been by your side most of the night in case you needed me." With a yawn and a tender smile, Judy murmured, "Can we go to bed now, please?" Ever the gentleman, John offered to retrieve their bags for more proper bed preparation. Still, Judy, overcome with a longing for simplicity and raw connection, interjected, "No, John, please let's just undress completely and go to bed, cuddle, and sleep, please, nothing else, okay?"

With that, they moved together as if in a dance that only they knew the steps to. When the lights were turned off, only the glow from the outside bathed the room in a soft, silvery light. Their movements were unhurried and relaxed as they helped each other shed the layers that separated skin from skin. Each touch and kiss was a silent promise of trust and affection.

Finally, bare and unguarded, they slipped beneath the cool sheets of the bed. Their bodies entwined effortlessly, a puzzle that had found its missing piece. A final kiss, gentle and lingering, sealed the night before they surrendered to the embrace of slumber.

At that moment, as the world outside continued, John and Judy lay in a fortress of tranquility and love. The trust that enveloped them was as accurate as the sheets that draped their forms, a testament to love both tender and fierce. It was a trust that could weather any storm, an excellent and unbreakable bond. The first light of dawn entered through the mansion's main bedroom curtains, casting a warm glow over the room. Judy's eyes fluttered open, the previous day's excitement lingering in her heart like the sweet aftertaste of a fine wine. The mansion, with all its history and whispers of the past, now held a new treasure, a memory of unbridled joy and love that she shared with John.

She gazed upon him, his chest rising and falling gently with each breath, his features softened by slumber. It was in this tranquil moment that Judy's love swelled within her, a tidal wave of affection that she knew would only grow as the years unfolded. John, her beloved, with the lineage of mystery and the unexpected inheritance that brought them to this very room, lay there as though he were part of the mansion's design, a prince in his castle.

Judy felt a gentle urgency as the clock on the mantle ticked toward their morning plans. "Good morning, honey, wake up; it's Sunday morning," she whispered, her voice a tender caress in the quiet room. The morning light danced upon her skin as John stirred, his eyes opening to the vision of her, a sight more enchanting than any sunrise.

"Good morning to you, honey," he replied, his voice tinged with the warmth of a man who had found his heart's counterpart. His smile blossomed like the first bloom of spring, an expression of admiration and devotion. "You are just as beautiful in the morning as at night."

Judy's heart fluttered as she leaned in, her lips meeting his in a kiss that held the promise of forever. As the sheet slipped, revealing the silhouette of her form, John's eyes sparkled with a playful recognition. "Honey, you do remember that we have nothing on, don't you?" he teased, his tone light and loving.

Her shy smile was the key that unlocked John's deepest feelings and captured his heart. "I know," she whispered back, her voice laced with the certainty that comes with true love. "I also know I love you." Their kiss deepened, a passionate declaration that words could never fully capture. Time seemed to stand still, and the world outside the bedroom walls faded. But the promise of the day ahead, a visit to Bluff Field Airport to gaze upon John's plane, beckoned them with the thrill of shared adventures yet to come.

"Honey, it's time to shower and get dressed so we can eat breakfast and go to the airport," Judy said, her voice tinged with reluctance to end their tender embrace.

Judy smiled and said, "I'm going to shower; look the other way." As she stood, the morning light illuminated her, giving her an elegant and beautiful appearance. John put on his bathrobe, opened the bedroom door, and retrieved the clothes Molly had left the night before. When Judy finished her shower, she could dress while he took his shower.

As Judy descended the elegant staircase to the mansion's kitchen, a sense of eager anticipation fluttered within her chest. The morning light poured through the vast windows, casting a warm glow over the marble countertops and the polished silver appliances that sparkled in the spacious kitchen, a culinary dream. She found Molly, the ever-attentive housekeeper, already busy with the morning's duties, her hands gracefully gliding over the surfaces as she prepared for the day ahead.

"Molly, where do we keep the eggs?" Judy inquired, her voice light and cheerful. She wanted to whip up something special, perhaps to surprise John with a breakfast creation, a gesture of appreciation for all the moments they had shared within these walls, a token of her love.

Molly turned to her with the smile of a confidante, the bond between them tangible in the comfort of their exchange. "Ms. Judy, please allow me to take care of your breakfast. What would you like me to prepare for you and Mr. John?" she offered, the kindness in her eyes mirroring her words.

Judy's heart warmed at Molly's willingness to serve, but she knew the joys of a simple gesture, the intimacy of crafting a meal for a loved one. "Oh, I don't mind doing it," Judy assured her, but she saw an opportunity to share in Molly's ability to bring another layer of connection to the table. She proposed a delightful alternative. "I don't know what we fancy this morning. Let's do this; you surprise us. Fix whatever you'd like, and we'll love it. What do you say?"

The proposition seemed to take Molly aback, her concern endearing as she pondered, "But what if Mr. John doesn't like it?" Judy's smile grew playful and reassuring as she replied, "Mr. John will like it, or he can fix his own breakfast." Her laughter tinkled through the air, a light-hearted challenge. Molly, now with a mischievous glint in her eye, agreed, "All right, Ms. Judy. Would 9:00 be suitable for the two of you?" Judy assured her with a nod and a grateful smile, "Perfect, Molly. We can't wait to see what you come up with."

Judy then returned to their room, her steps light, anticipating Molly's culinary treat, adding a spring to her stride. "Honey, breakfast at 9," she chimed as she entered, the promise of a new day wrapped in the scent of fresh linen and the soft rays of sunlight that kissed their sanctuary. John's laughter met her announcement, his voice rich and deep, "Yes, dear, I'm on it." The familiar banter is a dance of words they have perfected over time. When the clock neared the hour, they descended together, hand in hand, two souls in harmony, making their way to the heart of the home. The kitchen now exuded the mouth-watering scents of a feast lovingly prepared. Poached eggs, link sausage, creamy cheese grits, robust coffee, and a vibrant fruit awaited them, a picture of affection and care.

"Is this what you've been doing, my love?" John inquired, genuine care coloring his words as he beheld the spread before him. Judy's heart swelled with pride for Molly's hidden talents, now on full display. "This is all Molly's masterpiece. I merely asked her to treat us to her favorites, and oh, what a magnificent job she has done," she beamed, giving Molly a nod of thanks.

Their breakfast was a symphony of flavors, each bite a testament to their shared lives, the sweetness and spice mingling in a dance upon their tongues. Complete and ready to embrace the day, they ascended once more to prepare for their journey to the airport, their next grand adventure.

As they left for the day, Molly asked, "Ms. Judy, what would you like for dinner tonight?" Judy looked at John and asked, "What do we do? I do not know how to answer that." John said, "Molly, can we call later and let you know what we plan to do?" "Yes, sir, Mr. John, that will be fine."

As the December sun broke through the morning haze, an air of anticipation shimmered around John and Judy, the mansion's silhouette fading behind them. They had just spent their second night together within the walls of John's newly inherited estate, the air still echoing with unspoken promises and the tenderness of newfound intimacy. In the solace of the car, the world outside seemed to stand still, abuzz with silent questions about their future.

As John and Judy drove to the airport, they would pass by the Poplar Bluff cemetery. John asked, "Honey, we will pass by the cemetery where my father is buried. Would you mind if we stopped at his grave for a few minutes?" Judy, with tears in her eyes, said, "Honey, I will be honored to visit your father's grave with you." Judy hugged him tightly as they stood by the grave. "Honey", as Judy hugged him tighter, she said, "I hurt for you, I can't imagine the pain you must be going through. I know you didn't know about your father until a few weeks ago, but to lose him now and your mother, all in one year, is unimaginable." They walked back to the car, hugging and wiping the tears from their eyes, and headed to the airport.

Judy's voice, glistening with uncertainty and excitement, broke the silence. "They are expecting us back tonight," she said to John, her mind wandering through the network of possibilities. "What are we going to do? Should I keep living with Kathy? Will you be staying at the lodge? Should I keep living with Kathy, and you stay at the mansion? Should we both move into the mansion and start anew?" These are discussion items on the ride from the mansion to the airport. They were so happy that they just talked and laughed as they drove to the airport, with Judy sitting beside John. Judy said, "I love you." John smiled at her and said, "I love you too, honey; I can't imagine living without you." He had his arm around her and gave her a little squeeze, a loving hug. She smiled and said, "I could not imagine living without you either." She continued with her head tilted at him with a shy smile that always set him on fire. "What are we going to do about it, then?"

John said, "Honey, don't smile at me like that right now; that shy and beautiful smile sets me on fire, and I can't help it." Judy smiled at him and said, "Well, what are we going to do about this, sweetie?" John said, "Well, I know what I want to do, but I want to make sure we are together on this. After we leave the airport, why don't we go back to the mansion or somewhere private to talk and decide what we want to do."

Judy said, "I like that idea; I know what I want to do; I just hope they are the same thing." They smiled at each other and then turned into the airport parking lot. As they started to get out, John said, "Wait a minute, sweetie." John leaned over and gave her a big kiss. "Now, I'm ready to go." Walking into the airport's embrace, the scent of oil and the distant hum of engines was a symphony to their senses. Entering the main office with an air of quiet purpose, John's voice blended with the morning bustle. "Good morning, we are looking for Mr. Bill," he announced confidently.

A figure appeared from a corner, casting a friendly shadow. "Good morning. Just a minute, and I will get Bill from the Roberts hangar. He's expecting someone around 10:00." Gratitude warmed John's response. "That's us," he acknowledged. The familiarity of his name attached to the hangar sparked a quiet pride. "Mind if we come along to meet him there?" The invitation was met with an unequivocal "Yes, sir." They followed their impromptu guide, weaving through the airport's heartbeat to arrive at the metal hangar sheltering John's airborne treasure.

The moment they stepped into the hangar, the world seemed to hold its breath. Judy's grip on John's arm was electric, a current of raw emotion that spoke volumes. The concern in John's eyes mirrored the love he felt, a love ready to shield her from any storm. But the storm was not one of fear; it was awe in the vastness of the hangar, amplifying her sudden stillness. John, attuned to her slightest nuance, reached for her with concern. "What is it, honey? Anything wrong?"

Her eyes, heavy with history and love for the skies, turned back to John. "Oh no," she breathed, a radiant smile chasing away the shadows of concern. John's heart surged as her gaze was a beacon of shared dreams and unspoken vows.

"Thank you, honey, for trying to protect me," she whispered, touching a feather-light affirmation of his unwavering support. Their moment was a silent vow, their connection to the thread sewing their futures together.

Bill's approach was a gentle interruption as he greeted John with a knowing chuckle. "No worries, John, I am Bill. And I reckon she is okay. It is the look of the skies calling; I have seen it many times in a seasoned pilot. I take it you are a pilot. Only a pilot will have that look," recognizing the passion in Judy's eyes. She was a pilot, her soul as free as the skies she soared through. Judy's eyes locked onto the plane, her heart recognizing the silhouette before them, a majestic Model 18 Twin Beech, wings poised like a guardian angel.

"Yes, about fourteen years," she confirmed, her voice rising in excitement, "flying single and twin engines. It's a Model 18 Twin Beech; it is beautiful." The revelation was an unveiling, a shared passion that added another layer to their evolving story. "I took my multi-engine rating on a Model 18 Twin Beech, but it was a tail dragger," Judy told him.

Bill continued, "I commend you for flying the tail dragger; that is an extremely difficult plane. If you mastered that, you have it made." Then Bill said, "Do you keep your logbook with you?" "Yes, I do; I always carry it with me," said Judy. Bill asked Judy, "Would you mind if I see your logbook?" Judy reached into her purse, pulled out her logbook, and handed it to Bill. He looked through it and said, "Judy, you have many hours in the Twin Beech tail dragger; this will be a breeze. A quick checkout, and you will be ready to go."

Bill said, "I'm sorry, John, this is rude of me. I noticed the excitement in this young lady, and I just naturally started talking about airplanes. My apologies." John replied, "That's okay, Mr. Bill. My apologies for not introducing her. Mr. Bill, this is my wonderful girlfriend, Judy Martin." Bill said, "John, you must be so proud to have a girlfriend who is a pilot; that is just amazing." "Yes, Mr. Bill," John said, "it is, and she is amazing, and I love her more every day. I am so proud of her." Judy looked at John with a big smile; in her mind, she thought, My love had just introduced me as his girlfriend. And, out loud to others, he stated how proud he was of me.

Bill, who runs the airport, is also a flight instructor and can give Judy a check ride in the Model 18 Twin Beech airplane. Bill said, "Well, I have the whole afternoon open for you, John. Would you like to take a ride in your new plane?"

John looked at Judy, who was smiling, and nodded. "Yes." John said, "Well, I guess that is a yes."

"Great," said Bill, "I will pull it out to the tarmac and do the precheck, and we will be ready to go. My wife is here in the office. Do you mind if she rides along? She has always loved this plane but has never had a chance to ride in it." John said that was ok with them. Bill said, "Thanks, I'll have someone bring her out here." We are in our 60s, so she moves a little slower." Then Bill turned to Judy and said, "Judy, I can go ahead and give you your check ride on this plane, and you'll be ready to go anytime you want to take her up."

Judy turned to John, smiled, and said, "Can I, honey? Only if you say I can." John looked into her eyes and said, "Of course you can, honey." With that, Judy jumped into action and began performing the preflight checks, using the book as one should, even though many people do not use the book and instead rely on memory. Once finished, she gave the book to Bill so he could check behind her; he took the book and said, "I watched every step you took; it was perfect; you were taught very well."

She smiled and said, "It was my father; he was also a pilot for an airline company." They all climbed into the beautiful Beech and prepared for takeoff. Judy opened the small sliding window on her side and yelled, "Clear prop," then turned to Bill. "Will you call out clear prop on your side, please?" Judy adjusted the radio dials and said, "Bluff Field traffic, Bluff Field traffic Twin Beech 49840, permission to start engines." Bluff Field traffic replied, "49840, permission to start engines granted, advise when ready to taxi." John is watching Judy with a smile, showing his pride in her. Judy yelled out the windows again to clear prop and started turning over the engines. Each engine started and was perfect. She looked at Bill; he smiled and nodded, giving her the go-ahead to taxi. "Bluff Field traffic, 49840. Request permission to taxi to the runway." Bluff Field traffic replied, "49840 taxi to runway five, hold short of takeoff position." Judy said, "Bluff Field Traffic 49840 taxi to runway five, hold short of takeoff position," and they started to move. In a few minutes, they were at the hold position; Judy did her engine run-up procedure and reported. "Bluff Field Traffic 49840 holding short at runway five." Bluff Field traffic replied, "49840 continue to hold, waiting for a single to land." Judy replied, "49840 holding." In a couple of minutes, over the radio, Bluff Field traffic replied, "49840, you are cleared for takeoff." Judy replied with a big smile, "49840, taking off runway 5." With that, she moved on to the runway, eased the power to three-quarter throttle, started down the runway, and then slowly went to full throttle. In a minute, they were lifting off. And she was doing great; John was so proud. Then he heard Judy say, "Bluff Field traffic, 49840, turning left downwind runway 5, staying local." Bluff Field traffic replied, "49840, report 5 miles out when returning; good day."

They were off flying, and Judy turned and looked at John, who was smiling so big. Judy was a beautiful vision in the pilot's seat, her hands steady, her gaze focused, mastering the flight as if she had done it a million times before. John's pride swelled in his chest with love and admiration as they flew through the heavens.

As the Twin Beech plane cut through the skies with the grace of a bird in flight, Judy's hands danced over the controls with practiced ease. At her fingertips, the world below seemed to unfold like a map of limitless possibilities, and today, she was exploring the seamless integration of man's ingenuity with the laws of nature, the autopilot.

With a flick of a switch and a steady gaze, Judy tested the system, assigning it a destination and watching with quiet approval as the aircraft obediently banked toward the new heading. Each change, each new direction, confirmed her mastery over this mechanical marvel.

John, her co-pilot in life, watched her with an intensity that seemed to transcend the mechanics of their journey. There was a language in his gaze that spoke volumes without a single word. Judy felt a spark, a connection, an unspoken dialogue between their souls. She responded kindly, her smile a silent sonnet, her nod affirming their shared experience.

The moment was fleeting yet eternally etched in the canvas of her heart. Judy's thoughts soared like the plane she commanded: "Oh lord, let him be mine. I love him so much." It was a silent prayer that she hoped would pierce through the veil of uncertainty and reach the depths of John's desires.

Her breath caught as she looked back and sent a kiss across the plane. Daring in its simplicity, it was a bold declaration without a sound. The gesture was like a comet streaking across the sky of their shared existence, blazing a trail of passion and longing.

The plane responded to her touch, aligning with the final destination as if it were in tune with Judy's heart. The 5-mile buzzer sounded, and the light blinked on, a beacon drawing them back to earth, back to reality. Yet, even as she called out their position and intentions to the air traffic controller, Judy's mind lingered on the possibilities, on the hope of what might come after they touched down. "Bluff Field, Twin Beech 49840 request straight in landing on runway 5," she announced with professional clarity. "49840, straight in landing approved," came the crisp reply. "See you on the ground."

The words were standard and routine, but they promised more than just a successful landing to Judy. They were an invitation to a future where her dreams might take root in the fertile soil of reality. As the plane's wheels kissed the tarmac, Judy knew that this was merely the beginning of a journey that she hoped would intertwine her path with John's forever.

Judy went through her shutdown procedures on the ground, and everything was quiet after a few minutes. "Fantastic," said Bill. "I do not think I have ever seen anybody fly that professionally. You were amazing, Judy," said Bill.

With a big grin, Judy said, "I guess I passed my check ride, Mr. Bill?" "Oh yes," said Bill, "with flying colors. Let me see your logbook, and I will sign off on it now." With that, Judy was ready to fly the Twin Beech. As they stood up, John said, "I'll wait for you just outside the door, honey; that will give you time to complete any necessary paperwork." I am so proud of you, and I love you dearly." "I love you, too, honey," Judy said with a big smile. "I'll be through in about five minutes."

Judy exited the plane in a few minutes with a smile so big she could not contain herself. She ran to John, wrapped him in her arms, and kissed him in the airport hangar. Then she said, "I don't care who sees us; I love you." With a big smile, John could hardly stop smiling to say, "I love you; I love you; I love you; I have never been so proud of anyone in my life." And kissed her again.

Bill walked up laughing and said, "John, I do think she likes the plane." Then he said, "You have a great plane and a fantastic girlfriend, and from the looks of things, she will probably be your wife soon. Congratulations, young man, on both."

"Thank you, Mr. Bill," John said. "How do we pay all the expenses for the plane? Do you send us a bill? Or what?" Bill explained, "I normally send a bill to the store at the end of each month, and Sarah typically sends us a check." "That sounds good," said John. He continued, "What must we do to fly the plane?" Bill explained, "Just call us and let us know when you are coming, and I will have the plane pulled out of the hangar, gassed up, and ready to go. When you return, park it on the tarmac and secure it with tie-downs. We will move it to the hangar as soon as we can." John said, "Can Judy and I walk back in for a minute?"

"Give us about two minutes; they are hooking up to it now to move it into your hangar," said Bill. John and Judy watched as they moved the Beech back to the hangar. After it was parked, they climbed aboard, sat down, looked at each other for a minute, and started laughing. They leaned over and kissed each other, and Judy said, "Honey, it just can't get any better." With a big smile, John said, "I don't think so either, but let's go to JJ's for an early dinner tonight and see if it gets any better." Judy said, "I would love to go to dinner tonight, Mr. Jenkins," as she kissed him. She continued, "It's 1:00 P.M. now; we can go back home, shower, and be at JJ's by 4:00 P.M." John smiled and said, "Home." With that, they got in the car and headed back to the mansion.

16

The Proposal

In the frost-kissed twilight of December 29, 1946, an undercurrent of anticipation hummed as John and Judy returned from their airborne adventures. The mansion rose to greet them, a steadfast symbol of the world they were building together, a world John was ready to seal with Judy that evening.

John's heart thumped with the promise of forever as Judy, the beacon of his affection, ascended the stairs to the main suite. Her elegance was effortless, accentuated by the sound of cascading water as she prepared for an evening that would be etched into the annals of their history. Meanwhile, John's footsteps echoed through the empty halls as he descended to the heart of their well-appointed mansion, his intentions as clear and sharp to him.

With a nervous but determined smile, John picked up the phone and asked the operator to dial JJ's Restaurant. This restaurant had woven its way into their love story, the place that held memories within its walls, and now promised to host a moment that would surpass them all. The reservation hostess recognized the voice of the new owner of JR's department store, a man whose name was rapidly becoming synonymous with prosperity and charm in Poplar Bluff. John's request was simple: a romantic table shrouded in the warm glow of candlelight, a solitary rose with petals as velvety and lush as the future he envisioned. As John conveyed his desires, the hostess knew it was more than a reservation; it was a prologue to a lifelong commitment.

"Mr. Jenkins," the voice on the other end was wrapped in hospitality, "everything shall be arranged to your exact request. Rest assured, this evening at JJ's will be the essence of perfection." As John hung up the phone, his pulse raced with the knowledge that he would ask Judy to marry him within hours. The flight they had shared that day was a mere foretaste of the ecstasy he hoped to offer her with his proposal. He envisioned her laughter, exuberant and pure, her eyes reflecting the candlelight, a symbol of the flame she had kindled in his heart.

John then asked Molly if the package he had ordered had been delivered. It was supposed to be delivered by a courier no later than 1:00 p.m. today. Molly smiled and said, "Yes, sir, Mr. John, the jewelry store delivered exactly at 1:00 p.m." John put his finger over his mouth, telling Molly this was a secret. She smiled, nodded, and put her finger over her mouth.

John prepared himself for the evening with the responsibility resting on his shoulders. He chose his attire with care, each piece a testament to the seriousness of his intent. Evening approached, and as they made their way to JJ's, Judy's eyes sparkled with the simple joy of an evening out, unaware of the magnitude of what was to come. The restaurant's ambiance embraced them, a symphony of subtle sounds and intimate lighting that set the stage for what was to come. As they walked up to the door, a line of people was already waiting to get a table.

Judy said, "Well, I guess we should have come a little sooner." John walked up to the door, and they recognized him, asking him to come in. Judy looked at John and said, "What's going on, honey?" They were ushered to their private table, a secluded sanctuary crafted with attention to detail, the candlelight flickering like the beat of a lover's heart, and the rose, oh, that rose, stood as if it held the secrets of the universe within its crimson folds. Judy was so surprised that she could hardly speak. "John, you must love me a lot to call ahead and set this up." She was smiling so much that a little tear formed in her eyes. She thought he must love me to do all this.

John reached for Judy's hand as they dined, and the world outside faded away. Her gaze met his, an unspoken yet lingering question, and in that quiet corner of JJ's, time stood still for a moment, destined to stay through the ages.

"Judy," John began, his voice a gentle caress against the backdrop of a world hushed in anticipation, "today soared above any dreams I've ever dared to dream, but it pales compared to the lifetime I want to spend with you." The ring, a glimmering testament to his unwavering commitment, caught the candlelight as he knelt before her. "Will you marry me?" Tears of joy came before the words could form, and as she whispered, "Yes," the very foundation of their destiny was cast. People in JJ's started clapping, many made toasts, a beautiful kiss to seal the proposal, and the promise of a future unfurled like the petals of the rose that saw their love's newest beginning.

As the night ended, John and Judy stepped into the evening, their hands entwined, hearts ablaze with a promise that would journey beyond the bounds of their December romance. As they approached the parking lot, Judy said, "Where is the car, honey? I thought we left it right over there." John waved his hand, and a 1940 Rolls-Royce Phantom III Limousine drove up. Judy stood there with her mouth open, unable to speak until John said, "Honey, close your mouth and say something." Judy said, "Honey, how did you do this? What is this? When did you do this?"

John smiled, laughed, and said, "I am so happy you liked everything tonight. I wanted everything to be perfect for you because you are the perfect person for me. I love you, sweetie," and kissed her. She looked at him and said, "Well, I guess our secret is out." In the coming years, this evening at JJ's will be a tale told and retold, a story of love found, a question asked, and the magic that unfolds when two hearts choose to beat as one.

Judy's eyes are still rimmed in the delicate traces of joyful tears, with the luminance that only love can show. She turned to John, her voice a whisper brimming with excitement, "Do you think we could…? I have to show Kathy!" John's heart throbbed in his chest; the thrill of their engagement was evident in every glance they shared. He nibbled on his lower lip, considering, before gesturing towards the front of the limo. "Let's ask David if he has time to swing by."

"David?" Judy inquired, her voice bubbling with anticipation as she leaned towards the partition. The limo driver adjusted his rearview mirror, his eyes meeting Judy's gaze. "Yes, Ms. Judy, where to?" She rattled off directions with the certainty of someone who had traveled that path a thousand times before. Each word told the story of a deep and genuine friendship, a bond forged in shared secrets and sisterly love. With a nod, David steered the limousine back onto the street, its powerful engine purring like a contented cat. The journey was short, but each second seemed to stretch into eternity, filled with thoughts of future promises and heartfelt possibilities.

It was early evening when John and Judy's limousine stopped before the ivy-clad entrance to Judy's closest confidante, Kathy's apartment. Upon arrival, Judy hurried to the apartment, her hand clasped in John's as they approached Kathy's door. Through the peephole, Kathy caught sight of the unmistakable outline of her friend's beaming face. Her heart skipped a beat; Judy had been crying, a mix of excitement and concern flooding her senses. The door swung open, and Judy wasted not a second. "Kathy, can we talk? There is something I need to tell you and show you!" Kathy's worry continued at the sight of Judy, her eyes brimming with unshed tears. They retreated to the sanctuary of Kathy's bedroom, a space filled with the echoes of past heart-to-hearts and laughter.

John, momentarily left in the gentle hum of Kathy's living room, could only imagine the scene unfolding as the telltale sounds of elation reached his ears, the sound of joyous shrieks and the unmistakable cadence of happy sobs. The walls of that apartment, thick with the history that only years of friendship could build, reverberated with the sound of a new life beginning. Judy's engagement to John, a man who cherished her very essence, was more than just a union of two people; it was a union of two hearts and two souls. After a time that seemed forever, the bedroom door opened once more. Judy and Kathy appeared, their eyes glistening with the tears of shared happiness, her hand clutching Kathy's as they floated back towards John. Kathy, finally seeing John, approached him with the warmth of a sister. Her congratulations came as a heartfelt embrace, a blessing upon the beginning of John and Judy's lifelong journey together.

John's heart raced as he approached Kathy, anticipating what was to come, causing his palms to sweat. "Kathy, may I borrow your phone? I need to call Sarah," he said, his voice tinged with a nervous excitement he could not entirely conceal. Sensing the urgency of his request, Kathy nodded and quickly recited Sarah's number. John's voice stumbled slightly as he gave the operator the number, the gravity of his impending confession weighing heavily on him. The line connected, and Sarah's familiar voice filled his ear. "Hello, Sarah, this is John. Could I possibly come over for a quick word?" he inquired, hoping his voice did not betray the fluttering in his chest. Sarah's response was warm and inviting despite her being amid entertaining guests. "Of course, John. Come on over. We'll talk in the study." John and Judy left Kathy's apartment and took the Limousine to Sarah's house. With Judy by his side, John walked up to Sarah's house, each step feeling more monumental than the last. They knocked, and time seemed to crawl as they awaited Sarah's response. The door swung open, and Sarah's smile was like a beacon guiding them into the warmth of her home. "Come in. The study will give us the privacy we need," she said, her voice a soothing melody amidst the confusion of his thoughts.

Sarah excused herself from her guests, and as they settled into the quiet sanctuary of the study, John's mind was a whirlwind of emotion. He opened his mouth to speak, but the words tangled on his tongue, his message obscured by a maze of nerves. Sarah's eyes twinkled with a knowing gaze. "John, you're talking in circles. It is as if there is something you are trying to say but cannot find the words. Perhaps you'd find your starting point if you started with Judy and I got engaged tonight." John's eyes widened in shock. "How did you know that's what I was going to say?" he stammered, the surprise etching across his face.

Sarah's laughter was like music, light and free. "John, for years, there wasn't much that happened in this town that your father and I didn't know about. I am happy for you both. I knew it would happen; it was only a matter of time." John's tension melted away, replaced by a profound sense of relief and joy. He and Judy exchanged a look of shared pleasure, their future together now unfolding like the petals of a blooming rose. Sarah's blessing was the final piece they needed, the perfect end to a day that marked the start of their lifelong journey together.

As Judy and John returned to the limo and headed back to the mansion, Judy said, "Honey, we need to go back to Mountain Home and tell my father and mother. I sure do not want them to find out from someone else. When do you think we could go? I will call them and let them know. I know driving there will be a long day, but I do not want to do it over the phone."

John smiled and said, "Well, my soon-to-be wife and my private little pilot, would you like to fly us to Mountain Home and maybe have your dad pick us up at the airport?" "Yes," Judy said, "I would love to do that, and it would tickle my dad to see his daughter fly in on a Twin Beech. And I will not tell him that I am the pilot; when he finds out, he will be so happy."

John said, "Ask him if Thursday would be okay; we can work at the store on Monday, Tuesday, and Wednesday to get most of the things we need to do, and then fly out Thursday morning and be there in about 45 minutes to an hour on the plane." We can then fly back late Thursday afternoon."

"I think that's a great idea, honey; I'll call them when we get home," said Judy. At that point, John smiled big, and Judy said, "Why are you smiling so big, honey?" John said, "Because I love it when you say when we get home." Judy just smiled and grinned with that shy little smile that made John's heart race with love.

The mansion's lights loomed over them as John and Judy stepped through its massive doors, the weight of the day's journey settling into a quiet, relaxing moment. With its sprawling space and plush furnishings, the main bedroom offered a sanctuary to refresh and regroup. With practiced ease, they moved about the room, each lost in their thoughts until they found themselves sitting side by side on the bed, the softness of the mattress a welcome reprieve.

John turned to Judy, his eyes searching hers for any hint of hesitation. "Are you sure before we call your father and set this up for Thursday?" he asked, his voice a mix of hope and nervousness. Judy's response was a smile, shy and tender, the kind that never failed to disarm him, to remind him of the depth of their connection. "Honey, I am surer about us getting married than anything I have ever done," she assured him, whispering between them.

Then, as if to seal her promise, she kissed him, a kiss that spoke of shared dreams and whispered promises, a kiss that had become their signature. It was a passion that had grown familiar yet remained as intoxicating as when their lips had first met. They lay back on the bed, allowing the playfulness of their affection to envelop them in intimacy, their kisses a prelude to the life they were about to begin together.

After a few stolen moments, they composed themselves, smoothing out the wrinkles in their clothes with hands that still trembled from the touch of the other. Hand in hand, they made their way downstairs, their hearts racing in anticipation of the call that would set the wheels of their future in motion. Judy approached the phone with confidence, but butterflies fluttered in her stomach. "Operator, could you get me Mountain Home, Arkansas, for Mr. William Martin?" she requested with a practiced ease. The line crackled to life, and soon, the familiar voice of her father filled the room. "Hey, Daddy, how are you doing? Yes, sir, doing good. Look, Daddy, I only have a few minutes. I am flying to Mountain Home this Thursday and wondered if you could pick us up at about 10:00 Thursday morning?" Judy's words tumbled out in a rush of excitement and urgency. "I'll be glad to, sweetie. Why an airplane? You said 'us'. Who is coming with you?" Mr. Martin's voice was a mix of curiosity and surprise. Judy hesitated, the enormity of what she was about to reveal making her heart skip a beat. "Sorry, Daddy, all the change I have. Gotta go. Love you, see you Thursday." The line went dead, leaving Mr. Martin with more questions than answers.

"Who was that?" Mrs. Martin inquired, her voice laced with curiosity. "It was Judy," he replied, the confusion evident in his tone. "What did Judy want?" Mrs. Martin pressed, her interest piqued. "I don't know," he admitted, the mystery of the conversation hanging in the air between them. "Who's coming with her?" she asked, her maternal instincts sensing the importance of this unknown guest. "I don't know," Mr. Martin repeated, a sense of wonder taking hold. "She just said she would see us Thursday morning, about 10:00, at the airport." Mrs. Martin said, "I wonder if it is a young man she is bringing home for us to meet. She has never brought a young man home for us to meet. What do you think?" Mr. Martin said, "I don't know." Then Mrs. Martin said, "Well, if it is, " Then Mr. Martin cut her off and said, "Honey, let it go. We will have to wait till Thursday morning and see."

As the Martins pondered the cryptic call, Judy and John shared a knowing glance, their secret safe for just a few more days. As the grandfather clock in the hall chimed the half-hour past ten, an air of contented anticipation hovered within the grand walls of the mansion. The evening had been a whirlwind of joyous announcements and heartfelt congratulations, and now John and Judy, the soon-to-be-wed couple, found themselves in the embrace of a rare, quiet moment.

"Well, honey," John began, his voice a soft baritone in the dimly lit corridor, "we have told everyone that we need to let them know we're getting married." What do we do now? I'm not quite ready for bed yet." Judy's eyes sparkled with mischief and warmth. "Why don't we sit down in the family room of the mansion and watch a little TV? We have not even been in the family room. What do you think about that?"

John's heart swelled with affection for this woman who, with her simple suggestions, could make an ordinary evening feel like an adventure. "Let's try it out and just crash and relax before bed." The family room awaited them, a testament to luxury and comfort with its plush sofas and richly woven rugs. Yet, despite the richness, a sense of home filled the space. They were trying to navigate the unfamiliar territory of the television set when Molly, the ever-attentive housekeeper, appeared like a fairy godmother, ready to grant their unspoken wishes.

"Can I help with the TV?" Molly offered a gentle voice of help in the quiet room. With her guidance, the once-silent screen came to life, flickering images dancing across its surface as they settled into the cushions, a world of entertainment at their fingertips.

"Ms. Judy, may I get you and Mr. John something to drink?" Molly inquired about her presence as a comfort in the daily changes in their lives. Judy's smile was one of gratitude. "Thank you, Molly. How about a glass of red wine for me and a beer for John? Will that be okay?" "I'll bring it right out, Ms. Judy."

John returned from a brief visit to the restroom to find Judy nestled into the crook of the sofa, her face alight with the soft glow of the television. He slipped beside her, his arm finding its familiar place around her shoulders. They had just begun to relax and snuggle close when Molly reappeared, a tray of drinks balanced expertly in her hands. "Your wine, Ms. Judy, your beer, Mr. John," she announced, placing the tray before them with the grace of a seasoned hostess. "Thank you, Molly," they chimed in unison, their voices harmonizing in the quiet room. "Will you need anything else, Ms. Judy?" "No, thank you, Molly," Judy replied, her heart full of the simple joy the evening had brought them. "Yes, ma'am. If you don't need anything else, I will retire now." "Thank you, Molly. Have a good evening," Judy called after the retreating figure of their housekeeper, her words carrying the weight of their sincere appreciation.

John turned to Judy, his gaze soft and full of admiration. "Thank you, honey. You think of everything." And as they settled back into the family room, the television softly playing in the background, they knew this was just the beginning. It awaited them a lifetime of shared moments, each to be cherished and a testament to their love. With its beauty and history, the Jenkins mansion now served as the backdrop to their unfolding romance, a story they would write together, each day bringing a new page filled with love and laughter.

John and Judy cuddled on the plush sofa and watched the Geographically Speaking show, an American travel series. They cuddled, sipped their wine and beer, and relaxed more than they had in a long time. After they finished their drinks, Judy took the glasses to the kitchen, washed them, and placed them on a towel to dry overnight. She returned to the family room and said, "Honey, I'm ready to go to bed; we'll have a big day tomorrow, picking up where we left off in our office and answering many questions about our engagement." We met on the train in Mountain Home, Arkansas. Before we left the station. So, we knew each other in Mountain Home before we came to Poplar Bluff, ok?" "That's okay with me, sweetie, but why?" John said. With a tear in her eye, she said, "John, I do not want anybody talking about me behind my back. You deserve a wonderful and upstanding wife, and I do not want people to think that" she teared up more now, "I am just a blond bimbo slut chasing you for your money. I could not take that."

John hugged her tightly and said, "I love you more than ever. We knew each other for over ten months in Mountain Home before I knew I had an inheritance." She smiled at John, laid her head on his shoulder, and let the tears flow. She was so happy, and so was John. They continued to watch TV for a while until John said, "Honey, wake up. Let's go to bed." They turned off everything in the family room and went to the main bedroom. John sat on the bedroom sofa to remove his shoes while Judy went to the bathroom to get ready for bed. John had turned off the lights, and the dim lights from outside served as the room's nightlight. She exited the room and stood by the bed, letting her robe slide to the floor. The light cast a slight glow on her perfect body, and she slid under the covers as John went to change for bed. In a few minutes, he came out, and at the bedside, he placed his robe on a chair near the bed and turned to face the bed. The glow of the outside light told Judy that he was the perfect man, and they would be married. John slid under the cover beside Judy and held her for a long time. He kissed her passionately and held her until they fell asleep.

As Judy rolled over and looked at the clock, her heart started pounding with the urgency of the morning. "Honey, wake up, wake up, honey, it's 7 A.M., and we have one hour to get ready and get to work!" Her voice was a blend of excitement and alarm that jolted John from his slumber as if he had been shocked. Judy said, "Sorry, honey, if we're going to make it, we're both going to have to get dressed at the same time in the bathroom." Her words stumbled over each other like playful puppies. John's reply was a chuckle, rich and warm as freshly brewed coffee. "Ok, honey, we just have to do what we have to do. Love you," and with that, he kissed her lips. It was not their usual lingering embrace, but in that swift peck was a promise of more to come, a testament to the love that thrived even when time was a luxury they could not afford. In a flurry of sheets and limbs, no time for bath robes, they leaped from the bed, their pulse racing with the sudden rush of adrenaline and noticeable shy glances at each other. They collided in the bathroom, a dance of toothpaste, ties, stockings, and shirts. Their laughter mingled with the steam from the shower, a symphony of joy in the chaos of the morning rush.

They ran down the stairs, a duet of urgency and determination, when Molly, the ever-observant housekeeper, met them with a smile as bright as the morning sun. "Here, I thought you might be running late, so I made you two egg sandwiches each. Now you can go." Her hands extended the precious gift of energy, the fuel for their day.

With a chorus of thanks, John and Judy snatched the sandwiches and darted to the car, their movements a ballet of efficiency. "Go to your door; I'll open my door this morning," Judy declared, her tone playfully commanding as they executed their routine with a new twist. The engine roared to life, and they sped down the road, the world outside their window a blur of winter's last stand. They weaved through the streets of the waking city, each traffic light a blessing, ushering them onward.

As they pulled up to JR's department store, the clock granted them a gracious reprieve; they had ten minutes to spare. They smiled, flirted, and laughed as they walked up to the third floor where their offices were. They shared a final, fleeting kiss, a seal on the promise of the coming evening. "See you somewhere sometime today; love you," John whispered, his words a vow. With a nod and a smile, Judy watched him stride toward his office, the captain of his ship, before she turned to face her day, the queen of her realm.

The morning sun streamed through the tall windows of JR's department store, casting a warm glow over the polished floors and the bustling employees preparing for the day. John Jenkins, the new owner of the iconic establishment, strode confidently through the halls, his steps echoing with the promise of a fresh start. As he passed through Kathy's office, his voice was a cheerful baritone, "Good morning, Kathy; hope you had a good weekend."

Kathy, ever the professional, looked up from her typewriter with a smile that reached her eyes. "I had a great weekend, Mr. Jenkins," she said. The formality in her tone was a testament to her respect for the structure that kept the store running like a well-oiled machine.

John paused, a playful glint in his eye, and took a few steps back. "Kathy, you were the first person Judy and I told that we were engaged." Don't you think you could call me John?" His request was more of a friendly nudge, a hope to bridge the gap that titles often create.

"No, sir," Kathy replied firmly yet kindly. "At work, there has to be a hierarchy for everything to flow correctly, and show respect for that hierarchy chain. That's very important; no company can exist, much less be successful, without a chain of command, just like the military. Her conviction was clear, and John could not help but respect her dedication to the principles that made JR's department store its institution.

Meanwhile, Judy, John's radiant fiancée, entered her new domain excitedly and apprehensively. Then, Sarah, the wise veteran of the store, appeared with a greeting that was both a welcome and a reassurance: "Good morning, Ms. Jenkins; I just thought I'd try it and see how it sounds. It sounds great to me."

Judy's laughter mingled with the morning air, a sound of pure joy, yet her words carried the weight of uncertainty. "Thank you, Sarah. I hope we are doing the right thing. I don't know if working with your husband is the right thing to do."

Sarah's laugh was uplifting to Judy. "Judy, John Sr., and I were not married, but everyone knew how we were, and it was as if we were married in everyone's eyes. You will call him John as any wife or fiancée would, and he will call you Judy, as it should be."

Judy's smile reflected her gratitude as she confided in Sarah about their upcoming trip to Mountain Home, Arkansas, to share their joyous news with her parents. Sarah's advice was a treasure trove of experience, reminding Judy that being a partner in life and business meant supporting and guiding each other through the storms and celebrations.

As Sarah embraced her, Judy felt a surge of confidence. She was the woman John deserved, the woman he had chosen to stand by his side. Sarah's words confirmed what Judy's heart already knew, and she was already the person she aspired to be, a beacon of love and support for the man she loved. A new day was beginning in the heart of JR's department store amidst the hum of activity and the scent of fresh merchandise. Hand in hand, John and Judy were not just business owners; they were the custodians of a legacy. With their union, the store's foundation was more vital than ever, a testament to the power of love, respect, and partnership.

The air was alive with enthusiasm as the doors opened to welcome the day's customers. John and Judy, alongside their dedicated team, were ready to usher in an era of prosperity and romance woven into the fabric of JR's department store. The future was bright, and it was theirs to write together.

On January 2, 1947, John and Judy flew on John's Twin Beech airplane from Poplar Bluff, Missouri, to Mountain Home, Arkansas, to visit her parents and inform them that they were getting married. As they board John's plane, they are excited that the flight time is about an hour compared to the eight hours it would take to drive. They got airborne and leveled out, and Judy activated the autopilot. With his charmingly boyish grin, John could not help but marvel at Judy's poise as she controlled the aircraft. She was a vision, her eyes bright with the same spark that had ignited his love for her. The autopilot hummed softly, a lullaby for the couple as they sipped coffee and shared laughter, the kind that bubbled up from a well of shared secrets and dreams.

They can get up, move around the plane, and talk to each other as long as Judy remains close to the cockpit in case the autopilot system fails. Judy gets the coffee out and pours another cup for both. They talk and laugh and drink their coffee, and then they get up to sit in the cockpit seats. They start walking to the cockpit seats, and then, as if drawn by an unseen magnet, they find themselves in an embrace, a kiss that bridges the gap between the busy days behind them and today. They have been so busy the last few days that they seem to have less time for each other. They kissed for a few minutes and then went to the cockpit. Judy sat in the pilot's seat, and John sat in the copilot's.

The timing was pretty good. About ten minutes after they sat down, they had to start descending and lining up for the runway at Mountain Home. Judy began calling into the airport radio and following the standard procedures for landing. The radio crackled to life, and Judy's confident and clear voice filled the control tower. On the ground, her parents' faces lit up with pride and wonder as they recognized their daughter's voice, a pilot, a woman charting her course. Mr. Martin told his wife that the voice she heard was Judy's, and she was piloting the plane. The plane touched down with the grace of a swan landing on a still lake, and as the engines moved to an idle, so did the anticipation in Judy's heart. After they landed and Judy parked the plane, as the ground crew directed her, she went through the shutdown procedures and opened the door. She looked at a scene that felt like something out of a storybook. She saw her father beaming with pride, her mother's eyes shimmering with unshed tears. Judy stepped out, with John right behind her. Judy ran straight to her father, hugging him, and said, "Daddy, did you hear me as I was bringing the twin beech in?" Her father, smiling big, said, "Yes, we did, sweetie, yes, we did."

Then Judy went to her mother and said, "Mom, I have missed you so much." However, life has a way of weaving the unexpected into the fabric of our stories, and the recognition that sparked between John and Judy's father was a twist that none could have expected. "Mom, Dad, I'd like to introduce someone to y'all. John, come up here."

But before Judy could introduce them, Mr. Martin said, holding his hand out to shake John's hand, "Hello, Sgt. Jenkins." John said, "Hello, Colonel Martin." Mr. Martin said, "I was very sorry to hear about your mother, John. I wanted to come to the funeral, but I was just unable to at the time." John said, "I understand, Colonel but thank you for the flowers." Judy looked so puzzled that she did not know what to say. She finally said, "Would someone like to tell me what's happening here?"

"Judy," her dad began to explain, "John was a gunner on my B-17 crew in Germany during the war. A lot of us owe him our lives. Ack Ack hit us hard on a mission one day, and the landing gear was stuck. Someone needed to climb down the landing gear and get it unstuck. Not enough room for a parachute, straps, or safety lines. One and only one slip, and you fall to the ground. John was awarded the Congressional Medal of Honor for his heroism." Mr. Martin wiped a tear from his eye and gave him a salute, and John returned the salute, which is the proper greeting for anyone who has won the Medal of Honor. Mr. Martin said, "I'm sorry, Judy, I didn't mean to steal your thunder." What did you want to tell us?"

Judy said, "Well, I don't know where to start after that; I was going to introduce my boyfriend to y'all, but it looks like there's no need to do that." Mr. Martin and his wife greeted John with a big smile and said, "We have a lunch table ready here at the Pilots Club, so let's go eat." Judy said, "Wait a minute, Daddy, there's more." Mr. Martin turned with a puzzled look and said, "I'm sorry, sweetie, what else did you want to tell us?" Judy said, "Daddy and Mom, this is John Roberts Jenkins, my fiancée. We got engaged Sunday, and I wanted to be here with you when I told y'all." Mr. Martin looked at John and said, "John, I owe you my life, but this is my daughter about whom we are talking. First, you had better not ever mistreat her; if you do, you will discover how mean an old man can be. Second thing, are you financially able to take care of her?" John said, "I promise, sir, I will never do anything to hurt her in any way. And yes, sir, I can financially provide her with a comfortable lifestyle. Sir, she already works for me." Mr. Martin looked at Judy and said, "Judy, I thought you were going to work at that big department store called JR's?" "I do, Daddy," she said. "John owns JR's Department Store, and the plane is his, too, but I get to fly it. Daddy, let's talk about it over lunch, ok?"

Mr. Martin said, "Ok, let's eat lunch; welcome to the family, John," as they shook hands. The lunch that followed was a feast not just of food but of stories, laughter, and joy from knowing you are exactly where you belong. As the talk continued, Mr. Martin said, "Judy, let's you and me walk outside for a minute." "Yes, sir." Standing up, she kissed John and said, "We'll be back in a minute, honey."

Mrs. Martin said, "John, you need to know something if you haven't figured it out." Judy is a daddy's little girl, even after graduating from college. There is nothing in this world that he would not do for her. He is not trying to change her mind; he wants to ensure she wants this. When he went off to war, it almost broke her heart not to be able to talk to him every day. When she left for Poplar Bluff, it almost broke his heart until I finally convinced him that this had to happen; he had to let her go. It has not been easy, but he has accepted it. He is just making sure."

Mr. Martin and Judy walked out on the restaurant balcony, where guests can watch the planes taking off and landing. For people who loved to fly, it was a beautiful sight. Mr. Martin said, "Sweetie, do you love him? Do you love him so much that you miss him, and it hurts when he leaves?" "Yes, sir, every time he drops me off at Kathy's apartment, I cry for a little while. I do love him so, Daddy."

Mr. Martin said, "Judy, this is a big step; all I have ever wanted is to protect you. That's why I have always closely watched you and your brothers. However, when you decided to move to Poplar Bluff, Missouri, and live with Kathy for a while, I tried to convince you not to. But your mother finally got me to understand that I had to let go sooner or later, and this was the time. That was the hardest thing I ever had to do."

"I know, Daddy," Judy said. "It was hard for me to; I have always known you would be there if I stumbled or fell. But this time, I had to go and test myself; I had to know what I was made of and if I could make it on my own. When I moved to Poplar Bluff, I was completely on my own. No one to pick me up or to lean on. Daddy, there is one more thing. I trust John with my life and want to tell you I have moved in with him." Mr. Martin said, "Judy, I don't like this at all; I just don't like this." "Daddy, stop, please stop and listen." "Okay, sweetie, I'm sorry. I know I need to listen more before I start talking. That is what your mother has been telling me lately."

"Well," Judy started, "for once, Mother is right. Daddy, I moved in with John about a week ago, and he made a promise to me that he would never try to do anything sexual until I point-blank told him I was ready. He even said I must say it and not just give a sign. He said that way, he would not misunderstand what I meant in any way. And, Daddy, he has been perfect to me every single day. If I wake up in the morning before him, I lie there and watch him breathe, his chest going up and down; it makes me so happy that I get tears in my eyes." Judy's father said, "Okay, it sounds like you have things covered without my help. Is his house big enough to hold all your stuff? You know, you have a lot of stuff, cheerleading trophies, softball trophies, and many other things." Judy said, "Well, that brings me to the rest of the things I want to tell you." Mr. Martin said, "You're not going to tell me that he needs money to help his business, are you?" "Daddy, you're talking." "Ok, I will hush," he said. Judy continued, "Here is a picture of his house." Judy pulled out a beautiful eight-by-ten picture of the mansion. "That is beautiful. Is it all his, or is it shared with others?" "No, sir," Judy said. "It is all his; it is huge. I do not even know how many bedrooms it has. Five people work at the mansion, which we call it, to keep it up and going. One person oversees everything, then two groundskeepers and two housekeepers. One housekeeper and one groundskeeper are husband and wife and live in the mansion. My boss and I also handle all the bookkeeping for the department store, including his personal books. Daddy, your soon-to-be son-in-law is a multi-millionaire." "Well, I'm glad he can care for you, but it's not about the money. Does he love you as much as you love him?" "Yes, sir, even more if that is possible. And, Daddy, I will always be Daddy's little girl. Just like I always have been."

Mr. Martin and Judy walked back into the restaurant and sat with everyone. As they sat down, he leaned over to Judy and said, "Is it ok to announce the engagement here at the pilot restaurant lounge with a toast?" "Yes, sir, we would be honored." Judy then leaned over to John and told him what was about to happen, and she said, "If you were toasted here, you were accepted." Mr. Martin stood up, started tapping his glass with his spoon, and said, "May I have your attention, please?" Everyone stopped and looked at him. "Many of you here know my daughter, Judy; it is my honor and pleasure today to introduce my daughter's boyfriend, and soon-to-be my son-in-law, John Jenkins." Everyone started to clap, and when the clapping stopped. "I also want you to know about my soon-to-be son-in-law, who served with me as a gunner on my B-17 over Germany. Also, I want you to know that on one flight, we were hit with some Ack-Ack and were going down, but due to some extremely heroic actions, this young man saved the plane and its crew. And for that, he was awarded the Congressional Medal of Honor." Many prior service personnel in the restaurant were familiar with the protocol of such an honor; they all stood up and saluted John, while the rest stood up and started clapping. John stood up, returned the salute, and nodded his head. He leaned over to Judy and said, "I wasn't expecting that." Judy said, "Well, my father believes in protocol. He has accepted you and us to be married; otherwise, he would never have toasted you. That is how much the toast means here." As they sat amidst the clinking of glasses and the murmur of conversation, John and Judy knew this was just the beginning. It was about 2 p.m., and it was time for Judy and John to leave for home in Poplar Bluff. They hugged everyone, said their goodbyes, and boarded the plane. Judy performed all her regular preflight checks, yelled out the window, and said, "Clear prop," before smiling at her father as she started both engines. She received clearance from the tower to taxi, opened the small window on the side of the cockpit, and waved at her father; he gave her their secret hand signal, telling her to call when she landed. She sent him a message to let him know that she would call.

Judy and John are in their Twin Beech airplane headed back to Poplar Bluff after telling her parents they are getting married. Judy, the pilot, is flying the course, so she turns on the autopilot. She and John are talking, and she tells John that she also told her father they were living together. He was unhappy but finally accepted that we loved each other. And I assured him we do. John, one more thing: I told him we have moved in together. She watched him to see how he would react, but no reaction. She began to get nervous, and then she got scared and started to cry. Judy knew she had to focus on landing the plane; she thought of her father and how distracted he must have been on some of his missions over Germany. She kept telling herself to focus until she had dried up her tears and gotten her mind back on the plane. She flew on to Poplar Bluff with no conversation and landed perfectly. John smiled and said Perfect landing. As John spoke with Bill about the hangar and other aspects of the airport, Judy finished her logbook entries and headed to the car to wait.

John returned to the car and said, "Hey, sweetie, I didn't know you were in the car." Judy said. "Can we just go to the mansion, please?" John could not understand what was happening; he said, "Honey, what's wrong?" She said, "Please, let's go." So, John drove a few minutes from the airport to the mansion. Judy got out, went in, went to the bedroom, and locked the door. When John reached the door, he tried to get Judy to open it, but she would not. He could hear her crying, but didn't know if he had done something wrong. He went downstairs and called Kathy. "Kathy, this is John; sorry to bother you. Judy and I have just returned from Mountain Home. Judy is in the bedroom with the door locked, and she is crying. I must have done something, but I have no clue what it is. She will not open the door and will not talk to me. Can you come over and see if you can figure out what's upsetting her? Thanks, Kathy."

Kathy arrived at the mansion about ten minutes later, and John met her at the door. "Please talk to her; this is breaking my heart to have hurt her somehow. I don't know what I've done to hurt her so I don't know how to fix it." Kathy went to the bedroom door and knocked. Judy said, "Just call me a taxi; I will pack and leave." Then Kathy said, "Judy, it's Kathy; please open the door." Judy said, "Is he out there?" Kathy said, "No," as she motioned for John to go downstairs. Judy opened the door, and Kathy went in; she then locked the door again. "Judy, why are you packing?" Judy said, "He doesn't want me here." "How do you know? What made you think he doesn't want you?" said Kathy. Judy started talking, but Kathy stopped her; she was crying so much that Kathy could not understand her. Kathy said, "Judy, Judy, Judy, please come over here and sit on the sofa and talk to me. We have been best friends for years. We talked about every boyfriend we have ever had, what we did on our dates, and Judy, we even talked about how they all kissed. Now, calm down and come sit beside me."

Judy approached the sofa and sat, trying to calm down, but it was hard. Judy said, still crying, "I gave him my heart, and I held back nothing. I loved him more than my own life; I would have given my life for him. But he does not want me anymore. We have been living together for several days now, and we have never had sex. I am not ready for that yet, and he said he was fine with that until I was ready, but that is not enough for him anymore, and he does not want me anymore." Kathy had difficulty following Judy, but she thought she understood. "What did he say?" "When we left Mountain Home, we talked a few minutes, and then I had to take off, and he had just told Daddy he would never hurt me, and now look at me." OK, Kathy asked what he said when you all talked on the plane after takeoff. Judy said, "Nothing."

Kathy looked at her and said, "Judy, what did he say that upsets you?" "Nothing, I just told you. I sat there for about ten minutes and opened my heart to him, even telling him that I had told Daddy that I had moved in with him. You know, my daddy, Kathy, that was not easy for me to do." Kathy said, "Yes, I know your daddy, and I will bet that was extremely hard to do. I'm glad it was not me telling him. That took a lot of guts to do that, Judy. But what did he say?"

"Nothing, like I said. After everything I said and told him I wanted to do, some of which was a little naughty, he did not speak to me or say a word. I was hurt and so embarrassed. I cannot believe it." "OK, I will be right back. Just sit here, and please, Judy, do not lock the door." "OK." Kathy went downstairs to see John; when John saw her, he jumped up and ran to her. "What is wrong? How do I fix it?" "Well," Kathy said, "on the way back, after y'all were leveled out and on autopilot, Judy started talking to you. She said some things that may have been a little naughty, and you did not respond. Then she told you about how she had told her father that she had moved in with you, and he hit the ceiling. And if you knew her father the way I do, you would know that was a mild statement she said. But she stood her ground and would not let her daddy interfere in any way; she loved you, and that was how it would be. After all that, you would not even acknowledge what she was saying. So now she believes that you think she is a terrible person and a slut. It is breaking her heart; she said she gave you her heart, all of it, and left herself wide open for you to come into her heart. I know some of this does not make sense, John; she is distraught."

John said, "Kathy, I never heard a word she said, so there is nothing there for me to judge her about. Next, I love her, and I would never judge her in the first place. Kathy, one thing you and she did not know about me until I met her father today is that I was in the Army Air Corps during the war. I served on the same B-17 airplane crew as her father. I did not know that until we saw each other in Mountain Home, on one of our flights with Colonel Martin, Judy's father, we were hit by a bomb that damaged our plane, and I was struck on the left side of my head with flying metal and hurt very badly. I said all that to tell you this: it's hard for people to notice because I've adjusted to it very well. That is, I am deaf on the left side. I have learned to adjust how I listen, but I struggle to hear on a plane or in a place with a lot of background noise. So, anything that was said in the airplane on the left side, I could not hear." Kathy returns to Judy's room, knocks on the door, and opens it. Kathy goes in, and Judy is sitting on the bed. She sits down next to Judy, and Judy asks quickly, "Well, does he hate me?" Kathy said, "No, he loves you more now than before. He was trying to hold back the tears in his eyes like a man sometimes does when he is about to cry, but does not want anyone to know it." Judy says, "Yes, I understand; if they just let a few tears drop, it would be much easier on everybody."

Kathy told Judy, "Now that I have let him know what's going on, he has a problem that he didn't want you to know about, and he is embarrassed and now ashamed to see you." Judy said, "Oh no, I didn't mean to hurt him in any way; tell him I'm sorry; I don't want to upset him." Kathy said, "Let me tell you the rest of what he told me. He told me that he was in the Air Corps with your father, and their plane was hit with a bomb. The explosion did a lot of damage to the left side of his head when he was hit with something, and he was hurt badly. He completely lost his hearing on the left side, but he learned to adjust to normal conversation. However, he cannot hear anything from the left in a noisy situation. He never heard you say anything after the flight took off. He thought you were talking to the towers or other traffic pattern people and did not want to get in your way. He knew if he asked a question, he could not hear the answer, which might get you sidetracked and not pay attention to what you needed to do."

Judy said, "Did he tell you everything about that flight with my dad?" "That's all," Kathy said. Judy continued, "He's being very modest; according to Dad, he did a superheroic deed, and everyone on board believed he would not live through the task he volunteered to do, but he managed to live through it. He saved the B-17 plane and all its crew, and for this heroic deed, he was awarded the Congressional Medal of Honor; I am so proud of him. I did not know he was hurt so bad; I need to go to him." With that, Judy ran down the stairs, calling him, "Honey, I am so sorry; I did not know you were hurt like that. Are you okay? What can I do to help you?" John said, "I'm fine; the main thing is, are you ok? I don't want you to get hurt in any way." Judy said, "No, honey, this is all my fault; I should have talked to you first to ensure what was happening. Please forgive me."

John said, "We just had our first argument and learned from it. Let's just let it all go and move on, ok?" Judy said, "Ok with me, my little honey bunch. How about you, Kathy?" Kathy said, "Oh my goodness, yes, me too." John said, "Thank you, Kathy; we would like to repay you with dinner tonight; it's not late, just a little after 5

P.M." Kathy said she couldn't tonight, but maybe another night. With that, Judy and John walked her to the door and said good night. Judy realized she needed to call her father and tell him they were home safe. She asked John if it would be okay, and John said, "Sure, honey, you don't need my permission to use the phone, whether it's local or long-distance." She picked up the phone and said, "Operator, could I have Mountain Home, Arkansas, please, for Mr. William Martin?" The phone began to ring, and then. "Hey, Daddy, I just wanted to let you know we've arrived home safely and are relaxing now; we'll eat shortly. I love you too, Daddy. Tell Mom I love her, too. Yes, sir, I suppose you can tell my brothers that I love them, too. Bye."

Later that night, John and Judy spent the evening lounging on the sofa, cuddling with each other, and watching TV. At about 9 P.M., Judy said, "Honey, tomorrow is Friday, and we were off yesterday and today, we may be a little busy tomorrow." We probably need to go to bed to get some rest." John said, "I think so, too, honey." With that, they went to their room and went to bed. They snuggled up close, kissed, and talked for a little while. Judy said, "Well, honey, when do you think we should get married?" John said, "How about tomorrow morning? We can get married, and then we can start our life together." Judy laughed, saying, "I wish we could, but you know we can't do that." John said, "Colonel Martin, your dad, was like a father to me during the war, and he stayed connected after the war. I could never do any-thing that would disrespect him." "Ok, then, when would you like to make plans for it?" John said, "Let's talk to Sarah tomorrow morning and see when a good time for us would be to be away from the store." Judy smiled and said, "I like that idea, honey; Sarah will know better than anyone when we should be away from the store for a few days."

"Honey, I love lying my head on your shoulder when we are cud-dling, but I do not want to hurt the left side of your head or your ear. Is that ok?" Judy said, trying to make sure she was not hurting him in any way. "Honey," John said, "you are not hurting me in any way. That is part of why I did not want to tell anyone about my wounds. I do not want people to feel sorry for me or make a fuss about the Medal of Honor. Honey, I want you to love me for who I am, not for what I have been through." "Honey, I love you for who you are, and I will try not to fuss over you too much, but it will be hard. I am so proud of you and love you more tonight than this morning. How long were you in the hospital when your plane finally returned to the base?" "Several months, but let's talk about you and not me. Where do you want to get married? What day of the week should we get married?" said John.

Judy started talking about the wedding, and John smiled at her. She said, "What are you smiling so much about?" He said, "It makes me happy seeing you get into this so deeply." You started talking and just kept going." Judy smiled and said, "OK, I'll stop until tomorrow when we talk to Sarah." With that, they kissed again, hugged, cuddled, and slept.

<h1 style="text-align:center">17</h1>

<h1 style="text-align:center">The Wedding</h1>

John and Judy arrived at JR's Department Store at 8 a.m. on this cold day, January 3, 1947. As they exited the car, John said, "Honey, as soon as I finish with some quick work I need to do, I will come to Sarah's office. Does that sound ok with you?" Judy nodded with a big smile, her heart jumping with joy. "Should I call you Mr. Jenkins or John?" she teased, smiling with that shy little smile that always excited John. "Well," said John, "after the JJ's steak and seafood restaurant proposal, I think everyone knows we are engaged. Don't you think so?" "Yes, you're probably right, sweetie." They laughed as they entered the store and were about to go down the employee's hall and up to their office when several people stepped out from around the corner and started clapping and congratulating them. The happiness of those around them touched John and Judy. After about ten minutes, everyone went to work; following a brief celebration, they proceeded to the third floor to their respective offices.

"Love you, sweetie," John said, his smile showing how much he loved Judy. "Love you too, honey," Judy replied, her voice like a whisper as they parted ways. When Judy turned into her office, Sarah came out to Judy's office and said, "Good morning, soon-to-be newlywed. How are you this morning?" Judy looked at Sarah nervously and said, "Sarah, I am so scared right now; I don't know which way to turn."

What do I do now? I do not know where to start. John said he would come down here shortly so we could discuss the date with you and hear your thoughts.

Sarah smiled and said, "Judy, I am touched that you and John think enough of me to ask for my opinion. Regarding dates, please note that we are closed on Sundays, and January is typically our slowest month. However, we have been running for almost a year without anyone to help me out, and we can manage for a week or so while y'all take your honeymoon. You and John must remember, after y'all are married, every plan you make is normally planned around the store."

As John entered his office, he said, "Good morning, Kathy. Did you have a good first of January? Well, except for yesterday!" Kathy looked up at John and said, "Yes, I did, Mr. Jenkins. How was your evening?" He smiled and said, "It was a great evening; thank you so much for helping us. With everything you did for us last night, why can't you call me John?" Kathy said, "No, sir, never, not at work. By the way, Judy told me that you were awarded the Medal of Honor while flying with her father. Is that right?" John looked down and said, "Yes, but let's let that go, okay?" I am going to Sarah's office shortly to discuss the best time for our wedding date. What do you think?" Kathy explained, "January and Sunday are probably the best times. The store closes on Sunday, and January is normally the slowest time of the year."

"Thanks, Kathy. Please ask Sarah if she has time for me this morning." John said to Kathy as he walked into his office. Kathy walked to John's door and said, "Mr. Jenkins, Sarah said she was in Judy's office, talking to her about it." Come on, when you get ready." "Thanks, Kathy; I am headed that way now."

As John walked to the office where Judy and Sarah were waiting, he wondered, should we do this quickly or wait several months? John wanted to go ahead and get married; he was eager to start his life with Judy. "Good morning, Sarah," John said as he entered Sarah's office. "I am sure you and Judy have already discussed a wedding date. What are your thoughts?" Sarah said, "Well, January is normally the slowest time of the year, so I would say January is the best month, and Sunday is the best day since we are closed on Sunday." John said, "That's the same month I think we should get married." What do you think, Judy?" Judy smiled and said, "We should run to the courthouse now and get married." After gasping for a second, John said, "Well, that would be fine with me, honey; we would have to face your parents or, more directly, your father. I do not think we want to do that."

Judy said, "Well, the dates will be January 12th or January 19th." Those are the two Sundays in January that will work out. Sunday the 5th is a little too close to get things set up. I will call Daddy and Mom and see what date works for them." Judy picked up the phone and said, "Operator, can you please connect me to Mountain Home, Arkansas, for Mr. William Martin?" Thank you. I will hold. Good morning, Daddy! How are you this morning? Yes, sir, we are doing well." She covered the phone and whispered to John, "He's asking about you." Is Mom around? Can you get Mom to pick up the extension phone with you?"

Mr. Martin said, "Okay, sweetie. Mom is on the other phone." Mom said, "Hey, honey, I'm here." This must be important to get us both on the phone at the same time." Judy said, "It is, Mom; we're planning the wedding and have Sarah with us. She started the department store with John's father years ago. Sarah says hey to y'all. Anyway, we are trying to set the wedding date, and I'm sure you'll understand that we need to schedule it around the store now, as it's crucial for us. The slowest time of the year is January, which means the 5th, 12th, and 19th are the best days for us. What about your schedule?" Mr. and Mrs. Martin said, "Well, we have something at the church on the 19th, so it would have to be the 5th or 12th, and the 5th would be hard to get everything set up, so my plan would be the 12th. We can handle everything here with the church, preacher, catering, and all your friends. Mom and I will take care of everything here." Judy looked at John and said, "Honey, what do you think?" John said, "I think that's great, but what about you, Judy?" Judy said, "Well, I have already said we should go to the courthouse, get married, and return to work. But you said no." Mr. Martin said, "I agree with John, no, ma'am. I know it will be quick, but I want to walk you down the aisle. John is the 12th good for everyone there."

"Yes, sir," John said. "We all agree the 12th is the best." Mr. Martin said, "Okay, that's it. The day is set for the 12th at 2 P.M. That will give us time to finish anything after church, set up the church, and get everyone ready." Is that time ok with everyone?" Everyone said okay, and Judy said, "That's a confirmed date and time." Daddy, we will fly there on the morning of the 12th and may have as many as ten people on the plane. Can you possibly get transportation from the airport to the church?" "Yes, I can take care of that," Mr. Martin said. Judy continued, "Thank you, Daddy; I will talk more about other stuff in a day or two. Love you and Mom. Bye."

Judy hangs up the phone, looks at everyone with the biggest smile imaginable, and says, "I'm getting married, I'm getting married. I love you, honey," looking at John. Judy started out the door and said, "Be right back," and was off. John, smiling, said, "She's going to tell Kathy." Well, we have a lot to do here. Sarah, I think we can take the airplane first thing on Sunday morning. The pilot and copilot will be Judy, and you, Kathy, and I will occupy the two seats following them. The last eight seats will be for Uncle James, Aunt Jamie, and their family. Could you please contact them and find out if they plan to attend? They may not want to go that far; I understand if they don't. After all, they don't know me. If they do want to go, they can fly with us. If they are not going, you can offer the seats on the plane to anyone else you'd like. I want to get Mr. Thompson on there if we can."

Judy walked into Kathy's office and said, "January 12th at 2 P.M., I'm getting married." They both squealed and hugged each other, and both started talking at the same time. Then, Kathy said, "I will give you a bridal shower here in the conference room. It is going to be fun. We have been discussing this for years, and you are the first. I am so happy for you." It was about 5:30 P.M. on Friday. John and Judy decided to go home and have dinner at home tonight. As they drove home, they discussed what they wanted for dinner. They would ask Molly if she could fix hamburger steaks covered with Swiss cheese, sautéed mushrooms, sautéed onions, gravy, and fries. They decided to have a glass of wine and a beer after finishing dinner, sit in the family room, and watch a little TV before bed. When they got to the mansion, Molly met them in the family room to find out what they wanted for dinner that night. They told Molly what they wanted and said they were going upstairs to freshen up and would eat dinner in about an hour. It would be around 6:30. John and Judy went upstairs to shower.

As John was showering, Judy said, "Honey, I am hanging your clothes on the hook. I am hanging mine behind yours, so don't knock mine down when you get yours." John said, "Thank you, sweetie." Judy leaned over as he stuck his head out of the shower to kiss her. They had a long, wonderful kiss, and John said, "Would you like to wash my back for me?" Judy said, "Sure, give me your bath cloth, and I'll wash your back from out here." She smiled with that beautiful, shy smile that John loved so much. Judy washed his back quickly and said, "Okay, honey, here's your bath cloth. Hurry and finish so I can take a quick shower."

John and Judy descended the sweeping staircase to the small dining room for dinner. The night was filled with excitement, not just for the meal, but for the life they were about to start together. Molly, the mansion's cook, had outdone herself; the hamburger steaks were covered with Swiss cheese melted over the perfectly seasoned meat. Sautéed onions and mushrooms topped the meat, and the thick gravy was poured over the entire dish. The sauce added a unique flavor to the dish. The golden crisp fries were the ideal side dish to a hearty meal. Dinner was filled with joy, marked by flirting glances and soft smiles; the smiles told the story, and no words needed to be spoken. They enjoyed the dinner, not just because of the food but because of the moment, this precious time together before the wedding plans swept them up again.

After they had finished their meal, they went to the family room, where Molly brought a glass of wine for Judy and a beer for John. They cuddled on the couch while watching the news and had minimal discussion about the wedding. As the clock chimed the late hour, they went upstairs, hand in hand, a silent agreement that the day had been another beautiful time in their story. In the privacy of their bedroom, their eyes locked, emotion reflecting on one another, and they kissed; this kiss was a promise, a memory, and a dream all at once. It was a kiss that spoke of the past and the present and gave joy to the future. Slipping beneath the cool sheets, they wrapped themselves in each other's embrace, the outside world melting away until there was nothing but the warmth of their bodies. Whispers of the wedding filled the room, speaking of flowers, music, guests, and vows. And as the night deepened, their conversation trailed off, their breaths slowing, until they finally drifted into sleep; the love that had brought them together would carry them forward into the dawn of their new life.

The days they had left before the wedding went by in the blink of an eye. They had so much to do that it was a rush to finalize the wedding plans and ensure the store was taken care of. Sometimes, it seemed like a circus, with everything happening at once. But the day before, everything came together, and they were ready.

The soft morning light slipped through the curtains, painting everything in golden tones, notably John, the one Judy cherished most, as he slept soundly, unaware that the long-anticipated day had begun. Our scene was set, with the furnishings bathed in warmth and harmony. This morning is a special day; we are getting married.

As Judy gazed at John, her heart swelled with love; it was as if every tender moment they had shared had led to this day. His chest rose and fell in a rhythm that sang the sweetest lullaby of love and commitment to her. She reached out, her fingers trembling with anticipation, and with the softest touch, she stirred him from his dreams.

"John, wake up," she whispered, with a melody of excitement. "It's our wedding day." John opened his eyes, his smile bright. "Good morning. Love you," he replied, his voice gentle. "Love you too, honey." Judy smiled, her words showing great happiness. "We've got a big day ahead of us. My wedding dress is at my dad's, so we need to get up, get dressed, and get to the airport to fly to Mountain Home." So, hand in hand, they rose with the day; the world outside awaited their story, a tale of love that would soar across the skies.

At the airport, the scene was abuzz with the excitement of friends ready to witness Judy and John's union. Judy, the bride, was not just the soon-to-be Mrs. but also the skilled pilot who would navigate their plane to the wedding venue. Sarah, her trusty co-pilot and confidante, was ready at her side, and both women were a testament to the strength and independence that defined them. John and Kathy, Judy's maid of honor and pillar of support, took their seats behind the leading ladies, their laughter and chatter adding to the symphony of prenuptial bliss. Mr. Thompson, John's attorney, Uncle James, his wife, Aunt Jamie, and her husband found their places in John's ten-passenger plane to carry them on this 45-minute flight to destiny.

The twin engines roared to life, a powerful hymn to the journey ahead, and the plane lifted off; so did the spirits of all aboard. The world below shrank away, leaving only the endless blue sky as their companion, symbolizing the limitless future ahead for John and Judy. Miles melted away beneath them, each one a step closer to the moment they would become husband and wife. As the plane touched down in Mountain Home, the excitement was visible, the air electric with the promise of 'I do's and forever after. Judy's dress, a vision of white and lace, awaited her, a garment that would transform her into the embodiment of every dream she had ever had.

Today, January 12th, 1947, was a day of love and unity that would forever be etched in the annals of their hearts. John and Judy, surrounded by those who loved them, were ready for a lifetime of love and shared as they took their first steps as man and wife.

The sun poured through the stained windows, casting patterns on the crowd. The air was filled with anticipation, and the sweet scent of lilies and roses adorned every pew. With her beautiful smile, Judy was a vision in her white gown.

Mr. Martin, Judy's doting father, was a pillar of strength. While standing at the back of the church, he asked her, "Sweetie, are you sure you want to do this. If not, you can walk away now, and I will take care of everything here. The limo is outside and will take you anywhere you want to go." Judy said, "Daddy, I will always be your little girl and love you, but I am getting married today." Mr. Martin was very emotional as he escorted her toward the future that awaited her at the altar. The whispers of awe that followed her graceful procession down the aisle could not overshadow the thunderous beating of her heart.

His voice, barely more than a whisper, was full of love and a hint of bittersweet surrender as he entrusted his precious daughter to John. "Please take care of my daughter. She is now in your hands." The words resonated with a father's love, a sentiment as timeless as time itself. John, the essence of a gentleman in his sharp suit, received Judy's hand with a reverence that spoke volumes. "Sir, I will, I promise you that." His voice was a vow, a sacred pledge binding him to Judy and the family she brought with her. The ceremony unfolded like a dream, a perfect blend of tradition and personal touches that made it uniquely theirs. Mr. and Mrs. Martin, their faces showing pride and emotion, bore witness to the union of two souls meant to be together. Mrs. Martin's tears were a silent testament to the love that filled the room, while Mr. Martin's misty eyes mirrored the joyous hearts of all present. As John and Judy exchanged vows, their smiles were beacons of pure happiness. They were two halves of a whole, embarking on a journey that was theirs and theirs alone, yet shared with all who loved them. The preacher's voice, solid and transparent, cut through the emotion, presenting the newlyweds to the world. "Ladies and gentlemen, it is my great pleasure to introduce Mr. and Mrs. John Roberts Jenkins to you." The proclamation was met with applause and cheers, celebrating the triumph of love.

Judy looked into John's eyes with a big smile and said, "I love you, my dear, sweet husband." And John said, "I love you too, my dear sweet wife." As the newlyweds made their way back up the aisle, the church bells rang, and the air was alive with the melody of new beginnings. Outside, the festivities continued with a table of finger foods, cake, and punch, each bite and sip a sweet reminder of the day's joy.

When the moment came for Judy to toss her bouquet, her heart fluttered with a secret hope. She positioned herself with a practiced glance over her shoulder, aiming for Kathy, her lifelong friend and confidant. The bouquet soared through the air, a fluttering symbol of love's next great adventure, and all eyes followed its arc, landing gracefully in Kathy's outstretched hands. The crowd erupted in another round of cheers; the significance of the catch was not lost on anyone. Kathy's surprised blush and wide smile were the perfect ending to a day overflowing with love and happiness. As rice rained down upon the couple, the air was filled with laughter and good wishes. It was time for John, Judy, and everyone on the airplane to return to the airport, load up, and fly back to Poplar Bluff.

Mr. Martin, family, and friends went back to the church to clean and get everything ready for the Sunday night service. Judy told her father to gather the family outside the church at a specific time and to look up. He gathered the family and a few friends, went outside the church, and looked up. At that time, Judy flew over the church and waved the airplane's wings. Mr. Martin smiled as he waved at Judy. Someone said, "You know she can't see you." Mr. Martin said, "It doesn't matter; she knows."

John and Judy, hand in hand, stepped into their future, leaving a trail of joy and hope in their wake. The love they shared was a beacon for all, a reminder that in a world of chaos, love is still the most potent force, and everyone knew that this was just the beginning of a beautiful, everlasting romance.

The engines hummed a soft lullaby as the plane descended gracefully through the clouds, bringing John and Judy back to the familiar embrace of Poplar Bluff. The flight, a mere 45-minute tour in the sky, was as smooth as their newfound love, a perfect metaphor for the seamless journey they had embarked on together. As the wheels kissed the tarmac, one part of their life had closed, and another awaited its eager beginning.

The air was thick with anticipation as the group dispersed, each individual carrying with them the shimmering memories of a trip that would be eternally etched in their hearts. But for John and Judy, the magic was far from over. Their homecoming to the mansion was a prelude to the symphony of their lives together and their love.

Molly, the head cook and an unwitting conductor of romance, received their request with a knowing smile: hamburgers and fries, a humble feast for a couple whose love was anything but. The family room would be their sanctuary tonight, a place of comfort and laughter, the echoes of their joy mingling with the soft flicker of the television.

As they ascended the grand staircase to the main bedroom, their laughter cascaded through the halls. "We are husband and wife," Judy proclaimed, her voice a tender caress. John's reply came with a grin that could outshine the sun, "I love you, my dear wife." And Judy said, "I love you, my dear husband." Their kiss, the first as a married couple within the walls of their home, was a testament to the promises whispered and the dreams shared. It was a kiss that spoke of forever, a seal on the vows that bound them as one. Time seemed to stand still, the world outside fading into insignificance.

With a playful gleam, Judy suggested they don their robes and descend to their cozy family room. Ever the doting husband, John agreed with a warmth that filled the room, "Anything you want, my dear." And so, hand in hand, they went down to where Molly had prepared their simple yet perfect meal. There, amidst the soft glow of the dining room, they dined not just on the food but on the presence of one another. Every glance, every touch, and every shared smile was a delicacy that far surpassed the food on their plates.

The evening had been nothing short of magical: a hamburger, fries, and laughter that danced through the dining room where John and Judy shared their first meal as husband and wife. The glass of wine and the soft murmur of conversation had been the perfect overture to the night ahead.

With a chorus of "thank you" to Molly that expressed their genuine appreciation, John and Judy ascended the grand staircase to their bedroom, where the rest of their lives awaited. The door clicked shut behind them, a soft declaration of their newfound privacy, and their lips met in a crescendo of passion, a kiss that seemed to capture the essence of their deep and enduring love.

The bathroom lights flickered on, casting a warm glow as they each took turns freshening up; the night rituals drew them closer together. The sound of running water and the soft shuffle of slippers on tile were the tender notes that filled the air with promise.

Back in the bedroom, the robes they wore slipped from their shoulders like petals falling from a rose, their vulnerability with each other a testament to the trust and intimacy they shared. Beneath the sheets, their bodies entwined, and their kisses deepened, a prelude to the symphony of love they were about to compose together.

With a flirting smile playing on her lips, Judy was the spark that ignited the flame tonight. Her words, "My dear husband, I am yours," were a tender contradiction of nights in the past, her eyes, and the soft press of her body against his, telling a story, one of readiness, of yearning, of love that could no longer be contained.

As they gave themselves to each other, the world outside faded away, leaving only the rhythm of two hearts beating as one. Love's melody filled the room, a harmony of sighs and whispers that crescendoed into the quiet contentment of shared fulfillment.

In the afterglow, they lay wrapped in each other's embrace with warmth and affection. The night whispered its approval, and the stars outside their window twinkled in celebration as sleep claimed them, two souls adrift on the tranquil seas of matrimony.

18

Delayed Honeymoon

Dawn's first light crept through the curtains, a gentle nudge that aroused the lovers from their slumber. They smiled at each other with eyes still heavy with dreams, and John said, "Good morning, my beautiful and sweet little wife." Judy smiled with that beautiful smile that John loved and said, "Good morning, my wonderful husband." A tiny little kiss, and they hugged and cuddled tighter.

In that gentle embrace of dawn's first light, they lay in the warmth of their newfound union. The world outside lay forgotten, its noises hushed by the whispers of their love. Her head rested lightly on his chest, rising and falling with the rhythm of his breath, a silent testament to the life they now shared.

The room, still draped by the early morning rising sun, seemed to hold its breath, as if nature conspired to prolong this sacred intimacy. A tender, feather-light, tentative kiss blossomed into something deeper, a magic neither could resist. It was as though their souls danced in joyous harmony.

Their hearts quickened, beating in perfect union, echoing the vows exchanged, not just in words but in the very essence of their being. In that moment, time surrendered, and all that remained was the pure pleasure of each other's presence, a sanctuary where passion kindled into a fervent blaze.

Wrapped in each other's arms, they explored this new world they had created together, a world where every touch was electric and every sigh a promise. The tenderness of their love soothed away the uncertainties and forged an unbreakable and profound bond.

In their silence, they found a language beyond words, a communion of souls. As the morning sun rose higher, casting light upon them, it bore witness to the quiet strength of their love, which would endure unwaveringly forever.

They lay cuddled for a little while. The silent communication of a shared life was already beginning. John and Judy decided to delay their honeymoon trip until March, giving them time to work and understand the foundation and inner workings of JR's Department Store. They will take two days off to move Judy's things to the mansion and attend to other minor tasks. The day beckoned with the promise of new beginnings as they prepared to venture out to JR's to talk with Sarah about their honeymoon plans. They knew that every step they took now was a step they would take together.

Before embracing the day, they needed to indulge in the morning's ritual of a refreshing shower and a hearty breakfast. To John, breakfast was not merely a meal but the cornerstone of a promising day. With this in mind, Judy descended the stairs, her thoughts already drifting to the scent of freshly brewed coffee. She approached Molly, their ever-reliable cook, and inquired with a gentle smile, "Could you surprise us with breakfast in about an hour?" Always eager to please, Molly nodded warmly, "Of course, Ms. Judy, it will be ready."

Grateful, Judy thanked her and returned upstairs, where the sound of cascading water accompanied her entrance. John was in the shower, and she quietly laid out their clothes, ensuring everything was in perfect order. He peeked from behind the curtain, his face bright with affection. "Is Molly going to have breakfast ready for us, darling?" he called out with a playful glint in his eye. Judy approached, pressing a tender kiss to his lips. "Yes, she is."

"Mind helping me with my back, sweetheart?" John asked, extending the washcloth toward her. With a knowing smile that spoke of shared mornings and unspoken promises, Judy took the washcloth and stepped into the warm, inviting steam, joining him in the sanctuary of the shower. After they both had bathed, Judy said, "We have to hurry for breakfast, honey." They got out of the shower and dressed for breakfast.

Judy said, "Honey, Molly has breakfast ready for us. We need to go to the small dining room." John said, "Well, Mrs. Jenkins," as he stuck out his arm for her, "let's go to breakfast." With a big smile, Judy replied, "Let's go, Mr. Jenkins." They moved in step down the winding staircase, and each step seemed to echo the rhythm of their hearts. The aroma of freshly brewed coffee and warm pastries drifted through the air, guiding them to the intimate embrace of the small dining room.

With her ever-present warmth, Molly laid out a breakfast that was nothing short of a culinary delight. The table was adorned with delicate china, and the spread consisted of scrambled eggs, grits, bacon, toast, and jam, accompanied by coffee and a small glass of orange juice each. This was a testament to her skill and affection. John and Judy exchanged a glance, their eyes filled with gratitude and admiration, as they showered Molly with heartfelt praise for her artistry.

As they enjoyed their meal, a mutual understanding developed, reflecting their shared appreciation for the simple things of life. After finishing the meal, they returned upstairs with a refreshed sense of purpose. In the sanctuary of their room, they discussed things they needed to talk to Sarah about when they went to the store. As they prepared for the day, their thoughts lingered on the moments already shared that morning, the silent promises exchanged, and the endless possibilities that awaited them beyond the threshold. Together, they would embark on the day's journey, hand in hand and heart in heart.

John and Judy's love story blossomed like a dogwood in spring. The newlyweds, having just exchanged vows yesterday in a ceremony as enchanting as a silver-screen kiss, were the talk of the town. Her grace and charm made John, JR's Department Store heir, and Judy the perfect match.

The department store, a treasure trove of goods and memories, stood as a testament to the legacy John had inherited on Christmas Day. It was more than a business; it was a community cornerstone where locals gathered to shop, share stories, and exchange laughter. And now, as the new owner of this treasured establishment, John was eager to honor its past while steering it into the future.

Judy, the supportive partner, stood by his side as they planned to take a couple of weeks from their duties in March to go on a honeymoon adventure that promised to be a model of romance and discovery. Their love was a beacon, guiding them through the responsibilities of their new roles.

Judy and John's visit to the store was not merely a routine check-in but a moment to dream with Sarah, the assistant store manager. Sarah's wisdom and experience with the Florida vacation house in Key West were invaluable, as she had been there several times with John's father. They wanted to review their plans with Sarah for planning purposes and to ensure their plan would work for the store.

When they arrived at JR's, they stopped by John's office to check with Kathy and ensure everything was in order, with no pending matters that required attention that day. When they walked in, Kathy said, "Good morning, Mr. and Mrs. Jenkins. How are y'all today?" Judy smiled with the biggest smile you could ever imagine and said, "We're doing great, Kathy." Thank you for asking." John asked Kathy if anything needed to be done before they returned on Wednesday. Kathy told him nothing was pending, and they would hold everything together for the next couple of days. John and Judy then went to Sarah's office.

"Good morning, Sarah. How are you this morning?" As Judy hugged Sarah, "Thank you so much for everything you've done for us in the last couple of weeks." Sarah told them it was an honor and a pleasure to help. She then began to tell them that the Key West house was a slice of paradise, where the sun danced on the ocean like diamonds, and the air was perfumed with the scent of salt and freedom.

John asked Sarah, "Sarah, can you come to my office for a few minutes to discuss the dates we have planned for our departure and return?" Sarah, looking excited, said, "Give me about five minutes to finish this report, and I'll be right there." John and Judy went to his office and told Kathy, "When Sarah arrives, please come in with her so we can discuss our departure and return dates." "I'll come right in, Mr. Jenkins," and then looked at Judy with a big smile and said, "Mrs. Jenkins, can I get you something to drink?" Judy looked at Kathy with a big smile, hugged her, and said, "Oh, Kathy, I love you so much." And Kathy said, "I love you, too, Judy."

John and Judy were talking in John's office when Sarah and Kathy entered to discuss the honeymoon. Sarah said, "We are all here now. Let's see if we can help put everything together for your honeymoon. John started, "As of now, we plan to leave on Sunday, March 9, and return on Sunday, March 23. That allows us to be here for the first week of the month, including the first and second Saturdays. How does that sound for everything at the store and for both of you?" Both Sarah and Kathy said that it sounded good to them. They didn't see any potential problems with that schedule.

With everyone agreeing on the dates, John and Judy began to outline the plans for the trip. Their eyes sparkled with excitement, as though they were already flying the airplane, soaring above the clouds, and leaving behind the familiar streets of Poplar Bluff for the excitement of New Orleans. Four days in the Crescent City, where the music is a language and the food a symphony of flavors.

Then, on to Key West, where the days would stretch out before them like the endless sea, filled with moments of bliss and peace that can only be found when two hearts beat as one. Sarah listened, her eyes reflecting the joy of the couple before her, and offered her advice. She spoke of the beauty of the journey, the importance of savoring each moment, and the wisdom in pacing their adventure to fully absorb the magic of each destination.

The return journey, a scenic flight from Key West to Montgomery, Alabama, promised a chance to reflect on the memories made and deepen their bond. A stopover in Mountain Home, to visit Judy's parents, would be the perfect ending to their honeymoon, a time to share stories and laughter with family before returning to the life they were building together in Poplar Bluff.

Finally, John and Judy stopped talking and asked Sarah and Kathy, "What do y'all think about our plan?" They both said that it sounded good to them. They didn't see any problems with those two weeks in March. John and Judy's honeymoon plans are more than just a trip; it marks the beginning of a lifetime of adventure. Their love was a journey; this was the first of many beautiful times to come. The two months they will work at JR's before leaving on their honeymoon would seem like an eternity, but it's a decision they agreed they needed to make first.

As they were getting ready to leave the store, John turned to Sarah and said, "Sarah, I'm thinking about stopping by the Ford Dealership and talking to Mr. Jimmy about a car for Judy. Do you think that would be ok?" Sarah said, "Of course, it will be okay, John." I know you and Judy love riding to and from work together, but there will be times when that can't happen, and Judy will need her own transportation. Your father and I rode together many times, but I still needed my own transportation. I think that's what you need to do, and the sooner, the better." "Sarah, could you please call Mr. Jimmy and tell him I will come by this morning? Please let him know I want to buy this car for Judy and do not want to trade my dad's car. I would really like to keep Dad's car." "John," Sarah said with tears in her eyes. "John, as I have said before, I know I am not your stepmother, even though I sometimes feel like I am. Hearing you say "My Dad's Car" brings tears to my eyes. Because I love your father, and I know he would be so proud to hear you say those words. I will call Jimmy and let him know." John said, "Thank you, Sarah, and I really do feel like your stepson, and I am so proud to say that."

As they left the store, hand in hand, the future seemed as bright and inviting as the morning sun that kissed the horizon. Once outside, Judy turned to John and said, "Honey, we haven't talked about getting me a car. I haven't asked or said anything to make you feel like I wanted a car." John hugged her and said, "Sweetie, I've been thinking about getting you a car before we got married, or even before we got engaged. I was thinking about it that long ago because I knew I already loved you that much."

John and Judy walk to the car, talking, and as John always does, he opens the car door for Judy. As they drove to the Ford Dealership, Judy asked John when he thought they might return to her dad's house to pick up her things and bring them home. John said, "Why don't we call your dad tonight and ask him if we can pick them up this Sunday afternoon? We can fly there, pick up your things, and still be able to spend time with your parents, talking, and maybe have an early dinner before we come back home." Judy loved that idea and said she would call Dad when they returned home.

The morning sun was beautiful on the streets as John and Judy drove toward the Ford dealership. The air was filled with new beginnings, a perfect reflection of the young couple's beginning life together. As they approached the dealership, Judy's eyes sparkled with anticipation, reflecting the excitement that had colored every moment since their wedding day.

John, the gentleman, held the door open for Judy as they entered the showroom. The scent of fresh leather and polished chrome reminded them of the promise of new adventures. Jimmy, the dealership owner and new friend to John and Judy, approached with a welcoming smile, his demeanor as polished as the vehicles he sold.

"Good morning, John, Judy," Jimmy greeted them warmly, tipping his hat slightly. "Sarah called and said that y'all were looking for a car for Judy." John said, "We are, but I'd like to keep my dad's car and buy the vehicle outright for Judy if that's okay." Judy exchanged a glance with John, her heart swelling with gratitude for this thoughtful gesture. She had always admired how John cherished his father's Ford Sedan, a link to his father's past, yet he was determined to carve out a new chapter for them.

"Judy, you and John look around at all the cars and let me know when you find the one you think you would like. You can take it and drive around for a while. If that's the one you want, I will sell it at my cost." Judy felt a sense of newfound freedom and independence as they walked through the rows of gleaming automobiles. She kept telling John how much she loved him and couldn't believe what he had done for her. And then, as they walked up to a 1947 dark blue-gray 2-door Ford Coupe, she stopped in her tracks. Her fingers brushed against the smooth curves, and she knew this was the one. It was more than just a car; it symbolized the life they were building together. Judy and John went to Jimmy's office and said, "Mr. Jimmy, I've found the car. It's a two-door coupe, dark blue gray, on the back row."

"That is a beautiful car, Judy. I know because I ordered that one especially for my daughter." Jimmy said with a smile. "I don't have to have that one, Mr. Jimmy. I can look at another one." Judy said with a hint of sadness in her eyes. But Jimmy told her, "I will order another one for my daughter; this one is yours. Here are the keys for it. It's almost lunch; take it to JJ's for an early lunch. You and John talk about it. If you still want it, bring it back and leave it with me, and I will get it ready for you to pick up late this afternoon." "Is that okay with you, honey?" Judy said, looking up at John with that beautiful smile he loved so much. With a big smile, John said, "It sure is, honey. Mr. Jimmy, we will be back right after lunch."

John and Judy drove the car off the car lot. Judy would not drive first; she wanted John to drive it to a large parking lot before she tried to drive. She was a little nervous about it and wanted to refresh her knowledge of the basics before taking the wheel. She did great and drove to JJ's for lunch, with John praising her the whole time for her good driving.

After lunch, Judy drove back to the Ford Dealership and told Jimmy, "Mr. Jimmy, I love that car, that's the one I want." Jimmy informed them of the purchase price, and John instructed him to send the invoice to Sarah at the store. Jimmy said, "Judy, you can pick up your new car later this afternoon." Judy looked at John; the air between them was charged with a mixture of excitement and contentment. With the promise of new journeys ahead, they left the dealership, the world outside seeming brighter and more vibrant than ever.

Their next stop was a sad one, the apartment Judy had shared with her friend Kathy, a place filled with memories of singlehood and sisterhood. As they gathered Judy's belongings, the quiet apartment echoed with laughter and whispered secrets of late-night conversations. Each item packed was a piece of Judy's past, now intricately woven into her future.

John watched as Judy moved through the rooms, her grace and strength evident in every step. He marveled at how effortlessly she transitioned from one chapter of her life to the next, and he felt an overwhelming sense of love and admiration for the woman he had just married. John and Judy loaded the last boxes into the car as the sun slowly set. Together, they headed to the Ford dealership to pick up Judy's new car.

Upon arrival, Judy's eyes fell upon the gleaming silhouette of her new car, its polished surface reflecting the fading light. It stood there, a promise of adventure and freedom, waiting for her to take the wheel. With the formalities of paperwork completed, Judy and John stepped outside, the cold evening breeze carrying the scent of possibilities.

John wrapped Judy in a warm embrace, their bodies swaying slightly as if moving to the rhythm of their shared heartbeat. He pressed a tender kiss to her lips, a silent vow of his unwavering support and love. "I'll see you at the house, honey. I know you want to stop by the store and show it to Kathy."

Judy's face lit up with a radiant smile, her eyes sparkling with excitement and gratitude. "Is it okay, honey? Do you mind? I really want to share this moment with Kathy." John chuckled softly, an affectionate glimmer in his gaze. "No, honey, I don't mind at all. I'll be waiting for you at home." Their lips met once more in a lingering kiss, a promise of reunion and the continuation of their shared journey. With a final glance filled with unspoken love, Judy slipped into the driver's seat of her new car, the engine purring to life under her touch.

As she drove away, the road stretched out before her, a ribbon of dreams yet to be unfurled. She was headed to the store to share her joy with Kathy, knowing that John would be there at the end of the day, waiting with open arms and an open heart.

Judy drove into the parking lot of JR's Department Store with a sense of anticipation fluttering in her chest. The afternoon sun kissed the sleek curves of her new 1947 Ford 2-door dark blue coupe, making the polished surface shimmer like a sapphire. Today was special, not just because of the car, but because she was about to share this moment with Kathy, her confidante and sister in spirit since their high school and college days.

She parked just below the window of John's office on the third floor, her heart beating a rhythm of excitement. She walked through the front door of the store and went to the third floor, to Kathy's office, outside John's office. The familiar scent of polished wood and the soft murmur of customers surrounded her, but the sight of Kathy made everything else fade into the background. Kathy's eyes widened in surprise, her smile radiant as ever.

"Judy! What a surprise! Did y'all forget something?" Kathy exclaimed, enveloping Judy in a warm embrace that spoke volumes of their shared history. Judy grinned, her eyes twinkling with a secret she could no longer contain. "Kathy, I have something I'd like to show you. Come to the window in John's office for a minute." Intrigued, Kathy followed her into John's office, their footsteps echoing the deep bond of trust and affection that had been forged through years of friendship. As they stood together looking out the window, Judy said, "What do you think of that dark blue 2-door Ford coupe in front of the store, Judy nodded toward the car, her voice tinged with pride and disbelief.

Kathy's eyes widened, glancing from the car to Judy and saying, "Judy, that is a beautiful car, why?" Judy's smile widened, her heart swelling with emotion. "It's mine. John bought it for me today." Kathy's eyes sparkled with delight as she looked at Judy, understanding the depth of the gesture. In that moment, the car was more than just a vehicle; it was a testament to love, a tangible symbol of affection that transcended words. Their laughter mingled with a symphony of friendship that would last a lifetime.

Judy and Kathy hurried downstairs to the front door and went to look at the car. "Judy," Kathy said, "That is a beautiful car. I am so happy for you." After Kathy finished looking over Judy's new car, they hugged and said goodbye. Judy got in, started her beautiful new car, and headed toward the mansion. In this moment, as the road unfurled before her, Judy knew that the journey of their lives had only just begun.

She couldn't help but smile; she was so happy that she didn't know how to express it, except to shed a few happy tears. With its grand silhouette etched against the twilight, the stately mansion stood as a beacon of their shared dreams. As Judy approached, her heart leapt at the sight of John standing amidst the swirling snowflakes in the cold and snow, watching her drive up.

He was smiling so big, it would be hard not to see the smile. She pulled up behind John's car, parked, jumped out, and ran into John's arms. They hugged and kissed for what seemed like an eternity. Finally, John said, "Honey, pull your car in front of mine, and if we go anywhere tomorrow, we'll use your car." Judy returned to her car with a playful spirit, moving it in front of John's. In the following minutes, Judy again found herself enveloped in his arms, where the chill of the snow vanished, leaving only the warmth of love's embrace. Their kiss was tender and lingering, a silent vow in the stillness of the evening. In that moment, everything was possible, and the world was theirs to explore, hand in hand, heart to heart. They walked up to the mansion door. As they walked to the door, John told Judy, "Honey, please remind me when we get inside, and after we call your father, to ask Molly to get us keys to the mansion. One day, Molly may not be close to the door to let us in."

As they were about to knock on the door, Molly opened it and said, "Good afternoon, Ms. Judy, Mr. John. Can I help you with anything?" John smiled at Molly and said, "Molly, I hate to ask, but can you ask David and Michael to help me get some boxes and bags out of my car?" "I will be glad to, Mr. John. If I can have the keys to both cars, I will have them pull the cars around to the garage area, bring all the boxes to your bedroom, and place them inside near the walk-in closet. What would you like for dinner tonight, Ms. Judy?" "I'm not sure, Molly. I will let you know shortly."

Judy said as she looked at John, "I'm going to call Daddy and let him know about Sunday. Operator, can you please connect me to Mountain Home, Arkansas, for Mr. William Martin?" The phone rang a few times, and then, "Hello, this is Will Martin." "Hey, Daddy, it's Judy." "Hey, sweetie, how are y'all doing today?" as he told Mrs. Martin that Judy was on the phone and to get on the extension. "We are both doing fine, Daddy."

Not knowing Judy was on the phone, Molly walked into the den and said, "Ms. Judy, both cars have been unloaded and parked in the garage. Do you need me for anything else?" Judy smiled at Molly and said, "Thank you, Molly. We will be going to JJ's for dinner. Daddy, I wanted to let you know that we'll fly home on Sunday and load what we can into the plane. Then, we'll spend some time with you and Mother if you have time on Sunday." Judy's Mom said, "Who was that parking your car, Judy?" Judy smiled and said, "That was Molly, the primary housekeeper. She had two grounds workers move the cars from the front of the house to the garage in the back and unload the things I brought from Kathy's apartment." "Judy," John said, "ask the colonel if it's okay to come early for church, then maybe lunch at the pilots club, our treat this time." Judy smiled, laughed, and said, "Colonel, John wants to know." "I heard what John said, sweetie." Mr. Martin said as he laughed. "John," Judy said, "Daddy said that would be great, and we'll discuss who will pay for it after lunch. He will help load the car, take everything to the plane, and load it for a safe flight. Thanks, Daddy. Love you and Mom. Yes, sir, my brothers, too."

19

Honeymoon The Days Before

When John and Judy were married, they decided to wait two months before embarking on their honeymoon. John's inheritance gave him his father's pride and joy, JR's Department Store. They both worked long hours during the two months after their wedding, trying to learn as much as possible before leaving on their honeymoon.

It was Friday morning, March 7th, two days before they were supposed to leave on their honeymoon. The morning sun cast a warm tint across the room. It was a soft and tender awakening, the kind of morning that promised the world outside would hold its breath just for them. In the quiet sanctuary of their bedroom, Judy leaned closer to John, her voice a gentle melody as she whispered, "Good morning, honey."

Her touch was soft, wakeful, and he stirred beneath her hand, a smile playing upon his lips before his eyes fluttered open. "We need to get up, sweetie," she continued, her words a sweet nudge into the day. "We should try to get to work a little early this morning. We said we would try to get everything we needed to finish before leaving work today. That way, we can spend Saturday double-checking everything and hopefully start packing Saturday afternoon. Honey, if you let Molly know we'd like some sandwiches to take with us for breakfast, I'll lay out our clothes for today."

John nodded, the allure of her voice and the promise of the day ahead drawing him from the comfort of their bed. There was something profoundly beautiful in their routine, an intimacy found in the simplest acts of love. "Okay, honey," he replied, his voice warm and filled with the affection that seemed to linger in the air between them. "I'll tell Molly to fix us a couple of egg sandwiches. We should be ready to leave for the store in about an hour."

Their exchange was punctuated by a tender kiss, a shared moment that spoke of promises and dreams, of a life woven together with love and understanding. As John turned to leave, Judy watched him go, her heart swelling with a passion that felt as vast as the sky. The anticipation of their upcoming honeymoon was a whisper in the back of their minds, a promise of new beginnings and adventures yet to come. But today was about the present, the life they were building together, and the love that filled every corner of their world.

As John returned, the room was filled with a comfortable silence, punctuated only by the gentle hum of water cascading down in the adjoining bathroom. Ever thoughtful and meticulous, Judy had already laid out their clothes, a testament to her caring nature that never ceased touching him.

As John stepped into the bathroom, he found Judy standing by the shower, her hand under the stream of water, testing its warmth with careful precision. The steam swirled around her, framing her in an arousing mist, and when she turned to him with that radiant smile that had captivated him from the very first moment they met, his heart skipped a beat.

"Molly is making us two sandwiches each," he informed her, the words coming out in a soft murmur as if not to disturb the intimate atmosphere. "They'll be ready in an hour, honey."

Judy's smile widened, a blend of affection and playful flirtation. "The water is perfect, honey. Would you like to join me?" she asked, her voice a sweet whisper that wrapped around him like a tender embrace.

Without a moment's hesitation, John stepped forward, the world outside fading. The warmth of the water enveloped them as he joined her under the shower, their bodies close, hearts beating in synchrony. Their lips met passionately, reaffirming the love that had grown between them through shared moments and whispered promises. In that steamy sanctuary, time paused, highlighting the deep bond shared by two souls connected through love.

As they finished dressing, a soft intimacy lingered between John and Judy, a testament to their bond. John's eyes met Judy's, a tender smile playing on his lips. "Would you like to take your car, Mrs. Jenkins?" he inquired, his voice a gentle caress.

Judy returned his smile, a warmth spreading through her chest. "Yes, I would love to take my car, Mr. Jenkins," she replied, her words carrying the affectionate cadence of their shared life. She reached for her purse, preparing to head downstairs, the soft rustle of fabric the only sound in the room.

Before they descended the stairs, Judy paused, a thought occurring to her. "John, would you please speak with Mr. Wainwright about arranging for someone to pick up the car at the airport on Sunday after we leave and return it on Sunday, the 23rd?" Her voice was considerate yet firm, a reflection of her practical nature. "I don't like leaving either of our cars at the airport for two weeks." John nodded, his gaze steady and reassuring. "I will ask him to take care of it. Good idea, sweetie," he agreed, his words a promise. Together, they turned towards the door, their steps in unison, a testament to the life they were building together.

As the first light of dawn filtered softly through the curtains, John and Judy descended the stairs, their hands intertwined, to savor the comforting aroma of breakfast prepared by Molly. The kitchen was filled with the warm glow of morning, and Molly greeted them with a smile, her presence as steady and reassuring as the walls of the home they cherished.

"Molly," Would you please ask Mr. Wainwright to come here for a minute? "Yes, sir." Molly walked back into the kitchen. Mr. Wainwright's office, which was used to run the household, was just off the kitchen, and Molly delivered the message as requested. Mr. Wainwright walked in and said, "Mr. John, what can I help with?" John began, his voice carrying a gentle authority. Could you have someone pick up the car at the airport on Sunday and bring it back on the 23rd?" There was a quiet reliance in his request, a testament to their trust in him.

"Of course, Mr. John," Mr. Wainwright replied, his voice firm with promise. "I'll have David and Michael ensure everything is handled seamlessly." His words were a tone of certainty, and John nodded appreciatively, his gratitude unspoken yet deeply felt.

With her soft, pleasant voice, Judy added, "Molly, we'll be dining at JJ's tonight, so we will not be here for dinner." Her words had a lingering sweetness, a gentle reminder of the evening's promise. "I understand, Ms. Judy," Molly responded, her smile a silent blessing as they departed.

Outside, the world was awakening, the day full of potential and whispered secrets. They entered the garage, and Judy started the car; a playful glint danced in her eyes. "Honey," she teased, her voice a gentle caress, "aren't you going to snuggle up close to me while I drive to the Department Store?"

His heart swelling with affection, John obliged with a smile as warm as the morning sun. He slid across the seat and nestled against her, his head resting on her shoulder, a perfect fit. Their laughter mingled with the engine's hum, creating a symphony of shared joy that echoed through the car.

As they glided down the road, the world outside became a blur, insignificant compared to their tender closeness. "Honey, I love you," John murmured, his voice a vow that transcended the ordinary. "I don't care what people think or say if they see me cuddled up next to you."

As the morning sun cast its glow across the bustling streets, Judy and John pulled up to JR's Department Store, the city's heartbeat of commerce and dreams. With a graceful perfection, Judy parked the car and turned to John, her eyes sparkling affectionately.

Ever the playful romantic, John leaned over slightly, a teasing grin on his lips. "Honey, are you going to come around and open the car door for me?" he asked, his voice filled with a warmth that only deep love can bring. Judy's response was a symphony of joy, her smile a melody that resonated with John's heart. "Yes, I am, sweetie," she replied, her tone as light and enchanting as a spring breeze. "I'll be at your door in just a minute."

Judy gracefully exited the car and made her way around to John's side. As she opened the door, she extended her hand to him, her gesture as elegant as it was loving. "May I help you out, kind sir?" she asked, her voice a soft caress. John took her hand, feeling the electric connection that always seemed to spark between them, and together they laughed a sound as pure and joyful as the ringing of church bells. Arm in arm, they strolled toward the department store's entrance, their steps in perfect harmony.

Sarah and Kathy looked out the window at John and Judy as they drove up. They both started laughing, and Sarah said, "Well, that must be nothing but true love for Judy to get out of the driver's side and come around to open John's door." "Yes, it is, " said Kathy, "and they hugged and kissed like they had no care in the world. What a perfect couple they are together. They can almost complete each other's statements." They laughed again and went back to work.

John and Judy paused inside the store amidst the symphony of commerce and the gentle hum of conversations. John drew Judy close, and they shared a tender kiss, a silent promise of love and devotion. "If I don't see you before lunch," John murmured, his voice a whisper meant only for her, "I'll come by your office for our lunch at JJ's. Love you, sweetie."

Judy nodded, her eyes locked onto his. "I love you too, honey," she replied, her words a gentle vow as she turned to head to her office. Her heart already counted the moments until they would be together again.

John and Judy decide to order lunch and have a working lunch to get more done at the office. A little after three in the afternoon, Judy came to John's office and said, "Hey, honey, today went a lot better than I thought it would. I have finished up everything I needed to do." "That's great, sweetie; I just completed my last item. We can call it a day if you're ready." John told her as he closed the book he was working with. John smiled at Judy and said, "Would you like to walk through the store, just to look around and pick up a few things we may need on our honeymoon?" The word honeymoon lingered between them, a whispered promise of adventures yet to come. Judy smiled and replied, "I think that would be a great thing to do, honey. It would help us pick up what we need and allow us to spend time with the employees."

With a shared purpose, they tidied their workspace, each movement a step closer to their shared future. A few minutes later, they walked arm in arm downstairs to the sales floor. As they wandered through the store's aisles, their laughter mingled with the hum of daily life, creating a symphony of connection. Employees greeted them with warmth, their smiles reflecting the couple's joy.

With their items chosen, they headed to the checkout, blending seamlessly with the everyday bustle of the day's business. The cashier rang up their items, and they paid with ease. Their employee discount was a gentle reminder of the life they were building together. Finished with their shopping, they headed to Judy's car and went to JJ's for dinner.

As the afternoon sun had set, John and Judy found themselves at JJ's, the restaurant that cradled the memories of their first tentative steps into love. Over T-bone steaks, salads, and baked potatoes, they relived those moments of the past.

Later, at home, with the world outside their window a quiet spectator, they changed into the comfort of nightclothes. The living room welcomed them with the promise of relaxation and quiet companionship. With her intuitive understanding, Molly had already prepared a beer for John and a glass of wine for Judy, their drinks a testament to the rhythm of their life.

They settled on the sofa, the glow of the television casting soft shadows. Their hands were entwined, and their hearts beat as one. After their drinks, Judy went to the kitchen. The clink of glasses was a gentle exclamation point to their evening. Judy washed the glasses and placed them on a towel to dry.

As she left the kitchen, she bid Molly and David goodnight as they ate their evening meal at the table in the kitchen, as they did every night. Judy walked into the living room. She smiled at John and said, "Honey, I'm ready for bed. We still have to go to work tomorrow to check and ensure everything is completed and that we are okay with going on our honeymoon." John said, "ok, sweetie." As he stood up, he offered his arm to Judy, and they headed to the bedroom, toward the promise of shared dreams and whispered secrets.

The sun peeked through the clouds this serene Saturday morning. March 8 was not just another date on the calendar; it was the day before John and Judy would embark on their much-anticipated honeymoon, a journey into the heart of their shared future. Their first stop was Rivers Run Lodge, a quaint retreat nestled amidst whispering pines and a winding river, where the crackle of the fireplace and the aroma of freshly brewed coffee mingled in the air.

Their breakfast began with scrambled eggs and hickory-smoked link sausage, grits topped with cheese, toast, coffee, and orange juice. Over breakfast, they discussed their plans for the day and Sunday.

After they finished at JR's, they planned to go home and start packing. They would pack most of the things to take in the two large suitcases, and the small suitcase would be reserved for the essentials they would need that night. This would leave only the small suitcase to pick up in the morning. If they had time today, they might go ahead and take the two large suitcases to the airport and put them on the plane.

As they talked, their eyes would meet, speaking a language of love that only they understood. The world outside faded into oblivion, leaving just the two of them, wrapped in their love. After the last sip of rich coffee, they knew it was time to return to reality. They left the Rivers Run Lodge and headed to their next destination, JR's, the bustling hub of Judy and John's professional life. Together, they would make a final check before their departure, ensuring that everything was in place.

Upon arriving at John's office, they talked to Kathy first, whose smile was as bright as the morning sun. "Judy," she exclaimed, her voice filled with genuine joy, "I'm thrilled for you. We've been dreaming of this moment since our college days." Their embrace was tender and filled with the shared history of years gone by, a silent testament to friendship and loyalty.

Watching the emotional exchange, John gently urged, "Let's go see Sarah and make sure everything's in order for our two-week trip." Kathy, an integral part of their circle, joined them, and her presence was a comforting reminder of the support that surrounded them.

As they strolled down the corridor to Sarah's office, Judy and Kathy lagged slightly behind. Their conversation was a lively exchange of excitement and anticipation. The air buzzed with their animated chatter, a melody of joy that echoed through the halls.

Entering Sarah's office, they were met with her warm, welcoming smile. "Y'all look so happy and excited," she remarked, her eyes twinkling with shared joy. John, ever diligent, said, "Sarah, do you think everything is in good shape for us to leave for two weeks?"

Sarah's reassurance was immediate and heartfelt. "Oh, yes, we'll be fine. The two of you go on your honeymoon and leave your worries behind. The store, and all of us, will be here, eagerly awaiting your stories upon your return."

When they left Sarah's office, they went to the sales floor to buy two large suitcases and one small one, each symbolizing the adventures that awaited them. They carried with them the excitement of a new adventure, their honeymoon. As they left, all the employees wished them a safe trip and a great honeymoon. As they were walking out the door to the parking lot, Judy said, "Honey, I am so proud of you and the way the employees admire you so much." "Sweetie," John said, "it's not just me; it's us, Sarah and Kathy." As they drove off to the mansion, John smiled and said, "But my dad is the one who started it all. It really starts with him."

As the garage door closed behind them, Judy and John exchanged a glance, a silent acknowledgment of the sanctuary they had returned to, a world that was just theirs. Their footsteps echoed softly as they ascended the stairs, suitcases in tow, with each step a rhythmic reminder of the journey they were about to undertake.

In the bedroom, bathed in the gentle afternoon light, John laid the suitcases open on the bed, their interiors gaping like empty canvases, ready to be filled with the clothes of their shared adventure. Judy lightly touched his arm, her fingers trailing down to his hand, a gesture that spoke of countless shared moments. "Honey," she murmured, her voice a soft melody, "I'm going downstairs to let Molly know we'd love hamburgers, fries, and tea for lunch in about an hour."

John turned to her, capturing her gaze with eyes that held a depth of affection words could never fully convey. He kissed her, a gentle promise of love and gratitude, and whispered, "Thank you, my dear little wife, you're the greatest."

Upon her return, the suitcases lay open and ready. Their laughter filled the room like a familiar song as they packed each item for their journey.

As they finished packing, Judy's voice laced with excitement and practicality, said, "Why don't we go eat, and afterwards, we can double-check the bags just to make sure everything is packed? We can take the two large suitcases to the airport and put them on the plane if you'd like. After that, I can lay out our flight and file our flight plan, even though it's not required. We can ask Mr. Bill to ensure the plane is fully fueled. That will save a lot of time in the morning."

John, ever the supportive partner, smiled at her with an admiration that seemed to deepen with each passing day. "Great idea, sweetie," he replied, his voice warm with affection. "Let's go eat lunch and then put your plan into action." Together, they descended the stairs once more, hand in hand, their hearts filled with joy and the promise of a future bright with possibility.

As the sun cast a warm glow over their dining room, John and Judy shared a quiet meal at the small table they had cherished since their first days together. The scent of freshly grilled hamburgers mingled with the crisp aroma of French fries, prepared lovingly by Molly. Judy savored each bite, her eyes sparkling with delight. "These are wonderful," she murmured, a soft smile playing on her lips as she glanced at John. He, in turn, nodded in agreement, his mouth too full to articulate his appreciation, but his eyes communicated everything she needed to know.

With lunch concluded, Judy's thoughts turned towards their impending adventure. "Darling," she said, her voice tinged with excitement, "let's get our suitcases and head to the airport?" Her anticipation was infectious, drawing a chuckle from John as he reached for the phone. "Certainly, I'll call Mr. Bill," he replied as he picked up the phone and asked the operator to call Bluff Field Airport.

John and Judy left their bedroom, carrying the two suitcases, and headed to the garage. "Sweetheart," John began, a playful note in his voice, "may I drive your car to the airport? I've yet to experience its charm." Judy's laughter was like a melody, warm and inviting. "Of course, Mr. Jenkins," she teased, "it's yours whenever you wish."

As they drove to the airport, the world outside seemed to slide by, leaving only the two of them in their private haven. Judy nestled closer, her lips grazing his cheek in a tender kiss before she rested her head on his shoulder, contentment washing over her.

As they arrived at the airport, the setting sun cast a gentle glow over the airport. The hangar door stood open, just as Mr. Bill had assured them. Their car rolled up to the hangar entrance, the hum of its engine fading into the background of the airport activity. Together, John and Judy worked to load the suitcases and carefully placed the hanging clothes in the small closet at the back of the plane. Every movement loading the plane was sheer joy, as they laughed, smiled, and kissed.

Once the last item was stowed, they walked hand in hand towards the modest office where Judy would weave her magic, crafting the flight plan that would carry them into tomorrow's adventure. Inside, the soft rustle of paper filled the room as Judy expertly navigated the charts and documents, her brow furrowed in concentration.

John, meanwhile, engaged Mr. Bill in conversation, his voice steady yet gentle. "Can we leave the car parked here until someone picks it up after we leave tomorrow?" he inquired. Mr. Bill, with a nod and a warm smile, reassured him, "Of course, you can, John. If you'd like, you can drive the car into your hangar and leave it there until you return. It's your hangar, John. You can use it any way you need to. I will make sure the hangar is always locked and secure. You will have nothing to worry about."

John returned to the office just as Judy looked up, a satisfied smile playing on her lips. "Perfect timing, honey," she smiled, her eyes meeting his with a spark that made his heart skip a beat. "I've just finished everything. Let's put these papers and charts in the plane, and then we'll be ready to go."

With everything secured in the plane, they returned home, anticipating tomorrow's journey, weaving an invisible thread of excitement between them. As they drove, the soft hum of the car's engine was a comforting backdrop to their conversation.

"Sweetie," John said, his voice threaded with affection, "remind me to tell Mr. Wainwright that we won't need him to have the car picked up. Mr. Bill said we could park the car in the hangar. The hangar will be locked after we leave, so the car will be safe."

Judy nodded, a soft smile gracing her lips. Her heart was filled with the knowledge that their journey was not just physical but an exploration of the depths of their shared dreams and the love that bound them together.

As the twilight deepened, casting long shadows over the sprawling grounds of the mansion, Judy and John returned home, the quiet hum of the engine their only companion. With a voice as tender as the evening breeze, John suggested, "Darling, let's take my car to the airport tomorrow. If our honeymoon gifts overflow, we can easily carry them back." Judy nodded, a smile dancing on her lips, as they pulled into the garage.

Entering the familiar warmth of the kitchen, Judy turned to Molly, their devoted housekeeper, and requested, "Molly, we'll come down for dinner in about an hour. Could we indulge in steak tonight?" Molly, ever diligent, replied, "Of course, Ms. Judy. I might need more time to send David for the steaks." Satisfied, Judy ascended the staircase, her heart light and full.

Upstairs, the gentle hiss of water echoed softly against the tiles as John prepared the shower. Before joining him, Judy laid out their nightclothes. Holding the shower curtain open with a playful grin, John offered, "May I hold the door for you, Ms. Judy?" She laughed softly, a melody that mingled with the steam, and replied, "You sure can, Mr. John."

When an hour and a half passed like a dream, they descended again, their fingers entwined, to find the dining room aglow with candlelight. The steak dinner was a symphony of flavors, each bite a testament to Molly's culinary talent. "Molly, that steak was exquisite," they praised in unison, their gratitude genuine and heartfelt.

As the evening drew to a close, Judy went to Mr. Wainwright's office and said, "Mr. Wainwright, there's no need to send David and Michael for the car. Mr. Bill said we could leave it in the hangar." Mr. Wainwright said, "Mr. John, I must apologize for not telling you about that. Your father and Ms. Sarah always parked their car in the hangar." "That is quite all right, Mr. Wainwright; You will be off tomorrow when we leave, so I just want to thank you for everything you do for us. We will see you in two weeks." "Thank you, Mr. John."

John left Mr. Wainwright's office, walked back to the kitchen, turned to Molly, and said, "Molly, tonight, we'll skip the usual nightcap. Sleep beckons us early. Good night, Molly." With that, he and Judy retreated hand in hand, leaving behind the glow of the dining room, eager to embrace the promise of dreams and the dawn of a new chapter together.

20

The Honeymoon

The first light of dawn had not yet touched the room as John stirred. His gaze fell upon Judy, her face serene in the soft embrace of morning. The world outside was still, a quiet promise of the journey they were about to embark on. He reached out, brushing a stray lock of hair from her face, his touch gentle and tender. Judy's eyes fluttered open, meeting his with a warmth that spoke of shared dreams and whispered vows.

"Good morning," she murmured, her voice a soft melody that played upon the strings of his heart. "Good morning, my love," John replied, his voice a deep, loving tone of promise. Today was the day they would finally step away from the department store and into a world just for them, where their love would guide them through uncharted territories.

John kissed Judy lightly, and Judy returned the kiss with a passion that took their breath away. Their passion enveloped them, an unyielding tide pulling them into a realm where time seemed to stand still. The world around them faded into a soft blur, leaving only the rhythm of their hearts, synchronized in a dance as old as time. Their love was a force, fierce and unrestrained, carrying them beyond the mundane confines of reality into a sanctuary of pure joy and unspoken promises.

In that embrace, they held each other, breathless and passionate. The air was charged with an intensity that spoke of shared dreams and whispered futures. As they held each other close, the quiet settled around them like a gentle lullaby, cradling them in a moment that felt eternal.

Judy and John lay in the afterglow of their shared passion. The morning was early, and the sun was not yet showing through the curtains. Their love, an unspoken vow, wrapped around them like a warm, comforting blanket. In the quiet of the room, Judy's voice, gentle yet resolute, broke the silence. "Honey, we need to start getting our shower and get dressed for the day. It's going to be a long day."

With a smile that spoke volumes of his affection, John leaned in for another kiss. "It sure is, my darling. When we leave the house, would you like to go to the Rivers Run Lodge for breakfast? It would be a great way to start our honeymoon."

Judy's eyes sparkled, "Yes, my love, I would love to go to the Rivers Run Lodge for breakfast. If you start the shower, I will lay out our clothes for today's flight." With a big smile, John rose to start the shower while Judy meticulously arranged their attire. As she joined him in the bathroom, she was greeted by the playful glint in his eyes.

"My dear, beautiful wife, your shower awaits you," John announced, his voice a tender caress, as he drew her into the warm embrace of steam and water.

Together, they stepped into the shower, the hot steam enveloping them. It was a moment suspended in time, where the outside world ceased to exist, and all that mattered was their profound love for each other. In that steamy sanctuary, their love soared to new heights, a testament to the journey they were about to undertake hand in hand.

As the water cascaded around them, they found solace in each other's arms, their hearts beating in perfect harmony. It was not just the beginning of a day but the dawn of a lifetime, where every moment promised to be an adventure and every day a new chapter in their unfolding love story.

As John and Judy descended the grand staircase, their fingers entwined. The air was filled with the soft echo of their footsteps, a gentle prelude to the day ahead.

In the cozy embrace of the small dining room, Molly awaited them, her warm smile a beacon of familiarity and care. "What would you like for breakfast, Ms. Judy?" she inquired, her voice a soothing melody harmonizing with the morning's quiet symphony. Judy returned her smile with one of her own, a radiant expression of warmth and gratitude. "We will have breakfast at the Rivers Run Lodge this morning, Molly. But first, a cup of your wonderful coffee will start our adventure if you have coffee made."

With a nod, Molly disappeared into the kitchen, soon returning with steaming cups of aromatic coffee that enveloped them in a fragrant embrace. The moment was quiet, shared, perfect, a ritual that spoke of countless mornings filled with love and simplicity.

The time for their departure was at hand. "Molly, just as a reminder, I told Mr. Wainwright that we will leave the car safely in our hangar at the airport and return on March 23. Thank you for everything that you and the staff do for us," John said, his voice rich with sincerity. Molly nodded, her eyes reflecting the deep connection that had grown over a short time. "You are very welcome, Mr. John," she replied, her smile a gentle benediction.

They ventured to the garage, where the car awaited like a patient steed ready to carry them to new horizons. As always, John opened the door for Judy, a small yet profound gesture that conveyed respect and affection. She slid across the seat, settling beside him, and nestled close. The car purred to life, and as they set off toward the Rivers Run Lodge for breakfast, their love was as enduring as the river's flow.

As the first light of dawn cast a gentle glow over the Lodge, John, ever the gentleman, held the door for Judy, their fingers intertwining as naturally as the breath they shared. John and Judy stepped into the dining area. Their presence was met with warm smiles and friendly greetings from familiar faces. The early morning sky painted a beautiful backdrop, promising a day filled with possibilities.

The lodge was alive with the sound of morning activity, and the air was tinged with the comforting aroma of freshly brewed coffee. They were guided to a quaint table by the window, where the view of the tranquil river outside seemed to mirror the calm contentment they felt within. As they settled in, steaming cups of coffee appeared before them, the rich, dark liquid a perfect prelude to the day.

"Isn't it wonderful?" Judy said, her eyes sparkling with the delight of newfound recognition and the warmth of community. "How have we become part of this place in just a few months? People stop and greet us like old friends." John nodded, his smile broad and full of quiet pride. "It truly is," he replied, the sincerity in his voice as noticeable as the love that radiated between them.

Their breakfast order was simple: a plate of scrambled eggs, sizzling bacon, smoked sausage, and toast adorned with sweet grape jelly. As they savored each bite, their conversation danced around dreams and plans, the anticipation of their honeymoon adding a spirited tone to their words.

Then, as the meal neared its end, Judy's expression shifted to tender seriousness. "Darling," she said softly, her gaze meeting his with earnest intensity, "when we board the plane this morning, I'd like you to wear headphones. It'll help us talk, and you'll hear me clearly, even with your hearing loss from the war on your left ear."

John's heart swelled with affection at her thoughtfulness, her words a testament to the depth of their connection. "You're the pilot of this journey," he responded with a loving grin, "and I'm more than happy to follow your lead."

In that moment, as they lingered over the last sips of coffee, the world seemed to pause, wrapping them in love and understanding. With a shared glance, they knew that this was just the beginning of an adventure that would take them to new heights, carried by the wings of their devotion.

As Judy and John drove toward the airport, their hearts brimming with excitement, they shared laughter as they embarked on a grand adventure. Their route to the airport took them by JR's Department Store. Judy looked at John with a big smile and said, "Honey, I know we have only been working at the store for two months, but it seems like a lifetime ago when we started. I feel sad that we won't be working tomorrow. I am not sad enough to cancel our honeymoon, but I am a little sad." John kissed her cheek and said, "Me too, sweetie, me too."

Upon their arrival, the sleek form of John and Judy's twin Beech airplane awaited them, poised and ready on the tarmac. Mr. Bill, with his ever-present warm smile, approached with an air of admiration. "John," he greeted warmly, "you can pull your car up to the plane, unload your luggage, and then park in your hangar." John's handshake was firm, a gesture of camaraderie and gratitude. "Thanks, Mr. Bill, for all you do for us. We truly appreciate it."

Judy placed the small suitcase on the plane. As John moved the car to the hangar, Judy immersed herself in the meticulous work of pre-flight checks; her movements around the plane were precise and confident. She was steady and assured, the kind of woman who grounded John in ways he had never known he needed.

After the plane's pre-flight was completed, Judy moved inside the office and checked the weather reports, her thoughts flickering to the love that had brought them to this moment. With a heart full of purpose, she turned to John, her voice carrying the weight of their passion. "Honey, we are ready to go. Mr. Bill has fully fueled the plane, which has about 1,200 flight miles of fuel and about 604 miles to New Orleans, LA. We have plenty of fuel, and I've completed all my pre-flight checks." Her words were a gentle reassurance, a reminder that together they could navigate anything.

When they boarded the plane, Judy sat in the pilot's seat while John closed and locked the door, with Mr. Bill checking it outside. John then came up front and sat in the co-pilot's seat. Judy handed him his headphones, saying, "Here, honey, put these on. You will be able to hear from the right speaker." John put the headphones on, smiled, and threw her a kiss. Judy looked at John and said, "Look out your side and see if anyone is around the prop. If no one is there, yell out, CLEAR PROP, turn to me, and give me a thumbs up. If anyone is near the PROP, turn to me and give me a thumbs down. Then, turn back to the right and yell out, CLEAR PROP, and wait until they are clear. Then, turn to me and give me a thumbs up." John completed his task and gave Judy a thumbs-up. Then Judy yelled on her side, "CLEAR PROP." Judy adjusted the radio dials and said, "Bluff Field traffic, Bluff Field traffic Twin Beech 49840, permission to start engines." Bluff Field traffic responded, "49840, permission to start engines granted, advise when ready to taxi." John is watching Judy with a smile, showing his pride in her. The engines roared to life. Each engine started and was perfect, thus beginning their new chapter: "Bluff Field traffic, this is 49840, request permission to taxi to the runway." Bluff Field traffic responded, "49840 taxi to runway 5, hold short of takeoff position." Judy said, "Bluff Field Traffic 49840 taxi to runway 5, hold short of takeoff position," and they started to move. In a few minutes, they were at the hold position; Judy did her engine run-up procedure and reported. "Bluff Field Traffic 49840 holding short at runway 5." Bluff Field traffic said, "49840 holding." In a couple of minutes, over the radio, Bluff Field traffic responded, "49840, you are cleared for takeoff." "49840, taking off runway 5," Judy repeated. With that, she moved on to the runway, eased the power to three-quarter throttle, started down the runway, and then slowly went to full throttle. In a minute, they were lifting off. And she was doing great; John was so proud. Then he heard Judy say, "Bluff Field traffic, 49840, turning left downwind runway 5 departing area on heading 180." Bluff Field traffic reports: "49840 departing area on 180, good day." He glanced at Judy, his eyes reflecting the depth of his emotions. "Honey, I love you," he declared, the words a simple yet profound truth.

Judy's smile was radiant, a beacon in the dimming light. "Honey, if you want to talk to me, press this button. I can only hear you if you press the button. And I love you too." Her voice was a melody, resonating in the cockpit and within his soul. With a touch of the button, John's voice filled the intimate space in the headphones, a whisper carried through the air. "Honey, I love you."

As the twin Beech effortlessly leveled off at 16,000 feet, the vast sky stretching infinitely around them, Judy set the altitude, heading, and speed on the autopilot for New Orleans and pressed the "engage" button. She turned her attention to John, her eyes twinkling with a warmth that rivaled the morning sun. "Honey," she said, her voice as soothing as a gentle breeze, "would you mind getting the coffee and snacks from the back? I'll prepare us a little something to enjoy."

John nodded, returning her smile with a tenderness reserved only for her. "Of course, darling," he replied, rising to fulfill her request. As he moved, he couldn't help but feel a rush of gratitude for these small, shared moments that made the journey not just one of miles but of hearts intertwined.

They sat together, sipping coffee and sharing laughter that echoed softly within the cabin, creating a world all their own, amidst the clouds. Judy glanced at him, her expression a mix of affection and anticipation. "We're set to arrive in New Orleans around 11 a.m., honey."

John's eyes lit up at the thought. "That's wonderful," he said, reaching for her hand, their fingers naturally intertwining. "Three hours feels like nothing when I'm with you."

Her laughter was like a melody, light and full of joy. "Indeed, much faster than driving," she agreed, squeezing his hand gently. As they continued their conversation, time seemed to suspend itself, each minute a cherished brushstroke on the canvas of their shared adventure.

John looked at Judy with wide-open eyes when he heard a buzzing sound from the cockpit's dash panel. Judy looked at him, smiled, and said, "Nothing to worry about, honey, that's the autopilot telling me we are within 50 miles of the New Orleans airport. I need to prepare some things for us to land." As the outlines of the city began to take shape below, Judy prepared for their descent, focusing on the task ahead yet never far from the man beside her. Together, they would touch down on runway 11, ready to embrace whatever awaited them next, but for now, John watched her with amazed admiration. She worked the landing like a pro. She is a pro, and he is deeply in love with her. As they taxied up to the parking area, they made a plan. Judy would arrange for the plane to be refueled and do her after-flight, while John arranged transportation to the hotel.

As Judy went through the regular after-flight checks on the twin Beech and made arrangements for fuel fill-up and tie-down for four days, John went to the office to arrange transportation to the heart of the French Quarter and the Bourbon Orleans Hotel.

John had arranged for the airport courtesy car to take them to the Hotel. As the courtesy car driver carried them through the bustling streets, the city's pulse echoed in time with their hearts. The Bourbon Orleans Hotel awaited, its facade a sentinel of history and romance. As they pulled into the hotel's loading and unloading area, the courtesy car driver said, "You can go ahead and check in, and I'll bring your luggage in." When the driver finished unloading the luggage, he said, "That's all your luggage, Mr. Jenkins. Here is a card with my name and number on it. Call that number if you need me to provide transportation while you're here. I'd be happy to take you on a sightseeing drive around the city if you'd like. At a minimum, when you are ready to return to the airport, call and let me know what time to pick you up. I will pick you up, and someone at the airport will have your twin beach pulled out and ready to go when you return. I hope you have a great honeymoon. Call me if you need anything."

Their room, perched on the second floor, was a haven from which they could gaze upon the vibrant life below, each moment an intimate dance of strangers and stories. Judy smiled at John and said, "I can't believe we are finally here, John, and in the heart of New Orleans, starting our life together in the most enchanting way possible. The

Hotel feels like it was plucked straight out of a storybook, mixing old-world charm and modern luxury. I am so happy, sweetheart."

As John and Judy looked around their cozy loft room at The Bourbon Orleans Hotel, they couldn't help but grin at each other. The room was perfect, perched above the lively chaos of Bourbon Street, offering a front-row seat to the city's heartbeat. They dropped their bags and walked out on the balcony, where the world seemed alive with every glance.

"Look at that," John said, wrapping an arm around Judy's shoulders. "It's like watching a movie, but with real-life characters and stories." Judy chuckled and leaned into him. "I know, can you imagine all the stories out there? Each person has their own little universe they're living in."

They stood there for a moment, letting the rhythm of the street seep into their bones. Music floated up, mingling with laughter and the clinking of glasses from the lounge across the street from the hotel. Judy looked up at John, her eyes shining with excitement. "This is going to be the best start to our honeymoon." John nodded, feeling the warmth of the moment filling his chest. "I couldn't agree more. Just you, me, and endless possibilities."

With the world bustling beneath them and the promise of new memories in the air, they knew this was just the beginning. The city was theirs to explore, and every moment was a chance to weave their own story.

They will spend the next four days exploring every nook and cranny, from hidden courtyards to bustling markets, savoring the city's rich flavors and history. But the best will be those quiet moments, just the two sitting on the balcony, sipping wine and beer as the world goes by beneath them. It felt like their own little paradise, a perfect beginning to the rest of their lives, a love story unfolding one chapter at a time, right on Bourbon Street.

Walking around the French Quarter that afternoon, they laughed and talked and agreed that this place sweeps you off your feet. Later that evening, they decided to go to Antoine's for dinner, the city's oldest restaurant, which had opened its doors in 1840. It was like stepping back in time, with the bonus of savoring some divine French Creole cooking. It's as if the flavors tell stories of old New Orleans, romantic, vibrant, and delicious.

On Monday morning, Judy asked John, "Sweetie, can we go for breakfast at the Café Du Monde. It's supposed to be a little coffee oasis that's been serving beignets since 1862." John agreed and they walked to the Café. John said, "Let's order the dark-roasted coffee with a hint of chicory. The menu says it will transform an ordinary morning cup of coffee into something special." Judy smiled and said, "Let's do it, honey," so they both ordered the powdered sugar beignets with the dark coffee. With a big smile, John said, "They're right, sweetie; the coffee is fantastic." Judy smiled, agreed, and said, "This place is where time seems to stand still, where every sip and bite we take seems to connect us to those who have sat here at the same table across generations.

As the days ticked away, they toured the French Quarter, dining at old, historic restaurants where each meal was a symphony of flavors. Lunchtime found them in the shadowed courtyards of cafes, where laughter mingled with the tinkling of wine glasses. As the sun dipped below the horizon, dinner became a romantic evening of candlelight and soft music.

On their last Wednesday afternoon, they visited Jackson Square, a timeless canvas on which artists have captured the city's soul. They meandered through the historic French Quarter, horse hooves echoing against the cobblestones as they rode in a horse carriage, transported through space and time. The very air seemed to hum with the words of Tennessee Williams, resonating from the walls where he penned "A Streetcar Named Desire." It had just been published that year.

As the first light of dawn began to show, Judy sat quietly on the balcony, cradling a steaming cup of coffee in her hands. Her gaze wandered over the awakening city below, where shopkeepers flipped open signs, and the aroma of freshly baked bread drifted through the air.

When John stepped out onto the balcony, the warmth of the morning embraced him. "Good morning, honey," Judy greeted with a smile, her voice as soothing as the coffee she offered. He leaned down to give her a tender kiss, a silent thank you for the peaceful start she had given him.

"Morning, sweetie," he replied, settling into a chair beside her. "How long have you been up?" "About an hour," Judy confessed with a soft laugh. "I thought I'd let you sleep in while I enjoyed the view. It's mesmerizing, watching the city slowly come alive."

John chuckled, a bit sheepish. "I should've been up to join you. It sounds like the perfect start to a day." Judy shrugged, her eyes twinkling. "We've got plenty of time, and each quiet moment is a blessing, right?"

He nodded, sipping the hot coffee that warmed him from the inside. "So, what's the plan to fly to Key West?" With a thoughtful pause, Judy calculated, "Well, if we leave around 11 AM, that gives us time for a leisurely breakfast and for the restaurant downstairs to pack some sandwiches for lunch on the plane. We should land around 2:30 PM."

John, ever the planner, topped off their cups and smiled, "Sounds perfect. I'll arrange for the courtesy driver to pick us up at 9:30 AM. That gives us plenty of time to get to the airport, check the plane, and be ready for takeoff by 11."

Their conversation flowed like the gentle rhythm of the morning breeze, easy and comforting. Once their cups were empty, they dressed and headed downstairs, hand in hand, ready to savor breakfast and anticipate the next adventure.

Before leaving, John called the driver, sealing their plans with a sense of excitement in the air. Their day was set, and the promise of what lay ahead shimmered like the distant horizon, full of possibilities and whispered secrets only lovers understand.

As the courtesy driver dropped them off beside their twin-beech airplane, Judy turned to John with a playful smile. "Hey, sweetheart, how about I handle the pre-flight checks while you load the luggage? Oh, and don't forget to find a life jacket for each seat. Your dad should have them somewhere since he and Sarah flew to the Keys all the time. You know, just in case we have to do a dramatic water landing," she added with a teasing wink.

John chuckled, clearly impressed. "You've got it all figured out, haven't you? I'll get right on it," he said, grinning as he started packing everything into the plane.

While Judy ticked off items on her pre-flight checklist with the precision of a seasoned pilot, John busied himself organizing the luggage and locating the life jackets. As always, they seemed to finish around the same time, a well-oiled team.

Once inside the plane, Judy pulled the door closed. Turning around, she found John waiting there, a familiar spark in his eyes. Without a word, they wrapped their arms around each other, sharing a kiss so warm and lingering that a couple of onlookers outside couldn't help but smile at their obvious affection.

Finally, they settled into the pilot and co-pilot seats, ready to embark on the next part of their honeymoon. Engines roared to life, and soon enough, they were soaring through the skies, leaving the world below as they made their way to Key West.

About half an hour into their flight, John unbuckled his seatbelt and rummaged through their stash, pulling out sandwiches for a mid-air lunch. As they munched away, they couldn't help but reminisce about their escapades in New Orleans, laughter bubbling up as naturally as the clouds passing outside. It was another day in their love story, flying high above the clouds.

The world stretched like a shimmering puzzle as they soared through the skies. John and Judy were nestled in the front seats of their plane, sharing laughter, whispers, and a few stolen kisses. Suddenly, a loud buzzing filled the cabin. John chuckled, his eyes wide with excitement. "I know, honey. That's the autopilot giving us a heads-up. We're about 50 miles from Key West, and it's time for you to do some of that pilot stuff you're so good at."

Judy grinned, that playful glint in her eyes. "You're right, honey. Time to do some of that "pilot stuff." John couldn't help but laugh as he started tidying up. "Alright, I'll handle the lunch cleanup and make sure everything is strapped down and ready for landing back here."

After a quick, lingering kiss, they got to work preparing for their descent. Before long, the plane was parked, and they were all set to dive into the second part of their honeymoon. They chatted with the ground crew, letting them know the plane would be parked and tied down until Saturday or Sunday of next week. "We'll give you a heads-up when we know for sure," John promised.

Just then, one of the airport staff approached them. "Excuse me, sir," he said, his voice tinged with curiosity. " Isn't this Mr. John Roberts' airplane? I think he was from Poplar Bluff, Missouri."

"Yes, it is," John replied, a soft smile on his lips. "He was my father. He passed away on March 10 of last year." The staff member's face fell, sympathy etched in his expression. "I'm so sorry to hear that. We heard he had passed away, but we weren't sure. Mr. John was a dear friend to many of us at the airport and in Key West."

John nodded, a bittersweet warmth spreading through his chest. "Thank you. He loved flying, just like we do. It's good to be here, carrying on his legacy." As they stood on the tarmac, John and Judy knew they were exactly where they were meant to be.

A touch of uncertainty crossed his face as John stood at the customer help desk in the pilot's lounge area. Just moments ago, he'd asked one of the friendly staff members if they could help him and his wife, Judy, get to his father's house. The staff member, a cheerful woman with a warm smile, nodded enthusiastically, "Oh, absolutely! We have a courtesy car available for your use. It's right here, and you can have it for as long as you need."

John blinked, clearly taken aback. "Really? We don't want to take a car that other guests might need. All we need to do is get to my dad's house."

The staff member chuckled softly, her eyes twinkling with a knowing look. "Oh, there's no worry about that. This car actually belonged to Mr. John Roberts. He and Ms. Sarah visited so often that they bought a car and left it with us. Mr. John had an agreement with us that we would do all the maintenance on the car as a condition for us to use it. We also understood that the car would be at their disposal when they were in Key West. As Mr. John's heir, I'm sure the car now belongs to you. They were old friends, and I'm sure, if you agree, we can continue with the same arrangement as before." John smiled, shook everyone's hand, and said, "It is so nice to meet so many of my dad's friends, and yes, if my wife agrees with me, we will agree to the original agreement." Judy smiled at John and said, "yes, honey, I agree with everything you said." She loved him so much that he would ask her to be a part of the decision to keep the agreement, and this was the first time he had asked her to help him decide on something his father had originally started.

There's something incredibly electric about the moments when two people connect without even saying a word. When John glanced over at Judy, she caught his eye. A little frown was on her face, but it was like a frown that couldn't hide a smile. Judy was happy that it seemed like everywhere they went, they were meeting people who knew and liked John's father, yet John was also telling them that his father had passed away. The staff member continued, "We already know where Mr. Roberts' house is, so we'll give you the directions. And to make it even easier, one of our ground crew can drive over, and you can follow them. He can help you unlock everything, open it, and answer any questions you might have. You see, we keep an eye on the house and check it weekly. Everything should be just perfect."

They hopped into the car with their luggage tucked neatly in the trunk. Following the crew member, John felt a wave of nostalgia and excitement. Judy squeezed his hand reassuringly, her eyes reflecting the same emotions, and said to John, "Honey, your father sure was liked and respected all over the country. Everywhere we go, it seems someone knows and thinks very highly of him." John smiled and said, "It does seem that way. I wish I could have known him."

John and Judy began the 25-minute drive from the airport to their new vacation home, filled with butterflies and excitement. The drive was serene, unfolding around them like an old, familiar story. As they neared the house, a sense of belonging washed over John. It was more than just a journey to see his father's place that he had inherited; it was also a journey and a future waiting for him and Judy to write together. It's like something out of a postcard when they finally pulled up. They were looking at a gorgeous three-bedroom, two-bath place, and it's got that classic conch cottage style of the early 1900s in Key West. There are big wrap-around porches, a cute little gazebo tucked into the side yard, and a balcony off the main bedroom on the second floor. The second part of their honeymoon kicks off in this dreamy, laid-back paradise. Days drift by like being carried on a gentle breeze, as the sunsets splash the sky with those jaw-dropping fiery oranges and deep pinks. They're walking hand in hand, toes digging into the soft sand, making promises under the glow of a sky that seems to understand the depth of their love. It's like time has decided to hit pause just for them.

They spend their days walking on beaches practically begging for a romance novel scene, their skin salty from the ocean, and their laughter mixing with the sounds of the waves and the seabirds. The night stars put on this incredible show, almost as if the universe is nodding along, approving of their love story.

And when they thought things couldn't get any more magical, they bumped into President Truman on one of their beach walks. The President of the United States, casually strolling along like he's in the neighborhood! It turns out he's got a house in Key West called the Little White House.

John and Judy had finished an unbelievable week and a half in Key West, soaking in the sun and living in that dreamy, romantic bubble. Judy and John seem to have found the perfect balance between adventure and intimacy.

What could be more delightful than starting your morning with a breakfast lovingly prepared by someone you love. When shared with the right person, eggs, grits, and bacon are a meaningful yet straightforward combination. And then, washing dishes together, turning a mundane task into something special with smiles, jokes, and those flirtatious glances. Those small moments build the foundation of lasting love together.

Driving back to the airport, they felt a bittersweet tug. They were saying goodbye to new friends, shared connections, and past friends of John's father. John felt a sense of pride as he and Judy met people who meant so much to his father and now meant a great deal to them.

Judy handled the flight plans at the Key West airport like a pro. John watches her with admiration, proud of the incredible woman he has married. The flight time from Key West to Montgomery, Alabama is about 3 ½ hours. Judy had fixed some peanut butter and grape jelly sandwiches for a snack on the flight. After a couple of hours, John went to the storage area in the back and brought the snacks for him and Judy to enjoy. They enjoyed the snacks while laughing and joking about the time in Key West.

John smiled as he heard the little buzz from the autopilot, signaling they were almost to Montgomery. It was a gentle reminder of how quickly time flies when you're with someone who makes your heart race.

Montgomery, Alabama, is a place where Southern charm meets history. Judy and John found themselves on what was supposed to be a quick fuel stop. The plan was simple: refuel quickly, grab something to eat, and return to the skies. But the city had other plans for them.

As they landed in Montgomery, they couldn't help but feel a sense of nostalgia, as if the air was filled with past stories. Their service crew at the airport had given them a solid recommendation, Chris's Hot Dogs. "You've got to try them," they said, "best hot dogs in the country." With a curious appetite, they drove the courtesy car downtown to the heart of the city for a Chris's Hot Dog.

The moment Judy took her first bite, her eyes lit up. "These are fantastic," she exclaimed, a hint of disbelief in her voice. "I've never eaten a hot dog this good." With a grin that could rival the sun, John nodded in agreement, savoring his hot dog.

After their meal, they wandered the streets, hand in hand, feeling the whispers of history all around them. The past was walking alongside them, sharing secrets and stories from long ago. In those brief moments, they weren't just tourists but time travelers, touching the edges of history as they discussed their futures.

So, what was meant to be a quick stop turned into an unexpected journey. Montgomery's charm enveloped them, offering a moment of reflection. They realized that life is not just about the destinations but about the beautiful pauses along the way. For Judy and John, this charming city became a cherished chapter in their love story.

It was mid-afternoon, and Judy had completed the preflight checks while John paid for the fuel. Judy called her dad and said, "Hey, Daddy, we are in Montgomery, Alabama, and will leave in about 10 minutes. Yes, sir, Dad, I've completed a thorough preflight check and am ready to go. Could you pick us up at the airport in about 2 ½ hours? Thanks, Daddy. One other thing: We are tired. Would it be okay if we spent the night with Mother and you tonight, and maybe go to church tomorrow before we leave for home? Thank you, Daddy, see you in about 2 ½ hours."

They said goodbye to the grounds crew and told them that Chris's Hot Dogs were fantastic, the best they had ever eaten. Judy taxied the twin-beech to the runway and moved into line for takeoff. In a few minutes, they headed down the runway and into the sky. After leveling off at 16,000 feet, Judy engaged the autopilot.

She smiled at John and said, "This is a short flight. We should be at Mountain Home at about four o'clock, and Daddy will meet us at the airport." John smiled and said, "That's great, we haven't seen them but once since we got married."

Judy smiled the same smile that he had fallen in love with. That smile seems to make his heart race with love. "John," she said, "I hope it is okay. I asked Daddy if we could spend the night with them and go to church with them tomorrow before we go back home." When Judy used the words "before we go back home," it raised his love for her even more, if that were possible. He smiled and said, "Honey, I can't think of anything better.

As the twin-beech got within 50 miles of Mountain Home, the autopilot started to buzz, telling them to get ready for landing. John smiled at Judy and said, "Honey, it's time for you to do your pilot stuff." Judy gave John a flirty smile and said, "Yes, my dear sweet husband, I am starting my pilot stuff now." They flew over Mountain Home, exchanging smiles and flirty glances, where their love began amidst the green hills and blue skies. A little while after that, Judy landed like the expert that she was. She knew her father was watching, so she tried to do everything perfectly. After all, he was the one who taught her how to fly the twin Beech when she was 13 years old.

Judy could see her father from the pilot seat window as she taxied and parked the plane. She slid the window open and waved to her parents. After completing the after-flight checklist and shutting both engines down, John opened the door and helped Judy down the plane's steps.

As Judy stepped off the plane's steps, she ran to her father, "Oh, Daddy, I have missed you so much." Mr. Martin hugged Judy, smiled at her, and said, "Honey, are you happy?" Judy smiled at her father and said, "Daddy, I don't know how to explain how happy I am. But Daddy, I will always be your little girl." John hugged Mrs. Martin, and she said, "Don't worry, John, she will get to me in a minute." Judy finally moved over to her mother, hugging her and telling her how much she had missed her. John walked over, and Mr. Martin said, "Welcome home, John." John replied, "Thank you, Colonel, thank you very much. It's nice to have some place to call home."

Judy's mother and father greeted them with a joyous embrace, their eyes sparkling with the reflection of the happiness that radiated from the young couple. It was a haven for their souls, where they could reflect on the journey that had brought them together. The familiar sights and sounds of the place where they had become husband and wife enveloped them in a comforting embrace, a gentle reminder that no matter how far they flew, this corner of the world would always be home.

"Mother has a big dinner waiting for us at home. Let's get your bags and head to the house," said Mr. Martin, his voice warm with anticipation. "That's right," Mrs. Martin chimed in with a smile. "I've got most of the things Judy likes, and John, I hope I've managed to get some of your favorites too. Over time, I'll learn what you like. Judy, your room is ready for you and John, so make yourself at home, John." "Yes, ma'am," John replied, feeling a rush of gratitude. Could they really understand how much this all meant to him, having no family of his own?

When they arrived, Judy and John took their bags to Judy's room, freshened up, and then headed down for dinner. The meal was filled with warmth and laughter, which only family can create. After dinner, they sat around, chatting comfortably, until Mr. Martin finally told his wife, "Dear, we should probably head to bed so they can go to bed also."

As they stood up, John had an idea. "Colonel, why don't you and Mrs. Martin fly back to Poplar Bluff with us for a few days? Call it a short vacation. We can fly you back at any time you're ready. Spend a few days in the mansion with us and see how your daughter lives?" Judy's eyes lit up. "Yes, Daddy, why not? The boys are old enough to take care of themselves. They're in high school. Please, Daddy?"

Mr. Martin chuckled, clearly considering the idea. "We'll think about it and let you know in the morning," he promised, his eyes twinkling with the possibility of adventure. He looked at his wife and said, "Well, dear, looks like we have something to talk about tonight."

Judy and John are whipping up a Sunday morning feast in the kitchen, and the aroma is making its way through the house, luring Mr. and Mrs. Martin to the kitchen. Mr. Martin walks into the kitchen, eyebrows raised, a hint of surprise in his voice. "Judy, what is this? I've never seen you in chef mode like this. Everything smells incredible!"

Judy chuckles, wiping her hands on a dish towel. "Well, it's not just my doing. John and I teamed up for this one. We've got poached eggs, scrambled eggs, grits, cheese grits, bacon, biscuits covered with butter and jam. Coffee's brewing on the stove, and there's fresh orange juice too."

Mrs. Martin joins in, her eyes wide with admiration. "Judy, this is impressive! I had no idea you had these skills." Judy grins, a little bashful but proud. "Mom, I owe a lot to you and Molly, our wonderful housekeeper and head cook. She's shown me the ropes in the kitchen. She's a culinary genius. But enough about that, let's eat and chat about you and Dad joining us for a week."

"A week, wait a minute, a whole week?" Mr. Martin repeats with a raised eyebrow, clearly caught off guard. "I thought we were talking about just a few days. I'm not sure if we can really be away for that long?"

"Alright, listen up, boys," Judy says, turning to her two brothers with a knowing smile. "You're a junior and a senior in high school now, right?" "Yes, sis, we know," they reply in unison, a hint of amusement in their voices. "So, can you take care of yourselves and each other for a week? And! make sure you actually go to school?" The brothers chuckle, nodding confidently. "Yeah, we've got it covered."

"Okay then, Daddy," Judy continues, focusing on Mr. Martin. "What is happening this week that can't wait until you return?" Mr.

Martin thinks for a moment before shaking his head. "Nothing that I can think of. What about you, dear?" he asks, glancing at Mrs. Martin. With a warm smile, Mrs. Martin replies, "Nope, nothing at all. We are going and that's settled. Now, how about we eat and get ready for church?"

"Well, I guess we're doing this," Mr. Martin says, sounding more convinced, his gaze softening as he looks at Judy. "Judy, it seems like marrying John and helping him run the department store has given you some impressive life skills." Judy grins, feeling a glow of pride. "It's amazing what love and a little bit of business can teach you."

Sunday mornings always had that special feel; everyone buzzing around after breakfast, getting ready for church. This particular morning, the air was filled with excitement. The two brothers decided to go ahead on their own, while John and Judy rode with Mr. and Mrs. Martin. Everyone at church was shaking hands with Judy and John, congratulating them on their marriage and thanking them for visiting the church. The church service ended with smiles on everyone's faces, and soon everyone was back home, changing their Sunday best for more comfortable travel clothes and gathering their bags for the trip to Poplar Bluff.

They all gathered at the airport lounge for a hearty lunch. It was the kind of meal filled with good food, laughter, and a feeling of closeness that only family can provide. Judy took charge as they boarded the plane, conducting the preflight checks with practiced ease. She even asked her father, for old times' sake, "Hey, Daddy, want to ride up front with me?" But Mr. Martin smiled warmly, "No, thank you for asking. You and John seem to have that under control. I'll sit back here with your mother and enjoy the luxury of being a passenger for a change."

There was a particular pride in his voice. Watching his daughter and new son-in-law work seamlessly together, reminding him of a well-choreographed dance. It was hard to believe they had only been doing this together for a few months. As Judy taxied the plane to the runway, hearts raced a little faster. Soon, they were all airborne. Judy and John were on the final part of their honeymoon, and her parents were visiting them at the mansion for a week, ready to savor their first vacation in years. It was one of those moments that felt perfect, the kind you tuck away in your heart to revisit whenever you need a reminder of how beautiful life can be.

Judy glanced back at her parents, sitting a couple of rows behind. The way they laughed and pointed excitedly out the window at familiar landscapes, they were on a joyful trip down memory lane. Her heart swelled watching them. Turning to John, she gently tapped his shoulder and nodded towards her folks with a smile.

"John," she said, leaning closer and pressing the button on her headset, "I just have to say, I love you so much for this. Inviting them to stay with us for a few days means everything to me. Really, I love you for doing that."

John turned to her, his face lighting up with a smile that could warm even the coldest hearts. "Judy," he replied, his voice tender, "there isn't anything I wouldn't do for you or your family. You know that."

And just like that, in the middle of the clouds, surrounded by the hum of the engines, Judy felt a sense of warmth and contentment, knowing she had someone who loved not just her, but the people she cared about most.

The 45-minute flight back to Poplar Bluff was a journey through the clouds, a bridge between the carefree days of their honeymoon and the exciting reality of their life together. As they descended from the heavens, they returned to the life they had left behind, now to be lived as one. As the sun dipped below the horizon, casting a warm, golden glow over the sprawling landscape, the Jenkins' private twin-engine Beech airplane touched down gracefully, marking the end of a perfect honeymoon that had whisked Judy and John away on a whirlwind of romance and adventure.

As Judy powered down the twin-beech, Mr. Bill and his ground crew hustled over, sliding chocks under the wheels with practiced precision. While Judy checked off the last items on her after-flight list, John opened the door and started to unload the plane. Mr. Bill had thoughtfully brought the car right next to them, making the job a breeze.

John was all smiles as he introduced the Martins to Mr. Bill. "Mr. Bill, meet Judy's folks, Colonel William Martin and his wife," he paused, awkwardly scratching his head, "I am so sorry, Mrs. Martin, I have never heard anyone use your first name."

With a warm laugh, Mrs. Martin put him at ease. "Oh, John, don't worry about it. Just call me Gloria. Everyone does." John blushed, clearly flustered, and Gloria chuckled, patting his arm. "Really, John, no need to be embarrassed. I hadn't mentioned it yet, so it's on me."

Mr. Martin said, "Alright, now that we've settled that, Bill, you can call me Will. That's what everyone calls me." Mr. Bill raised an eyebrow. "But I thought John called you Colonel? What's the story there?"

Will gave a nod, a hint of nostalgia in his eyes. "Well, that's a tale for another day, but here's the short of it. John was one of my gunners on the B-17 back in the war. Funny thing, I didn't know he was dating my daughter until she introduced him a few months ago."

As they finished loading the car, a gentle breeze rustled through the trees, promising a beginning with John and his new in-laws. Judy turned to John, her eyes sparkling with excitement and tenderness. "Honey," she began, her voice soft like the whisper of an old love song, "would you call Mr. Wainwright and let him know that Mom and Dad are coming with us? Please ask him to tell Molly to have a room ready for them, down the hall from us, in the last room on the left. It's far enough so we can still have our moments alone."

Ever the devoted husband, John nodded with a smile that spoke volumes. Their journey to the mansion was not just a drive through the picturesque countryside, but a weaving together of two families, binding them closer with love.

As Judy closed the car trunk with a decisive click, she turned to her parents, the Martins, with warmth in her voice. "Mom, Dad, we're ready to go as soon as John finishes a little task, and then we'll be on our way."

John reappeared, his presence a reassuring grin and nod at Judy. "I took care of everything, sweetie, and a little extra that I think they and you will like. Let's head to the mansion," he said, his words a gentle caress of reassurance.

As they drove through the rolling hills, Mr. Martin couldn't help but admire the beauty that unfolded before them. "My goodness, Judy, the countryside is breathtaking, and the mansion looks much grander than the pictures could ever capture," he remarked, his voice tinged with awe.

Mrs. Martin nodded, her eyes wide with wonder. "It's more than I ever imagined," she agreed, the excitement of the journey sparking a youthful gleam in her eyes.

Pulling up to the mansion, they were greeted by Mr. Wainwright, Molly, and Michael, a diligent groundskeeper. The estate's grandeur was matched only by the warmth of their welcome. Judy introduced her parents with a beaming smile: "Mr. Wainwright, these are my parents, Mr. and Mrs. Martin."

With a welcoming gesture and a kind smile, Mr. Wainwright responded, "Welcome to the mansion, Mr. Will and Ms. Gloria. I'll take care of all your luggage and show you to your room shortly." Mr. Martin looked surprised. "How did they know our names?" John looked at Judy and said softly, "That's the surprise. I told Mr. Wainwright to make sure everyone knew their names and to make them feel at home by using their first names. I thought they and you might like it." Judy said, "Oh my love, I do and I'm sure they do."

As the sun dipped below the horizon, casting a golden glow over the mansion, the air was ripe with promise and the undeniable thrill of new beginnings. Judy and John exchanged a glance, a silent vow of love.

As the afternoon sun drenched the estate's grounds, Judy felt a flutter of anticipation in her heart. She was eager to share this piece of her new life with her parents, a life she had woven alongside John with love and hope. The gentle rustle of the wind through the trees and the familiar scent of blooming flowers filled the air, reminding her of memories of simpler times.

"Mom, Dad," Judy began, her voice filled with affection, "let's stroll around the grounds. I want you to see the beauty surrounding us here, and then we'll take you inside to show you our home." Her eyes shone with excitement, but beneath it lay a whisper of nervousness, the desire for their approval mingling with the joy of their presence.

Mr. Martin, ever the pragmatic one, chuckled softly. "Judy, let's get our luggage settled in first," he insisted, his voice as comforting, steady, and reassuring as it had always been.

Before Judy could protest, Molly, the heart of the household, stepped forward with a warm, welcoming smile. "Mr. Will, I'll handle your luggage. You enjoy your tour of the grounds," she insisted, her tone leaving no room for argument. "Michael, please see to it that the Martins' luggage is placed in the last room on the left on the second floor, and Mr. John and Ms. Judy's luggage in their room." "Yes, ma'am," Michael responded dutifully, already moving to carry out her instructions.

As they meandered through the garden, Judy's soft voice told stories of the mansion's history and John's father's illustrious military career. Each word showed her love for John and their life together. Judy led the joyful little tour around the gardens and finally into the house through the garage. After finishing the first-floor tour, they ended up in the kitchen.

Molly's voice cut through the gentle murmur of conversation, a beacon guiding them towards the evening ahead. "Ms. Judy, what time would you like dinner, and what shall we serve?"

Judy turned, her smile as bright as the sun setting behind the hills. "Molly, could we indulge Mom and Dad with your famous hamburger steaks? They remind me of my childhood, and I'd love for them to enjoy it without lifting a finger."

Mr. Martin interjected, his modesty shining through. "Now, Judy, we don't want to impose. A sandwich would suffice."

"Nonsense, Mr. Will," Molly replied with a twinkle in her eye. "It would be an honor to serve you our renowned hamburger steak. Ms. Judy, it will take Maria and me about an hour to prepare everything. Would that be suitable?" Judy said the time would be fine. Mr. Wainwright said, "Mr. Will, Ms. Gloria, may I show you to your room?" He gestured graciously, ushering them towards the stairs.

Judy called after them with a tender smile and a wave, "Mom, Dad, we'll see you in an hour. Love you both." Her heart swelled with an overwhelming sense of gratitude and love, the kind that transcends time and place, binding them all together in this moment that brimmed with the promise of cherished memories yet to be made.

As the Martins followed Mr. Wainwright upstairs, the anticipation hummed between them like a gently plucked guitar string. Each step brought them closer to the room that would become their sanctuary for the next few days.

When Mr. Wainwright walked into the last bedroom on the left, Mr. Martin glanced at his wife, a glimmer of excitement and uncertainty dancing in their eyes. The room was expansive, its elegance understated yet profoundly welcoming.

"Mr. Wainwright, is this supposed to be our room?" Mr. Martin asked, his voice tinged with wonder. "This is extremely large." Mr. Wainwright nodded, his demeanor as polished as the mahogany banister they had ascended. "Yes, sir, Mr. Will, this is your room. Let me know if you need a larger or smaller room, and I can change rooms for you. You also have a walk-in closet and a lovely private bathroom. If there is anything else you need, please ask."

As Mr. Wainwright retreated, leaving them enveloped in the room's tranquil embrace, Mr. Martin turned to his wife with a tender smile. "Honey," he said, his voice soft and reverent, "I don't know how to describe this. Judy is wealthy beyond anything I could imagine. I hope she is happy and not letting the money go to her head."

He paused, searching her eyes for the answer he feared and hoped for. She responded with a smile that could warm the coldest of hearts, her eyes twinkling with an emotion that mirrored his own: love, pure and unguarded. "I'm sure she is level-headed with the money as well as John is. They both seem to be adapting very well with the newfound money," Mrs. Martin said with a loving smile.

"Let's freshen up and go downstairs for supper or dinner?" he suggested, his attempt at humor lightening the air. They both laughed, the sound blending with the gentle breeze blowing through the trees outside, as they turned towards the luxurious bathroom, anticipation for the night ahead still yet to unfold.

Together, they prepared for dinner, their movements synchronized in a dance only husband and wife of many years would know. With its grand luxury, the room became their stage, and they were the stars in that moment.

The soft clink of silverware and the gentle hum of evening chatter filled the air as Mr. and Mrs. Martin descended the grand staircase, their footsteps echoing against the polished wood. The dining room awaited them, with the inviting aroma of a perfectly seared hamburger steak drifting through the air. It was an evening like many others, yet tonight carried an undercurrent of significance, a conversation waiting to unfold.

Mr. Martin, with eyes as earnest as the day he first held his beloved daughter, turned to Judy. His voice, a blend of fatherly love and lingering concern, cut through their light-hearted chatter. "Judy, this question is for you and John," he began, his gaze shifting to the young man who sat across from him. Judy, radiant in her youth and spirit, instinctively interjected, "Daddy," her voice a soft plea, yet he gently signaled her to allow him this moment. "Judy, please let me finish," he urged, his tone as warm as the summer sun. "I know I am in your home now, but I must ask you and John something."

Turning to John, a man whose courage had been forged amidst the chaos of battle, Mr. Martin's voice softened with respect and paternal care. "John, I have only known you since the war, but I placed my life in your hands, and you did not disappoint. That speaks volumes of your character."

The room seemed to hold its breath, the weight of his words lingering in the air. "John," he continued, "I know from our time in service together that you did not come from money. You and your mother overcame tough times with sheer grit and love."

Mr. Martin paused, the air thick with anticipation and the unspoken bond of family. "Judy, when you talked to us in Mountain Home about getting married, you said that John was a millionaire, but we had no idea how much money he really had. From the looks of this house and the department store, it seems that you and he are worth a considerable amount. It looks like you both are now millionaires several times over. My question to both of you is, can you handle it now that you find yourselves with this newfound fortune? Will you remain grounded, keep your hearts intact, and not let the money change who you are?"

Judy reached for John's hand, their fingers entwining beneath the table, a silent vow in their shared touch. John's eyes met hers, a gentle current of understanding flowing between them. They were no longer just individuals navigating a world of uncertainties; they were partners, bound by love and the promise of a future untainted by the burdens of their past.

With a quiet determination, John nodded, his voice steady and filled with conviction. "Colonel, Judy, and I have weathered storms far greater than wealth. We will cherish and use it wisely, but it will never!, ever!, define us. Our love and the life we are building together are what truly matter. Colonel, we fell in love before I knew how much money was really involved."

Judy squeezed his hand, her heart swelling with pride and a love that deepened with every beat. Together, they faced Mr. Martin, united in their resolve, their love a beacon that would guide them through whatever lay ahead. And in that moment, beneath the glow of the chandelier, they knew that whatever the future held, they would face it hand in hand, their love unshakable and true.

Judy faced her father with an earnest tenderness in her eyes. Her voice trembled with emotion, each word woven from the depths of her heart. "Daddy," she began softly, her gaze steady and filled with love, "John and I, we truly fell for one another long before the weight of his inheritance ever shadowed our lives. It was an accidental discovery on a train, a love so pure and untethered by wealth or expectation. When we first met on that train, we had no way of knowing the paths our fates would take."

Judy paused, recalling the vivid memory of their first meeting, how strangers became lovers guided by an invisible thread of destiny. "He didn't know I was your daughter, and I was blissfully unaware of the legacy set to unfold. In those quiet moments, there was only us, two souls whose hearts had found home in each other."

Her father's eyes glistened with unshed tears, the weight of her words sinking in with each breath. She continued, her voice gaining strength with the certainty of their love. "It wasn't until the day the will was read that the magnitude of it all became clear. Kathy had spoken of changes at the department store, hints of a future neither of us could have imagined. When John walked through that door, the truth instantly unveiled itself."

Her heart swelled with the recollection of that pivotal moment, a mixture of surprise and unwavering affection. "Yet, Daddy, even as the figures and fortunes were revealed, nothing altered the essence of what we share. Our love remained steadfast, in a world often clouded by material concerns."

Judy's voice softened to a whisper, a vow sealed in the sanctuary of her heart. "And I promise you, come what may, our love will endure, timeless, unwavering, and as boundless as the stars that quietly watch over us."

Following Mr. Martin's inquiries regarding John and Judy's recent financial gains, the discussion at the dining table transitioned into a mix of light-hearted laughter and more serious exchanges. Throughout the meal, both Mr. and Mrs. Martin expressed their compliments toward Molly's culinary skills. Mr. Martin remarked, "Molly, this hamburger steak is exceptional. It's been a while since I've had one this good." He then turned to Mrs. Martin, adding, "Mother, your version is excellent, but this one matches up well." Mrs. Martin laughed, "Indeed, honey, this is quite good, potentially surpassing mine."

The group shared a moment of laughter before John directly addressed Molly: "Tomorrow morning, we will leave early for the store, probably about 6 AM. Please fix some egg sandwiches for Judy and me to take with us. If David can arrange it, please have him take the Colonel and Ms. Gloria to the store at their convenience. And please make sure he can drive them wherever they need to go afterward." Molly acknowledged with a broad smile, replying, "Yes, Mr. John."

As the evening settled in, Mr. Martin stretched with a contented sigh, the kind that only comes at the end of a truly satisfying day. "Judy," he said, his voice warm and gentle, "it's been such a wonderful day for us. If you and John don't mind, your mother and I will head upstairs. We're ready to call it a night."

Judy wrapped her parents in a soft hug, the kind that communicates everything words cannot. "Of course, Dad. Good night," she whispered, feeling the comforting weight of their love linger even as they headed to their room.

Turning back to the living room, Judy smiled at John. "Molly, John, and I will have our evening drinks while catching up with the news," she said, a note of relaxation in her voice. "After that, I'll take care of the glasses. You can take it easy now. Thank you, Molly, for everything you do for us." "Yes, Ms. Judy," Molly replied, a warm smile gracing her face as she prepared their drinks. Moments like these, wrapped in the cozy routine of home, truly mattered.

With drinks in hand, Judy and John settled into the couch, enveloped in each other's comforting presence. They watched the news, but really, it was just an excuse to be close, to savor the moment when the day's busyness faded away.

Once the program ended, Judy took the glasses to the kitchen. The sound of running water was soothing in the quiet house as she washed and laid them out to dry. Then, with fingers intertwined, she and John made their way upstairs, the familiar path to their sanctuary.

In their bedroom, they lay on the bed, the room around them fading as they focused solely on each other. In this peaceful embrace, whispers of love exchanged in the dim light, they finally drifted off to sleep, hearts full and content.

Judy and John were up early the next morning, just like they'd planned. They grabbed the egg sandwiches Molly had whipped up for them and headed straight to the department store. The place was already buzzing with the energy of a new day, and as they walked in, they spotted Kathy and Sarah, who were already there.

The four of them exchanged hugs and the usual "How was the honeymoon?" small talk before diving into the day's work. It was just past 8 A.M. when John, sitting comfortably at his desk, casually called out, "Hey, Kathy, could you try to get Mr. Bill at the airport on the line for me?"

"Yes, sir, Mr. Jenkins," Kathy replied, as efficient as ever. John couldn't help but chuckle a bit; Kathy and Judy were such great friends, yet she kept it formal at work, calling him "Mr. Jenkins" even though they knew each other well.

Moments later, Kathy, sitting at her desk, said, "Mr. Jenkins, Mr. Bill is on line three," her voice cheerful as always. "Thanks, Kathy." John picked up the phone, his voice warm and friendly. "Hello, Mr. Bill. How are you today?" I'm doing great this morning, John. How about you?" Mr. Bill's voice crackled through the line, full of life.

John laughed and said, "I'm well, thanks. We had to come back to work to get some rest! Sorry to bother you, but we didn't get a chance to clean out the plane before heading home yesterday. Could someone take care of that? I'd be happy to pay extra." Mr. Bill reassured him without missing a beat, "Already done, John. It's part of our service for your father; no need to change a thing. Just let us know when you're flying it back in. And hey, if Judy teaches you to fly the twin-beech, I'll gladly give you your test ride when you're ready."

"Thank you, Mr. Bill. Talk to you later." John hung up, a satisfied smile on his face. It was the morning when everything felt right: friends at work, plans in motion, and a little romance lingering in the air, even as they went about their busy day.

John was working at his desk when he heard a squeal from outside his office. It was Kathy, and she was clearly excited. "Mr. Will, Ms. Gloria! Oh, I've missed seeing you both so much," she gushed. Her enthusiasm was infectious. John couldn't help but grin as he got up and went into Kathy's office to greet his in-laws.

"Hey, glad you stopped by," he said warmly before turning to Kathy. "I'll be back in a few. Just going to take my in-laws to see Judy at her office." With that, they strolled down the hall and rounded the corner.

John popped his head into Judy's office. "Honey, got a minute?" he asked. Judy beamed at him and teased, "Well, of course, Mr. Jenkins," before bursting into laughter.

John walked into Judy's office with her parents behind him. As she hugged her mom and dad, Sarah popped out of her office to say hi. After a few minutes of catching up, she headed back to work.

"Mom, Dad, how about lunch at JJ's Steakhouse?" Judy suggested. "We can head out early and catch up over a good lunch." Mr. Martin nodded, "Sounds great, but we'd love to check out the department store first."

John, remembering their packed schedule, quickly added, "Perfect. Kathy can give you a tour while Judy and I wrap things up here." They all headed back to John's office. "Kathy," he called, "can you show Judy's folks around the store?" Then he leaned in and whispered to her, "If they want to buy anything, just charge it to my account." Kathy grinned, "Absolutely, Mr. Jenkins. I'd be happy to." And just like that, everyone was off, the day's excitement buzzing.

"How big is the store, Kathy?" Mr. Martin asked, throwing a curious glance around. "Well, Mr. Will," Kathy replied with a smile, "it's a three-story building. The top floor houses our offices, meeting rooms, and storage. But the first and second floors? They're all about the shopping."

Just then, Ms. Gloria, who had been eyeing a particularly large pot, said, "Honey, look at this! I've been searching for a pot this size forever. Can you get us a cart, just in case we need it?"

Kathy chuckled. "No worries, Ms. Gloria. I've got it covered." Turning to the clerk, she said, "Jane, could you put this on Mr. Jenkins' account and have a runner take it to my office, please? Thanks a bunch. Alright, Ms. Gloria, let's dive back into shopping." Mr. Martin furrowed his brows slightly. "Kathy, is that okay? It doesn't feel right." With a reassuring smile, Kathy nodded. "Mr. Will, this is exactly what Mr. and Mrs. Jenkins instructed me to do." Mr. Martin smiled and asked Kathy, "With John and Judy owning the department store, why do they charge everything to their account?" Kathy looked at Mr. Martin and said, "Well, Mr. Will, they own everything here, including the building. They are very serious about keeping up with everything that comes in and goes out of the store. That way, they know exactly how the store is doing financially, and it lets us know if we are losing any inventory due to any losses. If they get anything, they pay just like any other employee."

"Alright," Mr. Martin relented, "but Gloria, maybe don't go too overboard. And Kathy, why do you keep calling them Mr. or Mrs. Jenkins? You guys are like family. You and Judy have been inseparable since school days, even through college." Kathy smiled softly, a hint of nostalgia in her eyes. "Yes, sir, Mr. Will, Judy, and I go way back. We're best friends, and always will be. But here at the office, there's a chain of command to respect, and that's important."

After an hour of wandering and selecting items that Ms. Gloria always wanted, they made their way back to Kathy's office. The desk was now a colorful heap of items, including purchases they had made, and a few extras that John must have snuck in. "Looks like we've done quite a bit of shopping," Kathy remarked with a laugh, a warm, contented glow lighting up her face.

It was a typical Thursday evening. The sun had dipped below the horizon as John, Judy, and her parents gathered around the cozy dining room table. The aroma of a delicious home-cooked meal filled the air, and the conversation flowed as easily as the wine.

"You know, Judy," Mr. Martin said with a chuckle, "we've had such a lovely time here, but if we don't head back soon, we might never leave. This life of having our room cleaned every day and meals served is dangerously tempting!" Judy grinned. "Why don't you just stay another week then?"

"Oh, we'd love to, sweetheart, but we can't. We actually need to get back to reality. Any chance you could fly us home tomorrow?" Judy exchanged a quick glance with John, who nodded thoughtfully. "We can do that," John replied, "but it'll have to be later in the day. Remember, we've got that bank meeting at 4 PM about the city park donation in honor of my dad."

"Right, right," Judy said, her face lighting up with an idea. "Excuse me for a minute." She stood up from her chair, walked to the living room, and called Sarah. After a quick chat, she returned, looking pleased.

"Daddy, here's a thought: Sarah can fly you both home tomorrow morning if John agrees. She'll be back by mid-afternoon. And get this, you can even be the pilot for the twin-beech with Sarah as your copilot! How does that sound?"

Mr. Martin's eyes twinkled. "If John's okay with it, count me in! I'd love to take the controls again." John nodded, smiling. "Fine with me, after all, you're the one who taught Judy how to fly." With plans settled and spirits high, they all returned to their meal, savoring the moment and each other's company.

Judy piped up with a grin as they cruised down the highway and headed to the airport. "Hey, Mom, Dad, I quickly called the boys before they left for school. I told them to leave a car waiting for you at the airport, with the keys tucked away in the pilot's lounge. That way, you won't need to mess around with cabs."

Once they arrived, Sarah was there, waiting with all the things they had bought at the store. They loaded everything onto the plane, waved to them as they started taxing to the runway, and watched the twin-beech soar toward Mountain Home. The touchdown came quicker than expected. Mr. Martin, never one to skip a good meal, insisted, "Sarah, you have to join us at the pilots' lounge for lunch before heading back to Poplar Bluff."

Sarah nodded happily, never one to turn down an invitation or a meal. They settled in at the pilot lounge, enjoying a spread that was as delightful as the company. Sarah couldn't help but tell them how well Judy and John handled the department store. "Honestly," she said, with a teasing twinkle in her eye, "They're doing an even better job than John's dad and I did."

After lunch and a lot of laughter, Sarah returned to Poplar Bluff, pulling into the department store just as John and Judy were about to head to the bank. John caught sight of her, and a smile broke across his face. "Sarah! Perfect timing. We were heading to the bank to make the donation for the city park in memory of my father. You knew Dad better than anyone. We'd love for you to come with us." Sarah smiled and said, "Give me a minute to freshen up, and I'll be ready to go. This is an honor for me to be with you and Judy to honor your father's legacy in Poplar Bluff."

We often think the big, grand moments make a relationship special. But really, it's those little, everyday things that truly count. Judy and John had their honeymoon travels and all that came with them, but what really tells the picture of their love are those quiet, unassuming moments where they share a look or whisper something sweet and silly. Their journey isn't about how far they've gone but how deeply they really know each other after the journey ends.

As they settled back into the rhythm of life, the department store, a testament to their hard work and dedication, was more than a business; it symbolized their commitment to each other and the community they cherished. Six days after their honeymoon, it was as if they'd never left. It's a bit like clockwork. That night, as they cozied up under the covers, Judy turned to John, flashed him that soft, flirting smile of hers, and said, "Good night, my love."